READER REVIEWS

"*Incident at Cougar Creek* is a masterfully woven eco-thriller that fuses mystery, romance, and mythology against the haunting beauty of California's central coast. Mary Flodin's prose pulses with authenticity, from vivid environmental detail to her nuanced portrayal of trauma and resilience. Both a gripping page-turner and a profound call for empathy toward people and planet. Highly recommended,"

The International Review of Books.

"I'm a Licensed Professional Counselor, specializing in PTSD. In *Incident at Cougar Creek,* I found that the author accurately and sensitively portrays characters who are dealing with unresolved PTSD resulting from the trauma of military combat and rape. This eco-thriller has plenty of page turning, entertaining, edge-of-your-seat twists and surprises, but also reveals the urgent need for conservation of wild California's fragile central coast ecosystem, and elevates serious concerns about missing and murdered Indigenous people. A timely and meaningful read."

Rachel Pfotenhauer MA, LPC

"*Incident at Cougar Creek* is an intricately plotted, deeply engaging murder mystery and love story that will compel the reader's attention from the story's beginning right to its very end. The story is set in California's central coast, with excursions to both Southern California and San Francisco. As a former Santa Cruz County Supervisor who represented that county's North Coast for twenty years, I can testify to how profoundly and powerfully the mystery and majesty of this under-appreciated part of the California coastline has been made into an essential element of the gripping trajectory of Flodin's story."

Gary A. Patton, Santa Cruz County Supervisor (1975-1995)

"Mary Flodin's new book, *Incident at Cougar Creek*, is a fast-paced cli-fi-eco thriller full of action and intrigue that made me want to keep turning the page. *Incident at Cougar Creek* delivers an exciting narrative full of twists, turns, and tense chase scenes threaded through with a profound and satisfying love story, along with vivid setting elements and factual details that reveal the challenges of protecting the natural world."

Anna Citrino, author of *Stories We Didn't Tell*

INCIDENT AT COUGAR CREEK

MARY FLODIN

Cover artwork design copyright © 2025 by Niki Lenhart
nikilen-designs.com

Published by Paper Angel Press
paperangelpress.com

ISBN 978-1-969655-47-0 (Hardcover)

FIRST EDITION

10 9 8 7 6 5 4 3 2 1

"The extraordinary, rapid growth of the Homo sapiens population, coupled with its voracious appetite for planetary dominance and resource consumption, had put every measurable biological and chemical system on earth in a state of imbalance."

THE COMING PLAGUE:
Newly Emerging Diseases in a World Out of Balance
Pulitzer Prize Winner Laurie Garrett (1994)
Farrar, Straus and Giroux

INCIDENT AT
COUGAR CREEK

Eyay e'Hunn — My heart is good.

PROLOGUE

APRIL 10, 2018
SAN DIEGO COUNTY, CALIFORNIA

S INCE CHILDHOOD, twenty-year-old Delfina Cuera had known the secret trails from their home at the Ma Tar Awa Viejas Trailer Park, on the outskirts of San Diego, up to the ancient Kumeyaay ceremonial site on Viejas Mountain.

This April evening, mother and daughter performed their sunset prayers and rituals in peace and solitude, as they had so many times before.

Twilight faded the bright blue Southern California sky to pale indigo. Far below to the west, the lights of San Diego twinkled awake.

★   ★   ★

Just as the last glint of sunlight vanished over the horizon, hot, dry, Santana winds rushed fiercely across the mountain. Like sinister, angry giants bringing mayhem from another realm, the Santanas boomed across the land, causing the very air to tremble and crack. Venomous wind demons kicked and hurled everything in their path, forcing the spirits of earth to shake and flee in terror before them.

The Satanás!

Enraged wind whipped Delfina's hair across her face. She protected her eyes with a raised hand, squinting to see better.

In the dim moonlight, Delfina perceived something strange happening to her mother. Ramona's body was weirdly changing.

Frozen in horror, Delfina watched Ramona shape shift—subtly at first, then all at once. The transformation was so radical, so grotesque, that Delfina could not doubt what she saw, although her mind would not make sense of it.

Delfina felt a rising irritation from deep inside her own body—an itching in her very bone marrow. Inflammation boiled through her blood and flesh. She needed to burst out of her skin, as if it no longer fit. A terrible pain gripped her. All her bones felt like they were breaking. Fur sprouted from her skin. She fell to the ground. Her hands and feet turned into large paws with sharp claws.

What's happening to me?

She screamed.

But the sound that rose from her throat was not human. It was the howl of a wild animal.

She heard her mother's voice in her head, shouting, "Delfina, run! Hunters have found us. Follow me. Run!"

The young puma leapt twenty feet straight up the cliff face and clawed her way across crumbling rock. She struggled to keep up with her mother as the two of them ran for their lives through the night.

The hot dry Santana wind threw gritty rock dust in her eyes. She blinked frantically. Her mother wordlessly instructed her to memorize the landmarks, to remember her way in the dark through this ever-dwindling corridor of mountain wilderness.

I must keep my vision clear.

They fled toward the reservoir along a mountain ridge trail that Delfina had never traveled before.

The farther into the wilderness the cougars ran, the harder the devil wind blew, sending waves of pressure rippling over their fur, as if an enormous invisible monster were trying to push them back, prevent them from reaching their destiny.

A loud crack sizzled through the air overhead. Like cupped hands slapping both sides of her head, pressure smashed into Delfina's eardrums with a violent burst. The world went silent, but the young puma kept running.

The Santana winds blew harder, faster, hotter. She squinted against swirling sand, dodging sharp thorns of barrel cactus, cartwheeling tumbleweeds, and crashing limbs of scrub oak trees.

A loud whistling squeal rang in her ears. Then the fierce crack of another rifle shot racked the night, followed by men's laughter.

The zing of a bullet buzzed Delfina's head like an angry yellow jacket, ricocheting off a rock just inches from where she stood at the edge of a cliff. A spark flew off the granite, igniting drought-dry chaparral. Within seconds, the devil winds had whipped fire all around her.

The sound of her mother's voice screamed inside her head.

"Delfina! Jump!"

Delfina leapt off the cliff into a canyon river gorge a hundred feet below.

1

**SIX YEARS LATER, APRIL 14, 2023
SANTA LUCIA COUNTY, CALIFORNIA**

FIVE HUNDRED MILES NORTH of San Diego, under an ancient stand of coastal oaks, California Fish and Wildlife Officer Colin Dawson knelt over the dying mountain lion.

Wavering streams of light and dark filtered through the dense oak canopy, throwing ghostly patterns across the ground. Mangled shadows insinuated their fingers over the big, beautiful puma, its fur the color of California's golden hills.

The cougar thrashed, gushing blood.

Colin leaned in closer to assess the wound and determine whether he could do anything to save the animal.

He watched, horrified, as the fur on the cat's head grew long, black, and shiny. The puma's ears lost their fur altogether, rounded, and moved down to the sides of the head. The wildcat's face changed shape, like a plastic mask being pulled and remolded before his eyes, until she became human. Paws transformed into human hands and feet, and breasts swelled on the cat's now furless chest.

Colin's brows pulled together. His jaw clenched. His heart roared like a firestorm in his ears.

The cat, still writhing and bleeding, had morphed into a naked woman.

Colin stared at the dying woman's face. From deep in her journey through the dark forest of death, she looked back at him, into his soul. Her green eyes pierced him through and through, as if she had known him forever, as if they were kin.

He trembled, mind whirling.

She spasmed, a single tear ran down her cheek, and her eyes became glassy.

Has she stopped breathing?

Suddenly she gasped, then took a noisy rattling breath. The rattling stopped. Silence. For a moment, the earth seemed to cease spinning; the constant chatter of creation paused. Colin felt for a pulse. Nothing. She was gone. A wave of deep sadness overwhelmed him.

His forehead throbbed.

Incredibly enough, this was not the most horrible thing he'd ever seen. But too weird.

Am I losing my mind? Did I just have a break with reality?

Proximity to violent death, the smell of all that blood—those are PTSD triggers. I must have hallucinated.

He squinted at the corpse. *But the cougar had seemed so real.*

No. No. She definitely was never a mountain lion. You imagined it, Colin.

He checked his smartwatch—Thursday, April 14, 2023. 3:56 p.m. Pacific Daylight.

So sad. This woman appears to be about my mom's age.

Leaves rustled behind him. He froze. Icy tingles along his spine awakened Colin's military combat instincts.

Her killer could still be nearby.

Colin looked over his shoulder.

Just a blue jay.

Shaking off spiderwebs of fear, keeping senses alert, he opened the voice memo app on his watch. He noted the time of death, then resumed his examination of the body, recording his observations, careful not to touch the woman.

"The arrow is lodged deep in her chest, probably all the way through. Not a clean entry. The flesh is ripped to shreds. I observed blood pumping out along the shaft like a gusher as she died. Massive blood loss. The arrow must have penetrated her heart. What caused those spasms, as if she were having a seizure?"

Colin examined the projectile, lightly touching it with his gloved hand. "This is no ordinary arrow. Looks like one of those hundred-dollar-a-pop jobs, engineered for a high-tech sniper crossbow."

His adrenaline spiked. "The kill shot must have come from close by—no more than a hundred meters, maybe as close as fifty, half a football field away."

His fingers wrapped around the grip of the Glock in his holster. Turning his head, he checked his six. Held his breath. Listened.

Silence.

Colin took a deep breath, and continued recording his observations. "Calluses, scratches, cuts, and dried blood on her hands and feet. Debris under her nails. These scratches and cuts don't look like defensive wounds. More like what you'd get if you were scrambling on your hands and bare feet over rough ground." He switched off the voice recording.

"You poor woman," he spoke out loud to the lifeless body. The trees seemed to lean in, listening. "How did you hurt your hands and feet like that?" Even in death, her presence emanated grace, nobility. "Who are you? Who did this to you? Why?"

Glancing around the clearing under the oaks, Colin scanned for signs that she may have been killed elsewhere, had crawled, or been dragged here, to die.

Chiaroscuro highlights and shadows heightened the shocking bright green of tall understory grasses, sprouting hallelujahs of rebirth and regeneration through the dense brown mélange of leaf litter.

The sound of nearby Cougar Creek meandering downhill soothed Colin's nerves.

On hands and knees, the wildlife warden moved his head side to side, up and down, until he caught sight of a blood trail beginning about ten feet from the body.

He stood and planted a marker where the trail began.

Tapping his voice app, he noted, "The forensic team will have to confirm, but it appears to me the victim was running, being chased. I've placed a flag where the arrow hit her. She dragged herself farther until she collapsed, then died there, where I found her. This looks to me like a typical hunting scenario. Except the prey was human."

A wave of vertigo surged through him.

He fell to his knees, his hand coming down hard on spikey fallen oak leaves.

A metal object pushed against his palm. Colin plucked it out of the leaves, drawing it close to his face to examine.

Jewelry? He turned the object around, studying it closer. *No. This is a broken piece from one of those telemetry collars the Puma Research Project uses.*

Colin's forehead wrinkled. He spoke again to the woman growing cold in the brittle leaves. "Did someone capture you, put a tracking collar on you?"

A stream of bright crimson ran down his wrist into his palm.

What? Is this her blood or mine? Wait. When did I take my gloves off? Did I cut myself on this broken collar when I fell? Crap. I've compromised evidence with blood from my cut.

He untied the kerchief from his neck, used it to wipe the blood off his wrist and hand, then wrapped it around his wound. With his smartphone, he photographed the object his hand had landed on, making sure to get a clear shot of the string of numbers engraved into the metal. Then he rummaged an evidence bag out of his knapsack, secured the metal-and-plastic piece in the bag, and labeled it. He placed an evidence marker where he'd found the object.

Spidey-senses keyed up, tingling down his back, Colin remained hyper alert. He couldn't shake the feeling of being watched. A predator could at this moment be sneaking up behind him, drawing a bow to take a shot.

Using the radio on his vest, he contacted dispatch for backup. From the Fish and Wildlife repeater, the dispatcher would ping all appropriate agencies, starting with the Sheriff's Homicide Division.

It would take at least an hour for the Santa Lucia County Sheriff's team to get all the way up here to the Cougar Creek Coast Ranch, ten miles north of Playa Azul. Meanwhile, Colin was at high risk, a vulnerable target. More so than usual. Cal Fish and Wildlife, with budget cuts and unfilled vacancies, was spread too thin. As the sole wildlife warden in charge of patrolling the entire northern half of this county, with its miles of coastline and thousands of acres of coastal and mountainous parks, Colin was often alone in isolated areas without any backup. But finding a dead woman with a high-tech sniper arrow through her heart made today feel even more dangerous than usual.

Nevertheless, he stood his ground, methodically taking photos of the body, close-ups of the arrow, the wound, the victim's hands and feet, and blood on the leaves where he presumed the arrow first struck the victim. On his phone's Notes app, he registered photo log notes.

The forensic team would take more professional and thorough photographs later, but Colin knew it was important to capture as much evidence as he could in these first minutes proximate to the victim's time of death, while the crime scene was still pristine.

When he got back to the road and his truck, he would radio the Sheriff's Homicide Division directly and talk them in. This location was one of those places where GPS didn't work very well. It wouldn't be easy for the Sheriff's team to find.

Colin dug a roll of caution tape out of his pack and cordoned off a perimeter around the body.

He started to leave, then hesitated. Returning to the woman, he knelt and whispered, "I'm sorry this happened to you."

Gently, he closed her eyes.

Finally he stood, brushed the leaves off his pants knees, and hurried to get out from under the oppressive oaks. Inside his skull, his footfalls on the earth reverberated like an echo chamber, as if someone were prowling around in his brain. His boot nicked a wild chanterelle hidden in the leaf litter, the musty odor triggering memories of time served in Afghanistan. He glanced over his shoulder. Black silhouettes of gnarled trees loomed over the body like ghouls.

When he stepped out of the shaded grove onto the ranch road where his truck was parked, oblique rays of late afternoon sunlight pierced his eyes. He blinked up at the sky, took a deep breath of fresh coastal air, and gazed down the mountain to the shimmering sea.

A whale spouted, then another—tiny white umbrellas of spray erupting out of glassy ocean far below. California grays were passing the Central Coast on their annual migration from Baja to Alaska. The explosive crash of distant breakers rumbled like bombs blasting through a tunnel inside his head.

He rubbed his forehead, fighting down another wave of dizziness and nausea. A cold gust off the ocean cut through him like an ice knife. Memories washed over him.

Thundering bursts of gunfire roll through the tunnel. It is March 11, 2012. Panjwai, Afghanistan. Shitstorm. Clusterfuck. Slaughter.

Me and my squad find the house that intel had ID'd as sheltering terrorist insurgents. We kick the door down. Musty odor of old prayer rugs, cumin and baharat, smoke choking the air, blood, burnt flesh, terror. Our mission: clean the site—eliminate the threat; bayonet all bodies, even if they already appear to be dead; leave nothing alive.

A young woman lies no longer breathing on a mat in a dark corner of the room, the veil fallen away from her face, glazed eyes open, a forever silent baby cradled in each arm.

Oh, God! You're from another culture, but you could be my sister. Both of us are part of one human family, all genetically related. Sapiens? What a misnomer. Nothing wise about this. All slaughtered. Absolute destruction of what was once beautiful and good. What have we done?

The scene spins around him. He rises out of his body, looks down from a great height, through the smoke of war, at the dead woman and babies on a blood-soaked prayer rug.

Everything he thought he knew about war falls away. He gazes down at his small self below, the bayonet in his hand aimed to stab the lifeless woman and babies. In a blinding realization, he sees the truth: *I am nothing but a tool forged to wreak chaos,* **in the hands of a gruesome monster whose malignant reach extends across oceans and continents!**

★   ★   ★

A red-tailed hawk flushed out of the treetops, circling overhead with a haunting cry.

Snap out of it, Colin. That was ten years ago. You survived. You didn't kill the girl and those babies. It wasn't your fault. Move on. Breathe.

Colin inhaled the clean ocean air deeper, deeper, counting to ten, holding his breath while the flashback cleared, then exhaling and breathing in again, focusing on the sea shining far below.

Don't let the past drag you down. Keep going forward. Be in the Now.

He implemented the antianxiety protocol he'd been taught at the military hospital in Kandahar. Bending forward, hands on knees, he forced ten yogic *breaths of fire* through his nostrils, with eyes and mouth wide open, tongue stuck out like a Māori warrior. He straightened his back and scrubbed his face and head with his hands, palmed his eyes, drummed his fingertips between his collar bones to calm his amygdala and release serotonin, punched his chest and gut, and karate chopped down his legs and across his shoulders. He rolled his head to loosen his tight neck muscles, squeezed his shoulder blades together hard, did a few squats, then he gave himself a good wet dog shake, throwing off lingering guilt and shame.

Finally, he stepped into his truck, gulped down half the water in his water bottle, and unlocked his rifle from the rack behind his seat. Sitting with the truck doors locked, windows up, and his rifle across his knees, he radioed the Sheriff's office.

He connected with Homicide Division Lieutenant Carlos Rosa, en route with a SWAT team, detectives, deputies, and a forensic squad.

Sitting in his truck, scanning his surroundings for any activity, Colin talked the convoy up the Coast Highway from the town of Playa Azul, onto an unmarked turn north of the abandoned cement plant, then along a dirt road to the locked gate leading to the truck road that wound up the mountain to the crime scene.

2

LIEUTENANT CARLOS ROSA, head of Santa Lucia County Sheriff's Criminal Investigations Division, pulled his notebook and pen out of his front shirt pocket and focused his penetrating glare on Colin. "As the first person on the scene, tell me what you saw, son."

Colin was six feet tall, but the lieutenant, as grounded as a deeply rooted tree, looked down on him by four inches. Lieutenant Rosa, with his graying temples, buzz cut receding hairline, square jaw, pencil mustache, and stocky build, made Colin sweat. He didn't do well with authority figures in general, and Rosa looked a little like Colin's drill sergeant in Army Ranger RASP, one of the worst pricks he'd ever dealt with.

Colin swallowed and stole a glance at the body being photographed by the sheriff's team. I feel strangely protective of her, he thought.

The forensic pathologist, Dr. Mary Sandow, arrived and began her examination. She efficiently slipped on her nitrile gloves, pulled a hair net over her tight, gray Afro and knelt over the body. She visually assessed the victim before touching her, shooing away a swarm of yellowjackets that had already arrived to feed on the sticky blood.

Riding a wave of nausea, Colin turned away from the body to answer the lieutenant's question.

"What did I see? Well, I received a call from dispatch this morning that an alert had come in through our CalTIP line about a possible wildlife poacher here in the coastal reserve. When I drove up and scouted around, I discovered a woman dying, apparently from an arrow wound. I was too late. Nothing I could do, sir."

"What else, Warden? You said you found something?"

"Yes, sir." Colin studied the matrix of oak leaves and tall grass sprouts under his boots. Bright sunlight and black tree shadows striping the ground spun like a Secchi disk under his feet. His muscles tightened. He waited a beat until the vertigo faded.

"Sir, there was a problem. I was kneeling over the body trying to figure out if I could do anything to save the victim, but she died fast. And then I kind of—I guess I blacked out for a few seconds. I fell and my hand landed on a piece of evidence. Somehow, I cut myself. I don't remember taking my gloves off, but I ended up holding the evidence with my bare hands. I might have gotten some of my blood on it. I'm afraid I compromised the evidence, sir."

Colin hesitated a moment, then pulled the brown paper evidence bag out of his pack.

"I marked the spot where I found this," he said. "Right there next to the victim." Colin pointed to the evidence marker he'd placed near the body. "I think it's a piece of a broken telemetry collar, like the ones used to track mountain lions."

He handed the evidence to Lieutenant Rosa, who examined it for a moment, then passed it to a forensic tech to store in an evidence box.

"There's something else, sir."

"What is it?"

"I know I shouldn't have, but—before I could think better of it— I, I reached out and closed her eyes. Instinct, I guess. Her eyes were wide open. It just didn't feel right leaving her like that. Sorry, sir. I only touched her eyelids. That's it."

Lieutenant Rosa frowned. "You were uncomfortable leaving her eyes open, but apparently you had no problem leaving her naked, uncovered?"

"I, uh …"

Two ravens burst out of the top of the oak tree canopy. Cawing, they flew at the hawk circling overhead. The hawk disappeared over a distant ridge with the noisy ravens in pursuit.

Rosa squinted at Colin. "Tell me again what you were doing up here."

"Responding to an anonymous CalTIP, sir. A caller reported seeing someone off trail, dressed in camo with a bow and arrows, stalking a mountain lion. As you know, hunting of any kind is illegal in this national monument, and in California, cougars are a protected species."

"Did your caller give a more detailed description of the hunter or his weapon?"

"No, sir. The tip was left on a recorded line. I had no opportunity to ask questions. But I recognized the arrow in the woman's body from my Army Ranger days. It's the type used with a Condor crossbow by special force snipers. A high-tech killing machine."

Lieutenant Rosa's sharp gaze pinned Colin with penetrating scrutiny. "Anything else?"

The wildlife warden squirmed like a specimen under a microscope.

They'd never met before, but Rosa's reputation preceded him. He was known throughout law enforcement circles to be tough and shrewd, by the book but fair, outspoken, uncompromising, and relentless in his pursuit of truth and justice.

Should I tell Rosa that I thought this woman was a mountain lion when I first found her?

No way. For sure he'll think I'm a nut case or on drugs. Maybe even view me as a suspect.

I must have been hallucinating. Maybe I am crazy. But, hey, who wants to be normal? These days, normal is frackin' insane.

Was there anything else he should tell the lieutenant? He'd reported time of death, reviewed his visual findings and evidence markers. The only thing he'd left out was the part about imagining the woman being a mountain lion.

"No, sir. That's all I can tell you." He dug his water bottle out of his pack and drained it in a few gulps.

"You know this area pretty well, Officer Dawson?"

"Fairly well, sir. It's within my jurisdiction, but it's not like I can claim to know it all. It's a vast piece of mostly roadless land—nearly seven thousand acres—much of it untouched by human contact for the last hundred years. This is the second most species biodiverse hotspot in the continental U.S. Its habitats include native grasslands, coastal prairie with actively managed regenerative grazing, maritime chaparral, coast live oak woodlands, redwood and mixed evergreen forests, ancient uplifted marine terraces like this one we're standing on, coastal mountains formed by tectonic collision and subduction at the edge of continental and Pacific plate boundaries, sensitive watersheds including seven wild endangered salmon spawning streams—all on the brink of coming unzipped—marshes, deep jagged canyons, caves, a valley homesteaded by old hippie farmers, and—"

"Okay. Do you know the people—the residents and whoever else frequents this area? I noticed a line of locks with different initials on the gate down below."

"I know who those locks belong to, sir, and I'm familiar with some of the people who have keys to the locks. There's the inholding of homesteaders—organic farmers who settled here decades ago, before the Sempervirens Land Trust acquired the property and then deeded it to the Bureau of Land Management. Pleistocene megafauna herbivores grazed this area heavily up to about eleven thousand seven hundred years ago. Indigenous humans appeared here about one hundred thousand years ago, maybe even earlier, and cultivated the land's ability to produce incredibly abundant wild food plants and wildlife through managed grazing of the endemic herbivores like elk and antelope, and also through traditional fire wisdom—managed burning. Then in 1790, Europeans wiped out the elk and antelope, as well as the Cotoni band of Ohlone people and their cultural knowledge, and used this land for cattle grazing. So to answer your question, following the continuous history of grazing this land all the way back to prehistoric times, a ranching family who's been leasing pasture here for five generations to breed and sustainably graze beef cattle was 'grandfathered' in when the BLM took title. They have a lock too."

Lieutenant Rosa's eyebrows drew together. He stared sideways at Colin, then glanced at his watch. "All right. The farmers and the cow people can get in. Anyone else?"

"Well, the Cougar Creek Coast Ranch was slated to be opened to the public as a National Monument this summer, but it's been hung up by lawsuits over a flawed BLM watershed management plan, among other issues, so there's currently no official public access. Even so, locals from Clark's Landing, the nearby village, climb over the fence to hike. And the Santa Lucia Mountain Bikers Club has been aggressive about violating access restrictions, cutting the ranchers' fences and carving up the land with their trails."

"Local townies, hikers, and bikers." Rosa made another note in the small spiral notebook he had pulled out of his shirt pocket. "Who else?"

"BLM has access, the Sempervirens and the Amah Mutsun Ohlone Land Trusts, and Pacific Gas and Electric. PG&E's crews are here all the time, at the small substation up the road. They're hypervigilant about maintaining the forests for fire prevention ever since losing the lawsuit after those devastating lightning wildfires in 2020. Then there's the lock you and I used—pretty much all security personnel have a master key to it: Fish and Wildlife, sheriff, other city, state, and federal law enforcement, and CalFire."

Rosa shook his head as he wrote down this additional information.

"Oh, and also Cientox—the old cement plant—has a lock," Colin added. "The plant is owned by a Mexican corporation. It was shut down a few years ago for environmental violations. It's about a hundred-seventy acres of land right in the middle of the Cougar Creek Coast Ranch National Monument land. The plan is to eventually add it to the national monument property. But Cientox is still dealing with lots of issues to bring the area up to public safety standards before the feds can acquire it, so the Cientox people come up here from Mexico to work. They have some gnarly hazmat situations. And it's rugged. Densely wooded, with a narrow, eroding, one-lane gravel road winding above an enormous, deep, sheer-sided gulch with an abandoned rock quarry. Very dangerous. Not an area you want to let the public wander around in."

"Did you notice any suspicious vehicles or people in the vicinity when you arrived?"

"No, sir."

"All right. You'd better go and get that cut taken care of. I'll need you back here tomorrow morning to help with a grid search. Do you have a card with your badge number and contact information?"

Colin handed Rosa his card.

"Good." Rosa pocketed it. "Meanwhile, make me a list of names, anyone you'd expect to see around here, and bring it with you tomorrow. Sounds like we have a lot of people we'll need to interview."

With a wave of his hand Rosa excused Colin and moved on to coordinate with his criminal investigations team and all the people from other agencies who had responded to Colin's call. On the way to his truck, Colin noted city police, two highway patrol officers, and even a U.S. Marshal.

The site had the feel of a circus arriving in town, with people checking in and setting up tables and tents on the broad knoll next to the oak grove where the murdered woman's body still lay.

In Santa Lucia County, homicide was rare enough to be a big deal. And here, with the Federal Bureau of Land Management in charge, investigative jurisdiction could prove to be a tangled web. The FBI could show up. And although there were no known surviving Ohlone people from the small tribal band that originally inhabited this place, the Amah Mutsun Ohlone Tribal Land Trust had asserted a claim to this newly designated national monument land. Native Americans getting involved could really complicate issues. Colin's list of names for Lieutenant Rosa was going to be long. But would his list lead investigators to the killer?

Who murdered that woman? Why?

Anxious to be away from all these people, Colin retreated to his truck as Lieutenant Rosa shouted into his walkie talkie, "Keep those press people at the gate. No reporters allowed up here!"

Heading down the mountain, Colin caught a glimpse in his rearview mirror of something standing at the edge of the oaks watching him.

What the —?

The silhouette of a man with huge wings?

No. No. The light's just playing tricks with my eyes.

3

COLIN ROUNDED THE LAST steep blind curve before the bottom cattle guard and swerved, barely missing the unmarked white coroner's van on its way to pick up the body.

At the bottom of the hill, he waved to the city cops guarding the perimeter. They were engaged with a TV crew, blocking them from entering. One of the cops nodded to Colin, and he drove through the ranch gate with a sigh of relief.

Even though Colin, like all law enforcement personnel, was fully vaccinated against Covid and keeping up with boosters for new variants, he'd still felt uncomfortable with all those people swarming around. It wasn't fear of Covid. If he was being honest with himself, the extreme social isolation during the height of the pandemic had suited him. That was one reason he loved his job. It was usually pretty solitary work.

It had been a long day, starting at dawn as usual, and he hadn't eaten since breakfast. His body was demanding food, and he wouldn't mind throwing back a few beers as well, just to take the edge off finding that poor woman. But department regulations prohibited wearing a uniform while drinking alcohol, so first he'd have to swing by his house to change clothes and switch from the department truck to his personal vehicle.

He turned right on the coast highway and drove north for about two miles. At the organic strawberry farm on Mallard Road, he turned inland.

A short way up the one-lane road, winding past strawberry fields and a lagoon populated with hundreds of migratory shore birds, Colin pulled into the driveway of the small farmworkers' cottage he'd rented for the past four years, since first being assigned to his North Santa Lucia County post.

As soon as he walked through the front door of his house, he secured his two service pistols, his rifle, and his shotgun in the hidden safe in his bedroom closet. Unlike some of his counterparts in law enforcement, who were required to be armed at all times, he didn't usually carry a weapon when off duty.

The cut on his wrist throbbed painfully. In the bathroom, he stripped down to his boxers, tossing his uniform in the dirty clothes basket. Then he peeled his kerchief, stiff with dried blood, off the wound. He held his wrist under hot water from the bathroom sink faucet, clenching his jaw against the hurt as he watched blood spiral down the drain. Once the wound was washed with Hibiclens and rinsed, he doused it with seventy percent isopropyl alcohol straight from the bottle, sucking air through his teeth. He dabbed the skin around the wound dry with a paper towel and hastily wrapped it with sterile gauze. No time to do more now. He wanted to get to the brewery before they closed.

He pulled on faded jeans and a Surfriders Foundation "Coastal Defenders" T-shirt and traded his field boots for comfortable Velcro-fastening sneakers. Relieved of the sweaty band of the regulation Fish and Wildlife cap he'd worn all day, he gave his head a good rub to get the blood flowing. Glancing in a mirror reminded him that he should get a haircut soon in order to stay within CDFW grooming standards protocol. He finger combed most of the tangles out of his unruly curls and brushed a sun-streaked whorl away from his eyes. Leaning in closer, he squinted at his reflection. No gray in his hair yet. But was there a little white sprinkled into the tawny stubble on his face?

He tugged a 49ers ball cap down over his tousled, blondish hair, grabbed a windbreaker, his phone and his wallet, plucked his car keys out of the large abalone shell resting on a rattan table by the front door, locked the house, and headed out in his pride and joy—a classic candy apple red 2017 Ford Mustang Shelby GT350 Voodoo V8 convertible.

Back out on the coast highway, he continued north, watching for more whale spouts along the way. Low on the horizon, the sun spilled a brilliant shimmer of molten sterling across the wild ocean.

He spotted a red-tailed hawk circling above. Every few miles, a redtail showed up again—perched on one of the electrical wires spooling alongside the road, soaring above the organic strawberry, Brussels sprout, and artichoke fields that checkered the coast, disappearing over the redwood-fringed ridgetops of the coastal mountains.

For a moment, he imagined that this was the same hawk that ravens had flushed out of the oak trees above the cat woman's body. Was it tracking him? He dismissed the notion as crazy thinking, reminding himself that California's Central Coast had a healthy population of raptors, and redtails were the most common hawk in the area.

As he passed the elephant seal reserve at Año Nuevo State Park, the sun low on the horizon flamed out from under drifting clouds, momentarily blinding him. Memories flashed through his mind of his UCSL environmental studies internship at Año, leading people on hikes over sand dunes and through ancient Indian middens to view the giant pinnipeds' rookery. Fresh out of the 'Stan back then, Colin had been searching for something to give meaning to his life. That experience as an environmental intern at Año had clinched his resolve to become a Fish and Wildlife Warden.

★   ★   ★

When Colin reached the lonely tavern a few miles before Pigeon Point Lighthouse, at the southern edge of the small community of Pescadero, Colin turned off the coast road onto a dirt parking lot. He put the top up and locked his 'Stang, crossed the highway, and ambled down to the beach to watch the sunset.

Standing on the sand, facing the sea, he followed a train of thoughts leading from the poor dead woman to his deceased mother, whom he deeply loved and missed. The cat woman's emanation of strength and dignity, even in death, had reminded him of his mother and flared up the ache of existential loneliness he'd felt since her passing.

His shrink from Kandahar would point out that he'd had a lot of triggers today. He cleared and refocused his mind until he was fully immersed in the unfathomable beauty of light and color transforming sky and ocean.

Just as the dying sun melted gold into the sea, it ejected a small brilliant emerald jewel.

They say that one who has seen the green flash will never ere in matters of the heart.

Venus appeared like a sparkler in the twilight. "First star I've seen tonight … Wish I might …"

June 2013, Kandahar Province, Afghanistan. In a military hospital for PTSD, waiting to be discharged. I'll be going home soon. Someone's wife has shipped him a telescope. Without all the light pollution from big cities, the night sky here is intense—amazing beyond imagining. Midnight. We watch with special filtered glasses for about an hour while Venus—a little black dot—crosses the sun. They tell us this is the last transit of Venus in our lifetime. The next transit of Venus won't take place until 2117. Yeah. Pretty sure I'll be dead by then. If Venus is the Goddess of Love and she isn't going to transit again in my lifetime, does that mean I've missed my chance at ever finding love?

The bitter taste of depression sat on his tongue and constricted his throat. He'd been teetering for months on the edge of that black hole. *Clinical depression. If I fall back in, I might never get out again.*

Deepening sunset purples bruised the sky. Colin stepped up to the entrance of the funky Route 1 Brewery. Good cooking smells reminded him how hungry he was. A masked girl welcomed him in, handed him a menu, and gestured toward an empty table in a far corner of the room.

Public venues in the state had reopened after the latest mutant viral surge, but California—with one of the lowest infection and fatality rates in the country—still erred on the side of caution, requiring vaccination, regular testing and masking of food service workers, monitored observance of Covid cleaning standards in restaurants, and distancing protocols. But with no standardization of public health protocols nationally, much less globally, new Covid variants just kept on mutating. The Covid virus had gone endemic. It seemed to Colin, as a trained ecologist, that the pandemic was just one more broken strand in the unraveling web of life.

The *thunk* of Colin's shoes on the old wooden floorboards grounded him. He felt more solid, more in his body as he scraped his chair up to a small table in a dark corner of the room. Felt even better as the first swallow of craft-brewed Storm Surge Porter landed in his belly. Storm Surge. A house specialty—deep reddish black, with a hint of chocolate. Colin glanced around for the brewery owner, an old friend, but didn't see him.

A gust of cold wind blew through the tavern as a man with a flamboyant gay vibe swooped through the door. His copper-colored face and obsidian black eyes lit up as he greeted his friends. Out from under his bowler hat—adorned with a beaded band and hawk feathers—flowed long blue-black hair. Colorful ribbons streamed from the shoulders of his fancy shirt. He appeared to be in his early thirties—about Colin's age. When their eyes met, a hawk's piercing whistle shot through Colin's mind.

The man turned and moved toward a table on the other side of the room.

Colin downed the rest of his beer.

He watched the newcomer approach a table occupied by the typical North Coast crowd: surfers, next gen hippies, organic farmers, students, artist types. Mostly young Millennials and Gen Z, they were the usual fusion of Latinx, Black, Asian, Anglo. The man who'd just arrived put his hand on the shoulder of a beautiful Native American girl—*er, woman*—and whispered something to her. A sudden tear rolled down her cheek. She brushed it away with the side of her hand.

The group shuffled chairs to make room for the stranger. He sat next to her, holding her hand.

Colin moved to the bar to get another beer, and to get a closer look at the woman. She seemed familiar.

It hit him all of a sudden, and a shiver ran down his spine. She looked like the dead mountain lion woman, only younger.

She caught him staring at her. *Oh hell no. She's coming to talk to me?*

She walked toward him with the ferocity and grace of a stalking cat.

Sweating like the outside of his cold beer glass, he pulled his ball cap down over his eyes and peered into the depths of his dark porter.

She sat down on the stool next to him. Her complex, subtle scent enveloped him: sweet wild lilac, smoky sage, native prairie grasses under untamed open sky, piney woods, salty ocean spray, bee balm, the bright mineral tang of parched earth after a rain. Pure wild woman. Sensations inside his body pinged all over the map.

Colin forced himself to face her and smile. "Hello." He tipped the visor of his 49er's cap.

"Hi," she said. "I noticed you staring at me," she said. "Have we met?"

"Sorry, ma'am. I don't think so. Didn't mean to make you feel uncomfortable. Actually, I was looking at that guy you were talking to. I think I might have met him before. Mind telling me his name?"

The woman glanced back toward her table. "That's my cousin, Hawk."

"I apologize if I'm being too personal, but I noticed you were crying. Is everything all right?"

Her eyes welled up again, and a tear rolled down her cheek. She brushed it away with a long, graceful finger. "Not really."

"Mind if I ask what's going on?"

The beautiful woman lowered her eyes and twisted the colorful woven friendship bracelet around her wrist. There was no ring on her finger. Colin was afraid he'd blown it. He shouldn't have pried. None of his business.

She lifted her chin, and her eyes, still welling with unshed tears, met his. Eyes of unearthly, intense topaz—like deep ocean reflecting a clear blue sky—did not waver as she spoke.

"Hawk just told me that my mother was murdered." She whispered the words as if she didn't fully believe them. "I feel like I've been run over by a freight train. Sorry. I'm not thinking clearly. I shouldn't have imposed on you. I have no idea why I came over here. I felt weirdly compelled to talk to you. Everything seems so surreal. My mother can't just be gone without warning."

"I might have found her body," Colin blurted before he could think.

The woman gasped as if she'd been gut punched. "What? When?" She clutched the abalone shell hanging on a leather cord at her throat. "Where?"

"Up on the Cougar Creek Ranch reserve land, this afternoon. I'm a wildlife warden. I responded to a call about a mountain lion kill, and instead I found a woman. She looked a lot like you. Maybe your mom?"

Arms wrapped tight around her chest, she rocked back and forth on her seat, shoulders quaking.

"I'm so, so sorry." Colin resisted the instinct to take her in his arms and comfort her.

Careful. Don't touch people without permission. Especially this woman. She just lost her mother. Respect boundaries.

He felt really bad for her. She'd gone pale as a ghost and was obviously trying hard not to lose it.

"This might be a weird thing to say," said Colin, "but when my mom died, it helped me process and made things feel less surreal when I was able to talk about it. So, if you want to talk about your mom, I'm here for you."

Those intense topaz eyes confronted him. "Was she already dead when you found her?"

Colin didn't know what to say. He couldn't talk about an open investigation. He'd already said too much. Slowly, he slid his empty glass around on the bar, pushing it through rivulets of condensation with the caution of an explorer oaring through unknown territory.

Finally, the woman took a deep breath, sat up straighter, and pulled her shoulders back. "So, what's your name?"

"I'm Colin. Colin Dawson."

"Dawson? Sounds like an Irish name."

"Yeah." Colin laughed self-consciously, relieved that she'd changed the subject. "My grandma was the granddaughter of Irish immigrants. A hippie anti-Vietnam war activist who fell in love with a Black Navy helicopter pilot when she was eighteen. She got pregnant with my dad. Grandpa died in 'Nam, so Gramma went to live in an Oregon commune, where she raised my dad. Gramma and my mom raised me. Gramma claimed she had Native American blood, but I always thought that was just her hippie BS." Colin smiled at the memory. "My mom was a schoolteacher."

He paused to look into those topaz eyes and mentally kicked himself. He always either clammed up or talked too much when he was nervous, especially around women. And this woman had just found out her mother was murdered. "Sorry. That was probably way too much information."

"It's okay." Delfina smiled through her grief. "Do your mom and grandmother live nearby?"

Colin frowned and stared into the bottom of his beer glass. That ache whenever he allowed himself to feel the loss, usually stashed away deep in his chest, welled up and squeezed his heart. He nodded to the barmaid to bring him another beer. "Mom and Gramma both passed away during the first year of Covid, in February of 2020, before we even had a vaccine."

"Oh no. I'm so, so sorry." Sincere compassion shone from the woman's eyes. "What about your father?"

Amazing that she can focus on my bullshit at a time like this. Maybe she welcomes the distraction from her mom's death.

"Yeah. Gramma's son, my dad, was career military like his father. Died in Fallujah in '04 when I was thirteen. I enlisted because I wanted to be a hero and serve my country like my father and grandfather. What a horrible joke. Gramma warned me, but I didn't listen. I found out, though. I love my country. I'm definitely still a patriot. But war is hell. There are so many contradictions. It felt like a betrayal of everything I believed in, everything I thought I was fighting for."

The barmaid filled Colin's glass with a fresh draft of Storm Surge Porter and plunked it on the bar. Colin took a long swallow to get rid of the bitter taste at the back of his throat.

"I'm sorry." The woman leaned closer, and he breathed in her subtle scent. She placed her hand on Colin's arm, her fingertips lightly touching the Orca inked on his bicep. Her touch was gentle, yet he felt as if a drowning person had grasped him and was holding on for dear life. His muscles twitched.

Her touch was like fire. He realized his feelings were inappropriate given Delfina's circumstances, but how long had it been since a beautiful woman had touched him? The fact that the four years of extreme social isolation during the pandemic was coming to an end sank in. He swallowed and pulled away.

"How old are you?" she asked.

"Well, I was born in 1991. Played football and surfed in high school. Enlisted in the Army in '09 when I was eighteen. Did two tours, two years in Afghanistan. Honorably discharged in 2011. Spent a little time in a military hospital in the 'Stan, then took four years to get my B.S. at the University of California's Santa Lucia campus, two years in the Cal Fish and Wildlife Academy, and I've been a Wildlife Warden since 2017. You do the math."

"Whoa, thirty-two. You're an old man."

Colin was impressed. She was smart. A woman who wasn't math averse.

"Well actually, thirty-one. I'll turn thirty-two this summer. But come on. This isn't fair," he said. "You know my whole life story, and I don't even know your name yet."

"Nice to meet you, Colin. My name is Delfina Cuera." She shook Colin's hand.

When their hands made contact, electricity zapped through his core from head to toe. He sucked in air, as if they'd both just fallen out of a helicopter and he was holding on to her for dear life.

He took a swallow of beer and pulled himself together.

"Greetings, Delfina. Are you from around here?"

"Depends on what you mean by here." The haunted look in her eyes gave away her emotional turmoil. Colin recalled his feeling of numbness and disbelief when his mother and grandma first died, and how he'd relied on upbeat behavior to disguise a grief too overwhelming to reveal, especially to strangers. His heart broke for her.

"By 'around here,' do you mean Planet Earth, the USA, California, Santa Lucia County, or this lonely tavern out on the dark edge of the wounded coast?"

Colin shifted on his barstool. "Sure. All of the above."

"Well, it's complicated. My mother and I belong to the Kumeyaay Nation." Delfina spoke of her mother as if she were still alive.

"Sorry, never heard of them."

"Our ancestral territory includes present-day San Diego County, California, and the northern part of Baja California, Mexico. Anthropologists say we've been in California at least twelve thousand years, but according to our legends, we've always been here."

"I'm a third-generation Californian, so why haven't I ever heard of the Kumeyaay People?"

"Third generation, huh? My people have inhabited the regions of Southwest California and Baja Californio Norte for six hundred generations at least. But like I said, it's complicated."

"Please, enlighten me. Oh, by the way, can I get you something to drink, or eat, or … anything? I haven't had supper yet. I was planning on getting a meal here."

"I didn't think I was hungry, but —" Delfina looked over her shoulder at the people she'd been sitting with. A waitress was delivering food to their table. "I guess I could eat something."

"Great." Colin smiled. "Oh, here comes my brother-in-arms, James. He owns this place. We spent some time together in the sandbox."

A stocky man with a square jaw reached across the bar and the two men fist bumped. "Hooah."

"Yo, brah, great to see you. Wait a minute. Who's your beautiful friend, Colin?"

"James, this is Delfina Cuera. Delfina, meet James Owens."

"It's a pleasure," said Delfina. The forlorn and stoic shadow around her eyes belied her false cheerful tone of voice.

"So, Delfina, let me entertain you with my brother James's incredible slow food saga."

James polished the bar modestly while Colin introduced him. "James is an organic hog farmer, as well as a master brewer. Totally into the whole sustainable slow food movement. He feeds the spent organic hops from his beer brewing operation, along with his family's organic kitchen compost, to his pasture-raised happy hogs. He raises them from birth to slaughter with certified humane practices. Then he serves the pork with his organic beer here at his tavern. *Voilà!* Full circle. The guy's a genius. The hops gives his pork the most incredible flavor. You've gotta try the pulled pork on a San Francisco sourdough roll. It's insanely delish."

Delfina wrinkled her nose. "Thanks, but I'm vegan. I'll have the veggie lentil burger, sweet potato fries, and a glass of water. And a Golden Gate Lager, please."

James's smile shone like a lighthouse beacon. "Never seen you in here with a woman before, Col. Makes this a special occasion. Did you show her your high school football MVP trophy and your Silver Star and Purple Heart, yet?"

Colin pulled his cap visor down to shade his eyes. "Cool it, James. We just met."

"Tell you what—tonight, dinner is on the house. You were sitting over in the corner, right? I'll bring the food out to your table."

★   ★   ★

While they ate, Colin asked Delfina to tell him more about the Kumeyaay People.

"There are twelve remaining bands of the Kumeyaay Nation. The conquering Spanish called us Diegueño. We currently own federally recognized Kumeyaay Reservations in San Diego County and Kumiai Indio tribal rancherias in Baja, Mexico."

Colin dipped a garlic fry in barbeque sauce. This was interesting, even though it sounded like a spiel she delivered to audiences.

"Of course many of us, like me, don't live on reservations anymore. We're 'assimilated.'" Delfina made air quotes around the word. "We go to college, have jobs in high tech and white-collar professions." She paused to take a sip of her beer, then squinted at him. "Do I sound like a Native nerd? Sorry, but not sorry."

"I get it. I'm the same way when someone asks me about being a wildlife warden. It's like they push a button, and I can't stop spewing information. Go on, please. I'm interested. What kind of work do you do?"

"At the moment, I'm a farmworker. But this fall I'll be going to grad school. After high school I went to Kumeyaay Community College for a year, then to UC San Diego for a year, then transferred to UCSL in 2018. Graduated with a double BA in Environmental Science and Poli-Sci in 2020, just before the pandemic locked things down. I postponed grad school. Been working at Agua Pura, an organic farm here on the coast, biding my time until the pandemic runs its course."

"Poli-Sci. Sounds like you're on a law school track?"

"How'd you guess?" She sounded defensive. "Maybe you think you can stereotype me, but I don't care. I'm proud of being the first in my community to go to law school. I've been accepted to Berkeley School of Law. Fellowship with a full ride. I start this September."

"Congratulations. That's awesome. I bet you're going to specialize in tribal law, right?"

"Of course." Her eyes flashed fire. "Tribal and environmental law. No way I would get a fancy law degree and then abandon my people. Did you know that legally, reservations are separate, sovereign nations? We have our own constitution; we're governed by our Kwaaypaay—our spiritual leader, and an elected council. Yet our people still get in terrible situations off the rez that require representation by attorneys licensed to practice in the US justice system. For example, some of our traditionals— elderly Kumeyaay who've stayed on the reservation all their lives—barely realize there's a border between the US and Mexico. So, when they cross the border along our traditional wilderness trails to visit family in Baja— the way we've done for centuries—and then try to travel home again, they often get stopped and detained. They have no papers. Most don't speak English. Currently, ten of our Beloved Elders are in prison. All of them over eighty years old, with critical health conditions. They need to be home with their medicine and their families. It's an outrage."

"Sounds like a mess, for real."

"Oh, you have no idea. What's going on at the border is monstrous. To be clear, the problem is the former president's racist policies and the extreme right-wing border police. ICE sometimes even arrests us Indigenous

Natives—the First People of this land—claiming we're 'illegal immigrants'! It's outrageous. They are the immigrants, not us! And the way they separated undocumented migrant children from their parents and kept the kids in cages is beyond anything I ever thought I'd see in the US in the twenty-first century. Things are getting more humane now under the Biden administration, but there's still so much to sort out."

"So that's why you and your mom moved up here to the Central Coast?" Colin felt Delfina flinch when he mentioned her mother.

She glanced down at her bracelet. Colin wondered if her mother had given it to her. "Every day it felt more dangerous to live down south as an Indigenous person," Delfina said. "We have family here, and when we heard that Santa Lucia had declared itself a sanctuary county we decided to move."

"That was in 2018? So, how old are you, Delfina?"

"Born in '97. You do the math."

"You're twenty-six?"

"Yes. But wait. Why do I feel like I'm being questioned by the police?"

"Whoa. I'm not the police. Just a fish and wildlife warden, off duty, ma'am." Colin put his hand over his heart. "I'm interested in what you have to say, that's all. If it's not too weird, I'd like to be your friend, Delfina, okay?"

Delfina's eyes met Colin's, reminding him of the way her mother's eyes had touched his soul as she died. "Thank you," she said.

"Of course," said Colin, reaching in his pocket. "In fact, here's my card. This has got to be a rough time for you. Please feel free to contact me anytime. I'll do anything I can to help you."

Delfina took the card. "Thank you. I will."

"Mind sharing your contact info with me?"

Colin couldn't believe he was being so forward. He wasn't usually so brash as to ask a woman he'd just met for her phone number. He felt guilty, but this was official business. Lieutenant Rosa would expect him to get her information.

"Okay. I'll text it to you when I get home and have cell service."

"Hey," Colin blurted, "if you're not going to finish those, could I have them?" Delfina laughed when he reached over and grabbed her remaining sweet potato fries.

"How was your veggie burger?"

"Very good, thank you."

The man called Hawk stepped up to the table and stood at Delfina's shoulder.

"Everything all right, Cuz?"

Delfina nodded.

"My friends and I will be leaving here in thirty minutes or so. If you like, I can meet you at your house and stay with you tonight," said Hawk. "I don't think you should be alone."

"That sounds like a really good idea. I'll meet you there. You know where the extra key is, in case you get there before me, right? I'm so grateful for you, Hawk." Delfina shivered even though the evening was warm.

Hawk turned from Delfina and stared directly at Colin. Colin wondered how Hawk knew that Delfina's mother had been murdered.

The memory of the hawk flushing out of the oaks at the murder scene, and the multiple hawk sightings on the way up the coast, niggled at the edges of Colin's mind.

Has Hawk been watching us all evening?

As Hawk returned to his friends' table, that strange image Colin had hallucinated just as he left the murder scene—a silhouette of a huge man with wings—played again like a stuttering vintage black and white film clip in Colin's mind. A hawk's scream pierced his brain like an arrow.

Delfina's voice brought Colin back to the present moment. "I'm thinking a visit to the ocean would help me feel better right now. Would you like to take a walk?"

4

B LACK NIGHT ENGULFED Delfina and Colin as they stepped outside. Up and down the coast for miles in all directions, wild nature reigned over the dark—free to carry on the essential rhythms of nocturnal life undisrupted by human structures and artificial lights.

Turning their backs on the bright little tavern, sole human outpost in an obsidian abyss, Delfina and Colin gazed at stars spilled over the sky.

"Diamonds on black velvet," said Delfina.

She pointed to the brightest diamond, blazing like a jet circling over the Pacific on its approach to San Jose International. "That looks like a plane."

"Nope," he said. "It's Sirius."

"It's serious all right."

"No. I mean that bright light is a star called S-i-r-i-u-s. The brightest star in our sky. Orion's faithful hunting dog, Sirius, a.k.a. the Dog Star."

"I was just joking with you, Colin. I know Sirius. We Kumeyaay are big on astronomy. Orion is a Hunter in our cosmology too. We call him Kwechnyay."

"Oh, hey, look over there, low above the ocean to the west." Colin pointed to a red-green-yellow-orange-blue sparkler. "Venus. Keep your eye on that. In a few minutes she'll disappear over the horizon."

Delfina nodded. "See that faint dot about three fingers above Venus? That's Mercury."

Colin studied Delfina with growing appreciation, and smiled. "He'll soon be following Venus over the edge."

"Come on," said Delfina. "Let's cross the highway and go down to the beach."

"Careful. Are you okay in the dark without a flashlight?"

Delfina yelped as she ran across the deserted highway ahead of Colin.

Her forlorn yowl sounded like the existential cry of a small creature in the dark issuing its challenge to the omnipotent mechanism grinding up lives in the never-ending wheel of time.

"Hey, wait for me!" Colin shouted.

★   ★   ★

Barefoot, they walked along the water's edge toward bright Capella in the arms of Auriga the Goat Boy. They took little notice as the constellation slowly tumbled over the edge of night into the void.

Alone with Delfina in the middle of nowhere, Colin felt a moment of panic. What should they talk about?

"The pandemic years were unbelievably awful," said Delfina. "I'm so relieved it's finally at least kind of behind us. I guess it was especially bad for you."

Over her shoulder, the Big Dipper poured stars and planets into the ocean.

"Losing my mom and gramma sucked, of course," said Colin. "But I'm pretty much of a loner so, in terms of the isolation, not so bad. How about for you?"

"It's been tough, especially for my mom."

There it was again. She spoke as if her mom were still alive.

She's in denial. I should be straight with her, tell her what I saw—what I thought I saw. But how can I? What should I say? What am I allowed to say without violating investigative protocol?

"Sorry," said Delfina. "I'm feeling kind of numb. I don't know if this is a normal reaction when someone you love dies, but I kind of feel like I'm not ready to take it in yet. I'm afraid that once I completely open to what's happened, I'll just lose it."

They walked along in silence, listening to the waves shush over the sand.

"Was she alive when you found her?" Delfina's voice was tight and strained, as if she halfway didn't want to know the answer to the question she'd just asked.

Colin kept his head down, trudging darkly through soft sand. His heart drummed in counterpoint to the rhythm of the waves.

"Say something, please."

"Yes. She was alive. I watched her die."

Delfina cried out—a few short, sharp wails—small fists pounding against the fortress of death.

Colin waited, alert. Night wrapped thicker around him. His heart beat louder. Gentle waves rattled small rocks and shells in and out over the sand.

Finally, Delfina spoke. Her angry voice broke through the night as if kicking in a door. "Did she say anything? Did my mother talk to you before she died?"

Colin hesitated.

Finally, he answered. "No."

"How did she die?" Her voice wavered with grief. "Do you think she was murdered?"

Colin wanted to cry, scream, run away. He didn't want to be the one to tell her. And professionally, it would be a breach of protocol to disclose details of a police investigation. Yet, this woman deserved the truth.

He turned and planted his feet full stop in front of her. The top of her head was level with his chin. Glimmers of starlight shone in her braided blue-black hair. She looked up and her eyes met his. His resolve to maintain professional boundaries crumbled.

"Yes, Delfina, your mother's death is being investigated as a homicide."

Drops of starlight rolled down her cheeks. "How do you know?"

"I'm sorry, but I don't how to say this except to put it bluntly. There was an arrow through her heart." The bloody image flashed through Colin's mind. "The sheriff's office had taken custody of the scene by the time I left. I was asked to return tomorrow to assist with the investigation."

"No!" Delfina covered her face with her hands and sobbed.

"I'm so sorry." Colin again fought the impulse to gather her in his arms. He shoved his trembling hands in his pockets and gazed up at the stars.

When her sobs subsided, Delfina whispered, "Was there anything else?"

"What do you mean?"

"Do you have any idea who killed her?"

"It's not my investigation, Delfina. The sheriff's office is in charge. At least for now."

"For now?"

"Yeah. I mean a US Marshal showed up before I left, and some state police were milling around with the city cops. The national monument is federal land, so I wouldn't be surprised if the FBI stepped in to supervise the whole team at some point. I assume it's going to end up being a multiagency response."

"But you were there first, right? You were alone with her when she died. I can tell you're an intelligent man, Colin. Didn't you notice something? Anything? Were there any clues?"

Colin took a deep breath. *Should I tell her?*

"Okay. I did find a broken piece of a tracking collar. The kind the Puma Project uses to track mountain lions. It seemed odd. The reason I was at the ranch was because someone reported seeing an illegal mountain lion hunter."

"Colin, I think there's something you're not saying. Please."

Oh, fuck. This is where she's going to find out how crazy you are. Sayonara, mi cariño. It's been a nice fantasy amigo but there's no way this beautiful, amazing woman will want to be around you when she figures out you're batshit looney tunes. Fuck.

"All right. I didn't want to tell you because if I do, you'll think I'm a psycho and you'll probably never speak to me again. But all right. All right. I had a hallucination, I think. Okay?"

"What kind of hallucination?"

"So, when I first found her, um, I didn't see a woman, not a human at all. I found a mountain lion dying under the oaks. Under the trees it was dark and shadowy, you know? With the sun and clouds making these wavy patterns all over the ground and over the body, and, well ... I—I have PTSD from my time in Afghanistan. So sometimes flashing lights can trigger me to have hallucinations. Anyway, I thought I saw a mountain lion. I got in close. I knelt next to the body, and it still looked to me like a puma, a cougar. It had an arrow stuck through its heart, and it was thrashing around, in pain, bleeding out fast. And then, while I watched .. . Okay, this is really bizarre, okay? But while I knelt there by the puma, it—she—just started to ... I don't know what to call it. She seemed to morph, just change shape before my eyes, and, and … she turned into a woman. The mountain lion turned into a woman. She looked like you, but older. She looked into my eyes like she knew me, like she could see into my soul, and then she died. I'm so sorry. Please don't judge me, Delfina. I'm really, really sorry about your mother."

Delfina didn't make a sound. She stared at him. Waves crashed on shore like distant enemy fire. He feared he might have an episode, a flashback. He started his breathing exercise and soundlessly chanted his mantra.

The world spun around faster and faster. *Vertigo.* Colin lost his balance and toppled onto the sand.

Delfina sat down next to him and took his hand. "Colin? It's okay. Hey, maybe it wasn't a hallucination."

Colin fought his way through a dark tunnel, toward the light, back to her.

"What? Delfina, what are you saying?"

"It's complicated. Never mind." Delfina put the back of her hand to his forehead. "You don't seem to have a fever. You've been vaccinated, right?"

Colin nodded. "Of course. I don't have Covid."

"Are you feeling better?"

"Yeah. I'm fine." Colin sat up. "Just got a little dizzy. James's porter packs a wallop."

"Thank you for telling me the truth about what you saw, Colin. It means a lot to me."

Colin sighed with relief. After all that, she wasn't running away from him.

"Whoa. Wait. Look up there. What is that?" Delfina pointed to a dotted line of lights blinking across the sky. "An alien flying saucer invasion? Maybe the Russians and Chinese are invading from space?"

Colin laughed, relieved for the out-of-left field change of subject. "Wow. Awesome." *She clearly needs this emotional space away from the reality of her mother's death.*

"It's so weird looking," Delfina said. "Like a Bay Area Rapid Transit rail train in the sky."

"It must be Elon Musk's SpaceX Starlink satellite train."

"SpaceX?" Delfina considered the lights twinkling across the sky with her full attention, as if the Starlink launch were the most profound event happening in her life.

"Yeah. Musk has been launching thousands of interlinked satellites to form an artificial internet 'constellation.' He plans to keep them in a low Earth orbit indefinitely."

"Oh yeah. I read about that, but this is the first time I've seen it," said Delfina. "It's amazing looking."

"He claims he's going to save the world by providing everyone on the globe access to low-cost broadband internet with his satellites."

"Most likely he'll make a ton of money off it."

"I think it's a good thing that everyone anywhere who wants internet connectivity can have it," said Colin. "But an artificial constellation? How is that not against the law?"

Delfina frowned. "Yeah. Right? Can he just fill up the sky with space junk like that? What about people who don't want internet access? And what about people who enjoy the night sky the way it is? For my tribe, the dark night sky is sacred."

Colin and Delfina watched the continuously regenerating asterism stutter across the night like a TV news chyron. When it finally disappeared, Delfina sighed.

"Colin, I need to see my mother. Can you help me?"

Colin nodded. "I can try. Her body will be with the coroner. Normally, in the case of homicide, they make next of kin wait to see the loved one until the forensic pathologist's investigation has been completed and the coroner has released the body to a mortuary. But I'll see what I can do. May I call you in the morning?"

"Of course."

"Great. How about if you just enter your contact info in my phone right now?" Colin handed her his phone.

Delfina entered her contacts and handed back the phone.

"Okay if I add your photo?"

Delfina smiled and nodded, and Colin took her photo.

"Please feel free to call or text me anytime, Delfina. I'll do anything I can to help you. The coroner is in the sheriff's headquarters in downtown Playa Azul, near Kind Peoples Marijuana Dispensary. If I manage to get you permission to see her, I should go with you. We can meet there."

"Colin, my mother practiced a traditional lifestyle as closely as she could manage. Our strict traditions do not permit disfigurement of the deceased. My mother's body must be handled with the utmost respect.

I understand that in the case of a homicide investigation, we shouldn't refuse an autopsy, but Mama at least needs a sacred ceremonial burial."

"I'll do everything I can to make sure that happens."

"I understand that you're not the police, but you can help me find out who murdered my mother, I know it. Help me figure this out. Please?"

Colin leaned in and looked closely at Delfina's beautiful face. What he saw was more than grief. She was frightened.

His forehead creased. "Delfina, do you think that whoever killed your mother might want to harm you too?"

Delfina shivered and gazed out over the pearl black ocean.

She turned toward Colin and whispered, "Yes."

5

COLIN WALKED DELFINA back to her car.

On the drive back down the coast to his house, his mind swirled with the day's dramatic events. The wound on his wrist burned and throbbed painfully.

As soon as he walked through his front door, he headed straight to the bathroom and a hot shower. Carefully, he washed his wound—reopened and bleeding—with disinfectant soap. Stepping out of the shower into his steamy bathroom, he toweled dry, then daubed away the blood at his wrist with sterile gauze until he could see the wound well enough to examine it.

This is a tooth puncture wound. Definitely not a human bite. It's cougar.

Oh, hell no. I can't remember being bitten.

Fuck. Now what?

Colin's mind raced, running through his options.

Tetanus shot? Nope. I'm up-to-date. Antibiotics? Not unless the wound starts showing signs of infection. Rabies? Fuckin' hell. Never take a chance with rabies. Always fatal unless treated in time. Hey, this is no big deal. Animal bites are an occupational hazard. I've kept up with my boosters. I'll just get the rabies protocol started as soon as urgent care opens in the morning. But how do I explain the bite?

Damn. Admit the truth. I was bitten by a mountain lion.

Colin irrigated his wound with Hibiclens and covered it with sterile gauze, swallowed an extra strength Tylenol tablet, then went to bed.

In his sleep, he sweated and shouted.

Burst of shrapnel! Burning. Stinging. Stabbing. Hurts like hell. Have to get my team through this.

He woke up, threw off his covers, made his way to the bathroom without turning on the lights, and splashed cold water on his face. Another frackin' nightmare about the skirmish that had earned him a Purple Heart and Silver Star. He didn't feel like a hero. He'd just done what was needed under the circumstances to make sure his squad came home safely. No hero. Just an angry, discouraged, damaged, lonely, exhausted kid in a thirty-two-year-old man's body.

He plodded through his house to the kitchen, poured himself a glass of cold filtered water, and carried it to the second bedroom he used as a home office. Placing his water glass on his desk, he sat and opened his CDFW laptop. He updated his timesheet, documenting his activities for the last several days.

Colin loved the freedom and autonomy of his job. As long as he worked a total of five eight-hour days a week and emailed his timesheet to his captain at the end of each month, no one questioned where or when he put in his hours. If he worked more than forty hours a month, he could put in for overtime. Captain Stevens, who supervised CDFW activities for five counties, rarely questioned Colin about why or how he chose to spend his time. Colin felt good knowing that his boss respected him and trusted his judgment.

When he'd finished updating his timesheet, he returned to bed and opened one of his books about PTSD and traumatic brain injury. He sat up in bed and read until his eyelids grew heavy and he was dropping his book in his lap. Then he forced himself to place his book on the side table and turn off the light. He tossed and turned until a few hours before dawn. Finally, he sank into a deep sleep.

At 6:50 the next morning, Colin rose with the sun, made coffee, and dressed in a freshly laundered uniform: beige Wildlife Warden

shirt and forest green pants. He tugged on his field boots, clipped on his badge, retrieved the weapons from his safe, readied his green CDFW truck for the day, and drove fifteen miles down the coast to the nearest urgent care clinic, on the west side of the town of Playa Azul.

Since he'd received his last rabies booster less than two years ago, he only needed to get two shots. He told the physician's assistant at the clinic that while responding to a Fish and Wildlife call, he'd been bitten by an injured puma, but the animal had shown no signs of rabies. *Truth.*

Heart racing, he signed the required paperwork agreeing to treatment. Hopefully, within the overburdened bureaucracy of public agencies, no one would put this bite report together with the murdered woman found at the exact same time and location.

After getting his first shot and making an appointment for the next, he stopped at one of his favorite taquerias for a breakfast burrito, checked his phone, then headed back up the coast to revisit the crime scene.

★   ★   ★

A squad of city cops stopped Colin at the entrance gate to Cougar Creek Coast Ranch Road. A young officer with a clipboard and an inflated sense of self-importance confronted Colin. "State your business, Warden."

"Fish and Wildlife Warden Colin Dawson. First on the scene of the homicide yesterday. Lieutenant Rosa requested that I report back this morning to assist with the investigation."

The officer logged Colin's name, badge number, and time of entry, then contacted the command post for authorization to admit.

"You're clear to enter. Command post is on the terrace 1.35 miles up the road. Lieutenant Rosa wants to see you ASAP."

With his truck windows wide open, Colin drove through the outer crime scene perimeter and up the ranch road. An ocean breeze carried the sound of lowing cows and newborn calves, and the faint, honest scent of free-range cow manure across the open coastal prairie, soothing Colin like a lullaby after the horror of yesterday's murder.

Despite the many times he'd driven this road, he was overcome by the beauty of the spring green hills gently rolling down to the sea, dramatically illuminated this morning by a changeable sky, the high cumulonimbus dark with the possibility of cloudbursts. Maritime currents from the northwest had blown a typical seasonal pressure front to the California coast.

Cerulean blue, sap green, California gold, seafoam white, magenta shadows—his soul drank it in, renewing Colin's deep love for his homeland.

His hippie gramma had been an oil painter, and he'd dabbled with oil painting a little himself, discovering his love of color while overseas in the military hospital. Apparently, art therapy was considered beneficial for people with PTSD. But Colin understood the limitations of using paint and canvas, or even a camera, to convey the powerful emotions called forth by the miracle of light and color on planet Earth. The best he could do was savor the beauty of this moment.

After the first cattle guard, the road sharply curved and steepened. Far below to the west, a kettle of about twenty turkey vultures soared in a slow circle above a deep erosion gully.

What are they feeding on? A calf stillborn or maybe mauled by a pack of coyotes, or by a mountain lion? Maybe the vultures are just cleaning up the afterbirth of a newborn calf. Or are they smelling yesterday's murder?

An image of Delfina's mother, dead eyes wide open, bloody body still warm, flashed across Colin's mind. He stomped on the brakes just before his truck veered over the cliff.

Yanking the gearshift into park and pulling on the emergency brake, Colin closed his eyes and took deep breaths until his equilibrium returned. Then he continued the drive up toward the command post.

Like waves, the coastal hills rolled up and up from sea level all the way to redwood-forested ridgetops. For eons, tectonic action from volcanic rifts offshore had been pushing the Pacific plate underneath the edge of the continental plate, forcing the coast to buckle, wrinkle, fold, crumple, thrust up, and form the coastal mountain range. Rocks containing fossilized underwater sea creatures were scattered over the tops of these mountains.

A little more than a mile up from the park entrance gate, Colin reached a natural terrace somewhat larger than a football field, covered with native grasses and spring wildflowers. The oak grove where Colin had found Delfina's dying mother stood at the edge of this grassy meadow. From this terrace, ancient oaks sprawled over the rolling hills all the way up to the ridgetop, where they gave way to Sequoia sempervirens, planet Earth's tallest trees.

A Federal Bureau of Land Management planning official, studying a map in a distant office on the East Coast, had designated this meadow of rare native wildflowers and endangered native grasses as the site of a future public parking lot for the new national monument. The Ohlone Native Land Trust, aligned with other conservation groups, had filed a lawsuit, asserting that the plateau had been a significant Native ceremonial site, likely containing important archeological relics and possible human remains that should not be disturbed. Moreover, the rare native grasses and wildflowers made this a sensitive ecological habitat for threatened and endangered fauna.

Cringing, Colin rolled his truck tires over the wildflowers and buried sacred relics. He parked in the sheriff's staging area with other official vehicles. The meadow was buzzing with activity.

Burrowing owls, grasshopper sparrows, bush rabbits, harvest mice, tiger beetles, and all the other wildlife intricately woven together in the fabric of this habitat had no doubt been frightened away by the commotion.

Colin glanced toward the oak grove. Yellow police tape, dripping and sagging with last night's condensed fog, cordoned off the inner perimeter of the crime scene.

Inside a large tent, Colin found Lieutenant Rosa speaking with personnel from several law enforcement agencies. Deputies managed communications and studied maps, charts, and computer screens.

An officer with a camera around her neck attached a photograph to a six-foot-by-six-foot magnetic whiteboard on wheels. *The murder board.*

The photographer smiled at Colin. "We're getting a mobile WiFi unit up here soon so we can set this up as a digital smart board. Meanwhile, the murder board is old school."

Colin approached Lieutenant Rosa and stood at attention until the lieutenant turned to acknowledge him.

"Colin Dawson reporting for duty, sir."

"At ease. What have you got for me, son?"

"Here's a hard copy list of all the people I can think of who have keys to the Cougar Creek Coast Ranch property, sir, as well as locals I know of who often hike here. I also emailed this to you as a Google Doc." Colin handed Lieutenant Rosa the list.

The lieutenant glanced at it and then, with a hard squint, scrutinized Colin. "Good. What else?"

"I—um, I met the victim's daughter last night."

"What! We didn't get an ID on the deceased until this morning. How the hell did you locate her daughter?"

"It was just random, sir. When I left here yesterday evening, after I stopped at home to change out of my uniform, I drove up to the Route 1 Brewery to get some dinner. I met a woman there who looked like the victim. Turns out, she's Ramona Cuera's daughter. Her name is Delfina. Delfina Cuera."

"You got her number, I hope."

"Yes sir." Colin's cheeks flushed. "Delfina's information is at the top of that list I gave you. She wants to see her mother's body as soon as possible. They're Native American. Her mother needs to have a traditional ceremonial burial."

"Did you explain to her that in a murder investigation it will be some time before we can release the body for burial?"

"Yes sir."

"I'll let the coroner's office know you're going to contact them to make a request for Delfina to view her mother's body. There's a good possibility they'll want her to come in to do a positive visual ID, but don't get her hopes up." Lieutenant Rosa's sharp eyes met Colin's head on. "Anything else, Warden?"

Colin squirmed. *This guy sees right through people. He can probably tell there's something off about me. Does he view me as a suspect?*

"I'm ready to assist on the evidence search today, sir."

"Good. Report to the lead officer at that table with the maps. She'll assign you to a team. We've drawn up a search grid of the entire seven-thousand-acre crime scene. At this point, I think it's unlikely that the killer is still here in the park, but drones are scanning the outer areas just in case. A SWAT team is standing by with ATVs in the event that a subject is spotted."

"Do you want me to stand by with SWAT?"

"No. I have other officers searching the grid of the immediate perimeter on foot. That's where I want you for now, Dawson. You're known to be a keen observer. We need something, anything, that will help us identify the suspect. I want every inch of this national monument photographed and sifted through with a fine net. You'll start in zone one, the innermost perimeter. This search must be thorough, meticulous, systematic. Remember, maintaining scene integrity is paramount. Make sure you wear protective clothing. Get a Tyvek jumpsuit and nitrile gloves at the search site. Don't forget to cover your shoes, too." Rosa squinted, hardening his glare a few more notches. "No screw-ups, Warden Dawson."

6

B Y 9:30 A.M., COLIN WAS BACK under the oaks where he'd found the dying mountain lion woman. Photographers and forensic artists were documenting the scene. A detective, two deputies, and a forensic tech spread out in a tight line alongside Colin to walk their grid, searching for hairs, fibers, fingerprints, trace evidence carriers, anything that might lead them to the killer. The white plastic Tyvek that everyone wore contrasted starkly with the natural greens and subtle browns of the oak grove, deepening the violation of nature's integrity.

Colin studied the dizzying leaf litter, straining to focus. *Positional vertigo.* He blinked and shook his head to clear his vision. The bright green spring grass shoots competed with young, vibrant rhizomes of poison oak sprouting up through a complex substrate of fallen dried oak leaves, wild mushrooms, and cow patties. Underlying all of it was an ankle-twisting minefield—soft, uneven earth pitted by decades of cows' hooves. He tried to ignore the sense of impending doom scratching at his lungs. He reminded himself that cow patties were not landmines rigged with IEDs set to blow up when stepped on.

"Halt!"

Colin flinched at the shout. The other searchers stopped and turned toward Detective Jamison, who was standing at the innermost search area, close to the yellow string outline of the victim's body.

Jamison had been working for the Santa Lucia County Sheriff's Department since he was a young deputy. At that time, Lieutenant Rosa had been his lead detective. Now Jamison wore the detective's suit and tie instead of a deputy's uniform. But Detective Jamison still had the wide-eyed credulity and dogged loyalty to Rosa, now a lieutenant, and to the rule of law, which had distinguished him since graduating from the academy over twenty years ago.

"I see the blood where Warden Dawson placed a marker yesterday," said Jamison. "Didn't see it at first, but now that the sun's coming through the trees at a different angle, it's more visible. Get the forensic techs and photographers over here, stat! This is where the victim was hit. Blood splashed and pooled. We should be able to determine the trajectory of the kill shot from this spatter. When the lab adds that data to an analysis of the angle the arrow hit the body, we can map where the killer was standing and track his probable escape route."

A forensic tech and photographer rushed to the site.

"Here's the blood trail the victim left as she tried to crawl away from her attacker." Detective Jamison shone a flashlight on the leaf litter. "Appears to be massive blood loss, now that I can make it out in this light. I want every leaf here examined, photographed, and, if relevant, bagged for DNA and other clues."

The forensic team followed Jamison's orders while Colin and the rest of his squad pursued their grid search.

Fifty yards from the flag marking where the victim was hit, one of the deputies found a footprint in the oak leaf litter. Colin, who was nearby, squinted to make out the subtle and delicate print. As Colin watched, forensic techs used hair spray to harden the shoe print in the oak leaves and prepare it for plaster casting.

Detective Jamison waved the search team forward. Colin took a careful step, and then another, looking down at the ground. Just in front of his boot toe, a drying cow pie bore a well-defined imprint of a shoe. "Here!" Colin raised his hand, and techs appeared to process the print.

Finally, Colin's team reached the center section of the inner grid—the area surrounding the yellow string that marked the outlines of the victim's body.

The forensic tech next to Colin stooped down, plucked something out of the leaf litter, and held it above his head.

"Found something!"

Colin's heart skipped. *Cougar fur.*

The tech turned to Colin, offering the fur for examination. "What kind of animal do you think this is?"

Colin shrugged and shook his head.

He had dreaded the possibility that people would question him, as the wildlife expert, and connect his report of a cougar bite with this incident. What could he say to explain the mountain lion fur?

He held his breath.

Colin felt a dank shadow loom over his shoulder. A chill oozed down his spine.

"Looks like puma fur to me," said a sinister voice behind Colin.

Colin turned to face a tall, gaunt man wearing all black—smooth, creased chinos, a long-sleeved shirt, and a black felt lawman's hat with a wide shovel brim. A shiny US Marshal star gleamed at his belt.

Before Colin could respond, a cowboy riding a bay roan quarter horse trampled through the trees into the crime scene. Officers shouted. Twenty firearms pointed at the rider.

The cowboy put up his hands. "Whoa. Hey! Don't shoot. Please. What's going on here?"

Detective Jamison aimed his Glock at the cowboy's center mass. "Dismount. Now."

Both hands still in the air, the cowboy stood in his stirrups, swung one chap-clad leg over his horse, and jumped lightly to the ground. Hands still held high, he repeated his question. "Can somebody please tell me what the heck is going on?"

Detective Jamison signaled for the other officers to stand down but kept his Glock trained on the subject. "State your name and business."

The cowboy touched the rim of his straw Stetson and smiled, showing his dimples. "Raphael Silva, sir. People call me Rafe. I'm Cow Boss, in charge of the cattle operation on this ranch."

Jamison holstered his weapon. "Officer Santana, please escort Mr. Silva to Lieutenant Rosa's tent at the command post for questioning. Careful where you let that horse step, cowboy. You're stomping around in the middle of an active crime scene."

The eagle feathers on Rafe's hat ruffled in the breeze as, head bowed, he led his horse away, following Officer Santana. A brown dog followed horse and rider like a shadow.

Colin's team resumed their meticulous culling through the oak grove understory for evidence and clues that might help identify the murderer and his—or her—motive.

Colin glanced around. That gaunt man in black, the US Marshal, was nowhere to be seen.

The forensic tech who'd found the puma fur had apparently tucked the evidence away and moved on to the next grid.

Colin needed a break. He'd been working at this tedious search for over two hours, and he wanted to follow up on contacting the coroner for Delfina. He informed Deputy Jamison that he would return, stepped carefully over the yellow tape, and with relief, walked out from under the oppressive oak grove into the midday sun.

7

LIEUTENANT ROSA RETREATED a few paces while the cowboy's horse released its fire hose into the grass.

"All right, Rafe. So, you were saying you didn't realize that you were entering a crime scene. Why were you in the vicinity?"

Amigo shook his head and stomped his foot. Rosa took a few more steps back. Rafe, standing at the gelding's shoulder, lightly held Amigo's reins, rubbed his forehead, and mumbled calming words. Once the horse quieted, Rafe flashed his baby-faced smile at Lieutenant Rosa.

"I'm sorry about all that, Officer. Yah see, being Cow Boss, I'm responsible for the safety of the cattle on this ranch. Night before last, I heard a lot of caterwauling, and then yesterday I got word of an incident in the oak grove, possibly involving a mountain lion. I just came to check it out."

"Got word? From where?"

"Someone texted me that there might be a problem with a wild cat."

"I'll need that name and number."

Rafe shook his head. "Sorry, sir. The text was anonymous. All I have is a number. I'll forward it to you as soon as I get to where I've got cell service."

"Tell me, Rafe, do you have much of a problem with mountain lions attacking your cows?" asked Lieutenant Rosa.

"Yeah. Of course. With the pumas protected by the state, their numbers are increasing. It's only to be expected that we'd lose a calf to them now and then. Can't know exactly how many. There's a lot of open country out here. Sometimes we don't even find the carcasses."

"I guess that makes you pretty angry?"

"Nah, it's just how it is. I personally think the cougars should be controlled, managed. My opinion is that with that Puma Project protecting them, their population is getting too high for an area like this. But I abide by the law. Truth be told, I'm more worried about cattle rustlers and mountain bikers than I am about the mountain lions. Used to be, when native elk roamed here and this land belonged to the Indians, the elk and the pumas managed to live together in balance. We nonnative humans are what's upsetting things."

"Rustlers?"

"Yes, sir. This may be the twenty-first century, but this here ranch ain't Silicon Valley. You're in California *country* now—a genuine part of the historic Wild West. Cattle rustling is still a thing 'round here. I admit, in California, cattle thieves are fairly rare these days, because they pretty much always get caught. Those bikers, on the other hand, they're a big deal. A real pain in my ass. They race down the hills every which way, upsetting my pregnant cows and nursing calves. They cut my fences and rip deep bike trails through the prairie that turn into bad erosion gullies next rainy season. Their bike trails and fence cuts cause my cattle to stray and get injured. What kind of people cut cattle ranch fences? But I'll tell you another thing that's really got me worried. Once they open this new monument to the public, all those city people doing who knows what to disrespect my girls and this land—well, that could become a very big problem."

Rosa noted the rifle secured in a scabbard on Rafe's saddle. He noticed a utility knife on Rafe's belt but didn't see a holstered firearm. "Are you a hunter, Rafe?"

"Yeah, no. I mean, every once in a while, for special holidays or whatnot, I'll go out with a bunch of guys, and we'll take a feral pig and hold a hog roast for our families and friends. I used to hunt for sport when I was younger, but these days I'm just too busy."

"You ever hunt with a bow and arrow, Rafe?"

"Nah. I do just fine with my daddy's huntin' rifle. I carry it for self-defense, in case I come across an aggravated mountain lion or wild boar."

"I'm assuming you know this area well."

"Like the back of my hand."

"I'm recruiting volunteers to help with our search effort. We have a lot of ground to cover. Are you available?"

"What are you searching for? What happened here, anyway?"

"Homicide."

"Homm a—a murder?"

"A woman was killed. We're collecting evidence that may help us ID the shooter and reconstruct the crime. We're searching for someone dressed in camo, maybe carrying a sniper's bow—on the off chance the killer is still hiding out there."

"My God. Yeah, yeah. I'd be happy to help out."

Rosa directed Rafe to the volunteer tent. Rafe tied Amigo's reins to a tree branch and disappeared through the tent flaps. The brown cattle dog followed at his heels.

Lieutenant Rosa turned toward a stranger approaching. Carlos Rosa's dark mood lifted when he recognized an old friend limping toward him from the nearby vehicle parking area. *George Chen.*

"Hey George. You got here fast. Why are you limping?"

"Stepped in a fuckin' cow pie." George bent to scrape wet manure from his shoe onto the tall grass.

Rosa suppressed a grin. Chen had the lean, wiry physique and tough-as-leather tan one acquires by playing years of tennis on country club courts. In his starched white shirt, Hermès tie, pressed trousers, suit jacket, and shined shoes, George was the quintessential FBI agent. He dressed with the same fastidious care and meticulous attention to detail that he applied to his investigations. George's vulgarity was completely out of character with his usual elegant, somewhat formal demeanor. Getting his expensive shoes covered with cow poo had hit a nerve.

"Stop laughing, Carlos. I know you were expecting me. If a crime occurs on federal land, the FBI is going to get pinged. So here I am. What have we got?"

Dark clouds overhead released the first drops of what promised to be a heavy spring cloudburst.

Lieutenant Rosa shaded his eyes with his hand and inspected the sky. "Let's go into my tent, George. I'll fill you in on everything we have so far."

8

C OLIN DUCKED INTO his CDFW truck and slammed the door
just as the squall let loose.

He squinted through his windshield into a field of swirling gray
mist. Shivering at the sudden temperature drop, he turned the truck
on and cranked up the heater, defrost, and windshield wipers.

Delfina's face floated on the other side of the misty windshield. A
familiar keyed-up feeling jittered through him, its tentacles squeezing
his chest. *Fear of emotional attachment.*

Can't breathe.

The tentacles tore him into ragged pieces. Part of him wanted to let
himself fall in love with this amazing woman. Part of him recoiled from
the risk of getting involved. He saw himself growing close to her, getting
hooked by physical intimacy, entangled in stifling emotional and financial
commitments, then trapped for life in a complicated web of addictive
codependency. It was pathetic and deluded to think he could ever be
truly happy in love and not turn the relationship into a dysfunctional
nightmare. He wasn't right in the head. He didn't deserve her. She was
too good for him. She could find someone better than a wounded,
damaged warrior struggling to heal from trauma. He was better off alone.

55

The sky darkened and heavy rain pounded the truck. Wind wailed like a banshee.

Delfina's face morphed into the face of the young woman he'd found dead in Panjwai. Colin braced himself, holding back panic, anticipating another flashback—an intrusive traumatic memory, his shrink had called it.

He recited the affirmations Dr. Bukhari had given him: *I didn't hurt her, or any woman. The war wasn't my fault. I'm not a bad person. It's okay to be happy.*

An intense craving to curl up and numb out with a bottle of whiskey rose through him. He shuddered as the sickness scratched at his insides with poisonous claws.

Booze is not a good idea, numb nut. Ride the wave of the crave until it passes.

Focus on the sound of the rain. White noise. Deep slow breaths. Count. He floated in a sea of gray with the dead woman and her babies. *I'm so, so sorry.* He choked back a sob. *How can I make it up to you? How can I help you?*

The woman became Delfina again. She stood beside her mother. Slowly the women changed, as if in a kaleidoscope, still beautiful but now they were mountain lions, running for their lives.

Cold fingers of fear slid down Colin's back. A creature devoid of light hunted in the shadows. Colin's eyes opened wide.

Delfina! You're in danger. I need to protect you.

He rummaged in the glove compartment for the small plastic container. Xanax. He rattled the pills in the container, thought about taking one. No way. He'd already gone through the hell of getting off this shit. No way he was going to start again. He tossed the pills back in the glove box.

I need to find a cell signal and call her.

★　　★　　★

The squall passed. Colin drove down the hill to the ranch gate, gave his name to the city cop maintaining the perimeter, and drove through. Turning left at Highway 1, he headed southeast toward town.

A few minutes down the highway, he slowed to twenty miles per hour at the edge of Clark's Landing Village. Pulling up to the curb on a side street next to the bakery, he shifted into park, and cranked up the heater, leaving the motor running. Another wave of rain blown in from the Pacific pounded the truck hard, turning into hail. The sound soothed. It felt like his brain was getting a carwash. He checked his cell phone. Good strong signal, lots of bars.

He dialed Delfina's number, heart thumping.

Her photo from his contact file popped up on the screen. His hands shook and he felt light headed.

The call went to voicemail.

"Hey, Delfina. It's Colin. Just wanted to check in and see how you're doing. I'm truly deeply sorry about your mom. Please let me know if there's anything I can do to help. Call me when you get a chance. Bye."

Next he dialed the coroner's office, hoping to arrange for Delfina to see her mother. He waited on hold three minutes before giving up.

Frustrated, he turned off his truck and zipped up his jacket. Pulling up his collar and holding his wildlife warden's cap down on his head against the wind, he sprinted through the squall into the bakery.

★ ★ ★

The warm aroma of just-out-of-the-oven cinnamon rolls and hot coffee wrapped around him like his mom's old down quilt. As usual, lunchtime drew quite a crowd to this popular coastal eatery. Hunger pangs propelled Colin toward a seat at the last empty table.

He rubbed his hands together to warm them and ordered a Reuben sandwich and a pot of hot tea.

A woman and a man left their group at a nearby table and approached him. Their rain ponchos hung over the chairs by their group's table. The ponchos dripped on the old wooden floor.

★ ★ ★

The pair standing in front of him looked young, probably under thirty. Maybe still in school? Both wore hats and jackets embroidered with Puma Project logos. Their disheveled clothing suggested that they had spent the night outdoors and hadn't showered, used a comb, or changed clothes in a couple of days. Windblown wisps of fine auburn hair escaped from the woman's braid, framing her tanned, intelligent-looking face. The man, who appeared fit and capable of scaling mountains, fording rivers, and performing wilderness rescues, had obviously not shaved in a couple of days. Both of them smiled at Colin with a friendly warmth and the light of open, youthful idealism.

57

"Excuse me, sir," said the woman. "We noticed you're with Cal Fish and Wildlife."

"Yes, that's correct."

"We're graduate students working with the Puma Project out of UC Santa Lucia. My name's Lili Armstrong and this is Jack Jordan. Our project manager, Niko Goodman, is the OG sitting over there at our table with the rest of our group."

Colin smiled at the OG handle. The man they'd pointed to was definitely not old enough to be an "original gangster." He looked fit and probably under fifty, with a cool professorial vibe.

"I'm Colin Dawson. Good to meet you, Lili and Jack. I worked with your group about six months ago, assisting in the capture and relocation of a mountain lion that wandered onto residential property. The Puma Project does important work."

"We heard about that. Thank you for your help."

"Of course. What's going on?"

"We recently collared a new cougar, but she's fallen off our GPS. It looks like she may have lost her collar. We're worried about her, and we were wondering if you've found anything."

Colin's temples throbbed. "Sorry, I can't tell you anything at this time. But I think the sheriff's department will want to reach out to you. May I have your contact information?"

Lili made a face, rolled her eyes at Jack, and mouthed the word "Sheriff?"

"Here's our card," said Jack. "Why would the sheriff want to talk to us?"

"Please let us know if you come across any news about our cat," said Lili.

Colin's Reuben sandwich and pot of hot tea arrived. He accepted the Puma Project card, slipped it into his jacket pocket, and said, "We'll be in touch."

9

LATER THAT AFTERNOON, Lieutenant Rosa and FBI Agent Chen drove down the coast from the crime scene to observe the autopsy.

In the Medical Examiner's Department at the Santa Lucia County Sheriff's Headquarters, forensic pathologist Dr. Mary Sandow completed the last X-ray of the decedent, switched on a video recorder, and began her visual examination of the body.

"Friday, April 15, 14:00. Victim is Ramona Cuera. Height: five foot eleven. Weight: one-hundred-twenty-two pounds. Native American. Dark brown eyes. Black hair. Forty-nine years old. Manner of Death: Homicide. Probable Cause of Death: Injury sustained by arrow, to be determined pending further examination. Body Temperature confirms Fish and Wildlife Warden's reported time of death: 15:56, Thursday, April 14, 2023.

"Unusually rapid onset of rigidity and low ADP postmortem possibly the result of premortem heightened level of physical activity, or a seizure disorder, ingestion of an unusual substance, or heavily insulating body covering."

"Insulating body covering?" Rosa stepped closer to Ramona Cuera's body, laid out on the stainless steel table. "According to the report, she was naked when she died, not wrapped in a fur coat. So many things about this woman's death don't make sense."

"If I may make a suggestion," said Agent Chen. "The FBI would support ordering not only the customary tox screens from the local lab but also an expedited screening from the National Medical Lab for unusual substances. If there is anything unusual in this victim's system, the National Lab will find it."

"Very good. Thank you." Dr. Sandow turned to her computer and ordered the tox screen from the local lab and an unusual substances screening from the National Medical Lab, which Chen signed off on.

Dr. Sandow drew blood samples, then continued recording her visual examination of the body.

"Hands and feet are heavily calloused and scratched. Dirt, small rocks, and wood splinters under the fingernails."

Moving the victim's hair aside, she discovered a tick behind her ear, which she captured and preserved for the forensic etymologist.

"No signs of vaginal tearing or any other indications of recent sexual activity."

The recording continued while Dr. Sandow described the penetration of the arrow through the victim's chest, and the surrounding wound. "At the point of impact, the skin and muscle tissue were not cleanly pierced, but torn—mangled."

Rosa took a closeup photo.

Dr. Sandow lifted her scalpel and began the internal examination, making a Y-shaped incision in Ramona's torso.

"Upon impact, the needlelike arrow tip expanded outward, opening razor-sharp blades that drilled a two-inch-wide wound channel. The arrow penetrated chest and heart, ripping muscle, shattering bone, and slicing arteries and veins along its path. It projects four inches out of the victim's back. This wound would have resulted in muscle and nerve spasms and massive blood loss."

The pathologist drew blood from Ramona's heart, exposed in the open chest cavity. She handed one of the tubes of blood to Lieutenant Rosa, as per protocol. Wearing gloves, Rosa placed the blood sample in a locking specimen transport cooler, which he would personally deliver to the crime lab as the victim's standard, to be compared against other blood samples the investigation might gather.

Next, Dr. Sandow gingerly removed Ramona's heart and placed it on a stainless steel tray to weigh. The doctor was especially careful handling the heart, as it had been so shredded by the arrow that it practically fell apart in her hands.

Looking straight into the video recorder, she pronounced the official COD: "Cause of death: Catastrophic injury to the aorta due to arrow wound."

10

AT 5:30 SATURDAY MORNING, April 16, Lieutenant Rosa sat at his shiny wood and chrome desk at the new Santa Lucia County Sheriff's Headquarters, his fingers wrapped around the hot Starbucks latte his old friend FBI Agent George Chen had just brought him.

"No sugar, right?"

"Thanks, George. And thanks for using your pull with the National Lab to expedite the special substances tox screen."

"The Agency was glad to help. Hopefully that report will come back soon and will produce something interesting."

George Chen surveyed the room. "Impressive setup, Carlos. Look at your tech! This new headquarters is a far cry from that cramped, windowless room in the county building of the old days, back when you were a lowly homicide detective with your cork murder board and that one Dell computer. This digital multimedia murder board is a beauty. It's as big as anything the Agency's got. Is it synced up to the mobile smart board at the crime scene? How did you get a WiFi connection up and running so fast up there in the boonies?"

"California got a pile of infrastructure money and federal pandemic relief funds. It helps that I grew up in Santa Lucia County, right on the edge of Silicon Valley. A couple of my college buddies now work in state government in Sacramento, and a few of my high school friends are in high tech over the hill in the Valley. I called in some favors to expedite internet and at Cougar Creek Ranch. We connected to satellite internet access and mobile phone service through Starlink. It's much faster than ground-based broadband or 5G, and we have unlimited data. Without it, we'd be groping in the dark on this investigation."

Chen raised an eyebrow and nodded. "You got internet connection through that SpaceX project of Elon Musk's? Interesting. Anything yet on the murder weapon?"

"Not a trace of DNA on the arrow, except the victim's. But the report from ballistics is useful. The arrow fits a specialized crossbow: a Condor R500 Sniper. We're talking about a real high-tech killing machine, built for extreme distance shooting. Blazing speeds and amazing accuracy up to two hundred meters. It handles more like a sniper rifle than a traditional bow and arrow. They were originally available only to trained military special forces sniper personnel, but now anyone can buy one. These bows cost over three thousand bucks. Arrows are a hundred dollars each. The killer's arrow was fitted out with a broadhead, an extra brutal attachment."

"At the autopsy, I saw the damage it causes, but tell me more about the broadhead."

"Not up-to-date on your modern archery, George? It's a device with a needlelike point that fits over the arrow tip. The broadhead has razor-sharp blades that spring open on impact, crushing and shredding a two-inch hole through the target."

"Hmm." George rubbed an index finger over his clean-shaven upper lip. "Sounds brutal. I think we can assume that the unidentified subject is not a casual deer hunter—not some yahoo who just decided to ignore the No Hunting signs, climb over the fence, and catch himself some dinner."

Rosa nodded. "It's unlikely Ramona Cuera was killed by accident. I'm not a profiler, but I think that whoever shot her must have wanted to inflict maximum pain."

"An unsub with a grudge against the victim?"

"Or a sicko who enjoys hurting people." Lieutenant Rosa stared into his half-empty coffee cup. "Possibly a contract assassin."

"We should be able to trace a weapon like that," said Chen.

"My thought as well," said Rosa. "I looked into it. Turns out, every one of these bows has a serial number, but unfortunately, the arrows do not. All we've got is an arrow, with no prints or DNA. It's not going to be easy to trace this murder weapon to a suspect."

"We should contact local gun shops, sporting goods, and outdoor stores and get a list of persons who have purchased a Condor R500 Sniper crossbow," said Chen.

"We can start with the local shops, but consider that there are thousands of retailers around the country selling these bows, and sellers are not required to keep records of crossbow purchases, much less purchase records connecting serial numbers to purchasers. Something might show up on a credit card receipt, but nada for cash purchases. And in any case, the killer may have bought the bow online, from anywhere."

"If you buy something online and have it shipped," Chen reasoned, "you must enter a physical address. And with something as expensive as that weapon, the seller would likely require a signature to prove receipt."

"It's a needle in a haystack, but we have to start somewhere," said Carlos Rosa. "We should limit the search to the last three years and start local, collect lists of Condor R500 Sniper bow *and* arrow purchasers from nearby brick-and-mortar shops, then move on to online stores."

"I'll have a couple of my agents assist your deputies. It's such an expensive, specialized weapon, there can't be that many out there," said Chen.

"Not so sure about that," said Rosa. "Maybe expensive, but readily available. Ballistics just requisitioned one from Amazon. No questionnaire required. Said it was as easy as purchasing a new T-shirt online. They'll have it in the lab by next week for testing. Once ballistics is able to work with the same type of weapon the killer used, they should be able to determine where the shooter stood and the direction he or she probably fled, based on blood spatter at the scene."

"Good. That will help us to target our search more precisely." Agent Chen stood, stretched, and glanced at his smartwatch. "Time for breakfast." George Chen had a surprisingly big appetite for a person so fit and lean.

"You don't get down here from San Francisco often, George. Do you have a favorite Playa Azul breakfast spot?"

"How about the Seabreeze Café? They're opened early, aren't they?"

"Excellent choice," said Rosa. "They open at six every morning. I wouldn't mind having a real breakfast for a change. Spinach and cheese omelet, potatoes, and bacon." Rosa placed his large hand over his belly and smiled.

"And one of their delicious homemade blueberry muffins. Warm enough to melt butter."

"Let's go. It's early enough we can probably still beat the crowd."

11

Sunday afternoon, in the undeveloped redwood-forested mountains on the upper University of California Santa Lucia campus, Hawk perched on a boulder, hugging his knees against his chest, wishing he knew how to comfort his cousin.

Delfina sat nearby on soft redwood duff, inside a circle of two-hundred-foot-tall redwood trees. Her back against a fallen log, she rested her elbows on her thighs, and bowed her head in her hands. Dark circles shadowed her red-rimmed eyes.

"You'll get through this, Delfina."

She raised her head and wiped the tears off her cheeks. "I can't believe Mama's been gone for three days. I feel like she's going to walk up that trail any minute. I can hear her voice in my head, so bright and strong. I just can't imagine I'll never see her again. I've never been apart from her, Hawk. I don't know how I'll make it without her. I miss her so much!" Delfina's shoulders shook as she wept.

"You can handle it, Cuz. Lots of people lose their parents when they're much younger than you. You'll figure it out. I did."

"It's too much. Mama gone, forever."

"Remember, Delfina, when Kumeyaay die, our spirit remains on Earth for a year. She's still here. You feel her, hear her voice, don't you? Has she appeared to you?"

"I guess I need to pay more attention. I've tried to shut down feeling my emotions so it doesn't hurt so much. I know I should open myself up, let it all in, let her in. I really need her right now."

"She needs you, too. You've got to be strong, for her sake and for all our people."

Delfina nodded and sat up straighter. "I don't even know what I'm supposed to do. I've never been to a traditional funeral. Will you help me?"

"Of course, sweetie. I'll do my best. You were only four when Great-grandfather died, but I was thirteen. I remember his funeral very well. The community held a burning ceremony. I can still see the flames and hear the people singing. He was kuseyaay, an important and revered elder, as is your mother."

Delfina nodded. "I knew her as the best mother ever, but I realize she was also a healer and an amazing community and spiritual leader. Everyone loved and respected her. She helped so many of our people."

"And she was dedicated to keeping our tribal traditions and ancestral knowledge alive. I've been talking with our aunties about how to help you with your mother's arrangements. We think she'd like it if we honored her with a special ceremony, one that follows our present customs but also goes back to the old ways. Does that sound right to you?"

"Sounds perfect. Just tell me what to do."

"I've been reading about early Kumeyaay spiritual practices," said Hawk. "We can figure this out. First, we need to gather her belongings. It's traditional to burn them along with her ashes in a pit, to send them with her to the spirit world during her Takaay. That will make her feel welcome and comfortable in the afterlife."

Delfina shook her head. "I know there were some things she wouldn't want burned."

"All right. Our aunties will help. We'll get through this."

"Wait. I can't bury all her ashes during the Takaay. I need to save some until I can take them to a secret place she showed me before we left San Diego. I know she won't rest until that's done." A tear ran down Delfina's cheek. "Who knows how long she'll have to wait for me to do that. Right now, I think it's too dangerous for me to go back."

"Time is different in the afterlife than it is for us. Don't worry about how long it takes you to complete your task, sweetie. Your mom knows you'll get it done. She won't mind waiting until the time is right."

"I'm afraid, Hawk."

"I see your fear, Cuz." Hawk hopped off his boulder, crouched in front of Delfina, and placed his hand on her shoulder. "You have reason to fear for your life. But I also see your courage. You are a survivor. Call on the medicine of Mountain Lion, your animal spirit. Take your place of power. Roar with conviction, with leadership. Even roar sometimes with love and laughter to balance the medicine. Delfina, what do you call a bear with no teeth?"

Delfina rolled her eyes and shrugged.

"A gummy bear."

Delfina laughed. "God, that was so lame!" She punched Hawk in the arm, and he rolled over on his back in the redwood duff, his hands and feet in the air.

"Yes, but it made you laugh." Hawk stood, brushed the redwood needles off, and sat on the log next to Delfina.

"Honestly, I'm not feeling any of it right now. Mountain Lion, the whole *changing* thing. Ugh." Delfina shivered. "I've only changed once. It was in San Diego. Men were chasing us, shooting at us, and it just happened. We ran all the way here as pumas through the mountains from San Diego. I've been terrified it would happen again, that I'd shift in front of someone. I have no idea how to control it. Mama taught me a little bit about it, but there's so much I don't know. When did you become a nāhualli, a shapeshifter? I don't even know the word for it in our Kumeyaay language. Do we have one?"

"I don't know. Sorry to say, I only know a few words of our traditional language." Like a bird preening his feathers, Hawk slid his fingers through the thin silk ribbons fastened in his hair, which he was wearing loose. The colored ribbons and black feathery wisps of hair fluttered in the breeze.

"I haven't had anyone to mentor me since Great-grandfather passed. Most of what I know I figured out for myself."

"Why does it happen?" asked Delfina. "How do you control the changing?"

"You'll learn to control it, Delfina. I'll help you. I was twelve when it first happened to me. Great-grandfather was alive then, and he taught me to live with it in a good way."

"I remember hearing the Old Ones whisper stories when I was little about some of our long-ago healers having the gift of speaking with the animals and even shapeshifting. But back then, I thought those stories were just legends."

"I used to think that too," said Hawk. "But I've since learned that for centuries, in each generation, there have been one or two kuseyaay with the gift, like Great-grandfather. And now something is triggering more of us to transform."

"But why?" Delfina lifted her eyes up along the two-hundred-foot length of the redwood trees encircling them. Like a wisdom council of ancient beings, the tall trees seemed to lean in above her, putting their heads together around a small sky hole of intense blue, as if the tree beings were gazing into a blue crystal ball.

"I don't know the biological mechanisms," said Hawk, "but it seems obvious that, with Mother Earth so out of balance, something would get triggered in our people, doesn't it? You and I are of the kuseyaay lineage. We're healers, hypersensitive to whoever needs our medicine. Mother Earth needs us now. I think we're supposed to align in council with our animal sisters and brothers to help stop the damage humans are causing."

"I know, right? Climate change, overpopulation, pollution, habitat destruction, diminishing biodiversity, ocean acidification, escalating violence, dehumanization, authoritarianism, genocide … How many more species will go extinct because of human's addictive hunger to consume and control?"

"It's getting worse, fast, Cuz. The bad shit, the consequences of human behavior, are being felt everywhere on the planet now, not just in poor, least developed countries. Wildfires, flooding, severe freak storms, drought, famine, intense record-breaking global heat waves, pandemics, hate crimes … Most people don't want to think about it, but no one's going to escape the chaos."

"I don't know anything about being kuseyaay, Hawk. I feel helpless to do anything right now, much less heal the world."

"You'll find your way. Mother Nature has a way of correcting imbalances. I'm convinced that's why more of us are shifting now. We need to trust the process."

"Will it always hurt so bad to change? The one time it happened to me was intensely painful."

"No. You'll get used to it. I kind of like the feeling now. It's like a surge of power running through me."

"You can change at will?" she asked.

"It takes practice, but yes. I can talk you through it. I think you should try shifting right now. You need to practice so you can control it. We're safe up here in the mountains this afternoon."

A pair of red tailed hawks carved slow circles in the cloudless blue sky, their calls ringing through the treetops.

"My hawk relatives are telling me no one's around. No hunters, no stalkers nearby. You should really go for it. Remember how amazing it feels when you've shifted, and your senses are so enhanced? You'll feel much better when you can just stretch out and run for miles."

"When you're in your hawk body, can you speak with other hawks?"

"Yes. In fact, now that I've been shifting for a long time, I can understand them, and most other animal species, even when I'm in my human body. My hawk community is really freaked out, I gotta say."

"I'm scared, Hawk. I miss Mama so much. I'm so grateful that you're in my life. I don't know what I'd do without you."

Hawk's forehead wrinkled. As her closest relative, he felt responsible for his cousin, especially now that her mother was gone.

"Delfina, there's something I should tell you."

"What is it? Tell me, please."

"I don't know how to say this gently, so I'm just going to come out with it." Hawk studied his cousin's face. He didn't want to hurt her more, but this needed to be said.

"Delfina, I was there when your mama was murdered."

Delfina's eyes opened wide. She gasped as if punched in the stomach.

"I hate how painful this is for you, Delfina. Should I not tell you?"

"No. I have to know."

"All right. I was in my hawk form, gliding on an updraft over the oak grove at Cougar Creek Coast Ranch. I noticed a hunter stalking a puma. The stalker was dressed in hunting camo and carrying a crossbow and arrows. At first, I didn't realize the puma he was following was your mother. Ramona, in her cat form, saw the hunter and started running for her life. She fell, and rolled over a cliff. I held my breath while I watched her claw her way up a sandstone rock face then slide down the other side and run along some bushes. She disappeared behind a thicket of coyote brush and came out the other side in human form. She kept running and dove behind a dense manzanita grove. Then she shifted again and leapt out from behind the manzanita as a puma. I didn't see the hunter take the shot, but I saw the arrow hit the puma. She ran a little farther, then collapsed under the oaks. I watched the camo guy run away, across the creek toward the highway. I stayed perched in the oaks above Ramona. I saw Colin find her. It seemed like he was trying to help. She bit him. I'm not sure if it was intentional or not. Then I watched her shift into your mom, into her human form, and die. I was powerless to help her. I was in shock. I almost fell off my perch. Such horror!"

Hawk held Delfina's hand and patted her on the back while she cried.

When the sobs subsided to hiccups, Hawk continued.

"Colin was right by her side, Delfina. He impressed me. He couldn't have known anyone was watching, and he must have been blown away and confused by what he witnessed, but he was so respectful, so honorable in the way he treated your mother. He spoke to her kindly, even after she died. The way he handled himself, methodically recording observations and contacting the sheriff, he seemed so intelligent and brave. When he left the ranch, I stayed in my hawk form and followed him. Your meeting Colin at the tavern—I think that was destiny, Delfina."

Delfina was trembling.

"What is it, Cuz?"

"Was there just one hunter?"

"I was so focused on your mother, I can't say for sure there was no one else around, but I only saw the one stalker."

"Did you see his face?"

"Sorry, no. I never got a good view of his face. It was painted with black and shaded by his hat."

Delfina looked down at her hands and whispered, "I don't know who or why, but I'm pretty sure that whoever murdered Mama is hunting me, too."

Hawk took Delfina's hands in his, looked into her eyes, and spoke gently. "Tell me why."

"It was six years ago in San Diego," said Delfina, "but I remember everything as vividly as if it were happening now, all over again."

12

ELFINA TOOK A DEEP BREATH and began telling Hawk her story. "Mama and I were at one of the secret ceremonial sites up on Viejas Mountain saying our sunset prayers.

Just as the sun sank below the horizon, powerful Santana winds came up.

Mama started shape shifting. There was so much sand blowing around I could barely see. I couldn't make any sense of what I was witnessing.

Then I started to change. It was terrifying, and horribly painful. My bones felt like they were breaking. Fur sprouted out of my skin. I fell to the ground. My hands and feet turned into large paws with sharp claws. I screamed, but the sound I made was the howl of a wild animal.

I heard Mama's voice inside my head, shouting, 'Hunters have found us. Follow me. Run!'

We ran toward the reservoir along a mountain ridge path that I'd never traveled before. Mama shouted inside my head that I needed to memorize every landmark and remember the way to return back again, at a later time, by myself, in the dark.

I heard the crack of rifle shots, and men's evil laughter.

A bullet zinged by my head and ricocheted off a rock at the edge of a cliff, just inches from where I was standing. A spark flew off the granite, igniting the dry chapparal. Within seconds, fire whipped all around me.

Mama's voice screamed inside my head, 'Delfina! Jump!'

I threw myself off the cliff into a canyon river gorge a hundred feet below."

★   ★   ★

The next morning, shadowy forms took shape in the predawn glow of the sky over El Capítan Reservoir. The river of stars spilling out of Hat-tat-kurr, the Milky Way, was beginning to fade. Ramona and Delfina sat at the mouth of a cave, gazing down at the last twinkling reflections of stars on the reservoir water far below. Mother and daughter looked out across the wild, undeveloped ecological preserve of the Kumeyaay Reservation, part of a critical and dwindling wildlife corridor connecting the Sierra Nevada mountains to Pacific Coast ranges from Mexico to Alaska.

Delfina breathed in the calming scents of coastal mountain sage and pearly everlasting that warmed in the rising sun. She held her hands in front of her face and examined them front and back. She had returned to her human form. Her skin tingled unpleasantly, and her muscles ached. She felt shaky and weak. A tantrum of dark thoughts and hazy memories clouded her mind.

"What happened to us, Mama?"

Ramona wrapped her arms around Delfina, drawing her close and rocking her as she had when Delfina was just a small child. Warmth and a sense of safety flooded through the young woman.

"Follow me, Delfina." Ramona stood and led her daughter into the cave. Sunlight illuminated their first few steps, but as they ventured farther in, cold darkness enveloped them, as suffocating as a black stygian shroud. Delfina could not see her own hand in front of her face. She became disoriented; panic welled through her.

Her mother found Delfina's hand in the dark and gently squeezed.

"Wait here, sweetheart. Don't be afraid. I'll be back."

Delfina closed her eyes and focused on her breath. Her heartbeat slowed, panic controlled.

Sudden light revealed Delfina's surroundings. Delfina's mother stood before her, holding a candle. Behind Ramona was an alcove in the cave's rock wall. On shelves in the alcove, someone had left candles and matches as well as other neatly stacked objects: dried plants, pottery bowls, baskets, blankets, shawls, folded lengths of cloth, and stacks of rocks in earthen colors. Delfina had been taught by traditional potters to recognize the rocks: ochre, umber, red iron oxide and hematite, copper green, serpentine blue and green; white zinc, feldspar, and kaolin; manganese and charcoal black.

On the cave walls all around them, flickering candle flame illuminated paintings. Delfina spun around, taking in the astonishing images.

The largest pictograph, repeated four times around the rock walls, was a blue and yellow sunburst.

Open hands with swirls in the palms, painted in various rock colors, gave the impression of many people gathered in the cave.

All around the cave walls, spirals of various sizes pulled Delfina toward them with such gravitational energy that she felt that if she got too close she might be sucked into the rock, pulled through into another dimension. Delfina wondered at the meaning of the rectangular and curvilinear designs in red, black, yellow, and white and the divided circles, spoked wheels, bold diamonds, chains, zigzags, insect-like figures, chevrons, straight lines, water waves, and dot patterns that Delfina recognized as constellations.

Interspersed among these designs, stick figures populated the walls—some displaying prominent genitalia—in various postures of resting, hunting, tending orchards and fields, and playing. Among the anthropomorphic pictographs, images of animals native to the traditional Kumeyaay lands grazed, leapt, crawled, and flew: bighorn sheep, mountain lions, coyotes, bobcats, deer, badgers, antelope, squirrels, cottontail rabbits, bats, rattlesnakes, scorpions, and tarantulas, birds, freshwater fish, and marine life. Plant images sprouted on the walls, and images of people apparently healing with plants.

Ramona handed her daughter a candle, and Delfina stepped closer to the wall to study the images in better light. A group of mountain lions seemed to jump out at her. Then a series of paintings came into focus, depicting a human transforming into a mountain lion, like the frames of a filmstrip.

Delfina's heart raced and her skin tingled.

Ramona stood at Delfina's back and placed a comforting hand solidly on her daughter's shoulder. More depictions of humans transforming into animals revealed themselves.

"Mama," Delfina whispered, "what is this? What does it mean?"

"Come, let us sit, and I will tell you."

Ramona arranged a stack of blankets for each of them on the packed earth around a small rock firepit. Inside the cold firepit, she placed their two candles and added several more, which animated the cave paintings with flickering light. Then she took an unpainted gourd water container and two unglazed earthenware cups from the alcove and poured water for Delfina and herself.

"I collected this water from a spring near the cave while you were sleeping. We call the healing water from this sacred spring God's Tears. We should both drink as much water as we can in the next twenty-four hours. Later I'll take you to the spring and show you where to find healing herbs to add to the water. They will help us recover more quickly from the transformation."

They drank the cold water in silence. Then Ramona spoke. "Now we need to pray and smudge."

Ramona lit a bundle of dried sage. With feathers from their four spirit protectors—eagle, hawk, raven, and owl—she guided fragrant threads of smoldering white sage smoke around their heads, bodies, hands, and feet. Mother and daughter sang a song of gratitude to the ancestors and spirit animals, asking for their protection and guidance. Ramona placed the still smoldering sage in a large abalone shell and set it in the candlelit fire ring. The women sat silently on their blanket cushions and sipped more water.

Finally, Ramona spoke.

"I have only been here once before. When I was a little younger than you, my grandfather brought me here. He was one of the last initiated kuseyaay, and he chose to pass his knowledge on to me. Kuseyaay have vast knowledge, wisdom, and power. I was only capable of receiving a small part of his teaching. I remember, at an early age, all of us children sitting around the fire, listening to the Old Ones tell their stories. Some of the stories were repeated often, some only seasonally or on special occasions like births, deaths, and significant natural occurrences. A few of our stories, as you know, are told only once or twice in a generation.

"As the kuseyaay told their familiar stories while I was growing up, they would sometimes intentionally leave out or misspeak a detail, and then the Elders would watch the children. There were always a few young ones who paid more attention and remembered more than the rest, and they would correct the storyteller. I was one of those children. I remembered every word of every story I heard—even if just once," said Ramona. "And I had a special connection to animals and plants and an affinity for healing. So, Grandfather guided me to become a kuseyaay cha'ak, a medicine woman. And then he chose me for something more. I'm only now beginning to understand what is expected of me.

"On the day Grandfather brought me here, he instructed me, as I did you, to remember every step, every plant and rock, every landmark, so that one day I would be able to find my way back here alone. Grandfather explained the sacred nature of this cave, that this is a place for acquiring power to do good, for healing, and peace. The loving Creator God Spirit, Maayhaay, gave us this cave, the spring nearby that weeps God's Tears, Viejas Mountain and other secret places. It is forbidden to talk about these places or say their names except on proper occasions. Viejas Mountain has been desecrated by the footsteps of many white people, with their TV relay equipment, Wi-Fi towers, and other things, but the mountain still holds power for ceremony in certain spots—places only we know.

"Before they flooded this canyon and built the reservoir, all of Mother Earth's land around here was wild. Sweet water gushed out of springs and flowed over the land in creeks and rivers that nurtured our people. But when white men took our land and our water rights, they flooded many sacred sites to make a reservoir so city people could water their lawns and fill their swimming pools and wash their cars and flush their toilets.

"In this cave and our other secret sacred places, long ago—in a time before memory—we were given our stories, songs, and dances, the way of herbs and medicine, and also teachings about all types of proper behavior. We were instructed to live in peace, to cooperate, and to help each other and all our relatives, including the four-leggeds, the winged ones, the plant spirits, and all beings.

"In Grandfather's time and before, only initiated kuseyaay were allowed to visit these places. But now there are no more kuseyaay living. Only a few of us still hold some of the blessings and wisdom from the Old Ones. It is up to us cha'ak to maintain the protection of our sacred places. Once every six years, one of us comes here to reweave the protections that keep this cave and the spring hidden, sacred, and full of power. I will teach you how we do it later so that you can carry on the task when I am gone."

"No, Mama! I don't want to think about a time when you're gone."

"None of us can refuse our fate, child. What happened to us last night was an event foretold since ancient times in our stories and songs and in these paintings. The Changing of the World is what called us here. There are things we must do now. While we stay, we will fast, only drinking water mixed with some herbs and a little kaolin for purification. Drink this, my daughter."

Ramona poured water from a painted gourd into Delfina's cup. She drank. The water was cold, chalky, and slightly bitter. Within a few minutes, the paintings on the cave walls surrounding them seemed to come alive.

"Now we must dance and sing." Ramona held out her hand, helped Delfina to her feet, and led her deeper into the cave, where the ceiling and walls expanded to form a large chamber. In niches in the chamber walls, the women found additional candles and lit them. The candlelight revealed even more magical cave paintings and a circular rut worn into the middle of the chamber floor from centuries of dancers.

"I will teach you the songs and dances, including the one that came to me last night in a dream."

The women prayed, expressing gratitude, inviting, and acknowledging the spirits of the Four Corners, of Sky World, and the world below, inside the earth. They sang and danced. Many voices seemed to sing with them. As they danced, Delfina felt as if she were flying, swimming, digging her sharp claws into a tall tree trunk. Sounds of animal cries, growls, howls, hoots, and tweets bounced off the cave walls. Finally exhausted, the women collapsed onto blankets spread on the rock floor and slept.

When they awoke, they returned to the first chamber and again drank God's Tears from the water gourd. From an alcove, Ramona took down a mortar and pestle, colored rocks, and paint brushes made of yucca sticks, soap plant fibers, and strands of animal fur.

Ramona spoke to her daughter while she ground the rocks and mixed the colored powders with water. "When we paint, our hearts must be pure so that all beings may benefit. The power of the sacred cave may not be used for ego, nor for power over others. One must seek power only to help others. Give me your hand, Delfina, and repeat what I say. Eyay e'Hunn—My heart is good. Haawka. May your spirit burn bright."

Delfina said the words.

Ramona spread open her daughter's hand and made a small cut across her palm. Delfina gasped.

"This is to bind the paint to the wall, and to the past and future," said Ramona.

Ramona turned Delfina's hand over and let a few drops of blood fall into each of the paint bowls. She bound her daughter's cut hand with herbs, then handed Delfina the knife.

Ramona looked into her daughter's eyes. "Haawka. Eyay e'Hunn."

Delfina cut her mother's hand and guided her mother's blood into the paint bowls.

When it was finished, Ramona swept her cut and bound hand over a blank space on the cave wall. "Here we will paint the story of what happened to us last night. Look into your heart, Delfina. Pray. Listen with your whole body to the voices of the cave. Open yourself to Father Sun and Mother Earth, to the hearts of the Kumeyaay People, to the Ancestors and all our Relations, to the light, the shadows, and the rock spirits. The images you are meant to paint will reveal themselves."

Mother and daughter painted all day and long into the night. After they finished painting, they slept. The next morning, they awoke to the smell of smoke. From the mouth of their cave, they gazed across the reservoir and watched a black cloud billowing into the sky.

"It's the wildfire those who hunt us started with sparks from their rifles two days ago. It still rages," said Ramona. "Although this fire will soon be contained, many of our animal relatives will die in it, and its aftermath. More frequent and deadly wildfires will follow, until everything Creator made is destroyed. Unless—"

"Unless we can change things. I know we can, Mama."

Ramona and Delfina stayed at the cave for nine days. Delfina learned many things about her people and her destiny. On the dawn of the tenth day, a heavy spring rain cleaned the smoke from the air.

"We must not return to our trailer at Ma Tar Awa, Delfina. It's too dangerous for us in San Diego now. We will Change tonight and make our way north across the mountains."

"We're not going back to our house? We're leaving everything? How will we survive with no money? No clothes?"

"We have family in Santa Lucia. They will help us."

13

EIGHT O'CLOCK MONDAY MORNING, April 18. The manhunt was still underway at Cougar Creek Coast Ranch. Inside the homicide investigation command post's main tent, Fish and Wildlife Warden Colin Dawson stood at attention.

It had been five days since Colin had found Ramona Cuera's body and met her daughter. *Delfina.*

Colin hadn't been able to stop thinking about her.

He saluted and addressed Lieutenant Rosa's back. "Reporting for duty, sir."

Carlos Rosa was examining a large topo map spread out on a table. He turned toward Colin just as a commotion broke out. Several officers were dragging a man through the tent door.

Colin flinched, ducked, and covered his head, expecting machine gun fire and exploding bombs. He straightened almost immediately, but Rosa's all-knowing eyes flashed through him for an instant, like a lighthouse beacon, before gliding on to illuminate the situation tumbling through the door.

"What's this, Officers?"

"We apprehended this man trying to sneak through a fence down by the highway north of the main gate, sir."

One city cop held the subject by his spandexed elbow while the other gripped the handlebars of an expensive-looking mountain bike.

"Let me go. Get your hands off me." The subject shook off the cop's grip. "I'm calling my lawyer. You have no idea who I am. If you damaged my bike, I'll sue. That bike's worth more than all of you put together."

Colin wondered why any man would dress that way in public, wearing tights and slippers like a ballet dancer. The guy was lean and pumped—upper body, quad, and calf muscles bulging—with an arrogant smirk and a fashionably macho three-day-beard stubble. But Colin sensed he was soft at the core—a pampered man-child, unprincipled and unforged in the crucible of lethal combat in defense of a cause larger than himself.

"Sir, you were trespassing," said Lieutenant Rosa. "Did you not notice the police barrier at the entrance?"

"I never use the entrance. Haven't you seen my online stories about new bike trails in Santa Lucia? I've been coming here for months. This is public property. Mountain bikers from up and down the coast will soon be swarming this place, thanks to my social media posts. I have thousands of followers. Get used to it. I drove down from the city, parked at a pullout north of the gate, and went through a hole my friends and I cut in the fence."

"You are trespassing," said Rosa. "This park is not yet open to the public."

"I'm entitled to ride here." The man waved his BodyGel-gloved hand in front of the lieutenant's face as if swatting away a fly. "One of my friends is the BLM field agent in charge of opening this new park. He's my BFF and an avid biker, and he gave me and a select group of friends permission to scout the property before it opens. We're advising him on the best routes for a network of bike trails we'll be cutting down the mountain to the coast."

"You breached an active crime scene." Rosa had his pocket notebook and pen ready. "We're going to need to ask you some questions."

"I'm not telling you anything until I have my attorney present."

"Very well. If you insist, these officers will read you your rights, arrest you, take you downtown, identify and book you, and put you in jail. Then you can call your lawyer. Maybe sometime later this evening. Up to you."

The bicyclist removed his helmet and glared at Rosa. "My name is Mikos Vadim."

"US citizen?"

"Of course. I was born in New York."

"And you currently reside in San Francisco?"

"I own a home in the Santa Lucia Mountains and a townhouse on the bay in South San Francisco, where I stay when I'm working. It's a far superior commute from my townhouse to my office than driving from Santa Lucia."

"What kind of work do you do?"

"I'm a software developer for a semiconductor company."

"Where were you last Thursday, April fourteenth?"

Mikos glanced at his smartwatch. "I was working at my company's headquarters in San Mateo. I take a company shuttle from my townhouse to and from work."

"Can you verify your whereabouts?"

"This is absurd. Of course. Here's my business card. My name will be on the shuttle list, and multiple colleagues can verify that I was on the shuttle and in the office that day."

"Are you a hunter, Mr. Vadim?"

"A hunt—hunter? Absolutely not. I'm vegan."

"Do you own any weapons?"

"Weapons? You mean guns? No."

"Any weapons other than guns? Do you own or use a crossbow?"

"No."

Colin's bullshit meter was flashing red. Mikos Vadim was a weaselly liar, if ever he'd seen one.

"Thank you, Mr. Vadim," said Lieutenant Rosa. "These officers will drive you and your bicycle down the hill to your vehicle now. Do not reenter the property or you will be arrested. And don't leave town. We'll be contacting you later for further questioning."

Colin stepped outside the tent and checked his cell phone for messages, pleasantly surprised to see he had a cell signal. A missed call from Delfina. His heart raced. He pressed the return call icon.

"Colin, thanks for getting back to me."

He took a deep breath and hoped he didn't sound too excited to be speaking with her. "What's going on?"

"I heard from the county coroner's office about an hour ago. They want me to come in this afternoon at one. I was hoping you'd meet me there."

"Of course." Colin wished he could teleport through the phone and put his arms around her right then. He told himself to be cool. He calculated that he could put in about three more hours here helping with the grid search, and still make it into town in time. "I'll meet you in front of the sheriff's headquarters at one."

14

OUTSIDE THE SPRAWLING new two-story Neo-Southwest-Colonial style sheriff's headquarters, Colin leaned over and polished a small dust spot off the hood of his department truck with his kerchief. Satisfied, he slouched against the truck, face turned up to the afternoon sun, to wait for Delfina.

His old truck, with over a hundred ten thousand miles, had finally been replaced last year with a brand-new forest green Chevy Silverado 1500 pickup. For a long time, the agency had had the money for a fleet upgrade, obtained through pandemic grants and the Biden administration's infrastructure funding. But Covid had stalled out big fleet orders from all the auto manufacturers. The excuse for everything these days was "supply chain shortages." Apparently, a massive global lack of computer microchips, a key component for manufacturing modern vehicles, seemed to have been the biggest problem. So, Colin was grateful he finally had a solid, up-to-date department vehicle.

When Delfina stepped out of her red VW Bug, his heart skipped a beat. She was even more beautiful than he remembered, but she seemed smaller, more fragile.

He met her under the arched entrance with a nod, two fingers to the brim of his CDFW uniform cap.

Together, they walked inside and stepped up to a reception desk. A deputy wearing an N95 mask handed them masks, took their IDs, and checked them in.

"You'll need to wear these masks inside, but before you can go any farther, we need you to take a rapid Covid test."

A white-coated tech swabbed their nostrils. They sat together silently in the waiting area for a few minutes until another masked, white-coated deputy greeted them, handed them temporary ID badges, and escorted them through sterile hallways and past closed doors. Finally, they stopped in front of a double sliding steel door marked Coroner. The deputy entered a code, the door shushed open, and they stepped inside.

The temperature dropped. Chemical smells of formaldehyde and embalming fluid hit Colin, sending his mind catapulting back to the military hospital in Kandahar Province, Afghanistan.

Delfina gasped when the smell hit her. She reached for his hand, bringing him back to the present. He entwined his fingers with hers.

The deputy glanced back over her shoulder and gestured that they follow. They continued through the antechamber and another security door. Inside the second space was another hallway. The deputy led Colin and Delfina down the hall and through an open doorway into an office.

Entering the office, they encountered a woman in a white lab coat seated in front of a computer. She pushed tortoiseshell glasses back on the bridge of her nose, stood, and stepped away from her desk.

The woman had a commanding presence—radiating intelligence, no-nonsense compassion, calm poise, and athletic grace—clearly a person with nothing to prove. She wore her peppered grey and silver hair in a short Afro. When she turned her head and smiled at Delfina, her gold earrings and diamond-studded wedding band sparkled under the LED office lights. As she held out her hand to Delfina, a gold smartwatch strapped around her wrist gave her an air of high-tech sophistication.

"Hello. Delfina Cuera?"

Delfina nodded and shook the woman's hand.

"You're welcome to take off your masks if you wish. Thank you for coming. My name is Doctor Mary Sandow. I'm the county's forensic pathologist." She turned to Colin. "And you are?"

Colin offered his hand. "Fish and Wildlife Officer Colin Dawson, ma'am. I'm assisting on the homicide investigation of Delfina's mother, Ramona Cuera. Delfina requested that I accompany her here." Dr. Sandow's grip was firm, her fingers long and graceful, and her fingernails unpolished but meticulously groomed.

"Very well. Please, have a seat, both of you." Dr. Sandow gestured to two chairs in front of her desk. She returned to her seat behind her desk and computer.

Delfina and Colin removed their masks.

"How are you doing, Delfina?" Dr. Sandow's voice conveyed sincere compassion, but her eyes were as clear and sharp as an eagle's. It was obvious to Colin that no detail would escape her notice.

Delfina shook her head and looked down at her hands in her lap.

"I'm very sorry for your loss. This must be so difficult for you."

Delfina raised her head. Her eyes, welling with tears, met Dr. Sandow's. "M-may I … May I see my mother?"

"Yes. Soon you will see her body and make a formal identification. But first I need to ask you a few questions if that's all right."

Delfina nodded.

"Do you mind if I record our interview?"

Delfina shrugged and Dr. Sandow switched on the recorder.

"You and your mother are Native American?"

"Yes. We are members of the Sycuan Band of the Kumeyaay Nation."

"Have either of you had COVID-19?"

"Yes. Even though we were vaccinated, both of us got it about six months ago. I think it was my fault. When UCSL went back to holding classes in person, I attended a colloquium on endangered local amphibians, and I was kind of careless about not wearing a mask in the classroom. But our cases were mild. The doctors told us we probably had one of the new variants. They prescribed Paxlovid, our symptoms cleared up, and we tested negative in about five days."

"Other than the Paxlovid, did your mother take any prescription medication— sedatives, barbiturates, or painkillers—Xanax, Adderall, Percocet, oxycodone, fentanyl?"

"No. My mother was healthy. She never took any medication."

"What about experimental drug use? Ketamine, marijuana, ayahuasca, LSD, psilocybin, cocaine, heroin?"

"No! My mom was clean and strict with herself about what she put in her body. She never did drugs. And I'm sure she wouldn't want any toxic death preservative chemicals injected into her now either. We have a strict burial tradition."

"I understand. We'll do our best to respect your needs. Did your mother work in or around a veterinary clinic or large animals?"

"No." Delfina's face paled, and she glanced at Colin. Colin sensed her heart racing.

"What's this about?" he asked.

"Results came back on a tox screen that indicates a high level of xylazine in Ramona's system."

Delfina shook her head. "I have no idea what that is."

"All right. Thank you." Dr. Sanborn made some notes on her computer.

"May I see my mother now?"

"Just one more thing." Dr. Sandow smiled patiently. "We received preliminary results on your mother's DNA analysis this morning. We found some anomalies. I'd like permission to collect your DNA—take a blood sample and a cheek swab."

Delfina's brows furrowed. "What kind of anomalies?"

"It's just a testing glitch, I'm sure. There appear to be epigenetic histone modifications in the protein structure of your mother's cell nuclei," said Dr. Sandow. "To be clearer, it's as if your mother has feline DNA mingled with her normal human mitochondrial strands."

Delfina glanced at Colin, fear in her eyes. He had no idea what to advise her. He shrugged his shoulders and shook his head.

"Sorry," said Dr. Sandow. "There's no reason to be alarmed. I just need to see if the anomalies in your mother's DNA also occur in yours. Will you permit me to take a cheek swab and collect a blood sample?"

Delfina touched the abalone shell at her throat. She took a deep breath. "Okay."

Dr. Sandow drew Delfina's blood, then swiped the inside of her cheek with a swab, which she placed in a sterile tube. Finally, she asked Delfina and Colin to follow her across the room to a large, curtained window.

She spoke into a microphone. "The next of kin is ready now. Open the window, please."

The curtain slid open, revealing a covered body laid out on a stainless steel autopsy table. A lab assistant stood by. At Dr. Sandow's order, he pulled the sheet down to Ramona's shoulders.

Delfina quaked silently. Colin wanted to put his arm around her but resisted, reluctant to invade her privacy.

Seeing Ramona's face again, he felt shaken. What kind of monster would murder this woman? He recalled the incredulity and sorrow he'd felt as he knelt beside the dying mountain lion turning into a woman before his eyes.

It was just a hallucination, he reassured himself.

After a moment, Dr. Sandow asked Delfina if she recognized the woman on the table.

"Yes." Tears streamed down Delfina's cheeks. "That's my mother, Ramona Cuera. But I thought I'd get to be in the same room with her. I want to touch her and tell her up close that I love her. I need to say goodbye in a good way."

"I'm sorry. That's not possible at this time. First, this is still an active homicide investigation; we can't risk contamination of the body. Second, the morgue is a dangerous place for an untrained civilian. You can't go in there. Once we release your mother's body, you will be in charge of how you want to handle things. I suggest you start making arrangements now."

"I don't even know what to do."

"You might want to contact a local mortuary. They will guide you through your choices for burial or cremation and help you and your family make plans. Once your mother's body is in the mortuary's custody, you will have the opportunity to say your goodbyes as you wish. When you select a mortuary, let us know which one. We'll contact them when it's time to transfer your mother's body, and the mortuary will contact you."

The lab tech signaled that he needed to cover the body.

"I'm sorry, but this is all the time we can give you. Ready, Delfina?"

Tears streaming down her cheeks, Delfina nodded. Dr. Sandow gestured to the lab tech, who pushed a button. The curtain slid closed over the window to Delfina's mother. Ramona Cuera was gone.

15

F ROM COLD RAIN SQUALLS last week to today's eighty-degree afternoon, the weather on California's central coast had been flip-flopping wildly this spring.

Drought-busting heavy rain, followed by warmer than usual sunny days had resulted in a prolific bloom of wildflowers on the Cougar Creek Coast Ranch. Lupines, poppies, sticky monkey flowers, buttercups, blue-eyed grass, Indian paintbrush, and wild lilac dotted the coastal prairie rolling down to the sea from the plateau where Sheriff's Lieutenant Carlos Rosa had established his homicide investigation command post.

Migrating birds following the Great Pacific Flyway—orange-crowned and Wilson's warblers, western bluebirds, golden-crowned sparrows, and violet-green swallows soared around the oak trees, filling the afternoon with song. Butterflies animated the air with splashes of color. A family of tiny harvest mice had taken up residence inside the command post's busy main tent.

On Tuesday afternoon, April 19, Lieutenant Rosa stood outside the command post tent, side-by-side with tanned and wiry FBI Agent Chen. Lieutenant Rosa wore a casual shirt with slacks and slip-on loafers. Agent Chen, usually a meticulous dresser, had stripped off tie and jacket, and unbuttoned his starched white collar. The temperature this afternoon, at eighty-three degrees, was far above normal for this time of year.

Chen held a white handkerchief to his nose, valiantly suffering from his pollen allergy. At five feet eleven, Agent Chen stood five inches shorter than Rosa's six feet four. And at one hundred fifty pounds, Chen was outweighed by Rosa's muscular hundred ninety-five. But the FBI agent, all lean, tough muscle, was as strong and as smart as a Doberman.

Rosa and Chen stood facing a tall, gaunt man dressed in black. Rosa and the stranger assessed each other from the same height, eye-to-eye.

Rosa handed back the man's badge and ID. "Very well, Deputy Marshal Kurt Stone. This all looks in order. Sorry it's taken us so long to officially welcome you to the team. You're from the San Diego district office? What are you doing up here?"

The man in black took his time replacing the ID in his wallet, which he slipped in the back pocket of his jeans. He hooked his U.S. Marshal star back on his belt, and adjusted his black lawman's hat to shade his eyes from the sun. "I'm working on a fugitive investigation relating to a fentanyl trafficking case."

Chen raised an eyebrow. "I hear a slight accent, but I can't quite place it. You're not a native Californian. Where are you from originally?"

"Texas."

"Tell us more about this case you're working."

"Probably not much more to tell than you already know. Fentanyl is a synthetic opioid, up to fifty times stronger than heroin and a hundred times stronger than morphine. Pharmaceutical fentanyl was developed for pain management treatment of cancer patients. But illicitly manufactured fentanyl is rapidly becoming our biggest cause of opioid deaths."

Chen nodded. "A decade ago, few people even knew about fentanyl, and now it's a national crisis. The number of fentanyl seizures and fentanyl-related deaths in California alone is unprecedented, and on the rise exponentially."

"Why are you here in Santa Lucia?" asked Rosa. "What's your angle?"

"San Diego County, where I've been working, is the epicenter for fentanyl trafficking into the United States. Mexican cartels, primarily the Sinaloa and the Jalisco New Generation Cartels, are stepping up manufacture of fentanyl for distribution and sale in the US by hundreds of pounds every month."

"And China supplies the raw ingredients," said FBI Agent Chen.

"That's right. Fentanyl precursor mixtures are imported mostly from China to Mexico, then the raw, unprocessed powder is pressed into pills or mixed into other drugs at massive, industrial-scale labs. Initially, drug trafficking organizations were adding small amounts of fentanyl to large loads of other drugs like methamphetamine and heroin. But now, straight up fentanyl pills and powder are being moved across the border."

"What exactly are we looking for?" asked Rosa.

"The pills mimic every imaginable prescription drug. But there's a new, candy-colored fentanyl product called Rainbow that comes in multiple forms, including pills, powder, and even blocks that resemble sidewalk chalk. Its appearance is a deliberate effort by drug traffickers to drive addiction among young adults and children. Fentanyl-related deaths among children have increased more than thirty-fold in the last ten years."

"We know that trafficking organizations will use anyone they can to help them move their product, including regular border crossers and even teens," said Lieutenant Rosa. "Is there a particular suspect you followed up here from San Diego?"

"We haven't ID'd any mules in your location, but we know there's an active distribution site somewhere nearby. I've been following a suspected fentanyl trafficker for the last two years," said Marshal Stone. "The trail led me here."

Lieutenant Rosa frowned. "That's bad news. Let's go on into the command tent and get out of the sun. We can have some ice water, sit down, and talk more."

As they stepped into the tent, a tiny harvest mouse scampered behind a filing cabinet. A yellow-bellied racer snake slithered after it, unnoticed by the humans.

In an instant, the snake struck the tiny mouse, grabbing it by the neck with its crushing jaws and coiling lightning fast around its body to hold it still.

Swallowing the mouse alive would take time.

Oblivious of the deadly drama playing out inside the tent, a burly officer with a big red beard followed Rosa and his companions inside.

Rosa glanced over his shoulder to see the newcomer standing face to face with US Marshal Stone. "Looks like our paths have crossed again, Bounty Hunter," said the red-bearded man.

Marshal Stone's mouth stretched into a gargoyle grin. He scowled down at the bearded man. "I'm no bounty hunter, Kozel. Bounty hunters are seedy characters with sketchy legal jurisdiction who think they're above the law. On the other hand, Federal Marshal is one of the oldest positions in the US Executive Branch, created in 1789 and originally composed of Revolutionary War heroes. Nowadays, with very sophisticated and effective police forces and intelligence agencies, we frown on bounty hunters, who are only a cut above vigilantes, like you, ICE."

"Yeah, yeah, yeah." The ICE Agent rested one gloved hand on the SIG Sauer at his hip and the other hand on his big belly, sagging like an inner tube over his belt. "Nice speech, Stone. Maybe you think you're a hero, but I'm glad to hear you don't think you're above the law."

"No one is above the law in this country, not even the president—or ex-president," said the man in black. Everyone in the tent within hearing distance laughed, except the ICE agent.

"I suggest you remember that yourself, Kozel," Stone continued. "Everyone's heard about the ruses you ICE men use to capture your prey. Look at you—wearing camo and a jacket that says *Police,* as if you're just a cop."

A city cop who was monitoring the tip line looked up. "Hey, not 'just a cop.' A little respect if you don't mind. And here's a heads up, Mister ICE Agent—you outsiders need to watch out for your excessive force racist bullshit. We've heard about the sadistic so-called policing that goes on down at the border. It won't be tolerated around here."

Kozel's eyes narrowed and his jaw tightened.

"Easy, boys. We're all on the same team," said Lieutenant Rosa. "We've been designated a Multi-agency Investigative Team. We're supposed to coordinate our efforts to identify and catch the bad guys, not attack one another. I'm going to need to see your ID and credentials, Agent Kozel. And be advised, both of you, that we will be contacting your supervisors and verifying who and what you claim to be. I'll also need a full written explanation from both of you, Stone and Kozel, justifying your presence here. I'm all for interagency cooperation, but I won't stand for people with personal agendas getting into the middle of my homicide investigation. It may be that the epicenter of the Central Coast fentanyl operation is somewhere nearby, but I'm not seeing any indication at this point that our homicide is connected to your fentanyl, Stone, or whoever it is you're tracking, Kozel."

"Did you do a background check on the victim when you ID'd her?" asked the ICE agent.

"Of course. No arrests or warrants, no gang affiliations, no history of violence, or bad credit. Not even a parking ticket."

"Any chance she was a drug mule?"

Lieutenant Rosa seared Kozel with his legendary X-ray vision. "Not a chance."

"I wouldn't be so sure about that," Kozel stroked his red beard. "Before 2017, Ramona Cuera and her daughter, Delfina, lived together in a small trailer park near UC San Diego, where Delfina was a student. Ramona worked at the Singing Hills Golf Resort, a luxury resort owned by the Sycuan band of the Kumeyaay. Ramona was the manager of the high-end restaurant there, and apparently made a very good living. She was active in tribal affairs with the Kumeyaay Indians. More than once, she accompanied elders across the border and back, supposedly to protect them. That put her under suspicion of being a mule. The San Diego PD recorded frequent incidents when she spoke out against what she claimed was police abuse of Native Americans. Bitching about tribal elders being wrongfully detained at the border for alleged illegal crossings, and a Native kid who she claims was profiled and roughed up during a stop and search. That little Indian girl even tried to convince us she was sex-u-all-y abused, and Ramona Cuera backed her up. Trust me, that Cuera bitch is a real fuckin' pain in the ass."

Kozel picked up a trash can and spit a brown gob of chew.

"And your point is?" said Rosa.

"That cunt stirred up some bad feelings among law enforcement. We'd been keeping a close eye on her. Then, with no warning, the dirty squaw and her little spawn, Delfina, just disappear. Recently, I finally caught their trail again. Found out she moved up here from San Diego with her daughter back in 2017, and they've been living together in town. Ramona was working at one of Santa Lucia's high-end tourist restaurants until the pandemic, but apparently hasn't had a job since Covid shut down indoor dining. I figure she had to be hurting for money. Maybe Ramona Cuera started moving fentanyl to make ends meet. Maybe the daughter, too. Heard Ramona was murdered. Good riddance. Where is the daughter, anyways? I need her address."

Rosa glanced sideways at Agent Chen, then glared at Kozel. "That's a need to know," said the lieutenant. "And you will speak respectfully about the deceased. Ramona Cuera, her daughter Delfina, and all women, will be respected when you're in my jurisdiction, Agent Kozel."

Kozel shifted his wad of chew to the other side of his mouth and raised the corner of his upper lip in an evil grin. "What do you think, Marshal Stone? Are the Cuera women the ones you're tracking?"

The gaunt man in black glared venom at Kozel. "That's a need to know."

Lieutenant Rosa had a sour stomach. He sipped his ice water. He wasn't happy about this Kozel character nosing around his investigation.

16

T HE NEXT DAY, Wednesday, April 20, Colin glanced over at Lieutenant Rosa in the passenger seat of his forest green CDFW Chevy Silverado. Colin rarely had anyone in his service vehicle with him, much less someone as intimidating as this guy. Talk about a strong father figure. *Uncomfortable.* Having been raised without a father, Colin didn't like the feeling of being under some male authority figure's thumb. Most of the ones he'd encountered, with the possible exception of his CDFW boss, Captain Stevens, were power-hungry, controlling, narcissists. As far as Colin was concerned, the jury was still out on Lieutenant Rosa.

Glad I cleaned out the trash and washed the truck this morning.

Rosa had asked Colin to drive him up the mountain to the Agua Pura Farm today. A preliminary ballistics' report had come in on the probable trajectory of the arrow that had killed Ramona Cuera. The report predicted that if the killer was still in the area, he was most likely hiding in the abandoned quarry, in fairly close proximity to the Agua Pura Organic Farm Community.

Rosa said he could "kill two birds with one stone"—interview the farmers and search the quarry area on the same day. Since the one-lane truck roads were confusing and poorly mapped, and since Colin knew the area and the farmers, Rosa had asked Colin to drive.

Colin was offended by the killing birds with stones comment. He cast another sideways glance at Rosa. He hated that he was escorting a mainstream sheriff's lieutenant into the center of the isolated Agua Pura community. These people had been alternative culture pioneers in sustainable organic farming since way back when organic farming was considered fringe. They had made it work, establishing local farmers' markets that were now an integral part of the Central California Coastal lifestyle. Off the grid in their secluded valley sanctuary, these farmers had lived close to the land for decades, working hard, enduring fires and droughts, doing without the amenities and support services of town life, and yet raising healthy, happy, well-educated kids who had become well-adjusted, creative adults living to their full potential and contributing to society.

Over the years, some of the hippie farmers had become professionals and social influencers in their own right, moving seamlessly between the isolated farm and professional day jobs in academia, environmental nonprofits, green tech, education, and local, state, and even federal government positions. And yet it seemed to Colin that there was something fragile about this community. They were like the endangered birds of the area, as sensitive to outside human intrusion as the wild ecosystem to which they belonged.

As Colin drove deeper up into the heart of Cougar Creek Coast Ranch, he sensed the arrow that killed Ramona still moving through the landscape, shredding and tearing into the soul of this sacred land.

About fifteen minutes uphill from the sheriff's command post, Colin stopped at a fork in the road and turned to Lieutenant Rosa in the passenger seat.

"If we took that fork farthest to the right, we'd thread up around the steep side of the canyon above the abandoned cement plant quarry. That road degrades and eventually becomes undrivable. Later we'll go back down the mountain and around the village, where there's an access road into the quarry on the other side.

"We'll go to the farm first. Up this way, along the bumpy curving middle fork, essentially around the other side of the mountain from the quarry, is the unmarked road to the farm. If you look up toward the ridge" Colin pointed "—you can see burned trees. The wildfires two years ago blazed along that ridge and right down to the edge of the farmstead. Some farmers lost their homes. There are real heroes up there who saved many of the dwellings, and even people's lives."

The partially paved one-lane truck road got bumpy as the asphalt paving degraded to dirt, rocks and gravel, with deep potholes and ruts. The road curved steeply uphill. Colin switched into four-wheel drive. Rosa gripped white-knuckled on the handhold above his window, grimacing at the cavernous drop just a couple of feet from the wheels of the truck tires.

The farther into the mountains they drove, the more the forest closed in around them. After about forty minutes of back-wrenching pothole bouncing, Colin took a sudden sharp-angled fork that turned steeply downhill.

They emerged out of the trees. Around another bend, Colin stopped the truck. Like Brigadoon, the farmstead appeared below, nestled in a ruggedly beautiful, enchanted valley sanctuary.

"There it is," said Colin. "Agua Pura Farm. Agua Pura pioneered an organic permaculture farming method that uses very little water and protects the crops with beneficial insects rather than pesticides. Everything they grow is hand-harvested. Their produce is sold as nearby as Santa Lucia farmers' markets and as far away as high-end grocers and restaurants back east."

"It's beautiful," said Rosa. "When we go in, we need to take it easy with what we say. Keep a lid on whatever fears the locals may be having."

Colin nodded. "Of course. Let's go on down and meet some people."

★   ★   ★

On the road down to the valley, Rosa seemed to take in every detail. Colin pointed out the solar array that powered the entire off-the-grid farm, a geodesic dome house, a yurt, several cabins, a teepee, two barns, greenhouses, and orchards. In the distance, little dots of farmers plowed a rectangle of dark brown earth. Beyond were colored squares of cultivated flowers: dahlias, asters, zinnias, cosmos, phlox, ranunculus, and more.

As Colin pulled his truck up beside an old barn, Rosa unfastened his seatbelt. Two friendly barking dogs ran to greet them.

"These are Phoebe and Hank's dogs." said Colin. "Their house burned to the ground in the fire. They're temporarily living off-site, but they're still farming here while they rebuild."

A tall, lean man with a blond braid ambled by, carrying a load of lumber over his shoulder. He gave the dogs a stand down sign with his hand, and the dogs quieted.

"That's Sun," said Colin. "He's Phoebe and Hank's green building foreman." Colin stepped out of the truck and Rosa followed.

A slender woman carrying a flat of snow pea starts appeared around the corner of a greenhouse. The gray in her hair bespoke her years, but her demeanor was youthful and radiant. "Colin, hello. What brings you out here this morning?"

"Good morning, Sarah. Sorry to intrude. Have you heard about the woman who was killed on the Cougar Creek Ranch property last week?"

"Unfortunately, yes. We did hear about the murder of Ramona Cuera. Her daughter, Delfina, has been working here part time during the pandemic. We all love Delfina, and when Ramona would come up to visit from time to time, we found her to be a lovely woman. This is a terrible thing."

Colin turned to the lieutenant. "Lieutenant Rosa, this is Sarah Amari." Then Colin turned to Sarah. "Sarah, Lieutenant Rosa would like to talk with some of you folks here at the farm about anything unusual you might have noticed around the area in the last few days."

"Oh. Okay." Sarah set down her flat on a redwood table and brushed a wisp of gray-streaked hair out of her eyes with the back of her hand.

"Thank you, Mrs. Amari," said Rosa. "I understand that Ramona Cuera's death has affected your community and I'm sorry for your loss. We're making our best effort to find the killer as quickly as possible. Have you noticed anything that might help us?"

"We haven't seen any strangers here in the valley as far as I know, but you're welcome to talk to anyone who's around today. People are working over there in the apple orchard you can talk with. And I was just going out to the field to do some planting. I can take you there to meet a few members of our collective, if you'd like. Do you think the killer could be hiding here on the land?"

"We haven't ruled out that possibility," said Rosa. "I don't want to alarm you, but obviously, the individual we're searching for is extremely dangerous. We need to find him—or her—before they hurt someone else. My team will continue to keep an active command post on the knoll near the site of the homicide for a while longer. The officers there are on alert and prepared to keep you safe. Here's my card. I can be reached any time, twenty-four seven by phone, text, email, or via 911. Sorry to interrupt your busy day, but I would like to meet as many people in your community as I can this morning. I'll follow you out to the field if you don't mind."

As they walked, Rosa asked who lived in the various structures.

"Everyone who lives here works on the farm. But a lot of our people have outside jobs for wages, as well. In the yurt up there on the hill is Alan Brody. The beautiful redhead watering flowers on the front deck is Alan's partner, Alexandra. He's an organic agriculture policy advisor, and she's a bigwig in California's organic certification program.

"Over there in the straw bale dwelling, Sparrow, a public school counselor, lives with her husband, Paul, a software engineer. They both commute to town for work, so they're not home today."

"Who lives in that old log cabin by the creek?"

"That belongs to one of our best orchardists, Sam Brown. His wife, Isabel, is a potter. About fifteen years ago, they sold their North Carolina farm, moved to Santa Lucia, and joined our collective."

"Exactly how many people belong to the Agua Pura Farm Collective?" asked Lieutenant Rosa.

"That's a hard question. A Vietnam vet by the name of Jake Nelson, along with several other families, bought the whole one hundred acres in 1983. Right now, we have about ten partners in the collective. But it's fluid. Two wonderful young people recently bought in and are building cabins farther up the mountain. We're so happy that a new generation of organic farmers is choosing our way of life. Ray de la Montaña would be the one to ask if you need specifics. He keeps track of those things. Kind of our self-appointed historian. He's a professor, an expert in coastal prairie habitats, agroecology, and the natural systems ecology of California's Central Coast. I think he's teaching at the university today."

"You say the community is fluid," said Rosa. "Is Delfina a member of your collective?"

"We consider her part of our community, but she doesn't legally own a share of the collective. Some of our farmers have invested money in the collective as partners and have legal and financial ownership in the farm. But the farm *community*—people who love Agua Pura and visit and help us farm, and who have even lived here for short-or-long-term stays—well, since our founding in the 1980's, that's a lot of people. Hard to say exactly how many, or to make a really definitive list of names. It's an organic community based on love of the land, trust, and shared values."

"Who lives in that teepee over there?"

"Oh, that's Aurora Bourne's teepee. She joined the collective about twenty years ago. She used to be a schoolteacher, but there was some kind of an accident right around the turn of the century. She almost drowned and she says it changed her. She quit teaching, became an artist and semi recluse, and bought in as a shareholding partner at the farm."

"Is she in there now?"

"No. She's been away for a few months. I think she's staying on an Indian reservation on Vancouver Island. She said she'd be back next fall."

Carlos Rosa's mind flooded with memories. He'd known Ms. Bourne years ago, when he was just a young detective working a trafficking, extortion, and multiple homicide case. The perps were caught, case closed, but his good friend Father Francis Hilman had been murdered. Body never found. Presumed washed out to sea. Ms. Bourne almost drowned. Rosa had sensed at the time that she and Father Francis were in love. Such a tragedy to lose Father Francis. Rosa would never forget him. Just luck that Aurora didn't die that night too.

"Mom!" A teen wearing bright red cutoff overalls and army surplus boots, with a blue Mohawk, and a ring through her nose, burst out of the barn and ran toward the group. She carried a quiver of arrows in a backpack and held a crossbow.

Craning her neck, she tilted her chin up to speak to Lieutenant Rosa. "I heard what you were saying, Sheriff. About a murder and a dangerous killer at large. I've been wanting to talk to someone official about this. Can I talk to you a minute, Sheriff?"

"Of course. What's going on?"

"See, some of my friends have been meeting up with this totally cursed looking dude after school. He's their plug—um, that means he sells them colored candies they call Rainbow."

The girl was skinny, with long legs, knobby knees and elbows. As she spoke, she flung her awkward arms at odd angles as if she were a rag doll.

"It's some kind of drug, you know?" She continued talking like a freight train speeding downhill without brakes. "Gets 'em burnt up real bad. Course, we're s'posed to keep it on the low key, you know, not tell The Man. But I'm worried about my friends, bruh. Fact. I think that shit's really dangerous, and probably the cursed dude who sells it is too."

"And you are?"

"I'm Frankie. Pronouns are they-them."

"And Sally's your mother?"

"Not my true blood mom." Frankie spoke with a slight lisping whistle through her braces. Her hands were constantly animated. "We call all the adults in the community mom or dad."

"I see. This is very valuable information, Frankie. And where exactly do your friends meet their dealer?"

"At the end of the road behind Clark's Landing, at the locked gate where the trail goes up along the creek to the old quarry."

"Looks like you're an archer?"

"Fact. Ever since I read *Hunger Games*, I've wanted to be as badass an archer as Katniss Everdeen. She's fire! She totally slays."

"What do you shoot at?"

"Only straw targets, Sheriff. Don't worry." She hopped up on a straw bale, as limber as a cat, but without the grace.

"Have you seen anyone around here with a crossbow?"

Frankie's eyes dropped to the ground, then she gazed up at the sky. She jumped off the straw bale, swallowed, and looked at Lieutenant Rosa's left ear.

"Nope."

"Let me know if you remember anything that might help us, alright, Frankie? Here's my card."

"Cool. Yeah."

Roosters crow, and teenagers lie, thought Colin as Frankie walked away whistling, her arms helicoptering. Frankie knows more than she's telling.

A mud-spattered red mini Jeep tractor buzzed up. The driver, a man in his mid-twenties with bright red hair, wearing dirty shorts, a black T-shirt, well-worn cowboy boots, shades, and a floppy cloth hat, grinned infectiously.

Colin waved. "Hey, Sam. How's it going?"

"All good, Col. Whatsup?"

"This is Lieutenant Rosa from the sheriff's office. Sheriff, Sam is one of the newest members of the farm collective."

"Nice to meet you, Lieutenant. Are you here investigating Ramona Cuera's murder?"

"That's right, son. I guess bad news travels fast."

"Yeah. If I were you, I'd look into those mountain bikers cutting up our land with bike trails."

"I guess mountain bikers aren't too popular with you folks."

"Honestly, I personally love mountain biking. It's a great sport. My friends and I go out a few times a month. But we already have hundreds of miles of great bike trails in the county, so I don't see the need to carve up Cougar Creek Coast Ranch for more at the risk of disrupting sensitive wildlife and threatening rare and endangered plants. Besides, that guy in charge of planning the trails is a real a-hole. He's got a bad attitude. Gives the rest of us mountain bikers a bad name."

★   ★   ★

Once Rosa had met with and questioned everyone present on the farm, Colin drove the lieutenant back down the mountain. They exited out of the Cougar Creek Coast Ranch gate, which was still being monitored by city cops, and proceeded south down the coast highway, to the historic whaling village of Clark's Landing.

"Are you familiar with the history of Clark's Landing, Lieutenant?"

"I'm a blank slate, son."

"Okay. Well, I'm a big fan of local history—a local history nerd, I guess you could say. May I tell you a little about the town while we drive?"

"Go ahead. Sounds interesting."

"Clark's Landing was founded in the 1860s by Captain John Clark, a whaler from the East Coast. Captain Clark established a shore whaling operation at Clark's Landing, and built a general store in the village out of lumber milled from the nearby redwood forests. In addition to whale oil for lamps, the Clark's Landing Cash Store sold ammunition, tools, clothing, feed for stock, and groceries for the small population living along the coast and in the mountains nearby. Besides whaling, the other primary business in town, established in 1906, was the Portland Cement Company. The village grew, adding a one-room jailhouse, a bar, a public bath house, a very small Catholic church, and a cluster of Victorian-style cottages. Some of those buildings still stand, including the church and the historically preserved jailhouse, where more than one drunken whaler once spent a night or two. At that time, every so often, a grizzly bear could be seen wandering through town. California grizzlies are now extinct, of course."

Colin drove past a grove of Monterey Pines and then an open stretch with a clear view of tourmaline-blue ocean.

"Beautiful view," said Rosa. "What's that crumbling wooden structure jutting out into the sea?"

"That's the remains of Clark's Landing pier, where whalers processed their catch. Steam-powered boats with bow-mounted harpoons allowed whalers to hunt efficiently. The dead whales were tied to the pier, the whale's skin and blubber would be peeled off in long strips and boiled down to make whale oil. Old-timers say the stench was horrible.

"By the early nineteen hundreds," Colin continued, "whale hunters had already so drastically depleted the population of gray whales that the California whaling industry dwindled to an end. The human population along the coast was growing, and new immigrants found agriculture and dairying more attractive than the dangerous and unpredictable work of prospecting for gold and hunting whales."

"My daughter's fascinated by whales," said Rosa. "She's been wanting my wife and I to take her whale watching."

Colin nodded. "I hope you'll do that, sir. It's a phenomenal experience. We're fortunate to still have them. Thanks to an enormous public outcry, California gray whales were declared an endangered species in 1972 and were protected by federal law under the Marine Mammal Protection Act and the Endangered Species Act. Nature is amazingly resilient," said Colin. "The whale population has rebounded, but they continue to be a fragile species, and they still need protection."

"You've mentioned before that a cement plant remains in the area. How about the Cash Store? Has that survived?"

"As the population grew through the first half of the twentieth century, Captain Clark's old Cash Store prospered. But in 1953, it was destroyed in a fire. In 1978, at the peak of the California Arts and Crafts Renaissance, the property was acquired by a local potter, who built a new business on the site. The New Clark's Landing Cash Store included a restaurant, a production pottery studio, and a pottery school. Since then, it's changed owners several times, but it's never permanently shut its doors."

Rosa gazed out the window. "I don't often get up this far north in the county. I'm appreciating this stretch of miles of beautiful, untouched open coast. Why hasn't it ever been developed? What gives?"

"Developers have had their eyes on this land for generations. Many development schemes have been proposed for this coast, including massive private commercial resorts, and even a nuclear power plant. We can thank generations of avid environmental conservationists, strong land trusts, and conservation-minded politicians who've worked hard to lock in legal protections, keeping this coast, with its treasure trove of rare coastal habitats and wildlife, free of commercial development and in the public trust forever."

Windows down, Colin and Rosa enjoyed a few minutes of fresh air and silence.

"We're almost there," said Colin.

"I've heard that the Cash Store has a good restaurant," said Rosa, "but I've never eaten there. My family usually heads to the south county when we want to go out to eat. Does the Cash Store still have a pottery?"

"Definitely a good restaurant, but no longer a pottery. Around the beginning of the twenty-first century, after the Trust for Public Land purchased the seven thousand acres of Cougar Creek Coast Ranch land and transferred it to the BLM, the owners of the Cash Store realized they were sitting at the edge of acres of exquisite public land, a beacon to tourists from all over the world. So, with an eye to the changing tastes of a new generation of tourists, they shut down the pottery studio and transformed the upper floors of their historic building into a high-end bed and breakfast, its rooms exquisitely furnished with period pieces from the nineteenth century whaling era. It was renamed the Clark's Landing Roadhouse Restaurant and Inn, and became what it is today—a bed and breakfast, watering hole, organic slow food restaurant, live music venue, and whale watching lookout, popular with tourists and locals alike.

"And here we are."

At the corner of Highway 1 and Clark's Avenue, Colin stopped, clicked on his left turn signal, and waited for a safe opening between oncoming cars.

Lieutenant Rosa rested his elbow in the pleasant warmth on the open truck window and gazed toward the ocean. An inviting path through a thicket of native willow led to windswept ocean cliffs overlooking the whalers' cove.

A Japanese tourist bus had just parked across the highway in the Roadhouse lot and was unloading. A group of people with binoculars, cameras, and floppy hats ran like a covey of quail across the highway toward the path to the cliffs.

When the coast was clear, Colin made a smooth left turn at the Roadhouse corner, across the two-lane undivided highway, onto the quiet street running through the center of the village. Only one block long and lined by quaint old beach houses, Clark's Avenue ended at the small hundred-fifty-year-old Spanish Catholic church.

At the church, Colin took a right. The road curved, then passed an art glass studio, which had for many years routinely dumped broken bits of colored glass into the creek behind the studio—until new regulations and an environmentally conscious community made them stop. Although the studio had long ago ended the dumping practice, beautiful sea glass still washed and tumbled on local beaches, delighting beachcombers.

Just past the glass studio, Colin turned left toward the mountains at the Old Coast Road. The Coast Road wound through a thick riparian corridor for a mile before the vegetation opened at a small housing development. Colin proceeded slowly along the quiet street, passing modest homes on the left and a wooded creek on the right. After the last house, vegetation once again threatened to overcome the narrow road, which continued through tangled riparian habitat for another half mile, and ended at a closed gate.

At the end of the road, Colin parked in front of the locked swinging steel barrier gate. The sign posted by the gate read, "No Trespassing. Property of the Cientox Cement Plant." Beyond the gate, the road turned to dirt and meandered up out of sight into the mountains. Colin and Rosa sat silently, each in their own thoughts, and stared through the windshield up the truck road.

Lieutenant Rosa unwrapped a stick of gum and folded it into his mouth.

"Cientox?" Carlos Rosa's forehead wrinkled.

"Cement is part of the history of this area. Ready for a little more local history?"

"Lay it on me, son."

"Okay. These mountains sit on an ancient seabed. Millions of years ago—"

Rosa leaned back and closed his eyes.

"—under the ocean along the San Andreas fault system, limestone and marble were deposited. Tectonic pressure and earthquakes lifted and folded these bedrock layers out of the ocean, forming mountains containing large deposits of comparatively pure, coarsely crystalline, white and blue limestone.

The Santa Lucia Portland Cement Company at the Clark's Landing plant and quarry mined this limestone to produce the cement that was used rebuild San Francisco after the great quake of 1906.

Cement kilns require extremely high temperatures to process the raw materials, so vast amounts of the surrounding old growth redwood forests, which were not yet protected, were cut and burned to fuel the kilns. Enormous amounts of water were also used in the production process. And as for the fresh, life-giving ocean air here on the cost, cement production ruins air quality, emitting large amounts of toxic substances into the air, including Sulphur dioxide and Carbon monoxide, which can cause or aggravate respiratory issues like asthma or cause damage to the central nervous system.

For a hundred years, everything in Clark's Landing—including houses, trees, flower gardens, cars, the school—everything was covered with cement dust from the plant. When children walked to school in those days, they left their footprints in the cement dust on the sidewalks.

It was not then known that the cement production process releases large amounts of carbon dioxide into the atmosphere, making cement a major industrial contributor to climate change.

The plant changed ownership several times.

In 2005, Cientox, a Mexican corporation, acquired the property, and took over the cement operation. But in 2010, the US Environmental Protection Agency permanently closed the plant because of its many, many hazmat issues. Now Cientox is just kind of stuck with it. They'd like to sell—to the state, the county, BLM, even to Clark's Landing. Public consensus is that the hundred-seventy-two acres of cement plant property, sitting in the center of the Cougar Creek Coast Ranch National Monument, should be added to the monument's publicly owned holding. But in order to sell, Cientox has to clean it up. That's a multimillion-dollar proposition. And no one will buy it for what it would cost Cientox to mitigate all its hazardous issues."

Rosa sighed sat up, and gazed at the overgrown road beyond the barrier. "This must be the road to the abandoned quarry where the kids meet their rainbow candy dealer."

Colin nodded. "The Cursed One."

"Ramona Cuera's killer could be hiding up there," said Rosa. "We need to get out a search party."

"Agreed," said Colin. "Although once searchers go in, the dope pusher will probably get spooked and stop coming to meet the youngsters."

"You're right. That crossed my mind too." Rosa stared up the road. "Before we rush in guns a-blazing, we need to do our homework, get a better idea of what's up there. Let's drive back down to those houses and knock on some doors."

Colin turned the truck around.

★　　★　　★

Halfway along the row of houses, Colin pulled up in front of a home with a man tending roses in the front yard. The man smiled and waved.

Colin and Lieutenant Rosa stepped out of the truck.

Colin tipped the brim of his cap. "Good afternoon. Beautiful day."

"Oh, sí. Es very beautiful today." The man smiled and looked up at the cloudless blue sky. "Es a good day to be alive."

Colin introduced himself and Lieutenant Rosa, then asked the man's name.

"Mucho gusto. Me llamo Jorge Escobar."

"Igualmente," said Rosa.

"Bienvenidos. Welcome to our neighborhood. You should go across the street and see the creek. Its name *es* Cougar Creek. Its water comes all the way from the top of the mountains. It is very beautiful and peaceful. The water is so pure, with little fish and frogs and so many birds in the trees, and shady blue green pools and waterfalls. Our kids love to play down there. All the people in our neighborhood enjoy it very much. We like to have barbacoa— barbeque with *mucho comida muy buena*, all together, in the grass over there next to the path that goes down by the water. You should go see."

"Thank you, Jorge," said Rosa. "Sounds like you've lived in this neighborhood awhile."

"Oh yes. Por muchos años. A long time." Jorge's smile was as beatific as the statue of the Virgin Mary in his rose garden.

A new SUV pulled into the driveway next door. A fit looking woman wearing a yoga outfit and expensive running shoes stepped out of the van on the driver's side. A bunch of laughing kids burst out on the other side, unloaded groceries from the back of the van, and disappeared into the house. The woman approached.

"Hi, Jorge. Is everything all right? I picked up that prescription for your wife. Is she feeling any better? What's going on?"

"Oh *sí*, Irene. Muchas gracias. Marta is better. No hay problema, todo está bien."

"I'm so glad to hear that." Irene turned to the officers and extended her hand. "Hello. I'm Irene Johansen."

"Good afternoon, ma'am. I'm Lieutenant Rosa of the Santa Lucia Sheriff's Department. This is Officer Dawson from Fish and Wildlife. We're investigating a homicide that occurred nearby. We just wanted to ask you folks if you've seen anything unusual in your neighborhood recently. Perhaps someone in the area who seemed suspicious."

"We heard that a body was found. It's terrible. I'm so glad you're here, Sheriff. There has been someone lurking around our neighborhood! A very scary looking man. Hispanic, with scars on his face and tattoos on his neck and arms. I've only seen him a couple of times, just glimpsed him sneaking through the trees. But my children have told me about him. Thank God they talk to me, unlike some teenagers."

As if on cue, one of the kids ran out of the house and stood at her mother's side.

"Are you a sheriff?" The blue-eyed girl craned her neck to look up at Rosa, brown freckles sprinkled over her pink cheeks. Her braces gleamed as she smiled. Thick ginger curls surrounding her face bounced like springs.

"Good afternoon, miss. I'm Sheriff's Lieutenant Carlos Rosa, at your service. And you are?"

"Oh, wow. Hi. My name is Lucy Johansen. I wanted to tell you something really important. My friend lives at Agua Pura. And she, um—they—carpool with me to school at Playa Azul Middle School. Clark's Landing doesn't have any secondary schools; only, you know, elementary. We were best BFFs all the way through elementary. So now our moms take turns driving us into town to middle school. We're going to be freshmen in high school next year!

"Anyways, Frankie stayed overnight with me a few weekends ago, and we saw a man hanging out at the end of our road, you know, by the gate to the quarry. He was really, really scary looking. Frankie says he's extra bad. We call him the Cursed One. So anyway, the day that Frankie stayed over, we hid behind the willows by the creek and watched him sell baggies of rainbow-colored candy that looked like Skittles. I did a research report on drugs for school, so I know the candy was really, you know, drugs. We watched him sell to kids who go to our school, and even some little kids. It really scares me that he's hanging around. Can you do something?"

"Thank you for telling me this, Lucy. We're aware of this individual, and we want to catch him. Can you tell me what he looked like?"

"I can't exactly remember. I was too scared."

"You are absolutely right to be scared. He's very dangerous. Stay away from him. Warn your friends, and tell your mom if you see him again, or anyone else who seems scary. Okay? Call me if you see him again. Here's my card."

"Oh wow! Okay! Nice to meet you, Sheriff." Lucy took the card and ran back into the house, her curls bouncing.

"Sometimes at night, my husband and I think we hear someone sneaking around outside," said Irene. "We had a security system with surveillance cameras installed last week."

"Have you reviewed your security footage?'

"Oh, yes. We look at it every morning. So far, nothing but a family of deer, a coyote, a few raccoons, and a skunk. Oh, and once, a beautiful little gray fox slipped by, nearly invisible in the night."

"Please contact me right away if you see or hear anything in the area, or see something on your security video that seems suspicious. Here's my card."

17

O N THE SAME DAY, up the highway at the Route 1 Tavern, Colin's friend James Owens polished his bar top—a salvaged two-hundred-fifty-year-old old growth redwood slab, fashioned by a craftsman friend into a work of art.

Today was a typically slow Wednesday afternoon, just a trickle of people dropping into the tavern since he'd opened at 11:00. A few locals. Some itinerant hippies working for the nearby semilegal pot grower. A few adventurous tourists looking for an off-the-beaten-path experience.

A red-bearded man wearing quasi-military getup shoved open the tavern door and let it slam behind him. He duckwalked pretend-casual, like an old-timey gun slinger—bowlegged, as if he had a sore crotch or a set of balls so big he couldn't put his legs together.

James's combat instincts triggered. *This guy feels unstable. Keep him in your sights.*

Red Beard sauntered over to a table in the darkest corner of the room, occupied by a man with a buzz cut. Buzzcut's yellow-trimmed black polo shirt gave him a preppy look. The word Defend was embroidered on his sleeve.

"Mind if I join?" Red asked Buzzcut, whose response was an OK hand gesture.

James folded a white bar towel over his arm, picked up a couple of menus and an order tablet, and approached the table.

"Welcome, gentlemen. Here's our menu. Can I get you started with anything? Maybe a drink?"

"Give me a dark stout," said Red Beard.

"I like those hoppy hazy IPAs, like the ones they used to have at Cider Riot in Portland," Buzzcut said. "Got anything like that?"

"We have both our home-brewed craft IPA and one of our best stouts on tap today. May I bring you samples?"

"Bring it on," said Buzzcut.

James returned with the beer samples. Red Beard grasped his glass. An OATH tattoo on the base of his thumb flashed in James's mind like a neon bar sign.

Fuck. I risked my life fighting to defend our democracy from these dickwads, thought James. Having white neo-Nazi racists determined to overthrow democracy in his tavern was worse than hosting a nest of typhoid-infected cockroaches.

James took the men's orders for pizza and beers.

They spoke together quietly while they ate. Both ordered another beer.

Now and then they became agitated, and their voices rose.

"BLM. Own the libs … antifa … the wall … Illegals … Jews replace us … Hitler … feminist cancer … election fraud … Soros. Who let those bitches vote? … total abortion ban … hunting rights my Second Amendment … Your semi-auto … Noncompliance … (laughter) … Government tyranny … Socialist clown show. Dark web. 1776. January sixth. Patriots. Recruit cops, Fresno training camp, Confederacy, Defend."

James surreptitiously took their photo.

When he brought the men their tab, Red Beard handed James his credit card.

"Thank you, Mr. Kozel."

As soon as they left, James sent their photo with a brief text message to his brother-in-arms, Colin Dawson: "Keep an eye out for these loose cannon Oath Keeper and Proud Boy wackos."

18

T HE NEXT DAY, Thursday, April 21, FBI Agent Chen set down a Starbucks latte and a blueberry muffin sprinkled with sugar crystals on Lieutenant Rosa's desk.

"Thanks, George." Carlos Rosa took a grateful sip of the latte and blinked at the tempting muffin on a napkin on his desk. "My wife would kill me if she knew I was drinking fancy Starbucks coffee and eating sugary muffins. She makes me eat a bowl of slow-cooked organic Scottish steelhead oatmeal every morning before I leave home."

Chen's laugh was little more than a polite sniff. "My wife's the same. Oatmeal every morning, even if it's just a few cold spoonfuls while I'm standing at the sink, if I'm in a hurry."

"Speaking of being in a hurry, it's already been a week since Warden Dawson found Ramona Cuera's body, and we still don't have a suspect."

"Shall we review what we know so far?"

Lieutenant Rosa opened a window on his computer, and the display popped up on the smart board wall.

"CSI is wrapping up their investigation around the immediate crime scene. We're continuing a wider search of the area. Never know—maybe our archer in camo is still hiding out in those hills."

Chen sipped his tea. "Unlikely. But we need a better description of Ramona's killer. We need to find a witness. How are the interviews going?"

"We have a lot of people on our list we still need to interview. It's going to take a while. Warden Dawson drove me up to the farm and over to Clark's Landing Village yesterday. We turned up information about a fentanyl dealer selling Rainbow to kids in the village. There could be a nest of fentanyl traffickers up in that deserted Cientox quarry. US Marshal Stone is following up, with the help of some of our deputies. Maybe Ramona was murdered because she somehow got crosswise with the fentanyl business."

"The FBI has plenty of resources to help with a manhunt," said Chen, "but we don't have an adequate focus for a search yet. Is Ramona's killer still somewhere in the seven thousand wild acres of Cougar Creek Coast Ranch, or in the adjoining cement plant acres, or did he flee to town, out of the county—or for that matter, out of state? All we know about this guy is that he was carrying a specialized crossbow and wearing camo. We need fingerprints, DNA, an article of clothing, some kind of lead."

Carlos Rosa set down his coffee cup on the desk. "What about motive? Examining Ramona Cuera's past may offer insight into why she was murdered."

Rosa made notations on the digital murder board to follow up on this line of investigation.

"What have we got from forensics?" asked Chen.

"The lab analyzed the casts of footprints found near the victim, including a perfect one taken from a cow pie."

"I assume they found the pie I stepped in, too?"

Rosa smiled. "They logged the print and identified it as yours. Did you turn your shoes into evidence? They looked expensive, and fairly new."

"It was no use keeping them. They were ruined."

"Sorry about that. Other than yours, the other prints found were from a size thirteen Belleville steel toe tactical boot manufactured within the last year."

"Excellent. A shoeprint can sometimes be more useful than a fingerprint for identifying an unsub."

"From these prints, we've got the size, design, mold characteristics, and sole pattern. Forensics also found a unique gouge in the outsole of the left shoe, and some small rocks—foreign to the crime scene—that were dislodged from the sole into the cow patty. This debris was similar to what was found under Ramona's fingernails."

"Sounds like enough to make a conviction-worthy positive ID, provided we find a suspect whose shoes match those characteristics."

"Let's hope the killer is not as fastidious as you, George, and doesn't throw his shoes away before we find them." Rosa took a bite of blueberry muffin and a sip of coffee, then brushed crumbs off his tie. "There's more."

"The arrow?" asked Chen.

Rosa nodded. "The shooter added a broadhead tip to the arrow— a brutal device, as you'll recall, with a needlelike point and razor-sharp blades that sprang open on impact, crushing and shredding a two-inch hole through Ramona's heart."

"Hmm. From that choice of weapon, can we infer that the killer desired to inflict maximum pain? Was the motive rage? Why?" Chen removed his glasses and polished them with his handkerchief.

"What about the search for suspects who purchased arrows for a Condor R500 Sniper bow within the last year? Have the resources the FBI brought in been helpful with that?"

"Yes," said Rosa, "but the joint task force is still combing through records. More people than I want to think about have bought military grade sniper crossbows over the last year."

Lieutenant Rosa sat forward in his swivel chair, pushed the muffin remains aside, and glared across his desk. "I think there's an elephant in the room, George."

"Which elephant is that?"

"Come on, George. Think."

Agent Chen gazed out the window at a pair of crows perched on the bare limb of a sycamore in the parking lot below. A row of newly installed EV chargers bounced sunlight into Chen's eyes. He frowned and shook his head.

"The mountain lion, George."

"Say more."

As Rosa enumerated each of his points, he tapped a bulleted section of text on his computer screen and brushed it up to the digital murder board that covered most of the wall facing them.

"Warden Dawson discovered the victim because of an anonymous tip about a mountain lion hunter. Dawson found a piece of broken mountain lion tracking collar near the body. Fur found near the victim has been positively identified as mountain lion. Puma Project researchers reported a missing mountain lion. That cowboy Rafe heard a puma caterwauling the night before the murder, and the next day got a text from a so-far-untraceable burner phone about an incident in the oak grove involving a mountain lion."

"Are you thinking Ramona Cuera was not the target?"

"Maybe she was killed accidently by an illegal mountain lion hunter."

"But why was she naked?"

"That I do not know." Lieutenant Rosa scrolled through the autopsy report on his computer screen. "Dr. Sandow's report has no indications of sexual activity."

"Okay. What else from the autopsy?"

"Dr. Sandow found unusually rapid onset of rigidity and low ADP postmortem. She lists several possible explanations: premortem heightened level of physical activity, a seizure disorder, ingestion of an unusual substance, or heavily insulating body covering. Also, the victim's hands and feet were calloused, with small cuts, scratches and dirt, small rocks, and wood splinters under finger and toenails. Sandow states that it's as if the victim had been wearing a fur coat while running on hands and feet, drugged, through the forest."

Chen stared at the crowded murder board, his meticulous mind clearly searching for pattern, for order. "Small rocks like the ones in the boot print."

"Yes. And the autopsy has other anomalies," said Rosa.

"Go on."

"A tick found behind the victim's ear had deer blood—not human blood—in its gut. Also, undigested deer meat was present in the victim's stomach."

"Meaning Ramona ate venison before she was killed?"

"The deer tissue was uncooked—raw meat. Not chewed, but apparently swallowed in large chunks."

"Running naked through the woods, wrapped in a fur coat, drugged, possibly forced to swallow chunks of raw deer meat. Perhaps some kind of ritualistic murder, then?"

Rosa shrugged. "Can't rule it out. We need to throw a wide net, consider all evidence, keep an open mind."

"And watch out for elephants in the room."

Lieutenant Rosa smiled.

"Anything else from the pathologist?" asked Chen.

"Yeah. Here's another weird one. Dr. Sandow's report mentions anomalous epigenetic DNA markers in both the victim and her daughter."

Chen raised an eyebrow. "Bookmark that. Why do I have a feeling there's more?"

"The tox screen came back from the National Lab. Results in under a week from the National Lab is a first, thanks to you, FBI Agent Chen."

"You're welcome. The lab found something of interest?"

"Yellow jackets swarmed the victim's body shortly after death and sipped her blood. Dr. Sandow captured several of the insects and had the contents of their guts analyzed. They found traces of xylazine. High levels of xylazine were also present in the blood sample taken from the victim's heart during the autopsy."

"Xylazine," said Agent Chen. "I looked it up. It's an essential large animal tranquilizer; a nonopioid, novel psychoactive substance. The DEA has recently noticed a sharp increase in the trafficking of fentanyl mixed with xylazine. It's being sold on the street as tranq dope. It's lethal."

"Sir, sorry to interrupt." A deputy stood in Lieutenant Rosa's office doorway. "Dispatch just radioed. There's a situation at Cougar Creek Coast Ranch."

"What kind of situation?"

"Remember that bicyclist you had removed for trespassing last week?"

"Mikos Vadim. What about him?"

"He's back with a group of guys and big tractors with front-end loaders. Claims they're authorized to work on grading bike trails right through the crime scene."

"Jesus, Mary, and Joseph! Tell the deputies up there to arrest the lot of them. Then run a background check on this Vadim character. Are you coming, George?"

"Meet you there. I have my muck boots in my car."

19

RAFE SILVA, the Cougar Creek Ranch cow boss, sat comfortably in his saddle watching deputies on the road adjacent to the sheriff's command center cuff Mikos Vadim and his gang of entitled mountain bikers.

While the bikers were being stuffed into a police van, they shouted threats of lawsuits, accusations of police brutality and unlawful arrest.

Meanwhile, beside the sheriff's tent at the edge of the oak grove, Marshal Stone and ICE Officer Kozel snarled at one another.

Rafe, mounted atop his quarter horse, sat nearly eight feet above the fuming men. Amigo pulled at his reins, rolled his eyes, and stomped. Rafe's dog barked and bared his teeth.

Kozel's index finger slid down the barrel of the Sig Sauer in his holster, his thumb disabling the retention device. He was a coiled spring, ready to draw and fire.

"I'm the patriot here," Kozel screamed. "I'm defending my country, while you Jews and woke libs try to turn the USA into a socialist clown show."

US Marshal Stone put his hands up, grinning his crooked gargoyle grin. "Hey, cool off, Kozel. No need to be defensive, okay? We're all on the same team here, man. Just trying to catch a killer."

Amigo stomped, reared, and whinnied. "Whoa." Rafe pulled back on his reins. "Zack, down." Rafe's dog stopped barking and lay down, head on his paws.

"Say, Officer Kozel," said Rafe, "how about if you lighten up that grip on your gun? Please? We don't want anyone getting hurt here today. Okay?"

Rafe took a deep breath. He watched the sun sparkle on the distant ocean. He was one with the breeze on his face and the power of Amigo's lifeforce between his thighs.

Kozel and Stone glared dangerously at one another. Long seconds ticked by.

Kozel's thumb, bearing an **OATH** tattoo, slowly moved back to reenable the retention device, securing the Sig in its holster. Kozel released his grip on the gun.

Rafe closed his eyes and silently thanked the saints above.

At the PG&E substation two hundred meters uphill from the sheriff's command center, a big rig screeched, winching the pair of tractor front-end loaders belonging to the bike trail crew back onto its flatbed.

★　　★　　★

Outside the sheriff's tent, Lieutenant Rosa strained to hear his phone over the big rig's metallic whine. He put the call on speaker phone and turned the volume to high.

"BLM Law Enforcement Dispatch. Do you have a crime to report on BLM-managed public lands?"

"Goddamn it! This is the head of Santa Lucia County Sheriff Criminal Investigations Division, Lieutenant Carlos Rosa. I need to speak to the Central Coast Field Manager right away!"

"Yes, sir. Just a moment please."

Another voice came over the speaker: "BLM Central Coast Field Manager Bob Budalo speaking. How can I help you, Lieutenant?"

"You sent heavy machinery into the middle of an active crime scene! What's wrong with you?"

"Sorry, Lieutenant. I had no idea. My associate Mikos Vadim informed me that your murder investigation on BLM's Cougar Creek Coast Ranch property was no longer active."

"Your associate?"

"Yes, I fast-tracked Mikos and his organization the contract to plan and build bike trails in our new park. We skipped all the tedious applications and paperwork. Back in the day, Mikos and I went to school together at Yale. He is so brilliant, and I'm new to California. I've been enormously fortunate to have him advising me on all the things there are to do in the area. What a playground we have here! Surfing, mountain biking, hiking, hunting, jet skiing, even snowboarding just a few hours away. My family and I are so happy to be here."

"Did you say hunting?"

"Oh, whoops. No. I—It just slipped out."

"Why would you say hunting?"

"Well, I did write hunting into the original draft management plan of the new Cougar Creek Coast Ranch National Monument. It seemed like a great idea to me. There's nowhere else in the region where a person can even go hunting. Can you imagine? No hunting? But—you know—*woke* Santa Lucia. There was such a big to-do. Huge public opposition. We had to take hunting off the table."

"Are you a hunter, Bob?"

"No. Well, I mean, yes, I personally enjoy the sport, but of course I follow Fish and Game regulations at all times."

"And you're saying that your friend Mikos told you it was just fine to bring heavy equipment and a trail building crew up here, into the scene of an active homicide investigation, and you didn't think to check with the sheriff's office?"

"Sorry about that. When do you think it will be all right for my crew to return?"

"Whenever our investigation is concluded."

"So … maybe a week? A month?"

"Check with my office in a month and we'll let you know. Don't assume your work can resume on the Cougar Creek Coast Ranch property until you have a direct okay from me, personally. Understood?"

"Copy that, Lieutenant. By the way, BLM has our own law enforcement officers, you know. We're spread pretty thin, but I could send a ranger or two over to help out, if you'd like?'

"No thank you."

"Oh, one more thing. We just received a memo from the Secretary of Interior's office informing us of a really big project newly designated for the Cougar Creek Coast Ranch property. Please keep this to yourself, but FYI, there's a lot more than trail building in the Coast Ranch's future. Maybe it's windy—wink, wink. Have a nice day. Bye for now."

★   ★   ★

FBI Agent George Chen stood outside the sheriff's tent, speaking with US Marshal Stone. Rafe scanned the area for Kozel. Nowhere to be seen. *Good riddance.*

The cowboy dismounted and led Amigo toward the tent. Zack followed at his heels. Lieutenant Rosa was putting away his phone, shaking his head.

"Excuse me, Lieutenant Rosa?" Rafe tipped his straw Stetson.

Rosa nodded. "Morning, Rafe. Seen anything suspicious while out patrolling your cow pasture? I hope you've been keeping an eye out for anything out of the ordinary."

"Always do. Nothing to report yet, sir. But I am concerned about my cattle. We have over a hundred head on the ranch. At this time of year, it's mostly pregnant cows, calves, and nursing mothers. I need my girls and their calves to be in a peaceful and safe place. Those big rigs bouncing over the potholes, with front-end loaders rattling along on top of the flatbeds like machine guns, that's not good for my cows."

Just then, the last of the trail builders' heavy equipment rumbled by, heading down the hill.

"It's handled," Rosa responded. "For now," he muttered under his breath.

20

THE FOLLOWING DAY, Friday, April 22, Sheriff's Homicide Detective Jamison parked the lieutenant's green-and-white on a tree-lined street in the town of Playa Azul.

"Here we are, sir," said Jamison.

At the front gate of Ramona and Delfina Cuera's small, freshly painted Victorian, Lieutenant Rosa and Detective Jamison ducked under a rose-covered arbor that led along a curving garden path lined with tulips, hyacinth, and daffodils.

Rosa nodded at the flowers. "Those are my wife's favorites."

Detective Jamison grinned. "They smell good. You planning to get her some for Mother's Day, Boss?"

"Remind me, when is that? I'll put it on my calendar." Rosa took a photo of Delfina's flowers and added it to his to do list.

"Nice place," said Jamison. "She and her mother own it?"

"Remarkably, yes. Nobody can afford to buy a home in Santa Lucia County anymore, but Ramona—er, now Delfina, owns this house."

"How did Ramona pull off buying a home in Santa Lucia on her own?" asked Jamison. "Think she was dealing drugs?"

Rosa shook his head. "No. I'm sure she was not. Agent Chen's people have given us thorough background information, including detailed financials, on the Cuera women. When she was young, Ramona married a white guy who came from wealth. He inherited a sizable trust from his grandfather, then became estranged from his family. Ramona never met his family. He died in a mountain climbing accident when Delfina was a baby. His trust went to Ramona. When she first arrived in Santa Lucia, she used money from the trust to pay cash for this house, hired an attorney, and updated her will, leaving everything she owned to Delfina, to be held in the trust."

Rosa and Jamison stepped onto the cottage porch and rang the front doorbell.

Delfina Cuera opened the door. "Lieutenant Rosa, good afternoon. What's going on?"

"We'd like to ask you a few questions, if we may, Delfina."

"Of course. Come in."

Delfina led Rosa and Jamison to the front parlor. A Native American man stood gazing out of the front bay window, thoughtfully stroking his feather earring. He turned to face Rosa and Jamison as they entered.

"Hello." The tall man's ribboned shirt, porcupine and abalone shell neck choker, beaded vest, and fringed moccasin boots were works of art. As he turned, some of his beads gleamed like crystals, refracting rainbows from the window light. Despite his lipstick and eye shadow, the dignified demeanor of this individual challenged anyone who might question his right to be who he was. His presence held no hostility or aggression; only wisdom and compassion animated his eyes.

"Lieutenant Rosa, Detective Jamison, this is my cousin Hawk. He's been helping me prepare for my mother's celebration of life."

Hawk put his hands together and bowed in greeting, then turned to Delfina. "Would you like me to stay or leave, sweetie?"

"I think I'd be more comfortable if you stayed with us. Thank you, Hawk."

Hawk took a seat in a corner of the room by the piano. He sat so still that he seemed to disappear.

Lieutenant Rosa settled on a Victorian loveseat and pulled his spiral notebook and pen out of his shirt pocket. Detective Jamison perched on the edge of a plush velvet easy chair.

"We're trying to understand who might have wanted to harm your mother, Delfina," said Lieutenant Rosa.

"You mean, what was the motive for her murder?"

Detective Jamison coughed.

"Yes," said Rosa. "I apologize for asking, but was she in a romantic relationship with anyone? Did she have an ex or a lover who may have felt jilted or betrayed?"

"No. My father died when I was a baby. As far as I know, Mama has never dated or had any intimate relationships since him."

"Do you know if she owed anyone money? Did she gamble or have any expensive habits? Was she in debt?"

"No way. My mother lived a disciplined, simple life. She didn't drink or gamble, do drugs, or anything like that. She didn't even wear makeup, and she sewed most of her own clothes. She was frugal. I didn't know until five years ago, when we moved to Santa Lucia and she bought this house, that she had a trust fund from my father. While I was growing up, she never spent any of that trust fund money. As long as I knew her, she worked hard and saved a large percentage of what she made to help me pay for school and to help members of our tribe who were in need."

"Did she have any social media accounts? Facebook, Instagram, anything like that?"

"None."

"What about friends, neighbors, coworkers? Could there be someone whom she made angry, who might have a grudge against her?"

"My mother was highly regarded at work, in our tribal band, and in the larger community. People depended on her. She helped people. Everyone who knew mama loved her."

Delfina looked at her hands, her fingers twisting the woven friendship bracelet at her wrist. "She did have some trouble with the local San Diego cops and the border police, though. They put her in jail a few times, even though she did nothing wrong. She's a US citizen. The Indian Citizenship Act of 1924 granted full citizenship to all Native Americans born within the territorial limits of the US. Our family have been residents of California since long before the Europeans arrived. Our roots are deep in this land, our ancestral home. We are the original people of the Kumeyaay land on both sides of the border. My mom was outspoken and not afraid to stand up for more vulnerable people in my tribe—elders, young women, defenseless kids." Delfina raised her chin. Her eyes, sparking fire, met Rosa's. "Some of the authorities didn't like her for that."

"Can you give us the name of anyone in particular who may have had it in for your mother?"

"Mama kept me away from her social justice work. She insisted that I stay focused on graduating from college. I never met any of the law enforcement people she dealt with."

"We haven't entirely ruled out the possibility that your mother's death was accidental. Possibly—say—a hunting accident." Rosa watched the young woman closely. Had he hit a nerve?

Delfina shook her head, eyes welling with tears.

"We are very sorry for your loss, Ms. Cuera," said Rosa. "Just a few more questions, if we may?"

Delfina nodded.

"Warden Dawson expressed concern that if someone murdered your mother, they might want to harm you as well. Do you feel that you may be in danger?"

"Yes."

"Has anything happened that would make you feel afraid?"

Delfina's face drained of color. She sipped tea from a delicate Haviland cup and carefully placed the porcelain cup back on its saucer.

For an instant, her eyes met Hawk's.

"There was an incident before we left San Diego, in 2017. Mama and I had just finished our evening prayers at a sacred site in the hills above San Diego when men with rifles started shooting at us. We ran for our lives. It was terrifying. We got away, but ever since, I've been afraid they'd find us again."

"How many men? Do you know who they were? Did you see their faces?"

"I think there were two or three, I'm not sure. It was already getting dark, and there was a terrible windstorm blowing dust and sand in my eyes. I didn't see their faces. I don't know their names, but Mama told me later that they were vigilantes. I got the impression it had something to do with a missing Kumeyaay girl that my mother had been trying to help."

"Are your mother's things still here in the house?"

"Yes. I haven't moved anything."

"With your permission, we'd like to take a look around her room."

"Of course," said Delfina. "It's down the hall, second door to the left. I'll take you there."

When Lieutenant Rosa and Detective Jamison entered Ramona Cuera's bedroom, it felt as if someone had just left the room moments before.

Rosa, not a particularly devout life-long Catholic, nevertheless crossed himself and whispered a brief prayer for the deceased.

The scent of burnt sage, sweetgrass, and copal imparted a sacred aura to Ramona's room. It was immaculate. Every object appeared to have been placed intentionally, as if in a museum of Native American art.

Ramona's bed was made with blankets woven in Native patterns. A framed photograph of Ramona and Delfina under an oak tree by a creek stood on the bedside table next to Ramona's cell phone. Handwoven baskets and red clay pottery were displayed on a bookshelf, along with books on Kumeyaay art, history, ethnobotany, and culture. Several large, colorful, framed paintings hung on the walls.

"Nice paintings," said Detective Jamison. "Who's the artist?"

"Thanks. My cousin Hawk painted those."

"Does Hawk have a last name?" asked Lieutenant Rosa.

"His family name is the same as mine: Cuera. But as an artist, he just goes by Hawk. I'll leave you two to look around. Let me know if you need anything."

When Delfina left the room, Rosa and Jamison stood still and observed for a minute.

A freshly wrapped bundle of sage sat in an abalone shell on top of the dresser. A filing cabinet stood next to the desk; the laptop on the desk was closed.

Lieutenant Rosa opened the filing cabinet drawer and thumbed through file folders: financial files, files pertaining to the house, work, health and other personal matters.

"Jamison, I think I've found something. Look at this."

Rosa moved the laptop aside and set a file folder down on Ramona's desk.

Jamison read the label. "Missing and Murdered. This could be important, sir."

Rosa opened the folder. On the first page was a printout of an article from the National Indigenous Women's Resource Center. The article described the work of a Canadian woman scholar who was researching and collecting data on missing and murdered Indigenous women in the US and Canada for her PhD thesis.

At the time the article had been written, a year earlier, the researcher's database contained over two thousand cases, including details such as the victim's age and tribal affiliation, whether or not they had been in foster care, were a victim of sex trafficking, had experienced domestic violence and/or sexual assault, police brutality or death in jail custody, and the race and conviction status of the offender, if known. Many of the victims in the database were unidentified Natives listed as Jane Does. A third of the missing or murdered were girls, eighteen years old or younger. Three fourths of the victims were known to have been murdered. The article estimated that at least twenty thousand unsolved cases from the last hundred years were not yet logged in to the database. It stated that one in three Native women would be sexually assaulted in her lifetime, three in five would be physically assaulted. Native women are more than twice as likely to be stalked than other women, and Native women are being murdered at a rate ten times the national average. The majority of the missing and murdered cases of Native women go unresolved and uninvestigated.

Rosa turned to the next page in Ramona's file folder: a list of fifty names of Kumeyaay missing and murdered women and girls. After most of the names, the word *missing* had been crossed out and changed to *murdered*. Rosa flipped to the next page. A photograph of a teenage Kumeyaay girl stared at him. She looked a little like Delfina. On the back of the photo someone had written: Stella Osuna, age: 15, date and location last seen: Cherry Coke Dance Club, San Diego, August 20, 2017, and the word, *missing*. The following pages in the folder were notes documenting Ramona's research, interviews, and contacts with law enforcement while attempting to locate Stella.

Delfina stood watching in the doorway of her mother's room. Hawk, much taller, appeared behind her.

"Ms. Cuera, we'd like to take a few of your mother's belongings into evidence."

Delfina nodded.

"One drawer of this cabinet is locked. Do you have the key?"

"Sorry. I'm not sure where that is. I'll have to look around for it."

Rosa wrote a reminder in his pocket notebook to follow up on Ramona's locked file drawer.

Rosa and Jamison packed up Ramona's cell phone, laptop, and several file folders, including the one labeled Missing and Murdered.

Once they had finished packing the evidence, Rosa turned to Delfina.

"Ms. Cuera, once again, I want to say I am sincerely sorry for your loss. We will do everything in our power to find out what happened to your mother and to bring the person who killed her to justice. You have my direct number. If you feel threatened at any time, day or night, do not hesitate to call me. And if you think of anything —"

Delfina seemed to stand taller than her five feet one. With a stiff back and her arms crossed in front of her chest, her posture made it clear that the grieving young woman was unhappy about watching strangers rummage around in her deceased mother's personal space. She was struggling to control her emotions.

"Thank you, Officers."

Delfina saw Rosa and Jamison to the door.

★   ★   ★

Driving back to the sheriff's headquarters on Highway 1, Jamison tapped the steering wheel to the tune of a song inside his head.

"Something on your mind, Detective?"

"Yes, sir. I'm thinking about what Miss Cuera said about the border police harassing her mother."

"Me too. Did anyone ever get a look at that red-bearded border patrol agent's badge or check his credentials?"

"Kozel? I don't think so, sir. Not yet."

"Make that a top priority. We need to take a closer look at him. And that mountain biker, Mikos Vadim, too. Might as well do a deep dive into U.S. Marshal Stone as well. I'll ask Agent Chen to have the FBI run background on all of them. I also want more information on that missing teen, Stella Osuna, who Ramona was trying to locate."

Rosa wrote in his pocket notebook, then drummed his pen on the notebook.

"Jamison?"

"Yes, sir?"

"Did you notice Miss Cuera flinch when I suggested a hunting accident?"

"No, sir, I did not notice that."

"Maybe it was just my imagination."

"Maybe." Jamison turned off the highway at the Soquel Avenue exit and drove east on the frontage road toward Headquarters.

21

"SIR, WE'VE INITIATED CONTACT with the San Diego Sheriff's Department to inquire about Stella Osuna, the missing girl Ramona was looking for," said Detective Jamison. "They said they'll get back to us next week."

Lieutenant Rosa turned to the FBI Agent. "What about you, Chen? Anything?"

"We don't have the requested profiles back yet on the ICE Agent or the US Marshal, but here's what the Agency managed to dig up on Mikos Vadim." Agent Chen handed Rosa a file folder and a flash drive.

Carlos Rosa inserted the data stick into his laptop.

Mikos Vadim's photo and the text of the FBI file appeared on the interactive smart board that covered most of the wall facing Rosa's desk.

Agent Chen wielded a laser pointer as he spoke. "Mikos Vadim. Born in New York City to a Serbian mother and a Russian father, Mikhail Prokhorov. Vadim is the mother's surname. Prokhorov, Mikos's father, is a multinational real estate broker, an oligarch. Just prior to the Russian invasion of Ukraine, before he and other Russian oligarchs were sanctioned and their assets seized, Mikos's father transferred a number of his high value properties to Mikos."

"Mikos isn't lying about being a software engineer," said Rosa. "Look at this. After graduating from Yale with a BS in computer science and economics, he worked for a semiconductor company in China a few years, then came back to the US and got an MS at Stanford in computer science, specializing in software theory. Currently, he's working as a semiconductor expert at the Silicon Valley headquarters of one of the largest wind turbine manufacturers in the world."

"Why does the FBI have so much information on Vadim?"

"As the son of a sanctioned Russian oligarch, Mikos came under scrutiny after Putin's invasion of Ukraine. Homeland Security only recently connected the father—sanctioned oligarch Mikhail Prokhorov—to Mikos Vadim and his real estate holdings. Take a look this Facebook page, Carlos."

Agent Chen opened the link. At the top of the page were photos of a younger-looking Mikos with a gray-haired man, presumably Mikos's father, in Africa, posing over a dead white rhino. Mikos held a crossbow. "Mikos deleted this Facebook profile several years ago, but the Agency's cyber team had no trouble restoring it."

"We need to pay Mikos a visit, George."

"I already have a search warrant. He's staying at his Santa Lucia mountain home this weekend. Here's the address." Agent Chen pulled up a Google map.

"I'll alert Detective Jamison to follow us with a team of deputies. Looks like this house is out in the boonies. How long is the drive?" Lieutenant Rosa glanced at his watch: eleven o'clock.

"It's only about thirty miles from here, but those winding mountain roads make for almost an hour's travel time."

"We should go tomorrow morning. I hope we don't run into any delays. I have to get back in time for my youngest daughter's quinceañera rehearsal at three."

"We should be okay," said Chen. "I'll drive."

★   ★   ★

The next morning, passing through the roll call room on the way out of the building, Rosa and Chen encountered ICE Agent Kozel. His flat-tire belly bulged out from under his flak jacket. He stood like a pile of rocks, scratching his mangy red beard and blocking Rosa's egress.

"May I have a word, Lieutenant?"

"Sorry. Not now, Kozel."

Rosa side-stepped around the ICE agent and spoke briefly with Detective Jamison. Then he and Agent Chen left headquarters and hit the road in Chen's bureau car.

★　　★　　★

Dense redwood forest lined both sides of the highway that twisted up into the Santa Lucia coastal mountains. Charred silhouettes of giant *Sequoia sempervirens*—trees that had burned two years ago in the 2020 lightning fire—stood in formation along distant ridgetops like an army of the dead, the blackened bones of their limbs raised in a doomsday warning.

Agent Chen expertly maneuvered around treacherous curves above steep drop-offs.

"This is more traffic than we had during the pandemic," said Rosa, "but not as much as before the Covid lock-down. I guess a lot of Silicon Valley tech people who used to commute over the hill to the Valley are now still working from home in Santa Lucia."

At the top of the mountain, views back down to the sparkling Monterey Bay were spectacular.

As they cruised down the other side of the mountain toward Silicon Valley, the navigation app announced a turnoff coming up.

Rosa squinted at the screen on the dashboard. "When we get to the bottom of the mountain and pass Lexington Reservoir, start keeping an eye out for the Highway 9 exit. It'll be off to the right, a cloverleaf that takes us north through the villages of Los Gatos and Saratoga, then up into the mountains again."

"All the way up the mountain, then down, and then back up the other side? That's a very circuitous route," said Chen.

"Wildcat Ridge is so far into the mountains, and so isolated, there just isn't a more direct road."

"Apparently Mikos Vadim doesn't want a lot of company."

"Are you sure you have enough gas to get us all the way up to Wildcat Ridge and back?" The lieutenant loosened his tie and ran a finger around the inside of his white shirt collar.

Agent Chen nodded. "More than enough."

Rosa rolled down his window and breathed in the fresh spring mountain air. "I haven't been over the hill and down this side of the mountain since before the big storms. Everything's so green."

Chen sneezed. "I hate these beautiful spring days. All this pollen triggers my allergies something fierce."

"Look at the reservoir! There's water above the high-water mark. I've never seen it this full."

"Those extreme storms this winter have ended the drought, for now," said Chen. "But the way climate chaos is accelerating, who knows what next winter will bring? More drought? Sea level rise? Floods? Fire?"

"I wonder what shape the roads are in up on Wildcat Ridge. Cal Trans did a good job of clearing all the downed redwoods from the highway last winter, but a lot of the smaller roads that washed out from the floods still aren't repaired. Did you check with the Highway Patrol, or Waze?"

"No." Agent Chen adjusted his sunglasses. "But I didn't see any alerts on Google map."

The navigation system announced their exit ahead.

Agent Chen rounded the cloverleaf and motored through the village of Saratoga along the wide treelined Saratoga-Los Gatos Road. They passed wineries, banks, trendy breweries, fancy restaurants, yoga-Pilates studios, and boutique clothing stores. At the edge of the village, the density of trees increased. Redwood, oak, buckeye, Western redbud, and California maple interspersed with old, nonnative ornamentals allowed only brief glimpses of grand mansions, each sitting on at least an acre of land, all with multimillion dollar price tags.

Four miles up the road, Agent Chen turned right and headed uphill, passing an eighteen-acre Japanese garden and teahouse, the historic Villa Montalvo estates with their world-famous gardens and a performing arts center, a Buddhist monastery, another winery, and a crystal healing meditation center. Winding farther uphill, they drove through three miles of unpopulated forested mountains.

Chen rounded a hairpin bend and stopped the car abruptly in front of a highway patrol barricade. A few yards beyond the barrier, the road had collapsed down the mountain.

"Good thing this vehicle has a tight turning ratio," said Chen. He executed a two-point turnabout, facing the car back down hill, and shifted to park. "What now?"

Rosa squinted at the nav screen. "No reception up here. Have you got an actual map?"

"In the glove box."

Rosa unfolded and studied the paper map.

"It looks like there's a narrow, unmaintained back road that connects to Wildcat Ridge. Should we give it a try?"

"Might as well." Agent Chen slowly headed back down the road.

"Detective Jamison and his team are probably about twelve minutes behind us," said Rosa. "I'll radio him via the CalNet repeater and let him know about our alternate route."

A mile downhill, Chen turned onto a steep one-lane byway that twisted back up the mountain.

The old asphalt road was cracked and full of potholes. Rosa clutched his seatbelt and peered out the window over the edge of the steep precipice.

This road could collapse any minute in an avalanche of mud and rock, taking us down the mountain with it.

Rosa wiped beads of sweat off his forehead.

At the top of the road, they connected with Wildcat Ridge.

The smooth, well-maintained ridge road skirted along the boundary of miles of roadless, forested, wilderness preserve. Undeveloped land blanketed the mountain with green all the way back down to the blue ocean sparkling far below.

Rosa let out his breath, released his white-knuckled grip on the seatbelt, and leaned back to enjoy the view.

22

WILDCAT RIDGE ROAD DEAD-ENDED at Mikos Vadim's gated driveway. There were no other structures around for miles.

Agent Chen reached through his car window and pushed the call button.

A male with a heavy Chinese accent responded. "Hello. How may I help you?"

"This is FBI Agent Chen and Sheriff's Homicide Division Lieutenant Rosa. We're here to speak with Mr. Vadim."

"Just a moment please."

The gate opened.

Agent Chen raised an eyebrow. "Did that seem too easy?"

"Yes." Rosa tapped a pack of gum thoughtfully, as if it were a pack of cigarettes.

They drove through the ornate metal gate and up a road that curved past horse pasture, vineyard, and an orchard in spring bloom. Rounding a blind curve beyond the orchard, they came to a driveway inlaid with decorative brick, and lined with crepe myrtle trees ablaze with pink blossoms.

Steering with one hand, Chen held his handkerchief over his nose until his sneezing fit stopped. The driveway ended in a circular parking area on a plateau at the top of the mountain.

Chen pulled his vehicle up beside a red Tesla Roadster and a gold Lamborghini Huracán Spyder.

To the side of the house was a helicopter parked on a helipad.

Rosa raised his eyebrows and Chen nodded. A grand staircase fanned up to the front door of a sprawling four-story Mediterranean Revival mansion.

Chen rang the front doorbell and a woman in her late twenties answered.

Her makeup, bleached hair, and short skirt gave her the appearance of a hooker dressed in a maid's uniform.

"Mr. Vadim is out by the pool." *Strong Middle Eastern accent.* "Please let me show you the way."

The maid led them down a tiled hallway and through a gallery hung with big game trophies and antique weapons. A wall-to-ceiling case held a collection of guns. Several crossbows hung on the wall. Rosa cleared his throat. Chen nodded.

Mikos Vadim stood with his feet in the water at the edge of an infinity pool, wearing gray, blue, and orange striped O'Neil board shorts and an unbuttoned white linen shirt with rolled up sleeves. The view behind him extended down the pristine forested mountain all the way to the sparkling sapphire-blue Monterey Bay.

"Agent Chen, Sheriff Rosa. What can I do for you today?" Mikos buttoned the middle button of his shirt as if it were a suit coat. He stepped out of the pool and gestured toward a glass-topped table and chairs under an umbrella. "Please, won't you sit? May I get you anything? A glass of water, a soda? Maybe a margarita, a mojito? Ah, my bartender makes a delicious pisco sour. Or perhaps a gin and tonic?"

"Thank you, Mr. Vadim," said Rosa. "We appreciate the offer, but we're fine. We'd just like to ask you a few questions."

"I'm all yours."

Agent Chen raised an eyebrow and glanced at Rosa. Rosa nodded back almost imperceptibly and cleared his throat.

"Thank you, Mr. Vadim," said Agent Chen. "I must say, I'm somewhat surprised at your gracious welcome, given the nature of our interactions the previous times we've met."

Vadim chuckled. "My attorney phoned and told me to expect you. He advised that I cooperate fully."

"Interesting. Well, then. Hmm." Rosa deferred to Chen with a nod.

"First of all," said Agent Chen, "there's the matter of your name. You go by Mikos Vadim, but the Agency has informed us that your father's surname is Prokhorov. Why not use his name?"

Mikos covered his forehead with his hand, shaking his head in faux chagrin. "You got me, Agent Chen." He raised his head and looked earnestly at the officers. "The thing is, I don't get along with my father. My mother's family is Serbian, and my father is very involved in Serbian politics. He desperately wants Serbia to take over Kosovo, which, as you probably know, is currently occupied by the Albanian Muslims. My father is extremely anti-Muslim. Because of his work to free Kosovo, he's formed close ties with Putin."

Vadim raised his hands and shook his head. "I'm not a fan of Putin. That's just not me. I'm proud to be American. Red-blooded, born and raised. I don't want anything to do with my father's politics. I do not want to be like my father. When I moved from New York to California, I changed. I realized I didn't want his name or anything to do with him anymore. I just wanted to start fresh, so I dropped his last name."

"But you live in your father's house."

"Ah, you figured that out. Yes. I suppose you already know that he's an international real estate developer. Because of his ties to Putin, he was sanctioned when Russia invaded Ukraine. He had to transfer all his US properties to me, including this estate and the controlling share of a cannabis company, or he would have lost everything. I had no say over any of his business transactions. He hid ownership of his holdings under multiple shell companies, hoping his connection to me wouldn't come to light, but I see that you have ways of finding out these things."

"So your name change has to do with hiding the transfer of sanctioned property from your father?"

"You got me again, Officers."

"Why are you living in your father's house, if you don't get along with him?" asked Rosa.

"Well, as you can see, it's a magnificent property. Given the opportunity, it would be ridiculous not to live here and enjoy it, don't you think?"

"That's understandable, Mikos," said Lieutenant Rosa. "But there's something else we're wondering. You told us that you aren't a hunter. That in fact you don't even eat meat—you're vegan. But on your deleted Facebook page, there are photos of you and your father in Africa with trophy kills of big game: rhinos, elephants, lions. Can you explain that?"

Mikos looked surprised. "I took down that page years ago. How–?

"Nothing online ever completely disappears, Mike," said Agent Chen. "The FBI has a preeminent cyber forensics team."

"Of course. The truth is, I did hunt with my father when I was young. But I'm ashamed of that now. As I said, I've changed. I really am vegan now. I don't kill things, for sport or for food."

The maid appeared. "Excuse me, Lieutenant Rosa. The police dispatcher just called with a message for you. Deputy Jamison wasn't able to make it up the road. His vehicles were too wide and heavy. He won't be coming."

Mikos Vadim turned to Lieutenant Rosa with a puzzled expression.

Rosa stood and smiled at the maid. "Thank you."

Agent Chen stood as well. "Well, that's all for now, Mr. Vadim. Thank you for your cooperation. We'll be in touch."

★   ★   ★

Two hours after the sheriff and the FBI agent left, Mikos Vadim put his feet up on his glass and chrome desk. In front of him, a bank of computer monitors blinked and churned out data. Glass walls on three sides of his home office afforded a view of forested mountains sweeping down to the bay.

Mikos spoke in fluent Chinese over the desk speaker phone. "I've got source codes, software development kits, chip designs, everything that you need from our top Silicon Valley semiconductor manufacturers to cement your lead in global wind turbine production. You will no longer have to buy semiconductors for your turbines from the US. With what I'm offering, you can launch a strategic economic attack on the entire world's wind industry. No. My employer will never know I sold you this information. No, they won't be able to trace it back to you. My hackers are better than the Winnti. Trust me. It's worth the price. And with your government backing, you can afford it. Yes, pay me in Crypto."

Mikos gave instructions for payment, then ended the call.

He rang for the maid.

Electricity buzzed through every cell of his body. This was the biggest deal he'd ever pulled off. Even bigger than his father's. Better than a big game kill. Fuck, he was turned on.

When the maid entered his office, she knew with one look what he wanted. He'd been grooming her since he'd brought her over to the States at age fifteen.

She bent over a side table, and he lifted her skirts. She wore no panties.

★   ★   ★

When he'd finished and was alone again, he phoned his attorney. "We're all set. You good? Oh, by the way, thank you for tipping me off that those cops were about to pay me a visit. How'd you know? Oh, so you're Kozel's attorney too? Tell him I appreciate it."

Next, he phoned his Yale college chum, Bob Budalo.

"Everything's in place, Bob. Soon, the Chinese will be in a position to sell wind turbines to the US for a fraction of the price anyone else is offering. If you can pull off that wind project contract on the new national monument land at Cougar Creek Coast Ranch, we'll get a very nice cut of the Chinese deal, plus a sweet bite out of the feds' big sustainable energy money trough."

"Don't worry," said the BLM field manager. "It's in the bag. Oh, hey. Speaking of in the bag, my boys bagged four wolves in Yellowstone. Cha Ching. Sold to China. I'm going to need to clean that money through your Mountain Bike Trail Stewards Go-Fund-Me deal."

"Yeah. No, wait. My accountant tells me that for now I can't run any more money through Bike Trail Stewards. It's got to go through my Orphans Fund charity."

★   ★   ★

Mikos wrapped up his morning business and left his office through sliding glass doors, returning to the pool patio. The afternoon sky was crystal blue, and the temperature an unseasonable eighty degrees.

A younger, shorter, skinnier, paler, skankier version of himself lounged in Mikos's favorite chair.

"Hey, Blatnoy, what's crackin'?" said Mikos's brother, baiting him as usual.

"Don't call me that, Kiki. It's Mikos, got it? Don't forget."

"Okay, okay." Kiki tugged on his nearly nonexistent goatee.

"Shit, brother. You look like a worm that's been living on amphetamines under a rock for a year. Put on sunscreen or you'll get burned."

143

Kristijan a.k.a. "Kiki" climbed out of Mikos's lounger and slunk over to a chair under an umbrella.

"Sunscreen? Nah, that's for pussies. I like to live dangerously. Speaking of which, I'm going to be gone for a while."

"Where to?"

"You don't want to know."

Vadim's bartender brought him a pisco sour and a plate of caviar, crème fraîche, capers, finely diced chives, and yeasted blini.

Kiki lifted his vodka and pomegranate on rocks for a toast. "Na Zdorovie."

"Cheers, little brother."

"Pardon, sir." Vadim's personal assistant stood by the pool in his formal suit, waiting to be acknowledged.

"Yes, Qiao Sung?"

"The funds for your software sale have been received. They are in your Crypto vault."

"Thank you. Anything else?"

"The Go-Fund-Me for your mountain bike trail building project has reached your one-million-dollar goal."

"Excellent, and?"

"Mr. Xiong, CEO of Shanxi Naipu Pharmaceutical Exports, would like to speak with you. They say it's urgent."

Mikos glanced at his watch. "Shanxi, China is fifteen hours ahead of us. That would be six in the morning for them. Put the call through. I'll take it in my office."

23

COLIN GLANCED AT HIS CELL PHONE in its holder on the dash. Ten a.m., April 25. It was a beautiful morning for a drive out to the Central Valley, and late enough that the Monday morning work commute had cleared. Virtually no one was on the roads.

He should be able to make it down to Fresno and back in plenty of time to shower, shave, and put on his new jeans and best shirt. Hopefully, he'd even have time to stop and buy Delfina flowers. This was the first time he'd been invited to her house, so he wanted to make a good impression. He could hardly believe she'd phoned and offered to make dinner for him. He should take a bottle of wine, too.

Lieutenant Rosa had asked Colin to personally meet today with Central Coast Field Manager Bob Budalo at the BLM regional headquarters in Fresno. Rosa explained that, as a Fish and Wildlife Warden, Colin might best be able to relate to the BLM guy. Rosa also mentioned that he thought something about Budalo seemed "off." Colin agreed. Something was way off about that guy.

Colin didn't know what Rosa was fishing for, but as far as he was concerned, Budalo was an idiot. The guy had no idea how to manage a natural environment held in public trust that was as sensitive and priceless as the Cougar Creek Coast Ranch National Monument. Budalo's management plan was all about throwing the land wide open to recreational activities destructive of the land and disruptive to the wildlife, while disregarding conservation—the actual mission put forth in President Obama's decree establishing the monument .

Snapping out of his reverie, Colin brought his attention back to his driving. In this car, it was too easy to let the speedometer climb over the legal limit.

He'd decided to get out of his department truck for a change and take his Mustang for a spin. This car was such a joy to drive. He'd found it for sale at next to nothing on a car wreck salvage website. It had taken him five years to restore it little by little, piece by piece, to near mint condition. He'd recently finished the project, hiring a friend who was an autobody pro to repaint it in the original lightning blue with red trim. When he cranked up the Voodoo V8, it sounded like a Ferrari.

Damn. The healing cougar bite on his wrist was itching and throbbing like crazy. Steering one-handed, Colin tore the bandage off his wound with his teeth, then raised his wrist up to his eyes. The itching, throbbing dark purple wound had spread and changed shape. It resembled a silhouette of a leaping puma, similar to the commercial athletic clothing logo.

No way am I'm gonna let this interfere with my enjoyment of this drive. Ignoring the discomfort, he tuned the radio to a California Country station and turned it up until he almost forgot about the puma on his wrist.

Enjoying the freedom of driving the open highway in a top-down convertible, wind blowing through his hair, he could feel Delfina's presence. He let the music carry him away with fantasies of how he would manage their first kiss. He knew it was too soon after her mother's death to come on to her like that, but hey—a guy could dream.

When the siren blared, Colin flinched. One pulse. A spinning red Highway Patrol light flashed in his review mirror.

The sign said speed limit was seventy miles per hour. He glanced at his speedometer. He had been keeping it well under that.

He needed to get his rising anxiety under control before it triggered an episode.

Initiate breathing protocol. Deep in through nose, exhale slowly out through pursed lips. Initiate rapid self-check.

Driver's license, registration, and insurance in my wallet. Check. Glock 22 at my side. My other service weapons locked in the safe in my trunk. Check.

Why are they stopping me? What did I do?

Warm spring morning in the Central Valley. I was sweating. Took my uniform shirt off and tossed it over there on the seat. Fuck. My badge is clipped on my shirt. Driving in just an undershirt.

Car's muddy. Should have washed it after the big storm. My CDFW ID decal is probably covered by mud.

Should have driven the Department truck instead of my personal vehicle. A classic, cherried-out 'Stang like this is bound to attract attention.

Jesus. I still have that sticker on my bumper from that failed Republican gubernatorial recall: No Newsom Recall. Keep California Blue. *Crap. I'm driving through California's deepest red zone. It's like I'm waving a red flag at a bull.*

He caught a glimpse of himself in his rearview mirror.

Oh, shit. I've been out in the sun a lot lately. My skin's as dark as it gets. I might look nonwhite to a racist.

The siren pulsed again. "Proceed immediately to the nearest exit and pull over." The amplified Orwellian voice chilled Colin to the bone.

A television news headline rolled in his mind. *Another lynching. Decorated war hero pulled over for traffic stop … beaten to death. Thoughts and prayers …*

Colin imagined his bloody, disfigured body rotting in an agricultural drainage ditch.

"Mother, help me." He felt his mother's presence. He thought of Delfina. A vision of her face hovered before him. His chest ached.

He clicked on his turn signal. Slowed down.

He stealthily slid his phone off its dashboard holder onto the seat next to him, then pushed Lieutenant Rosa's speed dial number.

Rosa answered on the first ring.

"Sir, I may have a problem. I'm on my way over to the Fresno BLM Field Headquarters, as per your request, to check out Field Manager Bob Budalo. I'm near Bakersfield, six miles south of Highway 152 on CA 99, about forty-five minutes outside of Fresno."

"What's the deal?"

"I'm being pulled over by Highway Patrol. I don't know what for. Sir, I've got a bad feeling. Gotta admit I'm afraid. This is an isolated area. Honestly, I think I've been profiled."

"Profiled?"

"I don't know, sir. I'm in my 'Stang, not my department vehicle.

Maybe it's the *Keep California Blue* bumper sticker on my car?"

"B-blue …? Oh. Jesus. Calm down, son. Keep your phone on and out of sight. Keep your hands on the wheel unless told to do otherwise. Stay polite and compliant. Do not resist. Try to keep your phone connected. Do not hang up. I've got your location. I'll be monitoring the situation."

Colin pulled off Highway 99 at Pistachio Avenue, turned onto a dirt road, pulled over, and stopped.

He threw his shirt over his phone, still connected to Lieutenant Rosa. His heart thundered.

Outside the Bagram Airfield, eleven klicks southeast of Charikar in the Parwan Province, Afghanistan. I aim my M16 at a car full of potential insurgents. Index finger over the trigger well—never inside it—thumb on the selector lever, ready to switch and fire. Dusty car window rolls down. Old man, woman holding a baby, a child staring, eyes huge with terror. My throat is raw from shouting. Get out of the car!

"Get out of the car!"

Colin gaped at the black hole of the gun barrel pointing at his face. He froze.

Click. Click.

"Out now!"

A second officer leans over the passenger door. Pistol cocked. "Move!"

Flash forward—a hundred percent into the present moment.

Colin blinks at his reflection in the cop's black sunglasses.

How did this escalate so fast?

The cop throws open the car door.

"Yes, sir." Colin raises his open hands above his head. "Yes, sir. I'm getting out, sir."

Colin slowly shifts his weight to his left hip, hands still raised, twists to inch his left leg out of the car, left foot searching for the ground, right knee starting to follow the left.

"Gun! Gun! He's armed!"

A cop grabs Colin's shoulder and neck.

"My eyes!"

It's Pepper spray! "I can't breathe!"

They yank him out of the car, officers yelling, "Out now!"

Grandfather! Colin's spirit reaches for the helicopter pilot who'd died in Vietnam—the grandfather he'd never met. Grandfather's face hovers above him.

The cops drag him by his feet, his head banging over dirt, gravel, sharp sticks. Colin gags, chokes, gasps, drools. *Don't resist.* He forces himself to go limp.

"On your stomach! Hands behind your back!"

The cops bend Colin's arms and shoulders at impossible angles. *Fiery pain of hell.* Colin flinches involuntarily.

Can't breathe.

"Stop resisting! This is your last warning. Stop resisting or we're going to tase you."

Colin did not resist.

The next moment, excruciating shooting pain zaps through his whole body. Angry killer bees crawling under his skin, flying around inside his head, stinging his flesh and brain.

"Taser deployed!"

Colin's body twitches, then goes still. He is utterly helpless, unable to move any part of himself. The cops, grunting and wheezing, roll him over as they cuff him.

If they tase me again, I'll probably have a heart attack.

Fierce pain. Eyes burning so bad. Yellow jackets stinging under my skin, in my flesh, buzzing my brain. Swallow the pain. Stay alive.

"We're gonna teach you a lesson, boy. We don't like you woke pretty boys with your fancy cars and your stinkin' Demo-*rat* bumper stickers drivin' 'round our county. We're gonna give you somethin' that'll make you think twice 'fore ever comin' through here again."

They beat him with fists and clubs.

Immobilized, hands bound, Colin cannot cover his head, his face.

They land blow after blow, kicking him in the ribs, the gut, kidneys.

He watches from above, out of his body.

They drag him to his car, prop him up against it in a sitting position. Colin sways. *Stay upright. Stay awake.*

Colin's world goes black.

Garlic. Its powerful, pungent odor saturates the air. No longer morning.

Water babbled over rocks in a small drainage ditch beside the road. The sun was high over the garlic fields. Buzzing bees pollinated almond flowers in the orchard nearby. A crop duster spraying a vineyard hummed overhead.

Colin wheezed and coughed. Blood oozed from his nose, his ear, from the corner of his mouth, tickled down his chin.

He was sitting on the dirt road, his back propped against his car, hot in the sun.

"What're you doin' here, boy?"

The officer with his face close to Colin's reeked of whiskey, cigarettes, and KFC. Greasy, fat lips. Grease-stained shirt covered a belly bulging out from under his flak jacket.

Waves of nausea.

Colin puked down the front of his bloody undershirt.

"Oh, shit. You stink, boy. The way you was twitchin' there looked like you was havin' a seizure. Don't you go gettin' a heart attack and die on us, now."

How many cops are there? Colin was pretty sure there were only two, but his eyes crossed, and he saw dozens of cops spinning around, as if through a kaleidoscope.

Did they find my phone? Is it still connected?

Are they wearing bodycams?

Colin squinted at the nearest cop's chest. There was a bodycam mounted on his flak jacket. *Is it on?*

Pinned above the cam, next to the Highway Patrol badge, was a patch embroidered with the words *Honor Your Oath. Defend.*

Oh, God. They're Oath Keepers.

"Where you think you're goin' to, boy?"

Colin struggled to speak. "BLM, sir. Fresno."

"BLM! So y'all plannin' to take part in that Black Lives Matter rally at City Hall?" Both officers laughed.

"Think again, boy. We have a well-trained militia at that rally, prepared to fight government tyranny and pick us off some of your kind. So y'all better just turn around and get your ass back to wherever you come from, right now, if you know what's good for you. Don't you come back, you hear? You ain't welcome 'round here, boy."

"Yes, sir. I'll leave now. Please …"

"Yo', Tad. Lookit here." A cop waved Colin's rifle in his face. "Found this in a safe in his trunk, plus another Glock and a shotgun."

"Whoa, now." The officer named Tad straddled Colin and bent down close to his face. "Why you got all them firearms for, huh?"

Tad shoved Colin onto his back, lifted his leg as if he were dismounting a horse, and pissed on him. Then he swung his steel-toed boot back, and sledgehammered a kick into Colin's ribs.

"You're in big trouble now, boy."

The other cop smashed Colin's face with the butt of his rifle, laughed, then stomped a heel into Colin's chest.

"Oh, oh. Think I heard ribs crack that time."

"Hope we didn't puncture a lung."

Both cops laughed like kids at a clown show.

Then they got to work on the beatdown in earnest.

The faint wail of sirens threaded through Colin's consciousness.

A siren yelped close by. An amplified voice reverberated through the vineyards and orchards and along the babbling drainage ditch that had once been a creek.

"Highway Patrol Officers Tad Bhin and Demitri Haley, cease and desist. This is the FBI You are ordered to release your prisoner and surrender to my agents."

Blood on their hands, uniforms, and faces, Officers Tad and Demitri hunched like bad dogs over Colin's limp body. As an FBI SWAT team swarmed them, the two men stood, hands raised. After being relieved of their weapons and cuffed, they were read their rights and led away to a secure vehicle.

"You will be escorted to the Fresno CHP Office," said Agent Chen, "where you will officially surrender your guns and badges and be relieved of duty. You will be held pending charges of professional misconduct, improper use of force, aggravated assault, and assaulting an officer of the law."

EMTs maneuvered Colin onto a stretcher. They slid the stretcher into an ambulance, and the ambulance raced away, siren wailing.

Colin blacked out.

24

ON TUESDAY AFTERNOON, April 26, a mountain lion perched on a sturdy limb, high in a hundred-year-old oak at the edge of the coastal mountain conifer forest. For his nap, the elusive, secretive puma had selected an ancient tree, survivor of both the forest fire two years ago and the tree-felling storms of last winter. This tree's limbs were sufficiently strong to hold the two-hundred pound, eight-foot-long puma.

Comfortably shaded from the unusually warm spring afternoon, M36—a four-year-old adult male—dozed secure in the knowledge that he was near the top of the food chain, an apex predator, and his tawny camouflage coat made him almost invisible in the thick forest canopy cover.

Yesterday at twilight, he'd taken down a large, healthy black-tailed deer. From the meadow where the deer had been grazing, the puma had dragged his kill here, under the trees at the forest's edge. Ripping and gnawing his way through fur, tough skin, and bones, he'd feasted on the deer's rich inner organs—heart, liver, lungs, kidneys. Now, the remains were hidden under leaf litter in a cache below his tree limb perch.

From on high, the cougar watched a gray fox discover his cache. The fox enthusiastically crunched some of the smallest of the deer bones. The little thief would probably find the messy digestive tract M36 had buried separately, and would steal that too. Welcome to it. As long as fox left alone the choicest pieces of the kill. M36 purred as he imagined enjoying his next meal—backstrap, tenderloin, and spinal column.

If he heard a mating cry calling him to one of the two females in his territory, or heard the challenging scream of a male intruder, he'd leave to take care of business, abandoning the remains in his cache to the foxes and any other little kleptoparasites, like bobcat, racoon, or skunk, who might come along. But if nothing disturbed him, he'd stay near his kill until he'd taken his time consuming all the valuable parts, nothing remaining but pieces of the pelvis bone, ends of the leg bones, and part of the skull.

Then he'd hunt again. Fortunately, deer were plentiful in his home range; he needn't encroach on another puma's territory beyond the two hundred fifty square miles he defended.

A fly buzzed his ear. He shook his head, jostling the bulky tracking collar he'd worn around his neck for nearly two years. Minor annoyances. He extended his long, curved, stiletto claws, and scratched them into the gnarly oak limb to sharpen them. Chunks of oak bark and lacy clumps of lichen fell to the forest floor. M36 languidly licked one paw clean, then the other, and settled into his nap with a full belly.

★   ★   ★

Cow Boss Rafe Silva rode under the cougar's tree, unaware of the sleeping catamount.

Big green eyes opened.

Amigo whinnied, tossing his head and pulling at his reins.

"Whoa. What's the matter, Amigo? Am I feeding you too much grain? Got a toothache?"

M36 recognized the horse—much bigger than any deer he'd ever taken down—and the human atop the horse, eagle feathers poking out of his hat. The dog would be easy, but hardly enough meat to be worth the trouble.

Amigo balked, rolled his eyes, and stomped. The brown dog pinned back his ears.

"Something's got you spooked."

Rafe looked up.

Overhead, through gaps between the oak leaves, green eyes met Rafe's baby blues.

★   ★   ★

"Colin?" An angel's face smiled down at him.

Delfina set down the cup full of shaved ice she'd been using to wet his lips.

"Where am I?" Colin asked.

"You're safe now," said Delfina. Her hand felt like a butterfly on his arm. "You're back in Santa Lucia, at Saint Francis Hospital."

Colin tried to turn his head to see his surroundings, but that proved impossible. He was in traction.

"What day is this? What time is it?"

"It's five o'clock Tuesday evening, April 26, Colin," said Delfina. "You've been unconscious since last night, when you were beaten up on your way to Fresno."

"Colin." Lieutenant Rosa stepped into Colin's field of view. "What do you remember, son?"

Flashes of light and dark. Pure pain. "Nah-n …"

"You were stopped by the highway patrol on your way to the Bureau of Land Management Headquarters in Fresno, remember? They beat you, son."

"Ug a humn." Colin closed his eyes.

"The officers who assaulted you have been fired," said Rosa. "They're being held without bail. They've been indicted on charges of official misconduct, improper use of force, aggravated assault, acting in concert, aggravated kidnapping and assaulting an officer of the law. Their case will be tried as a hate crime."

Colin tried to sit up. Delfina raised the bed to a sitting position. She and Lieutenant Rosa stood where Colin could see both of them. They both looked worried, angry.

Colin mumbled through cut and swollen lips. "How did you get to me so fast?"

"Agent Chen happened to be in the Central Valley close by, following a lead on the fentanyl investigation. Agent Chen, Deputy Jamison, Marshal Stone, and I have been sharing our location trackers with each other, so I was able to connect with Chen and alert him to your situation as soon as you called. The FBI maintains a SWAT Team at a field office near Fresno. Drawing on the resources of his agency, Chen was able to respond in time to save your life."

"They probably would have killed you, Colin," said Delfina, her voice breaking with emotion.

"Why are you here, Delfina? How did you know?"

"We were supposed to have dinner together last night, remember? You were going to come over to my house when you got back from Fresno. When you didn't show up and didn't answer your phone, I got worried. This morning, I called Lieutenant Rosa. He told me what happened and that you were at the hospital. I came right over."

A nurse entered to take Colin's vitals.

"Is there morphine in this drip?" he asked, nodding at the IV needle stuck in his hand.

"Yes, it's timed, but I can turn it up if you need more."

"No, I don't want it. Turn it off, please."

"You must be in terrible pain. I can bring you oxycodone."

"No, thank you. I don't want any opiates."

The nurse adjusted the IV to deliver fluids and electrolytes only, then left the room.

Lieutenant Rosa shook his head as he took in the extent of damage to Colin's cut, bruised and swollen face. "You stumbled into a snake pit, son. Agent Chen tells me that the Proud Boys and the Oath Keepers are running a 'militia training camp' near Fresno. They're recruiting law enforcement and military for their hate army. I didn't know. I'm sorry I sent you into that."

"I remember seeing an Oath Keeper patch on the uniform of one of the CHP officers who beat me up," said Colin. "Wait. That reminds me—Lieutenant Rosa, did they recover my phone?"

"Yes, and I heard everything. I was able to record the entire incident. Your phone is here. It's charging."

"Good. I don't think face recognition is going to work right now. My security key is 258360. Open it and take a look at the last text I received. I was planning to forward it to you. It's from my friend James Owens, who owns the Route 1 Brewery in Pescadero. He texted me a photo of that ICE agent, Kozel. I think Kozel is an Oath Keeper."

Rosa checked Colin's text, then phoned FBI Agent Chen.

"George, can you have your agency put a priority on that background check you ordered last Friday on ICE Agent Kozel? We need to do more than verify credentials. Dig deep. Find everything."

Detective Rosa put away his phone and turned to Delfina. "It would seem that there's no shortage of suspects for your mother's killer. We're going to figure this out, I promise."

★　　★　　★

White chin lifted from enormous tawny paws. Whiskers twitched. Fully awake, M36 watched the human, horse, and dog.

Rafe slowly raised his hands toward his chest to put light pressure on the reins; he subtly applied leg pressure. Silently, Rafe asked Amigo to back up.

Amigo placed his feet carefully, picking his way backward along the narrow rocky mountain trail. Dog followed like a shadow.

M36 didn't blink as he considered the intruders. He was still full from his recent meal.

Velvet fur the color of California hills in the summer rippled over taut muscles. The tip of his tail flicked. His haunches wiggled, readying muscles to pounce if necessary. He fixed his laser green eyes on the horse and human's awkward retreat.

Finally, they disappeared around a bend.

M36 shimmied down his tree and loped away in the opposite direction.

25

"HERE'S A FRESH ICE PACK, COLIN." Delfina held a bag of frozen peas wrapped in a tea towel.

Colin felt shy when she pulled up his T-shirt, revealing a muscular red, purple, and blue six-pack. Delfina settled the ice over his bruised ribs. His breath caught at the shock of ice on his inflamed abdomen.

"Sorry," said Delfina. She leaned in close to him. Her warmth folded around him like a healing blanket.

The contrast of Delfina's warmth, the cold ice on his skin, and the heat of desire flaming wildly through his body, made him light-headed.

"Wow. Barely a week ago I had just gotten invited to come over to your house for the first time and have dinner with you. Now I'm actually staying at your house, in your mother's bed? I'm grateful, but this feels kind of weird."

"It's only natural, Colin. Even though the hospital kicked you out because your insurance only allowed you to stay one day, you still need attention. You live alone. You don't have anyone else to take care of you. My mother's room was empty. So I'm happy to look after you for a while. You've been so kind to me, it's the least I could do."

"Thank you. But I hate putting you to all this trouble."

"I'm glad to do it. I'm just relieved your injuries weren't worse. A fractured rib, a dislocated shoulder, and lots of cuts and bruises is bad, but at least there's no permanent head injury, no blood clots or broken bones, and no evidence of cardiac complications from that Taser. And they say your handsome face isn't going to have any disfiguring scars."

Delfina gently touched Colin's cheek.

His heart opened tentatively, like a sea anemone ready to snap shut again at the first sign of danger. He explored this new feeling, these unknown currents. Could this be love?

"Lieutenant Rosa says that if the cops had tased you again, you could have died, Colin."

"Yeah, I definitely thought I was going to die, but not for the first time."

"James mentioned that you have a Silver Star and a Purple Heart. Mind telling me about that?"

"I assure you, I'm no hero. Just an ordinary guy. I did what anyone else would do under the circumstances."

"What happened?"

"You really want to hear the story?"

"Definitely."

Delfina helped Colin sit up a little higher against his pillows. She adjusted his ice pack and the covers. He met Delfina's eyes and took a deep breath.

"Okay. It was my first tour of duty in Afghanistan. I was assigned to a military police unit. Our job was to protect critical supply routes. We would go out in our Humvees and clear the route for IEDs or insurgents in front of the convoys coming through. In counterinsurgencies like Afghanistan, any routine patrol could turn into ground combat in an instant. It was nothing for my squad to get shot at every other day or so. One Sunday morning about nine, my team was escorting a convoy when we heard gunshots and explosions. The vehicle in front of us turned onto a side road, and right away it took a direct hit from a rocket-propelled grenade. I'll never forget the sound of that explosion. Everyone in that vehicle died. Friends of mine.

"Dozens of insurgents were firing on us. Three of my team members were shot, wounded. My squad leader and I ran toward the insurgents' trench line, took up a position, and started firing. Shrapnel tore up my back, but I just kept shooting. It was a major firefight. Lasted about forty-five minutes, but it seemed like an eternity. Everyone in my unit survived. I got a purple heart, along with all the other wounded guys on my team, and they gave me and my squad leader silver stars. But honestly, everyone just did what was necessary to survive."

"You've been through so much trauma, Colin."

"Yeah. War is hell. But at least in Afghanistan I got hurt doing something I believe in—serving my country. This thing," Colin looked down at his bruised and fractured body, "makes no sense. It's the twenty-first century, for fuck's sake. We elected a Black president. For a minute there, I thought America was done with bigotry and racism. But lately it seems like it's getting worse."

"I'm completely with you, Colin. I've marched and demonstrated with Black Lives Matter. In college, I went to every rally. But now we're sliding backward."

Colin shook his head. "The bad guys are trying to dismantle all the progress for human rights and environmental protection people made in the twentieth century. But you know what, Delfina? The good guys are going to win. The dying dinosaur is just lashing out in a final death gasp."

"I'm not so sure the dinosaur is dying. It may be stronger than ever. After Obama became our first Black president, I was never so naive as to think racism was over in the U.S. This country was founded on genocide, Colin. My people have been systematically slaughtered and disappeared since the first Europeans arrived on the continent."

Colin narrowed his eyes. "Racist violence seems embedded in America's DNA."

"At least the media covers attacks against Black Americans, as horrific as that is. But the epidemic of missing and murdered Native Americans has been going on for centuries, and most people don't even realize it's happening."

"True. It feels overwhelming. Any idea how we can fix it?"

"This may sound like an oversimplification," said Delfina, "but I think that, at its core, the issue is spiritual. It's truly a battle between good and evil, between love and hate, a war being waged on unseen levels. I'm not talking about religion. This is way bigger than our myopic little human religions. It's a war measured not in human lifetimes but in a geologic, maybe even planetary timescale."

"Well, um, thanks for sharing, but you lost me there, Delfina. Too far out for me. Sounds like a *Lord of the Rings* fairy tale. Sorry."

"I know. It's hard to explain. But what I'm talking about can be experienced through our ceremonies. For example, my people have a special healing ceremony for our combat veterans."

"Yeah? Tell me more."

"It's called Soul Retrieval. We believe that sometimes, when a person experiences a traumatic event, their soul jumps out of their body and runs away. The person's soul can be broken, fragmented, and parts of the spirit self can get lost, trapped in the unseen realms of the spirit world, unable to return to ordinary reality."

"I'm familiar with the concept," said Colin. "When I was in the military hospital in Afghanistan for PTSD, my shrink talked to me about dissociation and detachment disorder. I was feeling depressed and stuck, completely drained of energy, numb, and unable to focus or move forward. She gave me some tools to deal with it, like meditation, self-checks, and breathing exercises."

"Exactly. Soul Retrieval is another tool to help a person who feels broken get their whole self back and find their way home."

"Interesting. How does it work?"

"You start in a safe place, where you feel physically and emotionally comfortable. A healer guides you into a trance state. Then his spirit follows you into the unseen realms and tracks down the lost, fragmented pieces of your spirit. Often, the healer will even find fragments of soul that got traumatized in childhood and have been stuck, hiding in the spirit world ever since. The healer coaxes those traumatized parts of yourself, which may be scared, lost, angry, and hiding, to return with him to the ordinary world. Once he brings back all those pieces of your spirit self, he uses traditional medicine—song, prayer, herbs—to help you reintegrate the fragments back into your whole self. I received a Soul Retrieval a few days after my mother's death."

"Sounds awesome."

Delfina frowned and pulled at the woven bracelet around her wrist. *Did her mother give her that?*

"We haven't talked about it much, Delfina. But I hope you know that the sheriff, the FBI, the marshal, and everyone in their agencies are doing all they can to find your mother's murderer. I want nothing more than to protect you and bring that killer to justice."

"Justice? Honestly, I'm not holding my breath. You did hear me say that we have a crisis in this country of missing and murdered indigenous women? There's an egregious lack of legal protections for Native women. Violent crimes are ignored, excused, swept under the rug, or the victim is blamed. The majority of domestic violence, sexual assault, sex trafficking, disappearance, and murder cases are never even investigated or brought to court. It's nothing new. Violence against indigenous women has deep roots in colonization and genocide stretching back hundreds of years."

Colin moaned and closed his eyes.

"Oh God, I'm sorry. I shouldn't be haranguing you with all this political bullshit right now." Delfina leaned in close. She smelled incredible, like healing herbs and aromatherapy oils.

"It's time for you to give me back that ice pack and take your ibuprofen." She gently removed the no-longer-frozen peas from his chest. "I'm going to bring you a smoothie—full of good stuff to fight inflammation and boost your energy. And I've made some strengthening broth for later. Here, you've slipped down. Let's get you sitting back up a little more."

Delfina leaned over her mother's bed, put her arms around Colin, and helped him scooch up. He couldn't stop himself from looking down the front of her shirt. The beautiful rise of her breasts momentarily distracted him from the pain.

Once he was sitting, leaning against the headboard, he started coughing uncontrollably.

"Be careful. Here, hold this pillow against your chest and apply light pressure while you cough, to protect those ribs."

He held the pillow against his chest with one hand and coughed mucus into his other hand. *Embarrassing.*

"That's good." She handed him a tissue. "I'm glad to see there isn't any blood. The doctor said it's important to keep your lungs clear to prevent chest infections. Just be careful not to cough too hard. Now take ten deep slow breaths."

She took the pillow away, placed her hand gently on his chest, looked into his eyes, and counted to ten while he took deep slow breaths.

He wasn't sure if he felt dizzy because of the deep breathing or because of what he felt looking into her eyes.

"Perfect. Here's your ibuprofen and some water."

"I don't want any pills."

"I understand that you don't like to take drugs, Colin, but I have your hospital discharge papers right here, and it says, 'For rib fracture, adequate pain control is essential so that you can continue to breathe deeply and avoid lung complications, such as pneumonia.'"

"Okay." Colin took the ibuprofen. "Oh, hey, what's with that amazing mandala on the wall over the door?"

"I painted it for you. For your healing. It's Snake Medicine."

"Why snake?"

"Snake is a powerful totem animal for the Kumeyaay. Snake Medicine people are rare. Their initiation involves experiencing and living through multiple hell-fire snake bites, literally or figuratively, which gives them power to transmute all poisons, be they mental, physical, spiritual, or emotional."

"Yeah. That would be a great superpower. Sounds like an astrology horoscope."

"There's more. Snakes hold the power of creation, and … enormous sexual energy."

Delfina's eyes locked with his.

Seconds, minutes, years, lifetimes ticked away as their entwined bodies tumbled through a sensual ocean of love.

Colin swallowed. Returned from his fantasy, he licked his swollen lips.

Delfina offered him the water glass, and he drank.

Finally, he found his voice. "Why two snakes?"

"Two snakes intertwining around a spear represents healing." Delfina looked at her hands. Was she blushing? "On another level, it's similar to a yin-yang symbol. Complete understanding and acceptance of the male and female within each creates a melding of the two into one, producing divine energy."

"Beautiful." Colin's eyes were not on the mandala, but on Delfina.

"I'll be right back with your smoothie."

Colin admired her back end as she left the room: long legs like a pony's, the pert roll and tuck of her bottom under those tight blue jeans, hourglass hips curving from a thin waist and swaying with unaffected sensuality as she disappeared through the door.

He drifted off on a daydream. *Her legs squeezed around him, his hands explored her curves.*

26

T HE SIGN ON THE DOOR in the Interdisciplinary Sciences Building at UCSL read,

Santa Lucia Puma Project. Our lab combines rigorous field studies with state-of-the-art technology and quantitative techniques in order to answer cutting-edge questions in wildlife ecology and global change. We seek to better understand how climate change, habitat alteration and human harvest/hunting influence animal behavior, population dynamics and community organization, so as to better inform wildlife and habitat management and conservation. Primary areas of research focus are habitat fragmentation, climate change, overexploitation, genetics, and salmon-wildlife linkages.

At ten a.m., Thursday, April 28—the day after Colin moved from the hospital to Delfina's house—Environmental Science Professor and Project Director, Dr. Niko Goodman, along with conservation biology graduate students Lili Armstrong and Jack Jordan, huddled at a computer workstation studying GPS data on an interactive map. On the wall next to the workstation hung a colorful, detailed, three-by-four feet topographical map of California.

"M36's collar battery is nearly two years old, about at the end of its life," said Lili. "We need to replace it soon."

Niko leaned closer to his monitor and squinted at the numbered circles representing collared pumas being tracked on the GPS map. "Where is he?"

Jack zoomed in on M36's location. "Looks like he's been hanging out for a while in one of his favorite hunting spots, near the west fork of Bear Creek. Based on the accelerometer in his collar, he hunted, ate, cached his kill, and napped. Then something must have disturbed him. He left the site pretty fast. Odds are, he'll come back around to eat more in a day or so."

Lili stood and stretched. "Ready to go find his cache and set up a trap?"

★ ★ ★

Several hours later, the Puma Project truck bumped up Cougar Creek Coast Ranch Road, past the sheriff's homicide investigation tent, still manned by a minimal crew. Jack drove, passing the small PG&E substation, then turned west on an unmarked dirt spur that connected to Bear Creek Truck Road. Gunning the truck steeply uphill, Jack maneuvered around rocks and potholes for thirty-five minutes. Finally, they came to a pullout and parked.

They took their time putting together and checking their gear, then shouldered heavy packs and started the steep and rugged five-mile hike along Bear Creek up into the forested mountains.

The three researchers bushwhacked and sweated up the rigorous incline for two hours.

"I think this is the spot," said Niko, peeling the backpack straps off his sore shoulders. He set down the bulky trapping gear he'd been carrying and stretched his tall, lanky body.

Jack sat on a large boulder and pulled his water bottle and an energy bar from his pack.

Lili leaned her pack against a fallen log, checked her GPS/multi-GNSS device and the monitor that tracked M36's collar. "Yep, M36 has definitely moved on, but his cache should be right around here. It's a good bet he'll come back for another meal pretty soon."

Lili, Jack, and Niko stood still, senses alert, warily observing.

"Look, here's his scrape." Jack pointed to a conspicuous mound of leaves, dirt, and other forest debris under a tall old oak tree.

"Pee-yew! Strong cat urine stink. Definitely a cougar scrape," said Lili.

"Yep, and here's scat," said Niko. "He marked his territory. Let's get this in a collection vial."

"Scratch mark here, on this tree trunk." Jack took photographs of the scratch marks, scat, and scrape with his smartphone.

"Oh, God. Check out these tracks leading away from the tree. The paw prints are enormous," said Jack.

Niko knelt and placed his hand next to a paw print for size reference. "This is definitely our guy."

Jack took a photo.

"Claw marks where he shimmied down the tree, then dropped and took off that way in a hurry." Niko pointed upstream.

"Huh. This could be why he left. Right here." Jack pointed. "Tracks of horse and rider come up that trail, right up to M36's tree. Oh, shit. They stop, and back up. That rider was real lucky M36 had just finished a big meal."

"Let's find his cache," said Lili.

"Here!" Jack pointed to the flies buzzing around a telltale litter of fluffy deer fur, bits of blood-flecked tissue, and bone, near a heap of leaves, twigs, and bark. Part of a bloody deer muzzle poked out from under the pile.

"All right. Let's set up the trap," said Niko.

From high in the ancient oak, two ravens expressed their displeasure with deep, throaty *kraas*.

The researchers pulled on heavy gloves and set about the gory work of excavating M36's cache of deer remains. They placed a large wire cage where M36's cache had been, and wired the deer pieces to the inside back of the cage. Then they camouflaged the cage with the original cache's sticks, leaves, and bark so it would look and smell like M36's pantry. Finally, they hooked up a wildlife camera to monitor the trap and ping their devices when the trap was sprung.

"Now let's find a spot to camp," said Lili. "It's going to be dark in a few hours."

It had been a warm day, but evening chill was oozing up the mountain. Lili pulled on a sweater, zipped it up, and tucked the wispy hair escaping from her braid into a knit watch cap.

"I've been up here before," said Niko. "I'll lead the way."

Lili and Jack followed Dr. Niko's head of cougar-colored hair, bobbing above the dense forest understory of wild rose, tall ferns, wild lilac, poison oak, elderberry, thimbleberry, and huckleberry.

"Amazing how much this part of the forest has recovered in just the two and a half years since the lightning fires," said Jack.

"Nature's so incredibly resilient," said Lili. "If we just stop beating up Mother Earth, she'll heal on her own."

When they reached an area of level ground sufficiently distant from the cougar's cache, the team efficiently set up a small blind with ultralight tents and a minimalist cooking area. They made sure that GPS, phones, field camera connection, and collar tracking devices were charged and operating. As the sun set, Lili heated water over a backpack stove.

The temperature dropped and wind came roaring up the canyons, dangerously whipping branches overhead. The researchers pulled on parkas and wool gloves.

"This Windmaster is a great little stove, Lil," said Niko. "Most backpack stoves are hard to light and blow out in this much wind. I'm glad you suggested we add this to our gear."

They sat on fallen logs and hunched over their reconstituted hot meals in bags, sharing stories of previous adventures in the field.

Dinner over, they cleaned up, then organized everything they would need for a fast grab-and-run back to the cache. Finally, they crawled into sleeping bags and settled in for the night. A nearby pair of Great Horned Owls *who-who'd* them to sleep.

★　　★　　★

At dawn the next morning, M36 pinged the researcher's devices. The trap had been sprung. M36 was in the cage.

"Go time!" said Niko.

At the cache site, the researchers found M36 trapped, hissing, growling, screaming, batting, and ramming against the wire that caged him.

Niko loaded a long-handled syringe with xylazine and shot M36 in the hip with the anesthetizing drug.

Lili and Jack spread out a tarp in front of the cage. Once the drug took effect and M36 was immobilized, they covered his face with a breathable sleeve and gently maneuvered the heavy beast out of the cage onto the tarp.

They verified his ear tag, inspected the tracking collar and changed its batteries, then tested it to make sure it was working properly. Next, they measured and recorded overall body length, length of tail and limbs, inspected and measured his teeth and foot pads. They collected a blood sample to analyze genetic material and prior exposure to disease based on antibodies in the blood.

"This is one awesome mountain lion," said Jack. "These big feet definitely match the paw prints we found yesterday. And look at these huge fangs. Wow. His teeth are in perfect shape. My mother would be so proud of me if my teeth looked as good as his."

Wearing lightweight examination gloves, Lili stroked M36's fur. "He's so beautiful."

"We need to weigh this guy," said Niko. "Jack, how about if you and I lift him in his tarp and Lili, you read the scale."

"Ready, up." The men strained to lift and hold up the inert cougar in the tarp while Lili read the weight.

"Two hundred three pounds. M36, you're in the top one percent for weight, and all muscle."

Once they had collected samples and completed all their measurements, the team removed the sleeve from the puma's face and moved away a healthy distance to watch over M36 and keep him safe while the xylazine wore off.

"I wonder what happened to that female we collared last month," said Lili.

"I ran the blood sample we took when we caught her," said Niko. "There were SARS-CoV-2 antibodies in the blood."

"SARS-CoV-2? Meaning a human with Covid virus infected her somehow?" asked Jack.

"I'm not sure. Her DNA had some really strange anomalies."

"Look," said Lili. "He's waking up."

The team stood and watched as M36 got unsteadily to his feet, glared at the researchers, and growled.

Suddenly, he lunged.

Veering away from the researchers, he disappeared into the forest.

27

COLIN SUPPORTED his dislocated shoulder by wrapping his splinted arm around his bandaged ribcage. He used his stronger right arm and his legs to push himself up to sitting in bed.

In the hospital, they'd manipulated his shoulder back into place, but it was still hella sore. He was supposed to wear this splint for another week. Delfina had been helping him apply alternating icepacks and heating pads since he'd been staying with her.

He was going stir-crazy. Friday, April 29. He'd been stuck in bed since the beating, almost a week ago. Getting nursed by Delfina was amazingly sexy, but those sponge baths she gave him every day were giving him blue balls.

He had to get out of bed and get his life back.

Delfina was talking with someone in the next room. It sounded like her cousin, Hawk. Colin strained to hear what they were saying.

He gave up trying to eavesdrop and scooched over to the side of the bed, pushing through the pain. For a brief flash, he was back in the military hospital in Afghanistan.

His mind cleared.

He was sitting on the floor, leaning against the bed. Delfina and Hawk loomed above him, staring.

"What do you think you're doing, Colin? What's going on?" said Delfina. "You should have called me. Should I bring you the bedpan?"

"I don't want to use that anymore, Delfina. I'd like to use the toilet in the bathroom."

"I can take you," said Hawk.

Hawk leaned over and effortlessly lifted Colin to a standing position.

Colin swooned with vertigo. It had been a while since he'd stood upright.

Hawk held him steady. "You're okay."

Colin was surprised at Hawk's strength. He'd assumed that a man with his proclivities would be weak. That was clearly not the case.

"Ready?" Hawk gently eased Colin's good arm over his beribboned shoulder. They were close enough in height that it was a good fit, so Colin's aching muscles and ribs weren't overly strained.

As they walked to the bathroom, Colin fretted that it could be weird trying to take a leak with a gay man watching.

Hawk helped Colin into the bathroom. When he'd demonstrated that he could stand steady in front of the toilet by holding on to the sink, Hawk left.

"I'll be right outside if you need anything. Just don't fall."

★   ★   ★

Colin walked out of the bathroom on his own, wearing nothing but Delfina's embroidered Chinese silk robe, which had been hanging on a hook on the bathroom door. It was small for him and wouldn't close over his chest, but it covered the necessary parts, just barely.

Delfina and Hawk were waiting for him.

"Sorry. I had a little accident." Colin blushed and stuttered. "I'm afraid my boxers and tee shirt need washing."

"No problem," said Delfina. "I bought you a new set of clothes and some underwear a few days ago. Hawk helped me pick them out. The clothes you were wearing when you were attacked were ruined—torn and bloody. I'll just grab your, um, laundry and throw it in the wash. Hawk can help you back to the bedroom."

"No wait. I don't want to go back to bed. I just need be somewhere besides the bedroom, and I need to sit up for a while like a normal person."

"Are you sure you're ready?" Delfina had that look of nurturing concern on her beautiful face that Colin had grown accustomed to. "The doctor said it would take three to six weeks for your ribs to heal."

"Yeah, but he said I could move around, do normal activities, as long as I avoid anything intense. I'm so done with wallowing in bed all day long, Delfina."

"Okay."

Hawk helped him settle on a comfortable chair in the front parlor. Fresh flowers in a vase and the sun shining through the window lifted Colin's mood. He felt even better when Hawk handed him new boxer shorts to slip into. But pulling on a fresh T-shirt over his head was too painful a struggle to deal with. He resigned himself to looking ridiculous in Delfina's robe for the time being.

"Delfina and I were making final plans for Ramona's funeral," said Hawk. "It's day after tomorrow at the Agua Pura Farm. Would you like to come?"

"No, Hawk. That would be too much for him," said Delfina, returning from the laundry room with a heating pad for Colin's shoulder in her hand.

"Of course I'm up for it. I need to be there. I'll be fine. I'm going."

28

ON SUNDAY, MAY 1, as the sun set on Agua Pura Farm, thick cold fog rolled over the mountain like a slow-motion tidal wave. The fog-wave submerged a newly planted field and the dense hedgerows beyond, then oozed over a group of people huddled in a clearing up against the forest's edge.

Shrouded in damp and frigid white fog, people who had traveled from near and far to honor Ramona Cuera's life pulled warm jackets and shawls tight around their shoulders, snugged watch caps down over ears, and covered hands with gloves and mittens.

Colin hadn't taken his eyes off Delfina since she and Hawk had emerged from the ceremonial teepee nearby.

Delfina wore a long red dress that her mother had made, decorated with black and white ribbons and embroidered with traditional patterns representing cycles of earth and sky. Red ribbons twined through Delfina's black braids. A rabbit pelt robe hung down to her ankles. Fur-lined, beaded moccasin boots clad her feet. Her black, wide brim, open crown hat—made of buffalo fur felt, and decorated with an owl feather tied with red string and a turquoise bead—gave her an iconoclastic, edgy look. Although she was in mourning, Delfina emanated strength and nobility of body, mind, and spirit.

Colin sat on a log a little distance away from the funeral pit, warming himself at a campfire, in a circle of Agua Pura farmers and Delfina's friends and relatives. He had wanted to help dig the funeral pit, but the pain was too much. He put his hand in his coat pocket and rattled the plastic prescription vial that contained ibuprofen and the Percocet he'd been given at the hospital. He didn't want to take anything, but this was going to be a long night. He'd brought the pills just in case he couldn't manage the pain on his own.

Wrapping the rabbit skin robe tighter, Delfina turned her proud and stoic face to the spokesperson of Agua Pura Farm Collective, Ray de la Montaña. Tears ran down her cheeks. "Thank you again for allowing us to hold my mother's funeral here, Ray."

Ray took off a work glove, placed his large, chapped and calloused hand on Delfina's shoulder, and looked into her eyes with deep compassion. "I know that your mother would have preferred to have her celebration of life in her ancestral homeland, but since that was not possible, it's our honor to have Ramona's ashes resting in this sacred ground. Fortunately, with this fog, it's wet enough that I think we can safely go ahead with the ceremonial burning. Please tell us how to proceed. We're here for you, Delfina."

They stood at the edge of the freshly dug pit—ten feet deep, six feet long, and four feet wide. A lidded, unfired earthenware jar holding most of Ramona's ashes had been placed in the deepest part of the pit, and the pit filled with a layer of dried grasses and brush. Dry willow branches were stacked above the grasses in an open weave. Near the pit, a pile of cut branches and thick limbs waited to be added to the fire.

Delfina wiped tears from her cheeks. "My people have been cremating our dead forever, but obviously we can't literally burn a body in an open pit like we used to. And the old way of digging a pit with sticks, stones, and bare hands obviously isn't practical now either." Delfina looked up at Ray and smiled through her tears. "It was hard enough digging with picks and shovels. Thank you for doing this."

Ray nodded, brushing dirt off his work gloves and jeans.

Delfina lifted her voice to address all of the people gathered around. "More than twelve thousand years of Kumeyaay cultural traditions were suppressed by European incursion and colonization, and nearly lost altogether. In order to survive, our people were forced to stop speaking our language and practicing our traditions and customs. We had to adapt and assimilate into the ways of the colonizers. But now there's a resurgence in our cultural awareness. Today, with the help of teachers like Professor Stan Rodriguez of Kumeyaay Community College and other leaders, we're reclaiming and recreating our culture, based on stories our surviving elders have shared and on anthropological research. We build our future by honoring our past. We're still here. My artist cousin, Hawk, and I have planned a celebration of life for Mama that starts with modern Kumeyaay funeral practices and elaborates from there with what we've researched, prayed on, and dreamed. I hope my Kumeyaay relatives and friends will know that this ceremony comes from love, and that my heart is good. Eyay e'Hunn. May your spirit burn bright. Haawka."

Many of Ramona's possessions had been gathered and arranged nearby, ready to be burned, including a dozen unglazed earthenware pots, a rosary, clothing, a beaded hair ornament, several handwoven cooking baskets, and two large museum-worthy granary baskets. Breaking with tradition that required all of the deceased's possessions to be burned, Delfina had kept or given away the rest of Ramona's belongings, as her mother's will had specified.

"Traditionally," said Hawk, "Kumeyaay burned not only the deceased's body, clothes, and belongings, but even their houses. Our dwellings were made of willow."

The bottom of Hawk's heavy wool coat, as black as raven feathers and trimmed with red ribbon, brushed the ankles of his black boots. He buttoned the top button of his coat, turned up the collar, and tucked his braid under a royal blue silk kata, a Tibetan ceremonial scarf, which he wound around his neck and over his ears. One large condor feather adorned his black felt, open crown, wide brim fedora, worn low over his eyes.

"Today, some Kumeyaay even burn cars and motorcycles." Hawk did not seem to strain his voice, yet somehow it carried through the fog to all of those gathered around with a magical, hypnotic magnetism.

"Cremation and the burning of personal effects is supposed to happen no more than two days after death," said Delfina. "My mother has been kept waiting too long."

Colin shifted his weight on the log, took a sip from his water bottle, and leaned into the warmth of the fire.

Delfina turned toward Ray. "Ray, would you open the *Takaay* by introducing yourself and your land? After that, I'd like to address everyone for few more minutes, and then we can start burning my mother's things. I'm relieved and grateful that we're finally doing this. We believe that sending the departed one's personal belongings to the sky as smoke makes the afterlife more welcoming for the spirit."

"Welcome, everyone." Ray de la Montaña's voice resounded through the fog. He raised his open palms, and everyone present stood. Teenagers, who'd been at the ready, walked around smudging everyone with smoke from burning sage bundles while Ray spoke.

"We are honored that our farm has been chosen as the resting site for Ramona Cuera's ashes. Although we are exceedingly grateful to hold the deed to this land, we want to take a moment to recognize that the land on which we gather is the unceded territory of the Ohlone Tribe. The Amah Mutsun Ohlone Tribal Band, comprised of the descendants of Indigenous people taken to Missions Santa Lucia and San Juan Bautista during Spanish colonization of the Central Coast, is today working hard to restore traditional stewardship practices on these lands and to help us heal the land from historical trauma. We welcome members of the Kumeyaay and Ohlone Tribes, and all other Indigenous people who are present here today. We recognize that every member of our diverse Santa Lucia community has benefited and continues to benefit from the use and occupation of this land. Through this land acknowledgement, we affirm Indigenous Sovereignty and will work to hold our community accountable to the needs of Indigenous peoples. Delfina has told me that the Kumeyaay word for land and body is the same: *'Emat.* The human person is of the land and the land is of the human person. We are this land. Together, the land and the people watch over one another, and are One."

Shouts of "Ah Ho!" "Noso'n!" and "Eyay e'Hunn" were raised.

"Delfina, we consider you and your relatives to be a part of our Agua Pura Farm community. We honor and celebrate the life of your mother, Ramona, and grieve with you over her loss."

Delfina raised her hands over her head and began to sing a lament in a language unknown to Colin, wild and indescribable, part keening wail and part ancient psalm of jubilation and praise.

Colin's breath caught. Delfina seemed larger than life, a goddess. Over her head, a circle of starry night sky opened in the shredded fog.

Starlight poured down through tiny droplets of mist, refracting a rainbow all around her.

She's the most beautiful, powerful, pure woman I've ever met.

She dropped to her knees, forehead and hands on the ground, her song a faint lullaby. A Great Horned Owl hooted from tall redwoods nearby.

Delfina stopped singing. All was silent.

She rose and nodded to three white-haired Native women waiting by the funeral pit. The women elders walked clockwise around the pit from west and south toward the east, chanting and keening. The first scattered handfuls of pink beans on the ground from a basket, the second threw corn, and the last dragged a swath of blue calico. When they had circled the pit four times, the baskets with the remaining corn and beans and the blue calico were placed in the pit to feed and comfort the spirit of the dead.

Next, Ramona's friends and relatives, some of whom had had traveled from Southern California and even farther, placed her treasured possessions into the funeral pit, one by one. More brush and kindling were added on top. Finally, an effigy of Ramona's body was laid out on the funeral pyre, head to the north and face upward. The image had been made by Ramona's relatives of dried native grasses, woven together like a mat, with a large, red tomato placed inside the heart cavity. Head and face were made of dry, unfired clay, eyes of white seashells, pupils painted with black charcoal. Delfina had cut a handful of her mother's hair and, with spines from prickly pear cactus, had pinned the hair to the soft clay head of the effigy. More kindling and brush went on top of the effigy, then bunches of dried sage and sweetgrass.

Everyone stood as silent as statues in the mist. The Great Horned Owl hooted four times from the forest's edge. Delfina nodded, and Ray and Hawk lit the pyre.

As the flames rose, a Kumeyaay elder lifted his hands to the sky. "There is no death, only a change in worlds. Her spirit flies to Sky World now."

People sent up a ululation.

Firekeepers added larger pieces of wood, and the flames rose higher. Several people with gourd rattles started a rhythmic pulse. One elder began singing. Some of the other Native men and women who knew the death chant joined in, while rattles kept the rhythm.

Colin's cheeks flushed from the fire. The song went on and on. When it ended, a dancer dressed as a crow and another as a crane jumped and hopped around like clowns. The people laughed!

Laughing at a funeral? Colin's eyes widened in amazement.

Another solemn song began, and people again wept and wailed. Someone put a rattle in Colin's hand, and he instinctively found the rhythm. Firekeepers added more wood. The flames leapt higher.

Hawk sat on the log next to Colin. "These songs are called Bird Songs," Hawk explained. "Kumeyaay Bird Songs come from our ancestors. They're an important unifying tradition at Takaay—funerals, memorials, and other special ceremonies. A funeral sequence can include a hundred seventeen different songs and continue for as long as twenty-four hours. Many of our Bird Songs have been lost, which makes the ones that are still remembered even more precious. We're so blessed that some of our elder relatives who know the songs were able to come up from San Diego, and even a few from Mexico to honor Ramona with Bird Singing. Families who could afford it brought their kids so we can pass on our songs to the next generation."

The cycle of songs, punctuated by comical antics of crow and crane, went round and round, drilling deeper and deeper into a night seemingly without end.

As the hours passed, Colin felt his mind sliding sideways. He struggled to keep his eyes open. Crow and Crane's clownish antics grew even more outrageous. People dressed in other animal costumes joined the dance around the enormous bonfire as the rhythm of the Bird Songs grew faster and faster.

Hawk appeared in the middle of the dancers, covered in feathers, plumes on his shoulders, huge wings stretched out at his sides. He began to whirl-whirl-whirl-whirl and whirl.

"A Tatahuila—the Whirling Dance," someone said. Colin felt dizzy.

Are these dancers human?

No! Wait. Actual animals are dancing around the fire! Singing and blessing the people gathered round.

So many animals, here to honor Ramona and her family. I know them. Beloved animal friends. Highly sensitive, threatened residents of this land, too many of them too close to the edge of extinction. Wilson's and Orange-crowned Warbler, grasshopper sparrow, downy woodpecker, tree swallow, ferruginous hawk, Northern Harrier, Cooper's hawk, white-tailed kite, American kestrel, burrowing owl, short-eared owl, pigmy and saw-whet and great horned and screech owls, golden eagle, peregrine falcon, tricolored blackbird, olive-sided flycatcher, dipper, quail, marbled murrelet, band-tailed pigeon, American badger, red-legged frog, western pond turtle, Coho salmon, steelhead, tidewater goby, Pacific lamprey eel, Ohlone tiger beetles and rain beetles, and harvester ants, California giant salamander, the gentle yellow-eyed Ensatina, and Santa Cruz black salamander, newts, and tree frogs, lizards, the exquisite California kingsnake, San Francisco garter snake, rubber boa, ring neck and gopher snakes, yellow-belied racer, and rattler, dusky-footed woodrat, kangaroo rat, meadow vole, shrew mole, ringtail cat, long-tailed weasel, cavorting bunnies, skunks, and skinks, gray fox, black-tailed deer, deer mouse, fox, bobcat, mountain lion ... Agua Pura is a critical refugia *for protecting all this priceless biodiversity from climate change.*

Colin's heart warmed and expanded with love for all these beings, animal and human, dancing around the fire. A powerful certainty rose through him: protecting these beloved beings and their habitat was his life's purpose.

Flames leapt, the bonfire cracked, spitting red ash and fiery splinters of wood at the leaping dancers. Colin felt himself floating away, tethered like a kite by a thin silvery thread to his tiny body sitting on a log near the fire.

From this distance on high, the bonfire's weird red, orange, and black flames lit up the swirling fog—as if a mile-high oil derrick, far offshore, were exploding, raining apocalyptic fire. The enormous burning structure seemed to rise above the clouds and expand until it was an entire city of the future, pulsing in an unstable conflagration of fiery toxic gasses, on the cusp of erupting, engulfing everything at any second.

Screaming! Millions of beings, human and animal, were screaming in fear and agony.

Colin's spirit, still floating like a kite, looked down upon the circle of dancers and mourners around the funeral pyre. He saw his own body fall backward onto the ground, convulse, drool. A high-pitched tone pierced his brain. His skull was about to shatter. He struggled to hands and knees. Vomited.

A hairy, partly human monster pounced out of the flames. A horned buffalo headdress with coyote tails covered the monster's head and shoulders, a red and blue flag printed with a white rattlesnake flapped over its genitalia. With cloven feet, the monster stomped on a dancer, grabbed her by the neck, and twisted her head off, spraying blood everywhere.

Toggled to his silver leash far above the mayhem, Colin helplessly watched, frantic to protect the animal people below. The monster stuck its clawed fingers into his victim's viscera and painted its face with the victim's blood. Then, with a grotesque grin, it licked its bloody sharp nails.

In a horrifying parody of Crow and Crane's dance, seen vaguely through the fog, the monster laughed as it impaled dancers and mourners with a flaming spear, charring their mangled bodies black.

Nothing left alive.

Silence. A bleak eternity passed.

Colin's spirit dropped back down into his body.

Lying on his back on the ground, he rolled, pushed up onto his feet, and squatted in a defensive position. Wiping drool and vomit from his chin, barely breathing, he blinked, listened, squinted into the desolation, his heart as mangled, emptied, as desiccated as the scene around him.

Silent. Still. Slowly, he straightened. Deep breaths. All around him was burnt, tainted ground. Curled, brittle remains of animal bodies lay there, indistinguishable from the blackened remains of plants and trees. Annihilation.

Gray ash drifting through the air.

Colin choked, coughed, brushed away a tear crawling down his soot-smeared cheek. Unable to bear the horror, he closed his eyes.

He realized he had just witnessed his ultimate fear coming true: the complete destruction of life on earth, more horrible than his personal death or the death of a loved one, far worse than any scene of war he'd ever experienced: a vision of the last battle, pure evil triumphing over all life, all that is good, beautiful, true, and honorable. Was it an atomic holocaust, climate chaos, a comet from outer space? He couldn't say what that final death blow had been, but he was sure he had seen Evil win the war of the ages.

Why that vision? What did it mean? Was it up to him to stop it from happening? *You've got to be kidding.*

"Colin?"

He blinked.

Like a vision of heaven, Delfina stood before him. The sun was rising over the mountains. People with heavy rakes were moving dirt over the ashes and coals of the spent fire.

Delfina smiled. "Hey, that must have been an intense dream you were having. You were shouting about conservation mandates, data, and statutes."

Colin sat up, wiped his chin, pulled off the blanket someone had wrapped around him, and shivered.

He could still see the grotesque bodies of charred animals and little birds in his mind. "I realized last night that it isn't right to open this land to the public until we can get baseline data on all the sensitive species who live here, and then develop a scientifically solid species monitoring protocol. This park was established with a primary mandate of conservation, not public recreation."

Colin scrambled to his feet. With his good arm, he ran his fingers through his hair, scrubbed his face, patted his jacket, and brushed off his jeans. Had he only imagined being naked?

He painfully rolled his unbandaged shoulder, tried to swallow, slowly moved his head from side to side, held his ribs, and coughed. "I realize this sounds really trivial compared to the big picture of what's wrong in the world, but we need to do something to shift BLM's priorities before the Cougar Creek Coast Ranch Monument opens."

"Here, drink this." Delfina offered him a small red clay bowl filled with white liquid.

Colin looked sideways at the watery milky liquid in the offered bowl and gagged.

"Traditionally, after the burning ceremony, we would grind the calcined bones of the deceased to a fine powder, mix the powder with water and drink the mixture ceremonially from small earthenware bowls we call *ollas*. This drink was believed to ensure long life, without illness, and to endow those who drank with the virtues and qualities of the dead."

Colin frowned and wrinkled his forehead.

Delfina laughed. "This is not ground bones. It's actually just a little bentonite—white clay—we get from a local homeopath, mixed with an organic coconut water high in potassium and electrolytes, with ground chia seeds, and an organic cal-mag-zinc vitamin C supplement with a light pineapple flavor that we buy at the health food store."

Colin accepted the bowl and drank.

We're going to the temescal to sweat now," said Delfina. "Then there's a big feast. It's May Day, a cross-quarter day. A time of new beginnings. Do you think you're up to joining us?"

Delfina reached out her hand, and Colin let himself be led away.

29

C OLIN SNAPPED OUT of a deep sleep, his eyes open wide, his
mind fully awake.

"What the fuck!" Someone's hand was on his dick? He had a
gigantic hard-on. And he had to pee.

He scrambled out of bed and hurried to the bathroom. He stood
facing the john, trying to get the sex and urine functions of his plumbing
sorted while his mind whirled. Finally, he achieved the great relief of a
good long piss. But his brain still couldn't make sense of what had just
happened.

He glanced at the clock in the bathroom. Ten a.m., Monday, May 2—
the day after the all-nighter of Ramona's funeral ceremony followed by that
grueling sweat lodge and a big feast with a lot of people. He hurt everywhere.
He just wanted to go back to bed and sleep for another few days.

Bed. What happened there?

He struggled into the fresh boxers and T-shirt Delfina had left for him
on the shelf with the clean towels, then returned to Ramona's bedroom.

Delfina was curled up in her mother's bed—the bed he'd been
sleeping in for the last week. She was crying, her hands covering her face.

"Delfina?"

She didn't look at him.

"What's going on?"

Colin perched on the bed, at a respectful distance.

"Was I dreaming, or did you touch me, um, intimately?"

Delfina sat up and peeked at him, teary-eyed. Her red face was contorted in anguish and confusion. The thin nightgown she wore did not conceal the contours of her gorgeous breasts.

"Colin, I'm so ashamed. I don't know what happened to me. I came in to see if you needed anything. You were asleep, and you just looked so—I don't know, safe. And comforting. I got into mama's bed next to you before I knew what I was doing. I just wanted to feel closer to her. I miss Mama so much. But I didn't touch you, I promise. I'm sorry."

"Don't worry, Delfina. It's all right. I get it. Your mom's funeral was really intense, emotional. I'm glad you see me as safe and comforting. I want to be that for you. As for the other thing, well … I admit you turn me on, in my dreams. But I think we should take it slow, don't you?"

"Yes, of course." With both hands, Delfina wiped the tears from her face. She shivered and pulled the sheet and blanket up to her shoulders.

Colin swallowed. He noticed her silk robe on the floor. He crawled off the bed painfully, awkwardly, and fetched it.

"Maybe we can talk. Would you like to put this on first?"

"Yes."

He turned his back while she slipped on the dressing gown.

"Okay, you can look," she said. She sat cross-legged on the bed.

"The last two days probably took a big toll on you, Colin. How are you feeling?"

"I don't feel as bad as I thought I would. That sweat lodge was tough, but I think it ended up giving me energy. I actually feel pretty strong."

"Good. You should probably get back in bed, though." Delfina patted the mattress. The bed was a California king—with more than sufficient elbow room for propriety. "Sit here. Let' talk."

Colin climbed back into bed, careful not to tweak his fractured rib. He leaned on fat pillows stacked against the headboard and hoped he smelled okay.

Delfina's scent of sage smoke, wildflowers and salty ocean spray was intoxicating. Sitting cross-legged with no panties on, she was also emitting mind-blowing sex pheromones. It took all of Colin's self-control to resist reaching for her.

"I'm so ashamed, Colin." Delfina's cheeks were flushed. She turned away and looked out the window. "I don't know if I'll ever get over what I just did."

"There's nothing to be ashamed of, Delfina." Colin swallowed. He had a lump in his throat, remembering his own grief, as well feeling empathy for Delfina. "Grief is an unpredictable emotion. It sometimes makes us do things we don't understand. I'll never judge you. Truth. I'm flattered that your instinct told you to trust me, and you thought I seemed safe and comforting. I truly want to be that for you. I hope you'll always feel like you can trust me."

Delfina turned back to face Colin. Her chest rose and fell like ocean waves.

"Mind if I ask you a personal question?" asked Colin.

"Go ahead." A hero facing a dragon, Delfina met Colin's eyes.

"I've never seen any guys hanging around you, except your cousin, Hawk." Colin swallowed again, trying not to stutter. "I assume you don't have a boyfriend? Or girlfriend?"

"That's a correct assumption, Officer Dawson." Delfina tried to smile.

"Why aren't you in a relationship? You're so amazing. Intelligent, beautiful …" Colin's brow furrowed. "What's the deal?"

"Wow. You ask really hard questions." Delfina frowned and shook her head. She looked down and fidgeted with the friendship bracelet on her wrist, then took a deep breath. "It's secret. No one knows, except my mother—and the San Diego police."

"I promise I'll protect your secret, Delfina."

She studied Colin's face.

Finally, she took another deep breath. "Okay. It was my thirteenth birthday, thirteen years ago, my last year of middle school. It was a beautiful day in May, like today. My best friend Cathy and I had the same birthday. That day, we gave each other friendship bracelets, like this one."

"Wait," said Colin. "When's your birthday?"

"May 12. When's yours?"

"July 10. But please, go on."

"So anyway, our houses were on the same street, and after school that afternoon, we walked home together, as usual. We took a pretty path that skirted the edge of town along the base of a mountain wilderness area. To make a long story short, a man attacked us from behind. He grabbed us both by the neck and chloroformed us. We were both petite, and I could tell that he was an adult man, tall and strong. We never saw his face.

He blindfolded us and drove us to an isolated area in the mountains. I woke up while he was raping me, forcing himself into me. I was a virgin. It hurt, really really badly.

"I tried to fight back, and he beat me. I thought he was going to kill me. Then Cathy moaned. He stopped hitting me and raped her. Afterward, he left us there."

Colin reached for Delfina's hand, but she pulled away.

"It's a miracle we didn't die of exposure or get eaten by a mountain lion or some other wild animal. Just about twilight, some hikers found us, called 911, and we were taken to the hospital.

"My mom urged us both to go through a forensic medical exam. They got evidence from me, but my friend Cathy refused. The exam was humiliating. Turns out, I might as well have refused too. The police never did anything with my rape kit. My mom went to the cops over and over again, trying to get them to find my rapist, but they never did. My friend Cathy ended up committing suicide."

Delfina bowed her head and twisted her bracelet. A tear rolled down her cheek. "So that's it." She raised her chin. Her fierce, brave eyes met Colin's. "I've just avoided guys, or anything to do with sex, ever since then."

"That should never have happened to you, or to your friend," said Colin. "I'm so, so sorry."

Rage and sorrow boiled inside him. His heart broke for this woman. He was so choked with emotion that it was difficult to speak. He chose his words carefully. "I can only imagine how tough it's been for you to hold this secret. I know it took a lot of courage for you to tell me. Thank you for trusting me enough to share. I will always be a hundred percent here for you, to listen or help in any way I can."

The girl sitting on the bed next to him seemed as fragile as a wildflower. He was overwhelmed with a need to protect her.

"Please don't take this the wrong way, Delfina. I know you are a strong, capable, courageous woman, but please let me help keep you safe."

Delfina stared at Colin. Her eyes were clouded, and her face looked numb. "I guess we have something in common," she said. "We've both had horrible trauma. I don't want to diminish what you've been going through, but maybe I have some PTSD too."

"You probably do. I think a lot of people may be walking around with undiagnosed Post Traumatic Stress Disorder. In fact, it may be a global mental health crisis."

"I haven't noticed anyone coming around to see you since you took that beating," said Delfina. "I assume you're not dating anyone either?"

Colin sighed. He'd spent most of his life protecting himself from exposing his private life, his vulnerabilities and weakness. He wanted to be seen as strong, an invulnerable hero-type. He felt his usual defensive walls going up.

"Colin?" Delfina touched his hand and smiled. His resistance melted away.

All right, do this. She told me her big secret. It's only fair that I do the same.

"Yeah, well, you know that I was raised by two women, my mother and grandma, right?"

Delfina nodded.

"So, they were both hard-core feminists. They taught me the importance of healthy boundaries, never touch a person without permission, and no means no. By the time I got to high school, I understood that male chauvinism and misogyny are as ignorant as any other forms of prejudice, and that all people should be respected as equals.

"I was as horny as any other teenager, and I had plenty of good friends—male and female—who were sexually active, but sport fucking and using people for sex didn't appeal to me. I decided to be celibate until I actually fell in love with someone. Meanwhile, I put my whole focus on academics and sports.

"When I enlisted and served in Afghanistan, I saw guys bullying and taking advantage of women soldiers. I had a friend who was raped. It made me sick. It was just one of the many things during my time in the Army Rangers that caused me to feel like I was in way over my head, in a psychological, existential crisis. As you know, I got injured and ended up in the military hospital with traumatic brain injury and PTSD. So, there was no romance in my life at that point.

"After the army, when I went to college, I met a girl, a woman, who kind of took me over. She came on to me really fast and just acted like she owned me. I happily went along. She seduced me, taught me everything she knew about sex and lovemaking, and believe me, she was incredible— a real expert. I thought I was in love with her. In retrospect, I think I was addicted to her, and to the sex. But then, out of the clear blue, she dropped me. Just ghosted me. I never heard from her again.

"I went crazy over it for a while. I figure she got fed up with me because I'm so fucked up. I'm just not good relationship material. I'm definitely not worthy of you, Delfina. You deserve someone way better than me."

"No! Colin, that's not true. You are so sweet and kind, and strong, honorable, and heroic and brave. You're smart, and you know about nature, and you love the environment. And …" Delfina paused. She cradled his bruised cheek in her palm, then kissed her index finger, brushed it under his split lip, and dotted it on the dimple in his chin. "You're really handsome." With the gleam back in her eyes, she traced his tattooed biceps and ran her eyes across his abs. "Your body is smoking hot, Colin."

Colin's heart hammered against his chest. Intense desire gnawed like a burr inside him. But there was something else—a new sensation, a glimmer of hope that he might be able to attain actual happiness and true love, with this woman.

30

TWENTY-FIVE MILES NORTH of Clark's Landing, on Stage Coast Road in the coastal village of Pescadero, Duarte's Tavern was founded in 1894 by Frank Duarte, a Portuguese immigrant.

Duarte bought the building—constructed of old growth redwood logged from nearby forests—for approximately twelve dollars' worth of gold. He bought his first barrel of whiskey from a distillery in Santa Lucia and sold drinks for ten cents a shot or three shots for two bits. He'd set a barrel of whiskey on the bar for fishermen, whalers, cowboys, farmers, loggers, outlaws, and locals, who brought in their bottles to fill up. The original bar hasn't changed much over the almost hundred-fifty years since it was built in the 1890s.

Eventually, the Duartes added a larger, adjoining redwood building to accommodate a family-friendly restaurant, which is still operated, now by the fifth generation of Duartes. The restaurant is well known for classically prepared Dungeness crab, Pacific salmon, and other local catches fresh off the boat, as well as fresh steamed artichokes, delicious artichoke and green chili soup, and homemade olallieberry pie prepared according to recipes Mama Emma used in the 1880s. Duarte's has always opened daily at eight a.m.

On Tuesday, May 3, at ten in the morning, Agent Kozel—having started drinking at eight a.m.—exited the historic tavern, and slurred an insult at Rafe's dog.

"That's the ugliest fuckin' dog I ever seen."

The red-bearded ICE agent swayed and hocked a loogie on the sidewalk in front of Duarte's Tavern, just inches from Rafe's boots.

Zack, the dog, bared his teeth and growled.

Rafe held up his hand in a stop gesture. "Zack, settle."

The dog sat down quietly at Rafe's heel, but kept his ears pinned back.

"Hey … You're that cowboy from the Cougar Creek Ranch, ain't you?" said Kozel. "What cha' doin' up here in Pescadero?"

"I was born and raised in this watershed. I live a little ways up the coast, on San Gregorio Creek. Just picking up some breakfast pastries at the bakery. How about you, Kozel?"

"How'd you know my name, cowboy?"

"I watched your pissing match with the marshal by the sheriff's homicide investigation tent down the highway at Cougar Creek Coast Ranch. What're you doing here?"

"None of your fuckin' business. So how come you got such an ugly, vicious dog? He looks like a coyote, or a hyena." Kozel laughed like a hyena.

"Actually, I've never seen him growl at anyone until you. Zack's a purebred cattle dog: friendly, loyal, smart, great at his job, and just about my best friend." Rafe smiled at Zack, and the dog rolled his eyes and smiled back at Rafe.

"Have a nice day, Kozel."

Without waiting for a response, Rafe turned on the heel of his ranch boot and ambled down the sidewalk of the one-street town to his parked horse trailer.

Zack trotted beside him.

When Rafe greeted Amigo, the horse shook his head and stomped the trailer's floor.

"Vámonos." Rafe opened the truck cab door and Zack jumped in.

★   ★   ★

Rafe drove down a side street and pulled up in front of one the town's old but well-maintained Victorian cottages.

"Be back in a few," he told Amigo. The horse lowered his head and nickered.

With Zack at his heels, Rafe strolled up the garden path and through the front door and dropped a bag of pastries on his grandmother's kitchen table.

"Thank you, sweetheart," said his grandma. She turned from the sink, wiped her hands—age-worn but still strong—on her apron, and gave Rafe a hug.

Rafe's grandpa set a steaming cup of coffee on the table at Rafe's place. "Here you go. Glad you could set a spell with us this mornin'."

Zack drank from the cat's water bowl, then settled under the kitchen table at Rafe's feet. The resident cat, Meatloaf, retreated to the window seat, where he flicked his tail, plotting revenge.

Rafe dug into the pile of fluffy yellow just-cooked scrambled eggs, harvested fresh from his grandparents' coop, and the heap of fried potatoes, bacon, and assorted breakfast pastries.

"I'm proud of you for carrying on our family tradition, boy." Grandpa helped himself to more potatoes. "Cowboying for five generations here in California, and who knows how many hundreds of years back in the Azores? That ain't nothin'."

"Maybe someday you'll meet a nice girl and start a family," said Grandma, smiling lovingly at her son's child.

"My great-grandson would be a sixth generation California cowboy." Grandpa laughed. "Now wouldn't that be somethin'."

"Sorry Gammy and Pops, but it's pretty hard to meet girls out on the coast prairie. And anyway, the way things are changing—with BLM trying to turn our grazing land into a park for mountain bikers, plus mechanization replacing human workers, and drought maybe turning the prairie to dust— there may not even be cowboys by the next generation."

"At least these Danishes haven't changed yet," said Gammy. "Pescadero Bakery is still as wonderful as it was when I was a girl."

Rafe got up and poured kibble for Zack into Meatloaf's bowl. The cat laid his ears back, hissed, and jumped off the window seat. He snuck up behind Zack, who was enjoying his kibble, and—claws out— batted the dog's tail. Then he rapidly scooted outside through his kitty door.

Rafe returned to the table for a second helping of bacon and potatoes, and everyone except Meatloaf ate contentedly.

"Thanks for breakfast, Gammy and Pops." Rafe finished his last swallow of coffee and patted his stomach. "Love you. Gotta get going.

I need to check the fencing in the upper tree line. Think some of it might have blown down with all that wind we had last night."

★　　　★　　　★

The twenty-five mile drive down the coast to Cougar Creek Coast Ranch never got old. Rafe tuned his radio to a local California country station and sang along at the top of his lungs with Cody Johnson's hit song, "'Til You Can't." The lyrics lifted him up, strengthening his resolve to show his love to his family, appreciate his work every day, chase his dreams, and find the love of his life while he still had the chance.

Orange poppies and sky-blue lupines exploded along the roadside. He rolled down his windows and savored the fresh, salty air, heavy with a sweet lupine scent that evoked childhood memories of grape Kool-Aid.

Hundreds of migratory Sooty Shearwaters skimmed low over the ocean like a huge black cloud. Above, white cumulous cotton balls scudded across the lupine-tinted sky, casting shadows on the changeable water. Everywhere Rafe looked, the world felt vividly alive, sparkling like freshly polished crystal.

The truck and horse trailer cruised past Pigeon Point Lighthouse, Route 1 Brewery, Año Nuevo Elephant Seal Reserve, Costanoa Lodge, Pie Ranch, Rancho del Oso, Greyhound Rock, China Beach, the original organic strawberry farm stand, and the abalone research station. At Agua Pura Creek Truck Road, north of Panther Beach, Rafe turned inland, through a fragrant eucalyptus tree tunnel full of fluttering Monarch butterflies.

He unlocked a gate and parked his truck and trailer in a dirt lot next to a ramshackle old cheese barn.

"Hey, friend, we're here."

Amigo whinnied. Rafe asked him to back out of the trailer, then turned him out to the corral for water and feeding.

Once Rafe had curried and saddled Amigo, they rode out across the pasture. Rafe held cattle in this pasture several times a year for inspecting, tagging, sorting, vaccinating, and for deworming the new calves.

As he approached the pasture's far fence line, he squinted in disbelief. "Oh, hell no."

The fence had been cut.

Mountain bikers had trespassed into his cattle operation again, cutting his fences and carving a deep bike trail through his pasture. Good thing he'd discovered this breach before bringing the herd down here.

Anger and frustration boiled through Rafe. Those mountain bikers acted like they owned this land, like they could do anything they wanted. If he fixed the fence, they'd just cut it again. And Rafe's boss, Mr. DeCosta—whose family had held the grazing lease for this land for four generations—didn't want any trouble. Old DeCosta was worried that if he stirred things up, the new BLM manager might threaten to take away his family's lease.

Rafe was responsible for the health and safety of DeCosta's herd. Cut fences put the cattle in danger. What should he do? There had to be some way to rein in those entitled fancy bicycle motherfuckers.

Amigo whinnied nervously. "Sorry, Amigo. Don't worry. It's a beautiful day." Rafe patted the bay roan's neck. "Let's go see what else is going on out here today."

Rafe rode up toward the tree line along the east side of the creek, through the sweet-smelling coastal prairie. Zack gave a happy bark and ran on ahead, his head appearing and disappearing in the tall grasses as he leapt after a small flock of wild turkeys.

Wind blew the grass in whooshing waves. The cowboy buttoned up his heavy wool jacket, turned the collar up around his ears, and pulled the black wool Stetson he wore on cold days tighter down on his head. He rubbed his hands together, glad for his wool-lined leather gloves.

The weather this spring had been flip-flopping like a fish out of water. Cold one day and hot the next; sunny, then stormy. But the wildflowers on the coastal prairie were in full bloom today: Indian paintbrush, blue-eyed grass, buttercups, tidy tips, owl's clover. Like an artist's painting, color accented the many shades of green in the landscape with brush strokes of crimson and scarlet, cerulean blue, magenta, lemon yellow, violet, orange, and rose.

A fat, three-feet-long gopher snake slid away from Amigo's hooves through the grass. Since the 2020 fire, the rodent population had exploded in the regenerating environment, and with all the harvest mice and gophers had come many more snakes. Rafe kept his senses alert for rattlers.

Looking up, he watched newly arrived migrant Purple Martins making acrobatic maneuvers in the air above the tall grass to capture wasps and grasshoppers. A hunting Northern Harrier hawk glided low over the prairie and disappeared beyond a dip in the rolling land. Wind pushed across the ridgeline, making tall trees moan.

As Rafe rode higher, a distant hushed roar reached his ears from the white lines of giant waves crashing along the coast far below. He disturbed a covey of California Quail, and the birds rose around him in a loud whoosh of wings.

"Whoa." Rafe signaled Amigo to stop in front of another fence-cut, and a deep ugly scar in the ground where bikers had excavated more trail. A mama cow and her calf had wandered through the gap in the cut fence. They were crossing the creek onto a neighbor's property.

With a squeeze of his knees, Rafe urged Amigo to hurry after the wayward cow and calf. He caught up with them, herding them back across the creek, then wired the fence back together. He'd have to keep an eye on this. The bikers would probably cut it again.

He had no choice but to discuss this with his boss.

Black clouds that had blown overhead from the north released a sudden cloudburst. Rafe hunched his shoulders and faced into the squall. Waterfalls of rain poured off his hat brim.

He reached the tree line as the clouds blew by, the wind calmed, and the sun came out.

A shy bobcat hiding behind a tangled patch of poison oak blinked at him as he passed. Under the trees, forest flowers—sticky monkey, wild iris, and Solomon's seal—bloomed as if the present moment were all that mattered. Thick fallen branches, those dangerous heavy widow-makers, were strewn on the forest floor—evidence of last night's windstorm.

As Rafe rode deeper into the redwood forest, sky holes in the dense tree canopy afforded glimpses of blue above.

The trail narrowed and steepened.

The cowboy rounded a bend high above the riparian canyon, at the confluence of San Vicente and Mill Creeks. He checked his bearing on his smartwatch. He was about a mile above the old quarry, at 1,271 feet of elevation.

A soft sound turned his blood cold.

"Oh, no."

He squeezed back the reins and Amigo stopped.

Rafe tilted his head, and listened.

There it was again. He strained to hear.

"Help."

31

"**H**ELP ME."

Rafe peered over the edge of the cliff.

About sixty feet down the sheer three-hundred-fifty-foot drop to the old quarry, a young face peered out from under a pile of forest debris and fallen tree limbs. The tangle appeared to be precariously held in place by a large boulder partially buried in the earth.

"Help."

The narrow trail didn't present much elbow room. Rafe dismounted carefully and leaned over the side.

The boy's face was ashen, his eyelids nearly closed. Teeth chattering. *Hypothermia. The kid's fading.*

Rafe glanced overhead. *Helicopter rescue? Not enough time to wait for that.*

"Hold still." Rafe called.

The youngster's eyes opened but appeared unfocused.

"I've got you," said Rafe. "Don't move."

He pulled out the mini two-way satellite communication device secured in the side pocket of his pack and hit the button to send a preconfigured message: "Recipient: local rescue organizations alert via email and SMS. Critical / We are in a potentially life-threatening situation. Air rescue needed. GPS coordinates will track as I move. Please respond ASAP."

He clipped the device to his inside jacket pocket.

Then he grabbed Amigo's padded collar from his saddlebag. This was not the first time Rafe had needed to ask Amigo to haul something while out in the mountains. He'd come prepared. He slipped the collar over Amigo's ears and head and adjusted it to fit snugly against the horse's chest. Then he rummaged in his saddlebag for the hame—a pair of curved pieces of wood that fit into the collar. He attached the hame into each side of the collar, then brought ropes through the hame and the saddle, and down along Amigo's sides to a well-rooted Douglas fir tree. Keeping his eye on the angle of the trace coming from the hame down to the point of pull, Rafe wrapped the rope ends around the tree trunk using slip loops to rig a pulley that he would attach to himself. While he rigged Amigo with the improvised harness, Rafe spoke words of comfort and gratitude to his horse.

Then he set himself up for a body rappel.

Facing horse and tree—his anchor points—and straddling the rope, Rafe reached down, with his left hand in front of his body and his right hand behind, and pulled the rope up to his crotch. While still holding the rope in front with his left hand, with his right hand he brought the rope over his right hip, across his chest, and up over his left shoulder. He grabbed the dangling rope from behind his back and gave it an extra wrap around his right arm.

Carefully, he began his rappel over the edge. Zack watched anxiously.

With his back facing downhill, Rafe walked straight over the ninety-degree cliff backward, careful to keep his wrapped hip aimed downward. He used his left hand as a guide, breaking as needed by bringing the rope across his body with his right hand. As he inched down, he took care not to disturb the unstable ground.

When he got closer, Rafe recognized the boy as Johnny Taylor, a local high school kid from Clark's Landing who often walked alone around Cougar Creek Coast Ranch. Rafe had occasionally observed him talking to the cows.

The teen's breathing was shallow, erratic. Lips purple. Arms and legs were limp.

"What happened? Speak to me, boy."

Johnny tried to form words. He choked and gurgled.

"Rain—ran bo."

A mountain lion snarled from a rock ledge nearby. Zack bared his teeth at the cougar and growled.

"No! You can't have this one." Rafe grabbed a rock and threw it.

The puma pivoted and scrambled away.

Rafe turned back to the boy. "I've got you. It's okay. Stay still."

Careful not to dislodge the unstable pile of branches and debris from last night's windstorm, Rafe fashioned the end of his rope into a secure harness around the boy. Then, muscles straining, he lifted a large tree limb off Johnny's leg. The boy screamed in pain.

The boulder supporting the boy dislodged, and a landslide of debris tumbled three hundred feet down the mountain. It would have taken Johnny too, had he not been roped into Rafe's harness.

Rafe whistled.

Amigo began pulling. Slowly, as Amigo walked up the trail, the rope slid around the tree like an old mill turning, and Rafe and the boy were hoisted up the steep slope.

Once up top, Rafe quickly untied the boy, Amigo, and himself, laying Johnny on his back on the trail.

Shallow, erratic breathing. Pinpoint pupils. Cold, clammy skin. Purple fingernails. Was the kid trying to say rainbow? Possibly a Fentanyl overdose. Keep him awake.

Rafe made a fist and vigorously rubbed his knuckles on the boy's breastbone. Johnny's eyes opened, he groaned, and his eyes shut. Rafe tried rubbing his chest again.

Unresponsive. Rafe checked for a pulse. *Can't feel it.*

He made sure the boy's airway was clear, then started chest compressions and rescue breathing.

Finally, the kid gasped and started breathing on his own. Rafe rolled him on his side. The boy vomited.

While Johnny lay on his side, breathing shallowly, Rafe rummaged in his saddlebag for the naloxone that Lieutenant Rosa had instructed all deputized searchers to carry.

The cowboy injected naloxone into the boy's shoulder muscle.

As Johnny began to revive, chopper beaters sounded overhead. Rafe looked up. A search and rescue helicopter was lowering a member of the rescue team, with a harness to lift the boy to safety.

32

THE NEXT MORNING, Wednesday, May 4, a steady spring rain tapped at the windows of Lieutenant Rosa's office. The Pineapple Express—what meteorologists call an atmospheric river—was blowing in from over the Pacific.

FBI Agent George Chen put a tin of oatmeal cookies on Rosa's desk. "My wife makes great cookies. Healthy and delicious."

He handed Rosa a Starbucks latte, then nodded to Marshal Stone. "Carlos told me you'd be joining us this morning. Wasn't sure about your morning beverage of choice, so I just got you a straight coffee, dark, and some packets of cream and sugar."

"Coffee, black. That's perfect. Thanks, Chen." The tall man dressed in black languidly uncrossed his legs and leaned forward in one of Rosa's visitor chairs to claim his coffee.

"I wouldn't dare say this cookie is better than my wife's," said Rosa, "but … Umm. Chewy, raisins and walnuts, just the right amount of sweet … Umm." Rosa brushed crumbs off his tie and reached for a second cookie. "Exactly the midmorning boost I needed. Thanks."

"How's that youngster, Johnny Taylor, doing—the boy that the cowboy rescued yesterday?" Marshal Stone asked.

"He's still in ICU, in a coma," said Rosa. "Fourteen-year-old kid, by himself out in the mountains overnight in a windstorm, fallen over a cliff, leg crushed under a heavy tree limb. Hypothermia, dehydration, exposure, cuts, contusions, a fractured tibia. On top of all that, add a massive drug overdose. I hope he pulls through, but right now, it's anybody's guess."

"What in the world was he doing up there?" asked Chen.

"Do they know what drugs he took?" asked Marshal Stone.

Rosa skimmed the report. "Dextroamphetamine, amphetamine, fentanyl, naloxone, and—get this—a small amount of xylazine."

"Xylazine?" asked Chen. "The animal sedative found in Ramona Cuera's body?"

"That's right."

"This kid lived in Clark's Landing, right?" Marshal Stone reached for another cookie.

Rosa nodded. "We need to interview Johnny's parents, siblings, and friends."

"My surveillance at the gate where the drugs are being sold has been pretty lively," said Stone. "Two different perps regularly come down the mountain from the quarry area to the gate to sell. Some youngsters buy small amounts, and a few buy in quantity to sell at the high school. I have video, and good face shots of the dealers and buyers." Marshal Stone brushed cookie crumbs off his fingers and handed Chen a thumb drive. "I was hoping your agency could run these through facial rec."

"Of course," said Chen.

"Why haven't you brought the dealers in?" asked Rosa. "What are you waiting for?"

The squall outside intensified. Palm trees waved wildly in the howling wind. Rain pinged angrily against the windows

"The dealers are just little rats," said Marshal Stone. "I think they're coming from a camp up in that canyon, somewhere around the quarry. I want to locate and exterminate the whole nest. But I don't want to stir it up until I'm sure how the drugs are coming in. I've been following a suspected international fentanyl trafficker for the last four years. Her trail led me here. She's the apex predator, the one I want. Going in too soon runs the risk of scaring her away."

"The proximity of Ramona Cuera's murder and Johnny Taylor's fentanyl overdose makes me wonder if and how they might be connected," said Chen.

"Let's go over again what we know about fentanyl." Rosa pulled up a brainstorming app on the smart board. As Chen and Stone reviewed the facts, Rosa made notes on the board, putting key words and phrases in circles, and drawing arrows to connect related circles.

"I'll start," said Chen. "Fentanyl overdose has become a leading cause of death—especially for young Americans between ages eighteen to forty-five—since 2019, surpassing suicide, car accidents, COVID-19, and cancer, and topped only by gun violence."

"China is the primary source of the precursor chemicals for fentanyl manufacture," said Marshal Stone. "Illicitly manufactured fentanyl is controlled by the Triad crime syndicate and produced in China at massive, unregulated, industrial-scale labs, like Shanghai Fast-Fine Chemicals. Some Chinese fentanyl producers are actually subsidized by the Chinese Communist Party, which off-the-record, views illegal drugs as a vital part of its economy. The Chinese government is encouraging this industry through a series of tax breaks, subsidies, grants, and money laundering."

"But China is big and complex," said Chen. "Competing layers of the government are at odds with each other. For example, you might have a provincial official who wants to let these companies keep doing what they're doing because it brings in more revenue for the area, and another official with ethical objections who is trying to stop the flow of illegal fentanyl."

"Through an insider in Homeland Security's international branch of the FBI in Shanghai," said Stone, "I'm connected with an informant who's one of the good guys. With his help, I've was able to identify the kingpin I'm tracking."

"What else do we know about fentanyl?" asked Rosa.

"The DEA estimates that a kilogram—about two pounds—of powdered fentanyl from China can fetch several thousand dollars," said Chen. "But when the powder is transformed into thousands of counterfeit pills, that same two pounds can bring in millions of dollars of profits through street sales."

"Is China producing the counterfeit pills?" asked Rosa.

"No," said Stone. "The powdered fentanyl is shipped from China to Mexico for processing. It's mixed with whatever fillers are on hand: heroin, cocaine, methamphetamines, miscellaneous other prescription and over-the-counter medications, baking soda, sugar, starch, talcum powder, powdered milk, laundry detergent, caffeine, rat poison, and even animal tranquilizers like xylazine."

"Jesus, Mary, and Joseph," said Rosa. "It's worse than I thought. The public needs to be made aware of this. What kind of pills are we looking for?"

"These fentanyl-laced monstrosities are manufactured for consumption in various forms," said Chen. "Powders, drops on blotter paper that look like small candies, liquids packaged with eye droppers or in nasal sprays, and pills that look like real prescription pharmaceuticals."

"And Mexican cartels enlist mules to bring them into the US," said Rosa.

Stone nodded. "Traffickers use private cars, pedestrians, commercial vehicles, boats and planes to smuggle fentanyl into the United States through all ports of entry. They'll use anyone they can to help them move their product, including regular border crossers and even elderly people and teens."

"And China and Mexico are mostly to blame?" Carlos Rosa tapped his finger on his computer mouse, staring at his notes—with circles, highlights, and arrows—projected onto the interactive whiteboard.

"Chinese and Mexican cartels are the biggest players," said Stone. "But organized crime syndicates in Russia, India, Africa, Italy, and other countries are also in the game. The astronomical profits from traffic in drugs, humans, wildlife, and computer hacking, laundered through apparently legitimate businesses, are mostly taken in crypto. Since they're difficult to track, convertible virtual cryptocurrencies like Bitcoin, Ethereum, and Monero are popular with the money launderers, who leverage encrypted mobile communications apps like China's WeChat to move vast sums of money with great speed, discretion, and efficiency."

Chen stared at the brainstorming app on the smart board. "We need to fill this in with names and faces. I'm going to reach out to my contact at DEA. I think it's time we read the Drug Enforcement Agency into this investigation."

"Good idea, Chen," said Rosa. "Meanwhile, let's get back to our original question," "Is there any indication that Ramona's murder and Johnny Taylor's fall over a cliff may be connected? And if so, how?"

"And could either Ramona or Johnny have been users, and gotten crosswise with someone in one of the cartels?" asked Stone.

"From what we've been able to discover," said Chen, "it's unlikely that Ramona was a drug user, or involved in trafficking. Even so,

Romana's blood test detected xylazine, and Johnny had fentanyl and xylazine in his system."

"This mind map is as complex as a spider's web." Rosa shook his head.

Stone's gargoyle smile stretched enigmatically across his face.

33

ROSA AND CHEN AGREED it would be best, out of consideration for the distraught family, to go to the Taylors' home in Clark's Landing in an unmarked car and casual street clothes. They asked a female deputy, Officer Olson, to join them.

From the Coast Highway, they turned right at the Clark's Landing Roadhouse and motored up Main Street through the center of the quiet village. Main Street ended at the small historic church. Chen took a right and followed the curving road toward the mountains. Past the art glass studio, they turned onto Old Coast Road.

Chen drove along the overgrown riparian corridor for a mile. The inexorable creep of wild foliage gave way at the beginning of the row of houses, which Lieutenant Rosa and Warden Colin Dawson had visited two weeks earlier.

Chen proceeded slowly past modest, tidy homes on the left and the wild wooded creek on the right. Rosa recognized the house in front of which he and Colin had met SUV yoga mom Irene Johansen, her daughter with the boing-boing curls, and their Spanish-speaking neighbor, Jorge.

In front of the very last house before tangled habitat threatened to reclaim the road, Chen stopped and parked. In another half mile beyond this house, the road would end at the swinging steel barrier gate, where teens and preteens reportedly bought drugs.

"This is it," said Chen. "Johnny Taylor's house."

Rosa nodded. "Proximity to the buy site."

"So, Johnny Taylor is the youngest of three kids," said Officer Olson, reading from her notes. "His mom is a public school secretary. Dad's a plumber for a well-established company, earning union wages. They bought this home twenty years ago."

Chen shook his head. "Sounds about as stable as it gets."

"Let's get this over with," said Rosa.

They let themselves in to the front yard through a latched gate in a white picket fence, walked along a brick pathway through a well-maintained lawn to the front door, and knocked.

A middle-aged Caucasian woman opened the door.

"Mrs. Taylor? I'm Sheriff's Lieutenant Carlos Rosa. These are my colleagues, FBI Agent George Chen and Deputy Carol Olsen." The officers displayed their badges.

"Yes. Come in. We were expecting you. Thank you for calling first."

Gretchen Taylor's face, voice, and body language gave away the panic and grief she was holding in tight check.

She escorted Rosa, Chen, and Olson into the living room and invited them to sit.

Mr. Taylor joined them. His short hair was tousled and graying at the temples, his khaki slacks wrinkled, and his shirt untucked. His hands trembled.

"First," said Rosa, "we want to say that we are very sorry for what happened to your son, Mr. and Mrs. Taylor. Rest assured he's getting the best care possible. We're all hoping for the best."

Gretchen Taylor removed her glasses and wiped her cheeks and glasses with a handkerchief.

Ron Taylor sat next to his wife on the couch, his right hand on her knee. Their golden retriever, whose name tag said Lupe, got up from his bed in front of the fireplace, sat on Ron's foot, and leaned against his left knee. Ron absently scratched behind the dog's ear.

"Please excuse us," said Ron. "We haven't been sleeping. We're so worried."

"I don't understand how this happened," said Gretchen.

"We are doing our best to find out exactly what happened to your son and who is responsible," said Rosa. "May we ask you a few questions?"

Ron cleared his throat. "We're grateful you're here, Lieutenant Rosa, and we want to cooperate with your investigation, but I must mention that in order for both of us to be here while Johnny is in the ICU, we had to ask Johnny's grandparents to stay with him at the hospital. Gretchen and I need to get back to the hospital to relieve my parents as soon as possible."

"Yes, I understand, of course," said Rosa. "We'll make this as brief as possible. Shall we begin?"

Both parents nodded.

"First, we found drugs in Johnny's system. Were you aware that he was taking anything?"

The parents exchanged a meaningful look.

"Drugs? Are you sure?" Gretchen's brow furrowed. "As far as we know, Johnny is not involved in drugs."

"Have you noticed any changes in his behavior?"

"Our other two children are normal, and do fine in school," said Ron. "But Johnny was diagnosed with ADHD when he was in first grade. We've always had concerns about his behavior."

"After other interventions the school tried were unsuccessful," said Gretchen, "they recommended that we take Johnny to a doctor. The doctor prescribed Ritalin. After about six months on the drug, Johnny was having even more issues in school, and he was also experiencing troubling side effects. The doctor switched him to Adderall. That seemed to help. We kept him on Adderall all the way through elementary. But by middle school, his behavior seemed to have leveled out. We felt that he'd developed positive coping mechanisms."

"The doctor told us that he didn't need the Adderall anymore, so we stopped giving it to him," said Ron.

"I confess that during Johnny's middle school years I got really busy with other things." Gretchen twisted her handkerchief. "My job got very demanding, and I didn't pay as much attention to my baby as I should have. Things seemed to be going well for him. His grades were fine. And while his behavior at home became more withdrawn, we thought that was normal for a middle schooler. Honestly, we went out of our way to give him the privacy and agency we thought he should have by middle school.

I should have been more aware." Gretchen covered her face and sobbed. Ron wrapped his arm around her; Lupe put his head down on Ron's knee.

After a respectful interval, Agent Chen spoke. "According to the hospital, Johnny had traces of dextroamphetamine and amphetamine in his system, among other substances. These chemicals are components of Adderall. Is it possible that Johnny was continuing to medicate himself with Adderall, obtained without your knowledge?"

The parents looked at each other in shock.

"Oh my God. Do you think so? How would he get it?" Gretchen pulled away from her husband and put her hand to her mouth.

"How could we miss something like that?" asked Ron, his face aghast.

Lieutenant Rosa cleared his throat. "Does Johnny have his own bedroom?'

"Yes. Each of our kids has their own room."

"Are your other children here? We'd like to speak with them, too, with your permission."

"They're at soccer practice. They should be home soon."

"Would it be all right if we take a look around Johnny's room?"

"Of course," said Ron. "I'll show you upstairs."

★   ★   ★

At the door to Johnny's room, Rosa, Chen, and Olson slipped on plastic gloves and shoe covers.

"I'll leave you to it then," said Mr. Taylor. He and the dog, Lupe, retreated back downstairs.

The three investigators stood still at the doorway for a full minute, taking everything in, then entered and moved around the room, notating and photographing everything on the walls, surfaces of furniture, and floors.

No red flags. Everything looked pretty typical for a boy Johnny's age.

"I'll take the closet," said Rosa. "Deputy Olsen, search the drawers and shelves. Chen, how about if you check the desk and computer?"

"Here's his phone," said Chen. "I'll get the parents' permission to take the phone and computer back to headquarters."

After twelve minutes of searching, Deputy Olsen said, "Found something."

The deputy held up a sketchbook for Chen and Rosa to see. "I found this on the bookshelf."

A card fluttered out from its pages. She put the sketchbook on Johnny's desk. Rosa picked the card up off the floor.

"This is an art print by Hawk, Delfina's cousin," said Rosa. He turned over the card and read the handwritten note on the back. "Johnny, you're a gifted artist. Keep going. Never give up. Your friend, Hawk."

Agent Chen turned the pages of the sketchbook. "These are drawings and watercolors from Cougar Creek Coast Ranch. Not bad. Landscapes, flowers, trees, cows, birds, people."

"Bag it, and the card," said Rosa. "Let's keep looking."

Ten minutes later, Agent Chen held up a plastic baggie full of blue, white, and orange pills. "Found something."

Mr. Taylor appeared in the doorway. "Excuse me, Officers. My other two kids just came home from soccer practice. You said you wanted to speak with them?"

★   ★   ★

Pete was a senior at Playa Azul High. His sister Susan was a sophomore. They sat together in the living room with the investigators. Both of Johnny's siblings appeared clear-eyed, healthy, clean-cut, and focused.

"Were you aware that Johnny was taking drugs?" asked Lieutenant Rosa.

"Yeah," said Pete. "We found out about a year ago that he was scoring from some dirty gangbanger up the road."

"We told him to stop," said Susan, "but he got really hostile. He swore at us and told us to mind our own business."

"We threatened to tell our parents, but he cried and begged us not to. Said if we did he'd kill himself." Pete's face and tone revealed disdain and anger—not the emotions Rosa had expected from a boy whose brother was in critical condition in the hospital and might die.

"How did you find out he was using?" asked Chen.

"I was taking a walk along the creek with friends," said Susan. "We saw Johnny at the gate to the quarry road buying something from a guy in a black hoodie. It was obvious what he was doing. I told Pete, and we decided to talk to Johnny together."

"Johnny told us he wasn't taking drugs, he was buying Adderall." Pete rolled his eyes in contempt. "He said he still needed it to cope, and our parents had cut him off."

"He claimed he couldn't deal with his life without it," said Susan, "but our parents were too clueless to understand."

"We warned him that the stuff he was getting from that pusher was most likely fake, and probably dangerous," said Pete, "but he wouldn't listen."

"What do you know about the dealer? Can you describe him?" asked Chen.

"I didn't see his face," said Susan. "Just his back. It was only that one time. Since then, my friends and I have stayed away from that place."

"Are you sure the person selling drugs to Johnny was male?"

Susan shrugged. "Probably."

"Height? Build? Race?"

"I'd guess he was under six feet tall," said Susan. "His clothes were bulky so I can't say anything about build. Same with race. His skin was totally covered. I couldn't tell."

"Do you know of any other people who might be buying drugs there? Maybe some of Johnny's friends?"

"Johnny really didn't have any friends," Pete answered.

"It's true," said Susan. "He's a total loner."

"We know there are kids at school who get drugs at the gate, but my friends and I don't hang with any of them, personally." Pete's knee was bouncing up and down nervously. He glanced at his expensive smartwatch.

"We found a sketchbook in Johnny's room with drawings from the Cougar Creek Coast Ranch," said Rosa. "Did he go there often?"

"All the time," said Susan. "Lots of us townies from Clark's Landing climb over the fence to hike. Johnny spent lots of time there, wandering up into the hills. He liked to draw and paint, and take photos."

"And he liked to talk to the cows," said Pete.

"Photos?" Lieutenant Rosa made a note in his pocket notebook. "We didn't find a camera."

"He used his phone's camera," Susan said, "and uploaded everything to his computer."

"I don't mean to be rude," said Pete, "but can you excuse me? I have college applications to work on, and homework."

"Thank you both," said Lieutenant Rosa. "I think we're done for now. We're sorry about what happened to your brother. We're hoping he pulls through. If either of you thinks of anything else that might help us identify the drug dealer or shed light on who hurt Johnny, please contact me. Here's my card."

Pete had already left the room before Rosa finished speaking. He handed his card to Susan.

34

T HE FOLLOWING DAY, Friday, May 6, Delfina served Colin lunch at a pique assiette mosaic table on her patio. It was a quintessential spring day on the Monterey Bay, seventy-three degrees with a clear blue sky. Colorful majolica flowerpots on the patio bloomed with daffodils, crocus, tulip, and hyacinth. Anna's and Allen's hummingbirds zoomed overhead on their way to and from the hanging feeders.

Through a rose-covered arbor, Colin watched bright yellow goldfinches bathing in a birdbath. He took a deep breath, luxuriating in the beauty of Delfina's healing garden.

"It's hardly been two weeks since those cops beat you, Colin. Are you sure you feel strong enough to go to the barn dance tonight?"

Colin's forehead wrinkled. He ached for her to break through her reserve again, the way she'd surprised him after her mother's funeral. But since then, nothing of that sort had happened.

"A barn dance? Yes. Maybe not a barn raising," he said. "But getting out with you and doing a little dancing?" Colin licked his lips and smiled. "Yes, ma'am."

"Are you sure? The doctor said it would take about six weeks for your ribs to heal, and up to twelve for full recovery of your dislocated shoulder. Your physical therapy isn't even going to start for another two weeks."

Colin sat straighter and stretched his back. "As long as I don't go wild at the dance and try to lift you up and swing you around or anything like that, I'll be fine."

Delfina laughed. "That sounds fun, but definitely not this time."

Colin rubbed his hand over his still tender face. His two-week beard was past the bristly stubble phase—soft, but irritating. The fuzz over his upper lip, around his jaw and chin had filled out, but the beard still felt patchy on his upper cheeks and under his lower lip. "I'd really like to shave this off, but I think it would hurt too much right now."

"I kind of like it."

Delfina's smile flustered him.

He concentrated on finishing his soup and sandwich.

"Colin, Lieutenant Rosa called while you were napping to ask how you're doing. Your friend James, from Route 1 Tavern called too."

"Hmm." Colin raised his eyebrows. "That's nice."

"I'm looking forward to seeing my friends at the barn dance," said Delfina. "I asked friends and family not to come by while you were healing. I thought you could use the peace and quiet."

"Thanks. I wondered why the house was so empty."

"Colin, you've told me you don't have family, and you don't seem to have many close friends around here either. Are you lonely?"

"Nah. I like being alone."

"You're still having nightmares, aren't you?" she asked.

"Yeah. Just something I've learned to live with. One thing I'm not used to, though, is this damn cougar bite on my wrist. It just won't heal."

"Let me see."

Colin showed her his wrist, a raised blue-black scar in the shape of a puma spread across it. He rubbed it. "It constantly bothers me. It kind of itches and aches."

Delfina examined the scar. Her brows pulled together. "I can get you some salve that might help. Colin, I've been wanting to talk with you again about what happened when you found my mom. You said that at first you thought she was a mountain lion. Do you think it's possible that—?"

"Whoa. No way. I didn't say I thought she was a mountain lion. I said that at first I thought it looked like she was, but I know I was hallucinating. I'm not completely crazy, Delfina. My PTSD brain may be a little off, but

I've still got some grasp on reality most of the time. I know it is not possible for a human to change into an animal."

"All right. Just checking. So, are you ready to take that shower?"

"Yes, please. The sponge baths have been wonderful, but—." His eyes rolled back involuntarily as his body responded to the memory of her warm water basin, natural sponge, the medicinal soap that stung a little, her wild lilac scent and gentle salving caresses over his wounds and bruises. When she bathed him, his back would arch, his buns squeeze, and he'd strain his hips, praying for her to wrap her hand around his dick. All he could think about was having sex with her. But she'd hand him the sponge and a towel every time, leaving him alone to wash himself below the waist.

"A real shower sounds like heaven to me right now."

"Okay." Delfina stood, and moved the lunch things onto a tray at a nearby side table. "I have everything set up for you in the bathroom. Fresh washcloth and towel, the liquid soap that the doctor recommended, and the new clothes Hawk and I bought for you. Everything's there, on top of the bathroom cabinet. Probably be a good idea to leave the door ajar a little so I can hear you in case you need help."

"I'll be fine. Thank you again for going to all this trouble, Delfina. You've been amazingly kind and generous." The look on Colin's face did not hide his desire.

"It's been a pleasure," said Delfina.

Did he imagine that the word pleasure seemed to carry innuendo? She leaned in closer and squeezed his hand. Their eyes said things they weren't ready to say out loud.

Colin's face flushed. He longed to lose himself in her unexplored wilderness.

She released Colin's hand and picked up the tray. "You know where the bathroom is. Just holler if you need anything."

Delfina left the room, but her fragrance lingered. Colin's heart raced at the memory of her touch.

35

T HE MUSIC HAD ALREADY STARTED when Colin and Delfina entered Agua Pura Farm's Spring barn dance on the first Friday night in May, just after sunset.

Live fiddle, guitar, mandolin, piano, and recorder rocked the weathered wooden structure with old-timey Americana square dance and contra dance tunes—a blend of Appalachian, English, French, and Celtic folk music.

Most of the musicians were local, a few from farther afield up and down the coast—Monterey, San Francisco, and even a popular fiddler from Portland. A concertina and a dulcimer player had come all the way from New England to play in this dance, which had been an annual event for many years until the pandemic locked everything down. This was the first time in four years that the dance had been held.

The barn was crowded and overflowing with contagious ebullience. Some people, especially the elderly, still wore protective medical masks, but everyone was clearly overjoyed to be out dancing among family, friends, and neighbors again.

To help the crowd avoid stepping on toes, bumping into one another, or trampling the children as the music played, a homegrown caller sang out instructions to the dancers, who were arranged in several double lines, each with twenty or so couples facing one other.

"Balance to the right. Slide to the left. Catch hands and balance again. Slide to the right and swing your partner. Ladies chain. Left hand star …"

Chairs had been set up around the perimeter of the great room.

Colin and Delfina claimed two unoccupied chairs. For a few minutes, they were content watching the dancers.

The music ended, and people began milling around, some looking for a new partner, some heading to the tack room where a bar and dessert buffet had been set up, some heading to the restroom, and a few people stepping outside for a breath of fresh night air.

The caller announced that the next dance would be a waltz.

Colin stood in front of Delfina, feeling self-conscious in the new jeans and cowboy shirt with pearl-covered snaps that Delfina and Hawk had bought for him. She wore the prettiest blue dress he'd ever seen, with a red silk sash around her waist. Her long black hair shone. She was the most beautiful, exciting woman he'd ever met.

He put his right hand at his waist and, with a straight back, bowed forward from the hips. "May I have this dance?"

"I'd be delighted." Delfina laughed and took the hand Colin offered, and they walked together to join the other dancers.

Despite his usual anxiety and insecurity in crowds, Colin felt confident on the dance floor. His mother had insisted that he learn to dance when he was a boy. As much as he'd hated it at the time, he was grateful now.

Delfina fit in his arms as if they were made for each other. His left hand wrapped around an hourglass waist that flared out to sexy hips. She placed her left hand delicately on his shoulder in the classic waltz posture few people of his generation bothered with. He was pleasantly surprised that Delfina knew the classical old-school waltz. Their right hands joined, elbows bent like the spout of a teapot. They were a feather's wisp away from touching at the chest and hips. Colin felt electrified from the turn-on, and fought to keep his body from doing something embarrassing.

Her back was straight. He had forgotten that her head only came up to his chin. All the time he'd been laid up on her mother's bed while she was taking care of him, she'd seemed taller—so strong, her energy intense and powerful. But now that he was holding her, he realized how petite she was. Surges of yearning pulsed through him. He wanted to take care of her, protect her, be her man.

Dancing with her felt like floating over silky water, alone together in a beautiful safe bubble.

Her face was upturned, so close. He tingled with the realization that she was feeling it too. Should he try to kiss her?

He leaned forward. The space between their lips was but a fraction of an inch, yet the distance across that chasm between them seemed like light years—the distance between existential loneliness and loving connection. Light glinted on her lip like a lighthouse in a distant galaxy. He felt her sweet breath on his lips.

The music ended.

She took a step away.

"May I get you some dessert, or something to drink?" Colin offered.

"Thank you. I'd love a glass of water. I'm just going outside for a minute for some air."

"I'll find you." Colin headed to the tack room for Delfina's water and a beer for himself.

At the bar, he ran into his friend and army comrade-in-arms, James, who had donated beer for the community dance.

"Bro, your face is a mess. I heard about that beating you got from the Fresno County cops. They thought you were a woke lib on your way to a Black Lives Matter rally? Savage, man. I'm so sick of hearing about that kind of shit. So glad you survived it."

"Yeah. It was surreal. I'm recovering pretty well though."

"I saw you dancing with that beautiful Native American girl you met at my tavern. Are you and her a thing now?"

"She's amazing. She's been taking care of me at her house since the beating. I'd like there to be something between us. The chemistry is definitely there. But I'm not sure how she feels."

"I saw the way she looks at you. She's definitely into you, dude."

"I'd better go. Promised to take her some water. Great to see you, brother."

With a beer in one hand and a plastic glass with ice water in the other, Colin looked for Delfina outside under the stars. When he didn't find her there, he returned to the chair where they'd left their jackets. Delfina was not there.

The music had started. Colin's sharpshooter eyes scanned the room.

He spotted her. *Oh hell no.*

She was dancing with that cowboy, Rafe.

She was smiling and laughing, her cheeks pink, her long black hair flying around her shoulders, the hem of her blue dress flaring out above her thighs as she swung and twirled.

Colin's emotions and thoughts went careening all over the map. He struggled to get himself under control. He set Delfina's water glass down on her chair and rushed back outside.

The eerie trill of a Western Screech-Owl calling for his mate echoed through the dark.

Cold night air and the immensity of the stars in a black moonless sky helped him calm down.

Breathe. Deep, slow breaths. Count.

Of course she'd be attracted to Rafe. A real cowboy. A real hero. Everyone's heard about Rafe's epic rescue of that Taylor kid. Rafe is whole, unbroken, a real man. I was fooling myself to think Delfina would be attracted to a broken mess like me. She feels sorry for you, idiot, nothing more.

Colin finished the beer and tossed the bottle in a recycling can.

He lost track of time, his mind spinning through space. A shooting star flared across the sky. A coyote howled in the distance. A new Screech-Owl answered the first one's call. Their duet floated through the night, taunting Colin's aching heart.

He wished he could tear this stupid cowboy shirt with its mother-of-pearl snaps right off his back. She had tried to dress him up like something he wasn't, but now she'd found herself a real cowboy. He hated himself for falling in love with her. He should have known better.

"Colin?"

Delfina stood before him, looking like a goddess, her blue dress sparkling in the starlight.

"I got worried about you. You've been gone a long time. What's going on?"

"What do you think, Delfina?"

"Honestly, I don't know. I was having such a good time dancing, and being with my friends again, I kind of lost track of time. Sorry. Are you all right?"

"I'm fine. I saw how much you were enjoying yourself dancing with Rafe, so I just wanted to give you space to be with him."

"You what? Oh, my God. Are you jealous?"

Colin looked away, up at the stars.

"It was a contra dance," said Delfina, "not a waltz. For contra dancing, you don't really have a partner, you know that. You dance up and down the line with multiple partners, everyone dances together, even kids and old people. It's a community dance, Colin. What's going on? You don't think that Rafe and I—?"

"Well, Delfina, it sure looked a lot like that to me." Colin tried to blink away the tears stinging his eyes. He felt ashamed of his childish emotions.

"You have no right to be jealous, Colin. I can dance with anyone I want to. I'm a free woman."

"Of course I'm jealous. I feel like you've been giving me mixed messages. You dress me up in the clothes you want me to wear, like I'm your boy toy. What am I supposed to think? I was beginning to feel like we were kind of a couple. But now it looks like I belong to you, but you can be with any one you want. How is that fair?"

"I'm sorry if I misled you, Colin. I just thought that you needed help while you recovered from that beating. Since you helped my mom and me, I wanted to return the favor. But I don't have any desire to try to remake you into someone you're not. I do not think you belong to me. And I definitely don't belong to you, or to anyone."

"I get it. I absolutely understand that you're a free woman. And I think it's time that I get out of your way, Delfina. I should move back to my own house. I feel bad that I've already imposed on you so long. I need to get back to work, anyway. Thing is, though, I'm worried that if I leave you alone, something bad might happen to you. I haven't forgotten what you told me—that whoever killed your mom might come after you."

"I understand your need to move back to your own house," said Delfina. "Don't worry about me. I'll be fine by myself, honestly. Do what you need to do, Colin."

They drove back to Delfina's house in silence.

★   ★   ★

The next morning, Saturday, Colin woke at 7:30, dressed, and shoved the few belongings he had at Delfina's house into his backpack. Delfina and Hawk had retrieved his personal effects and his car from the police impound. Colin found his wallet and the keys to his Mustang in his pack.

When he walked into the kitchen, Delfina handed him a smoothie.

"Thank you," said Colin. "I mean it. Really, thank you so much for everything."

"Of course. I—"

"Delfina, when I saw you dancing with Rafe last night, I realized how selfish I've been. You need your space, to be with other people, to own your life."

"No, it's—"

"Goodbye, Delfina."

"Colin. Wait." Delfina grabbed him by the arm.

He turned, and felt as if he were looking into the face of his Destiny.

She reached up and touched his cheek. His eyes dove into that topaz sea. He leaned forward.

They kissed. The press of her breasts and thighs through her sundress burned up and down his body. A spell of timelessness enfolded them. He tumbled into a cosmic vortex of love and desire.

Reaching for self-control, he pulled himself to safety. He felt angry.

"Mixed messages, Delfina. I'll see you later. Bye."

<h1 style="text-align:center">36</h1>

“THANK YOU FOR MEETING ME, Colin,” said Lieutenant Rosa. It was a slow Sunday afternoon, the day after Colin had returned to his own home. There were only a few other people in the Clark's Landing Bakery. Colin and Lieutenant Rosa sat at a window table by the door.

Rosa maintained his stoic façade, but winced internally as he looked at the poor boy's bruised and swollen face. The black eyes had reached the yellow-purple stage; his split lip and cuts had scabbed over.

“I was surprised to hear you were out and about already,” said Rosa. “It hasn't been that long since the hospital released you. Are you sure it's not too soon for you to be back at work?”

“Thanks, but I'm fine, sir. I was going stir-crazy just lying around. I'm being careful, don't worry. I want to thank you again for saving my life, Lieutenant Rosa.”

“Of course. We were lucky that Agent Chen happened to be close by.”

Colin nodded and sipped his green drink through a straw. “What's on your mind? Why did you want to meet?”

“I'd like to go over your discovery of Ramona Cuera's body one more time. I thought you might have remembered something new. Any idea who phoned in that CalTIP? You said that all the caller gave you was a person in camo, a hoodie, and black face paint, with a crossbow, hunting a mountain lion? Were there any other details?"

"Sorry, sir. That was everything. It's an anonymous tip line. I've been over and over the whole thing in my mind. There's nothing else I can tell you. But that reminds me, I've been meaning to give you this card from the Puma Project researchers. I happened to meet them a while ago here at the bakery, and they wanted me to ask you to get in touch with them. A mountain lion they collared went missing, and they're hoping you might've heard something about its whereabouts. They don't know yet about the broken piece of tracking collar I found near the body. I didn't tell them. I figure it's up to you to share whatever you want about evidence in the case." Colin handed Lieutenant Rosa the Puma Project card.

Rosa put the card in his pocket and glanced through the window at the sparkling ocean across the highway. A strong wind scratched lines of whitecaps in the brilliant turquoise water. Rosa's mind wandered with the colorful sails of the wind surfers scudding over the choppy water. This case was jerking him around every which way, like those windsurfers fighting the gusts. He needed to get clarity, focus, steer for the shore, keep his balance. He needed a witness to Ramona's murder.

A bell over the bakery door rang. The door slammed shut on the heels of two teenagers. One of them walked directly up to Rosa's table.

"Oh hey, Sheriff. How's it going?"

Bright red overalls, army surplus boots, blue Mohawk, a ring through her nose, gangly arms and legs. The kid from Agua Pura Farm.

In point of fact, thought Rosa, he wasn't the Sheriff, just a lieutenant in the Sheriff's Homicide Division. But why quibble and possibly alienate this kid who stood grinning at him? Sweet face. No doubt much younger and more innocent than she, er-he, uh-*they* thought.

"Hello there, Frankie. Nice to see you again. What brings you down the hill to the bakery today?"

"Yeah, so my friend Lucy and I are studying together this afternoon. We have a big history test tomorrow. Our teacher says it's important that we learn history so we don't repeat our mistakes of the past."

Lucy was claiming a table for the teens' study session in a back corner of the bakery. Lieutenant Rosa recognized her—the girl with the boing-boing curls. Lucy lived on the road to the quarry, with the SUV yoga mom, Irene.

Come to think of it, he should check in with Irene about her home security surveillance and merge that with the data he'd received from

Marshal Stone's surveillance thumb drive. This investigation felt like a huge boulder rolling willy-nilly downhill. He needed to put on the brakes and catch up with Irene, and also with Marshal Stone. He turned the pages of his notebook and put stars next to earlier notes he'd made.

"Good for you, Frankie. I'm sure you'll do well on your test."

"So, I was wondering," said Frankie, "if you found that guy in camo with the crossbow that was hunting the mountain lion?"

Lieutenant Rosa's eyebrows knit together in surprise; his face wrinkled like a prune, and his jaw fell open. *Ask and ye shall receive,* thought Rosa.

"How do you know about that, Frankie?"

"I was the one who called in the CalTIP. I saw him. Oh, whoops." Frankie put her hand in front of her mouth and giggled. "I know the tip was supposed to be anonymous, but I guess I just let the cat out of the bag."

Rosa's mind raced. He caught Colin's eye. The warden coughed, but said nothing. "I'm grateful to you for coming forward, Frankie. That's brave of you. What exactly did you see? What do you remember?"

"Oh yeah. I totally remember everything. I was just taking a walk in the woods, doing some bird watching. And I saw a mountain lion in the distance. Up on a sandstone outcrop. We have sandstone and mudstone formations that were deposited by flowing water in the late Miocene. There's a raw outcrop of Santa Margarita sandstone near where I was walking, which is really interesting because its much older and usually underneath the Purisima Formation, but it got uplifted and flipped on top by ancient tectonic activity. Sometimes UCSL geology classes come and study it. I love geology, don't you?"

Lieutenant Rosa smiled and nodded. He didn't interrupt. Best to just let her keep talking.

"So anyway, this sandstone outcrop is a golden ochre color, just like the cougar's fur, so it was hard to see. Camouflage, you know? But I spotted it with my binoculars. I have super good binocs. It's really special to see a mountain lion. I haven't seen that many. So, I was watching it climb over the rocks and start down the hill. Then I saw this guy all dressed up in camo gear, with a gnarly crossbow. The dude was stalking it, the puma. It made me sick." Frankie looked over her shoulder and waved at her friend Lucy. Lucy's braces, with fluorescent pink rubber bands, glinted when she smiled back.

"Tell me more, please. What happened?"

"Okay. So, the lion seemed to spot the stalker and started running, then stumbled and rolled down a hill and clawed up a sandstone rock face, then kind of disappeared behind some coyote bush—you know, *Baccharis pilularis.* I don't like to get too close to coyote bush 'cause ticks like to hide in it and ambush warm-bloods that brush by. It was pretty early morning, so the fog was kind of coming in and out. Then I saw this woman. She seemed like she was just out enjoying nature, you know? I noticed she had something around her neck, though. She was tugging at it like she was trying to get it off. Then she looked back. I think she saw the stalker, 'cause she started running. At first, I thought she was wearing like, tan yoga pants and a tight T-shirt, but then I realized she was actually nude. The guy ran after her. Then the woman ran behind some manzanita bushes, and I lost track of her. I think the stalker did too, 'cause he stopped and looked around. Then the mountain lion jumped out of the manzanita and the stalker followed it. He must have hit it with one of his arrows 'cause I heard it scream. Mountain lions scream, you know. It sounds kind of like a woman."

"Are you sure the man shot a mountain lion?"

"Well … that's the part I'm not sure of. Maybe he shot the woman. I guess he did, since you found a dead woman."

"Do you think the stalker could have mistaken the woman for a mountain lion? Maybe he was just a hunter."

"That would be kind of weird. Possible, but it's illegal to hunt mountain lions in California because they're apex predators who keep the whole habitat healthy, and climate change and overpopulation are putting all our wildlife on the brink of extinction. So even if he thought he was hunting a puma, he'd still be a bad guy, right?"

Rosa nodded. "Did you see his face? A description would be very helpful. Height, approximate weight, skin color, identifying marks—tattoos, scars?"

"Yeah. I had my binocs with me, for birding, you know? Got a pretty good look at the psycho. He wore camo pants and a black hoodie, pulled up over his head, and black paint on his cheeks like he thought he was Rambo in jungle recon, ya know? As if. But I could totally tell he was white. Cawcashion. Didn't see any tattoos, but he was taller than the woman."

"Did he have a beard?"

"Don't know. A bandana covered his face from just below his eyes all the way down to below his collar. His eyes were spooky, though. Vampire-zombie-ish, like the walking dead. I'll never forget his eyes."

"How about weight? Fat? Thin?"

"Sorry. Couldn't tell. He had on this flax jacket that made him look puffy. But he could have been skinny underneath. Know what I mean?"

"Flak jacket?"

"Yeah. Flak. He creeped me out so bad I haven't been able to get him out of my head. I actually drew some pictures of him. If you want them, just come up to the farm and I'll give them to you. I hope you catch that motherfucker."

"Me too."

37

ON MONDAY MORNING, FBI Agent George Chen handed Lieutenant Rosa a flash drive.

"This is everything we could dig up on ICE Agent Kozel. As I mentioned when we talked on the phone this morning, your office must be secured before we can open these files."

Lieutenant Rosa straightened his tie and cleared his throat. "Rest assured my new office is secure. It was built to SCIF construction standards laid out in the ICD 705 Technical Specifications."

He pushed a button on his desk console. The door locked, window coverings rolled down, and a synth voice announced, "SCIF protocols activated. Monday, May 9. 11:10:39 a.m."

Agent Chen raised an eyebrow. "Impressive."

Rosa inserted the USB device into his desktop computer, and files appeared on the digital murder board on the wall.

"Sorry it took so long to get you this," said Chen. "Agency research personnel are overloaded, backed up, and as it turns out, this Kozel character has a lot of layers to unpeel. Fortunately, we were able to get the help of other DHS resources to reveal his secrets."

Chen used a Bluetooth pointer to navigate. He clicked to open a file marked *Top Secret.* Homeland Security Investigations | ICE, then opened a folder marked Aleksandr Kozel.

"In 1979, Aleksandr Kozel's parents and older brother—a baby at the time—lived in Belarus, not far from Chernobyl, near the Ukraine border. In 1986, when the Chernobyl nuclear power plant disaster occurred, the family was resettled in Sweden. Two years later, in 1988, they immigrated to the US, where Aleksandr was born. They lived in San Francisco with a wealthy uncle connected to Odessa—the dominant Russian organized crime group in the United States. We have evidence that Aleksandr was inducted into the Odessa Mafia in 2003, at age fifteen.

"Two years later, at age seventeen, Aleksandr, a.k.a. Alex and Al, moved to Arizona. He worked as a security guard in a shopping mall for a year in order to establish Arizona residency, then enrolled in Scottsdale Community College in Maricopa County. Continuing to work while attending school part-time, he received a certificate of completion in law enforcement in two years, then went on to complete his AA in Administration of Justice. Along the way, he joined Uncensored America, a far-right white nationalist, pro-Nazi student group.

"In 2009, at age twenty-one, Kozel enlisted in the army and served two years in Afghanistan. When his tour ended in 2011, he returned to San Francisco to attend his brother's funeral. The brother died of thyroid cancer, which doctors linked to childhood exposure to nuclear radiation from the Chernobyl nuclear power plant meltdown. Alex stayed with his uncle for a time, presumably renewing his ties with the Odessa crime family. We're still looking into what he did during that period.

"In 2012, he moves from San Francisco to Nevada. He works as a security guard for a year at a Las Vegas casino controlled by the Odessa Mafia. In 2013, he gets work as a hand on Clive Bundy's ranch. This is where his indoctrination into the radical right kicks into high gear.

"He starts training with a paramilitary group at Bundy's, and there he meets Stewart Rhodes. Alex is a vocal supporter of Bundy's views about a so-called bullying federal government, and Bundy's asserted rights to freely graze his cattle on federal land. In 2014, Alex participates in the Bundy Ranch standoff. After that, he joins the Oath Keepers and moves to a secret paramilitary training camp near the Arizona-Mexico border. Over the next few years, he's seen at more anti-government actions, increasingly menacing authorities under the guise of defending constitutional rights.

"In 2017, Alex participates in the violent neo-Nazi Unite the Right protest in Charlottesville, Virginia, where one of the white nationalists drove a car into a group of counterprotesters, killing thirty-two-year-old Heather Heyer and leaving nineteen others injured, five critically. Soon thereafter, he travels to Venezuela. In his online posts from that time, he expresses great admiration for Nicolás Maduro, Venezuela's corrupt fascist dictator."

Agent Chen opened a new folder, labeled Maduro. "Venezuela, by the way, is Russia's most important trading and military ally in Latin America. Besides his massively corrupt mismanagement of Venezuela's oil reserves, Maduro—the man that Aleksandr Kozel so much admires—is a global drug kingpin. The Justice Department indicted Maduro and four of his lieutenants on drug trafficking, money laundering and corruption charges in 2020, also charging two leaders of the Colombian revolutionary group FARC for colluding with Maduro to flood the United States with cocaine. Maduro's fascist rule is literally destroying Venezuela. The economy has crumbled; malnutrition and starvation are rampant; and with failing public services and widespread scarcity of medical supplies, Venezuela was ill-equipped to handle the Covid epidemic. Now, they are in the midst of a humanitarian crisis. Five million refugees have fled the country, many of them hoping for asylum in the US.

"Alex Kozel returned to the US from Venezuela in 2019, just before the Covid lockdown. In 2021, he was spotted at the January 6 Insurrection at the Capitol."

Rosa loosened his tie. "My God. You weren't exaggerating about Kozel having a lot of layers, George. For God's sake, what's next with this guy?"

Agent Chen clicked open another file. "After participating in the insurrection, Kozel headed to San Diego. He created a fraudulent online USAJobs profile and federal résumé, applied for a position with ICE, and actually got through the interview process and received a tentative selection letter. As you know, wheels grind slowly in our government's bureaucracy. It's a full year before Kozel's application is fact-checked and security vetted. Meanwhile, he spent a lot of time in chat rooms on the dark web, sharing farfetched conspiracy theories. During that period, he postured and play-acted at being an ICE agent, hanging around at the border with ICE agents who were suspected Oath Keepers.

"Ultimately, DHS/ICE completed their vetting, sent him a notice of ineligibility, and flagged him as a potential domestic terrorist. After that, he went underground … until this spring, when he turns up here, posing as an ICE agent, nosing around our homicide investigation, expressing interest in Ramona and Delfina Cuera."

Rosa tapped a new pack of gum on his desk. "I'm liking Kozel as the prime suspect for the murder of Ramona Cuera," said Lieutenant Rosa. "How about you, George?"

"Agreed. It's possible. But hang on, Carlos," said Chen. "I have more. The Agency has been monitoring a social media chat room on the Dark Web that Kozel frequents. He's been very active lately in a thread about blowing up electrical substations, with a lot of rhetoric about disrupting the deep state. We have evidence that one of the substations they plan to bomb is at the Cougar Creek Coast Ranch. They hate that the site is a protected national monument designated by President Obama and that it's public land leased for cattle grazing. They see attacking it as a symbolic gesture."

"Mother of God. Destroying that substation would take out the electric power grid for much of the Central Coast. We need to find Kozel before he does more damage."

"DHS and the Agency's resources are already searching for him," said Chen.

"I can hold him on charges of impersonating a federal officer while we investigate him for murder and conspiracy to attack critical government infrastructure."

"All good. But first we have to find him."

"Didn't I see him hanging around in the Sheriffs' Roll Call Room on the day we visited Mikos Vadim?" Rosa checked his pocket notebook. "That was on April 22. I didn't think about it at the time, but now I'm wondering if he might have overheard Detective Jamison prepping his team to roll on Vadim. Kozel could have been the one who tipped off Mikos Vadim's lawyer that we were coming."

"Could be. How do they know each other?"

"Hmm. Not farfetched, considering Vadim is the son of a Russian oligarch and Kozel is the nephew of a Russian mobster."

"We need to dig deeper," said Chen.

"Copy that." Rosa wrote in his notebook to follow up on who tipped off Vadim's lawyer and what, if any, was the connection between Mikos Vadim and Kozel. Then he flipped through his notebook pages. "Here he is. Kozel was seen another time a day later, on April 24, when Warden

Dawson's army buddy, James Owens, took a photo of Alex Kozel and his compatriot, and Kozel's credit card, at the Route 1 Brewery."

"Maybe there's a security camera at the tavern."

"If we get a clear picture of their vehicle's license plate, we can put out a BOLO. My people can do that today."

"We should identify the man who was with Kozel at the tavern," said Agent Chen. "I'll have the Agency run facial rec on that photo. We have access to more databases than you county cops. Which reminds me, the Agency still hasn't sent me the facial rec information I requested from Marshal Stone's stakeout photos. I'll see about expediting that, too."

Rosa rapped his knuckles on his desk. "We have to pick up Kozel, ASAP."

38

COLIN HADN'T SEEN DELFINA for a nearly week, not since he'd left her house the morning after the barn dance, their misunderstanding, and that goodbye kiss.

He'd phoned her every day, but she wasn't answering. He was crazy worried about her. What if something bad had happened?

Or is she ghosting me?

Of course she would ghost you, loser. After dancing with handsome heroic Rafe, she realized what a pitiful excuse for a man you are.

No! Stop the negative self-talk.

Delfina isn't like that.

We had a real connection. She wouldn't just ghost me. We're truly friends, if nothing else.

Colin parked his work truck in front of her house and painfully climbed out. It had been nearly three weeks since the beatdown. He hated how long it was taking to heal.

He rolled his shoulders, aggravating the ache but releasing some tension. His uniform felt uncomfortable on his skin.

He glanced at the old bite wound on his hand. It didn't look or feel right. The puma-shaped scar was deep purple with red veins, raised, and throbbing.

He walked around his truck, opened the passenger door, and picked up the bouquet of flowers he'd bought in town for Delfina's birthday. Today, May 12.

Confusing emotions bounced around inside him. He was embarrassed about the way he'd acted when Delfina danced with Rafe, ashamed that he felt jealous, hopeful that he could fix whatever it was that had gone wrong with their relationship. Even if it had to be a platonic friendship, he didn't ever want to lose her.

Trying not to walk like an old person, Colin limped up the garden path to Delfina's front door. The flowers along the path reminded him of her. His heart pounded.

★　　　★　　　★

The front door gaped open; its lock broken. Colin dropped the birthday bouquet on the doormat and put his hand on the service weapon at his hip. Cautiously, he entered the house.

What he saw when he stepped through the door was sickening.

Furniture was toppled, vases and glassware smashed, drawers pulled out and the contents thrown on the floor.

Colin scanned for blood. So far, none.

"Delfina?" He called her name as he rushed through the rooms. Everything in every room had been rifled through, defiled.

Fortunately, all of the valuable artifacts had been removed from Ramona's bedroom before the funeral. Colin's heart ached at the sight of the tossed mattress where he'd lain, recovering under Delfina's care after the beating. Ramona's dresser and desk had been ransacked, and her filing cabinet thrown on its side. One of the file drawers was still closed.

Colin pulled on it.

Locked.

In the kitchen, jars of raw grains and beans, dried herbs, home preserved jam, green beans, and tomatoes had been opened and spilled on the floor. The refrigerator door hung open. Judging from the state of the food inside, including a slimy head of butter lettuce and limp zucchinis, he estimated that the home invasion had happened more than three days before.

This was not just a commonplace robbery. Had the vandal been searching for something specific, or had this destruction been personal—an act of hate or rage?

Where was Delfina?

Colin's hand shook as he phoned Lieutenant Rosa.

"Sir, there's been a 459 Breaking and Entering at Delfina Cuera's house. I think Delfina has been abducted."

★   ★   ★

The next morning, Detective Jamison burst through Lieutenant Rosa's open office door.

"Sir, the forensic lab has a positive ID on the prints found yesterday at the Cuera home. There appear to have been two individuals involved in the B and E: Al Kozel and the man who was seen with Kozel at the Route 1 Tavern. His name is Bert Matsen. White nationalist, neo-Nazi Proud Boy, on the Federal Terrorist Screening Center watchlist. He and Kozel traveled together from San Diego to Santa Lucia a few months ago."

Rosa strode into the deputies' bullpen. "All right, everyone, we have their car license plate, and we've had a BOLO out on these two since last Monday. Where are they? We need to find them, now. Step up the search. Kozel and Matsen may have abducted our homicide victim's daughter."

★   ★   ★

That afternoon in Rosa's office, Chen and Rosa were comparing notes when a deputy rushed in with news.

"Sir, highway patrol officers just found Kozel's car."

"Where is it?" asked Rosa.

"Abandoned near the rollercoaster at the beach boardwalk parking lot by the San Lorenzo River."

"Abandoned?"

"Looks like an alternator failure caused a short circuit resulting in an engine fire."

"How long has it been there?"

"Hard to tell, sir. That boardwalk parking lot is so crowded with tourists, could be no one would have noticed a car left there for a few days."

"They may have stolen another car." said Rosa. "Detective Jamison, have your team look for reports of car thefts in that area within the last four days."

"There are multiple surveillance cameras at that location," said Chen. "The Agency should be able to see where they went, and whether on foot or in another vehicle. We'll find them."

"Any sign of Delfina Cuera?" asked Rosa.

"No, sir. They're dusting for prints and collecting DNA now. They're asking for permission to pry open the trunk."

"Tell them to go ahead."

The room went silent. Everyone waited for what—or who—might be in the stolen car's trunk.

39

T HE COMPULSION TO TRANSFORM and go south had come upon Delfina abruptly, right after Colin moved out of her house. She'd barely had time to grab her go-bag and drive up the coast to a safe place before making the transition.

In her puma form, Delfina traveled at night along forested mountain ridges, staying as far away as possible from the scent of humans as she retraced the path she and her mother had taken from San Diego north to Santa Lucia five years earlier.

She found her way along the fragmented wilderness corridor of connected mountain ranges back to the ancestors' cave, guided by memory and also by something else—intuition, or perhaps the spirits of her mother and her ancestors were guiding her.

She arrived at the cave in the middle of the night, shifted back into human form, and rewove the protections for the sacred cave, as her mother had taught her. Finally, she slept.

At dawn, when she awoke, Delfina sang a traditional song of gratitude and blessing, drank from the healing spring, and collected some of the sacred water, known as God's tears.

Next, Delfina prepared the paints as her mother had taught her. With prayer, she mixed God's Tears and a few drops of blood from her own hand, along with some of her mother's ashes, into each pigment. Then she painted. She depicted her and her mother's journey as pumas from San Diego to Santa Lucia County, their lives with extended family there, and then her mother's capture and collaring by the Puma Project, and the murder.

For three days, Delfina prayed, sang, and burned sacred herbs while she painted. She slept little, ate nothing, drank only water from the spring.

Once she'd completed all that the ancestors required of her, she shifted into her puma form and set off through dark night on the dangerous solo journey of return, across the broken and fragmented bones of the wilderness wildlife corridor that connects San Diego to Santa Lucia.

Her journey to the cave of her ancestors and back—more than five hundred miles each way on foot—took seven days. Until her final day of pilgrimage, Delfina fasted. But on that last day in her mountain lion body, her strength began to wane. She was compelled to catch and eat rabbits in order to complete her journey.

She circumvented Los Angeles, senses prickling with foreboding, by traveling across the San Gabriel Mountains. Near the Falling Springs wilderness area, she discovered the carcass of a female puma, decapitated, all four paws severed and removed. *Poachers' trophies.* Nearby, Delfina found the puma's den, flies swarming over the decomposing bodies of her three cubs.

When she finally reached the Santa Lucia mountains, Delfina followed the watershed along a network of spring-fed creeks flowing down to the coast. On an outcrop above Agua Pura Farm, she dug her claws into the soft sandstone to sharpen them, enjoying the sensation as she gazed at the stars.

At Agua Pura Creek, she skirted across hills in the moonlight above the coast highway, heading toward a cluster of houses north of Clark's Landing. The small housing tract had been built for cement plant workers nearly a century earlier.

The tidy homes sat at the edge of the coastal prairie in a square grid of three streets, each street two short blocks long, with four houses on each side of each block. Delfina had left her car and her clothes at the end of Third Street—the street farthest from Clark's Landing, next to a vacant barn and open field. The small barn stood at the transition from human structures to native grassland, the ecotone between human and wild.

Delfina hid in the grasses, ears alert, tail barely twitching, until she was positive that every soul in the small community was sleeping soundly. Stars glittered like diamonds on the black velvet dome. A Great Horned Owl broke the silence, hooting to its mate.

In the dark of night, the puma stealthily approached her car, relieved that it hadn't been towed or broken into.

The transformation between cougar and human form was easier now.

Delfina dressed in the dark—in jeans, T-shirt, running shoes, and a cap.

Just before dawn, ravenously hungry, nauseous from the rabbit meat, and desperate to flop down on her own bed and sleep, she slid behind the wheel of her VW Bug and took the coast highway south toward the home in Playa Azul that she had shared with her mother.

When she arrived, in the pale first light of Friday morning, she found her house cordoned off with yellow police tape. She ducked under the tape and let herself in. Everything in every room was smashed and trashed.

Hands shaking, she dug her cell phone out of her go-bag and turned it on. Luckily, the battery was at a hundred percent. She dialed her cousin, Hawk. The call went to voice mail.

A list of calls she'd missed popped up—three calls a day since the barn dance a week ago, all from Colin Dawson.

They hadn't spoken since their awful misunderstanding, but Delfina's heart surged with feelings for him. Without hesitation, she phoned him. Her call went to voicemail. "Hey, it's Colin. I haven't been sleeping, and I'm exhausted, so I'm going to try to sleep Friday until at least noon. Do not disturb unless it's a matter of life or death."

Trembling, Delfina drove to Colin's house.

40

T HE RADIO CONNECTION with officers at the site of Kozel's stolen car hissed static.

"10-12. Stand by."

"The trunk is opening."

More static.

"There is no body inside. Repeat. Delfina is not in the trunk."

Everyone in the room started breathing again.

Rosa's racing heart slowed. He hadn't admitted to himself until now how worried he was for Delfina.

More static.

"Jeez. Are you seeing this, sir? The trunk is full of contraband: a box of fentanyl products, ten kilos of dried sinsemilla buds, five wrapped pounds of—not sure what. A white powder. Cocaine? Heroin? And we've got two assault rifles, and a hundred rounds of ammo."

Jamison whistled. "That's a lot of expensive of product to leave on the table. Kozel and Matsen must have been in big a hurry to get away."

"We need to find Ms. Cuera, soon," Rosa spoke through the coms. "Hopefully she's still alive."

"Yes, sir," said Jamison. "The longer a person is missing, the less chance we have of finding her alive, right, boss?"

Rosa nodded, frowning.

"The Agency has been scrubbing security cameras near the car park," said Chen. "So far no sign of Kozel or Matsen. They may have been in the quarry at one time, but it's unlikely they would have doubled back from town where they ditched their car to head back up there now."

"Sir, maybe we should check with the harbor patrol," said Detective Jamison. "Could be they snuck away in a boat."

"Good idea, Jamison. Make it so."

"It's time to get their faces out there." said Agent Chen. "If you're all right with it, Carlos, the FBI can distribute wanted posters, with Kozel's and Matsen's faces, to post offices, liquors stores—the usual places. We'll also post their pictures online and on digital billboards around the state."

"By all means. Do it."

★　　★　　★

Lieutenant Rosa's phone rang just as Marshal Stone knocked on his office door.

Rosa nodded at Stone, and the marshal entered.

Rosa answered the call. He wrote *Lili Armstrong Puma Project, Wednesday, May 11* in his phone log, and pressed the speaker button on his phone console so that Agent Chen and Marshal Stone could hear.

"I appreciate your giving us a chance to examine that broken piece of cougar tracking collar you have in evidence, Lieutenant Rosa," said Lili.

"You're welcome," said Rosa. "Thank you for getting back to me. I presume you have some information that might help in our homicide investigation?"

"Maybe. We were able to identify the collar as belonging to our missing mountain lion," said Lili. "We trapped and collared her in the upper Agua Pura Creek watershed on Thursday, April 14, and released her the same morning, at ten o'clock."

"April 14. That's the same day Warden Dawson found the murdered woman, Ramona Cuera, at Cougar Creek Coast Ranch. Would you send me the exact coordinates where you collared and released that mountain lion?"

"Yes, of course."

"You tranquilize the cougars when you capture them, right?" Rosa asked.

"Yes."

"What kind of tranquilizer do you use?"

"Xylazine hydrochloride. XHCL."

"You draw blood and do other tests on the animal, correct?" asked Rosa.

"Yes," said Lili.

"Did you find anything unusual about this cat?"

"As a matter of fact, we did find anomalies."

"What kind of anomalies?"

"We found novel RNA codes, traces of Covid virus, and antibodies containing human DNA," said Lili.

"I don't know what that means."

"We're not sure either."

Detective Jamison interrupted. 'Excuse me, sir."

"What is it, Jamison?"

"Sir, CSI sent a message. As you know, they were able to map where Ramona Cuera's killer was standing and predict the direction of his escape, based on the trajectory of the fatal arrow. They've been searching along the likely path of the suspect's escape route, and just radioed that they found boot prints on the truck road up to the abandoned quarry. Could be a match with the print found at the scene of the homicide. They took plaster casts that they're bringing back to the lab. Maybe the killer's hiding up there in that quarry."

"Excuse the interruption, Lil."

"No problem, Lieutenant. I heard what your detective just told you. We do a flyover of our study area once a month to upload the GPS data on all our collared pumas. We're scheduled to fly over the quarry in two days, next Monday, the sixteenth. Maybe you'd like to join us?"

"I appreciate that, Lili. It could be very useful, but I'm not a fan of riding in small planes. Any chance one of my colleagues could ride along instead?"

"Absolutely. I just texted you the details of where and when to meet."

"Okay. We'll have someone there."

The lieutenant ended the call and turned to US Marshal Stone.

"Haven't seen you in a while, Stone. How's your fentanyl investigation going?"

The tall man dressed in black put away the cell phone he'd been noodling with, uncrossed his legs, and bent down to brush a speck of dust off his Tecova bison skin cowboy boots. His black lawman's hat sat on a table behind him. "Your office is pretty frickin' busy, Lieutenant. That's quite a confluence of news, about the boot prints and the quarry flyover," said Marshal Stone.

"Pieces are falling into place," said Rosa.

"I have a few more pieces to share with you. I want to thank Agent Chen for sending me the Agency's facial recognition information from Irene Johansen's home security cam in Clark's Landing. I synced it with my surveillance of the drug dealers at the quarry gate. I was also able to obtain drone footage of the quarry area. Last time I saw you, we were all wondering what connections there might be between Ramona Cuera's murder and Johnny Taylor's fentanyl overdose. I've uploaded everything I have to a secure video channel. I think I might have some answers. Also, unfortunately, more questions." Stone stood and gestured toward Rosa's computer. "May I?"

"Go ahead," said Rosa.

Marshal Stone typed in an encrypted URL, and his website popped up on the extra-large smart murder board on the wall. Stone clicked on a folder labeled Facial Recognition. A block of fifty thumbnail headshots appeared, and Stone scrolled through them. He stopped at a photo of Al Kozel and enlarged it. "I've had my eye on this individual for years. Al Kozel. He showed up on Mrs. Johansen's home surveillance video several times, as well as on my drone footage of the fentanyl camp. Kozel is an imposter. An ICE impersonator. He's deeply involved with a fanatical white nationalist, neo-Nazi, pro-Hitler, pro-Putin organization."

Rosa nodded at Chen. Chen raised an eyebrow.

Stone opened another folder. A video showed Johnny Taylor waiting at the Clark's Landing quarry gate to buy pills. A man dressed in camo pants and a black hoodie, with a knit mask pulled down over his face, appeared and spoke with the boy. Johnny shook his head and seemed to argue with the man. The man grabbed him and held a rag over his nose and mouth. Johnny collapsed, and the man loaded him into an old truck with no license plate, which was parked on the quarry side of the gate. The truck drove away, up the dirt road toward the quarry.

"Jesus, we've got the abduction on tape. Nice work, Stone."

"How's the kid doing?" asked Stone.

"He's alive," Rosa answered, "but still at the hospital in a coma. He hasn't been able to tell us what happened."

"Are there any camera angles that show the face of the man who took Johnny?" asked Chen.

"Unfortunately, no," said Stone. "The mask completely covered his face."

"'Now that we know that Johnny didn't wander up into the mountains on his own," said Chen, "we need to know why he was grabbed like that."

"It could just be a coincidence that Ramona Cuera's murderer and the person who abducted Johnny both wore camo gear, but ..." Marshal Stone's voice trailed off. He frowned.

"There's more." Stone clicked the black arrow on a video window and another movie began to play. "This is from the drone flyover of the quarry. First, the infrared imagery. Right here you can see the heat signature of people moving around and several patches of plants under cultivation. On this next video, you can see a tent village. I counted about twenty people working around the place. Look closely. These hombres are carrying AK-47s. And here, you can see people working in what we believe are illegal sinsemilla grows. Even though pot is now legal in California, the illegal operations bring in far more money than legal cannabis businesses. Here, beside the sleeping tents, you can see a large tent, which seems to be a group mess hall, and another big tent, probably used for drying and processing pot as well as storing other drugs and contraband."

Marshal Stone moved his red laser pointer. "Look at this."

"What is it?" asked Rosa.

"A helipad. This is where they're moving in fentanyl products and other contraband from Mexico."

"And you apparently think this is relevant to our homicide investigation because ...?" asked Rosa.

"I heard that Delfina Cuera was missing. I think she and her mother may be involved in the fentanyl trafficking. Maybe Delfina is there."

"We have absolutely no evidence of that," said Rosa.

"Wait," said Stone. He zoomed in to an image at the quarry camp of a woman with black braids, wearing a wide-brimmed hat and a poncho. "Look at her. Doesn't she look familiar? I think this could be Delfina Cuera."

"I'm not convinced." said Rosa. "But I'll tell you what—how about if you take that plane ride with the Puma Project on Monday and get a closer look? Let us know what you see. Watsonville airport, hangar B-9, 7:30 a.m."

41

C OLIN GLANCED at his bedside clock: 8:15 a.m., Saturday, May
14.

"What the hell?"

Another knock, more urgent that the first.

He didn't bother with underwear, T-shirt or shoes, just pulled on his old blue jeans and rushed to the door.

"Delfina!"

He grabbed her, wrapping his arms around her in a bear hug.

She trembled like a frightened kitten.

He guided her to the couch and helped her sit, then stepped back to look at her.

"God, I thought I'd lost you," he said. "I've been so worried. Are you hurt? Where have you been? What happened?"

Delfina put her face in her hands and sobbed. All the grief, fear, and tension she'd been holding at bay and had not allowed herself to feel since her mother's murder, came flooding out, breeching her self-control, toppling her tightly constructed walls of denial. Release finally came for her. She surrendered to the reality of her mother's death, and her own imminent danger. She opened to her vulnerability, and her tears flowed.

Colin sat next to her on the couch, took her in his arms, held her and rocked her.

"It's going to be okay," he whispered. "You're safe."

Delfina melted into the comfort and relief of Colin's strong arms for several minutes. Then she forced herself to move a slight distance away from him, and wiped the tears from her cheeks.

She explained that she'd traveled to San Diego to take care of urgent business pertaining to her mother. She left out the part about the cave and turning into a mountain lion.

"Why didn't you tell anyone you were leaving?"

"Everything happened so fast. I guess I was afraid that if I told anyone where I was going, there'd be a greater chance of being tracked. I'm sorry I worried you."

She put her hand on Colin's. "Thank you for caring."

He took both of her hands in his. "Are you kidding? Delfina, when I saw what happened to your house, I thought you'd been abducted, or—or worse."

He turned her palms up, and his forehead creased. "How did you get these cuts on your hands?"

"It's nothing." Delfina pulled her hands away. "Do the police know who broke into my house, or why? I found a bouquet of wilted flowers on my porch. Why would they leave flowers?"

"Oh, the flowers were from me. I came by to give them to you for your birthday." Colin blushed. "That's when I discovered you were missing and reported the break-in to the sheriff. Based on fingerprints and DNA, they identified the people who invaded your home. A guy named Al Kozel—an Oath Keeper who was posing as an ICE agent—and another man—a Proud Boy named Bert Matsen. Kozel was at the crime scene asking questions about you, right after your mother's death. The cops consider Kozel and Matsen to be suspects in your mother's murder. Do either of those names mean anything to you?"

"The names don't. But I know Mama had issues with some ICE agents. Maybe if I saw their photos?"

"I don't have them. But the team investigating your mother's murder will have them, and they'll want to ask you questions."

"You mean Lieutenant Rosa?"

"Yeah, and FBI agent George Chen. There's also a US Marshal named Kurt Stone helping with the investigation. Marshal Stone thinks there might be a connection between your mom's murder and a fentanyl ring he's been tracking."

"Fentanyl? No way. My mother and I have nothing to do with that."

"Of course not. But may I take you down to the Sheriff's Headquarters to talk to Lieutenant Rosa? Maybe later today, or tomorrow?"

"Okay. Later. Right now, I'm just too exhausted to think, Colin."

"Of course. Take your time. I'm really glad you came to me. I hope you'll stay here while we sort everything out. Please, let me help you, the way you took care of me."

Colin moved a stray wisp of hair away from her eyes. "Are you hungry? Would you like a shower? I can loan you clothes if you want, or you can just sleep here, for as long as you need."

"Thank you. I grabbed a few clean clothes when I went by my house. Right now, all I really need is a shower; then I just need to sleep. A long, long time."

"I have a second bedroom. It's a little messy, sorry. I use it as a home office and keep my gym equipment and surfboard in there. But the mattress is newish, so the bed is comfortable. While you're showering, I'm going to make a quick call to Lieutenant Rosa to let him know you're here, and safe. Then I'll put fresh sheets on your bed. You can sleep as long as you like. This way to your shower, madam."

While Colin made Delfina's bed, his mind replayed, over and over again, the relief he'd felt knowing that she was safe, and the feeling of holding her in his arms.

42

S UNDAY MORNING, outside Colin's kitchen window, a mama
hummingbird flew to her nest in the bougainvillea. Morning light
streaming through the window flooded the kitchen with golden warmth.

"These waffles are wonderful, Colin. Please pass the maple syrup.
And may I have that bowl of blueberries, too?" Delfina smiled.

She sat across from Colin at the kitchen table, wearing a yellow
sundress.

Colin blushed, hoping Delfina couldn't tell what he'd been thinking.

He passed her the syrup and blueberries, and poured himself
more coffee from the thermal carafe.

"You are truly a man of many talents," said Delfina. "Who knew
you could cook like this?"

"Thanks. Mom and Gramma were great cooks. They insisted that
I learn, and I discovered I enjoy cooking."

"Colin, I feel bad about taking advantage of your hospitality. I think
it would be more appropriate for me to stay with my cousin Hawk while
my house is sorted out. He's been renting with friends in Playa Azul near
my mama's place since he lost his home in the mountains to that last big

fire. I tried to reach him last night, but there was no answer. I think I'll go by today and see what's up with him. Honestly, I'm a little worried."

"He seems like a pretty capable dude. Why worry?'

"He's two-spirit, Native American, and a hawk. That's triple jeopardy."

Colin understood that two-spirit meant gay, but he wasn't sure what she meant about her cousin being a hawk. Anyway, with hate crimes escalating against anyone who wasn't a white, evangelical so-called Christian, straight male, he appreciated why Delfina was worried.

"Maybe you should hang out here today, Delfina. Be safe. I need to check in with my captain, and then I plan to catch up with Lieutenant Rosa. But please believe me when I say that you're welcome to stay with me as long as you want or need to. Mi casa es tu casa."

"Thank you." Delfina's eyes seemed wary. Was he trying too hard to hold on to her?

"I'm sorry I got jealous about you dancing with Rafe." said Colin.

"It's okay. I'm sorry if I came off like a bitch. To be clear, I'm not into Rafe. He's a nice man, but it was just a dance. I was never interested in dating him or hanging out with him, or anything like that. He's looking for a girl who will cook for him, do his laundry, and have his babies. Sorry, but not sorry. That isn't me. Anyway, I heard from a friend of mine that he met someone that night, and they fell madly in love. I'm really happy for them."

"Delfina, I understand that you're a completely free person. I acted like a petulant teenager who thinks people belong to each other. I promise that I know better. Healthy relationships are based on mutual respect and trust. I respect you, and will always honor your agency. I want to be clear, though, that if I'm in a sexual relationship with someone, I need to be able to trust that it's mutually monogamous."

"Back at you, Colin. I would never commit to an intimate relationship unless I was confident it was going to be monogamous." Delfina blushed. "And I completely trust that you would respect my autonomy no matter what. I don't ever want to change you, either … even though you did look amazing in that shirt with the pearl snaps." Delfina reached across the table, brushed her hand over Colin's, and smiled.

Her topaz eyes had changed to a more radiant, deeper blue. They shone with complete openness. And invitation?

43

U S MARSHAL KURT STONE pulled his unmarked black Dodge Charger into the parking lot of the small Valle Verde municipal airport at 7:30 Monday morning, May 16. It was already seventy-four degrees, with only a light sea breeze.

He left his usual black felt Kingman hat in the trunk of his car and settled a US Marshal ballcap over his buzz cut. He unbuttoned and pulled off his long-sleeved shirt, folded it, and placed it next to his hat and ranch boots, figuring he'd be more comfortable on a hot day like today in just a T-shirt, light cargo pants, and athletic shoes. He switched out his sidearm holster for a concealed-carry belt holster, which he fastened under his T-shirt. He slipped his Glock 43 and two loaded magazines into the holster. A smart phone and a slim wallet went in his pockets.

Striding across the nearly empty lot and around the small building that housed the airport terminal offices and a restaurant, he found a gate.

He raised his foot to stride through, and froze in mid-step.

The high-pitched buzz of a baby rattlesnake.

Instinctively, the marshal stepped back and stood as still as if he'd been turned to stone. He stared into the eyes of a northern Pacific rattler, coiled in the shade at the base of the gate, ready to strike.

Well aware that baby rattlers are even more dangerous than adults, Stone slowly tiptoed backward until he was clear of the snake's striking distance.

Continuing several yards farther along the cyclone fence, he found another opening and passed through.

He scanned toward the east, and spotted three people next to a plane in front of hangar B-9.

★ ★ ★

"Hello. You must be Marshal Stone. I'm Lili and this is Jack, with the Puma Project. This is our awesome pilot, Mark. He's been flying us around looking for mountain lions for the last eight years."

Stone nodded. He clocked the pilot, with his lean muscles and leathery skin, to be about the same age as him—in his early fifties. Most likely a retired navy or air force flyboy. Jack and Lili appeared to be typical easygoing grad student types. Jack looked like he was ready for a day at the beach—flip flops, baggie board shorts, and a faded T-shirt. Lili was dressed more sensibly, in tennis shoes, cargo pants, and a fleece sweater zipped over her blouse. Her blond hair was pulled back and braided. Pretty girl. No doubt also smart and capable.

"This is going to be a long flight," said Jack. "I hope you've got a big bladder. We have a few more things to do before takeoff, in case you want to use the restroom."

"Good idea. Be right back," said Stone.

"I'll show you where it is," said Lili.

She was chatty as she walked with him back to the airport terminal office building. "Every month, a couple of our biologists go up in a plane to locate all of our study animals and download the GPS information from their collars. Flying is the most efficient way to download the GPS data because we can cover much more ground than driving. We're really lucky to work with Mark, our pilot. He's the best. Here we are." Lili disappeared through the door marked Women.

When she reemerged, Stone was waiting for her. They walked back to the plane together, Lili talking all the way. "People with weak stomachs or small bladders don't do very well on these telemetry flights because the plane often has to circle above the animal for many minutes while the collar download is completed. To find all of our study cats—about fifty total—ranging from Corralitos to Palo Alto, it takes several hours of zigzagging up and down above the coastal mountains."

"I assume we'll have time to get a good look at the area of interest to my investigation—over the abandoned quarry at Cougar Creek Coast Ranch?"

"Oh, definitely. We track about twenty pumas in the redwoods around the Cientox Quarry."

As they returned to the plane, Lili unzipped her sweater, revealing pert little breasts under a tight white blouse.

"Hey," said Jack, looking up from a contraption he was tinkering with on the outside of the plane. "We're about ready to take off. Just finished attaching these antennae to the wing strut so we can listen for the pumas' location pings and download their data once located."

Mark completed a final walk around inspection of his plane. "A-okay. Ready to get airborne, crew?"

"Marshal Stone, you'll sit in back with Jack," said Lili. "He'll be on his computer, monitoring incoming data. I'll be in front, listening for VHF signals from puma collars. Once I hear one, I'll ask Mark to fly closer to the target animal so our receiver can communicate with the animal's collar."

Stone climbed into the back of the Cessna 172 Skyhawk, followed by Jack and his computer gear. Lili hopped into the front, and they all fastened seatbelts and slipped on headphones so they could communicate with one another over the engine noise inside the small plane.

Mark checked the ASOS for the latest weather report, tuned in to the CTAF, and then drove the plane to the longest of the two runways. As they bumped along the runway, picked up speed, and lifted off, Stone was viscerally aware of how lightweight the Cessna was. Through his window, he watched the ground recede. Buildings, cars, roads—all the material creations so important to humans—weirdly shrank.

The plane made a large circle, flying over checkered and striped farm fields toward the coast. Once they reached their cruising speed at an elevation of a thousand feet, Mark turned the plane landward, and they followed the Pajaro River up to the forested Corralitos watershed.

Lili had her headphones on, listening for VHF signals. Jack leaned toward Marshal Stone and gestured out the window. "From a thousand feet up, the impacts of habitat fragmentation and loss are really evident across the coastal mountains. Look down into the trees and imagine a puma moving through the forest. Anywhere they can go is not very far from a road or trail. With this bird's eye view of where 'civilization' begins and 'wilderness' ends, it's really impressive that pumas manage to have so little interaction with humans."

"I can see what you're saying, but why do you people think mountain lions are so important? Honestly, where I come from, and in fact, in every state in the nation except California and Florida, they're considered vermin."

"Unfortunately, that's the mindset of a lot of people," said Jack. "The thing is, mountain lions, sitting at the top of the food chain, are essential to maintaining healthy habitat in the ecosystems where they're endemic. In healthy ecosystems, all populations of plants and animals living there are connected in a delicate balance. Remove an apex predator or keystone species from the ecosystem, and the whole system will inevitably collapse."

"Why?" asked Marshal Stone.

"Mountain lions regulate and balance populations of deer and small wildlife, which helps native plants and shrubs that would otherwise get overeaten, critically reducing the overall supply of food for all the creatures in the habitat." said Jack. "Mountain lions are one of the best examples of an ecological engineer."

"Engineer?" asked Stone.

"Meaning they help keep entire ecosystems functioning properly. For example, mountain lions help reduce Lyme disease, keeping tick numbers down by reducing deer and mouse numbers. They cull out weak and sick animals, and also cut the time deer and elk spend browsing along streams, which helps protect our waterways from contamination, and from both droughts and flooding."

The boy spoke fast, as if he were lecturing students and had a lot to say. "Plus, the carrion mountain lions leave behind provide food sources for countless wildlife species. All that helps maintain biodiversity and keep ecosystems intact and resilient to the consequences of climate change, such as the intensifying droughts and wildfires."

Lili's voice came through the plane's coms. "Oh no!" The researcher's voice cracked with emotion. "Headquarters just radioed to tell us not to look for M58's signal. They got an alert from Highway Patrol that M58 was hit and killed early this morning while trying to cross Highway 17. They're bringing his body to the lab."

"M58 is a young adult male sired by M36," said Jack. "His telemetry data has been showing him wandering farther away from his natal area recently, straying increasingly close to human development. Young males aren't allowed to stay in their parents' territory. The parents force them to move out and establish their own range. But the young are often naïve to the dangers of getting too close to humans."

"Habitat fragmentation and loss from all the human development in California's coastal mountains is putting our pumas in danger from human interaction, limiting their hunting range, and causing them to become isolated from other mountain lion populations," said Lili.

"Habitat fragmentation is also leading to less genetic diversity," said Jack.

"So what?" quipped Stone.

"Genetic diversity is essential to the long-term survival of all animal populations, including humans, by the way. It makes a species more resistant to disease and other environmental hazards. A lack of diversity in the mating pool for mountain lions could lead to inbreeding and eventual extinction."

"We need to develop wildlife corridors that allow them to live safely in their own habitat," Lili added. "Restoring connectivity among mountain ranges would bring new animals in to exchange their genetics and increase the probability that our local puma population will be able to live on well into the future."

"Thanks, Professors," said Stone. "I'll keep all that in mind."

"We're flying over the Cientox quarry now, Marshal Stone," said Jack. "Mark is decreasing altitude so you can get a better view."

Stone craned his neck to look out the window, confirming what he'd seen on the drone footage. An illegal pot grow littered with trash, empty fertilizer bags, beer and booze bottles. A helipad. A village of small tents and two large tents. About twenty-five people moved around the place.

Stone raised his binoculars. He could clearly see the faces of the two men he recognized from his surveillance video: the maggots who sold fentanyl to kids at the gate.

"Bingo! There's the one I've been looking for. The woman with the straw hat and black braids." She looked up. Stone aimed his telephoto and took a picture. She yelled something.

Three men in camo gear pointed M16s at the plane.

Stone shouted at the pilot. "Mark, get us out of here now! We're about to take hostile fire!"

The plane turned sharply and rapidly gained altitude. Stone looked back to see puffs of smoke popping from the rifles.

★　　★　　★

"Oh my God! I can't believe that just happened," said Lili. "This is America, right?" Lili held her hand over her mouth. Her eyes were wide with fear.

"Why are you surprised, Lili," asked Jack. "You do know where they got those M16s, right?"

"What do you mean?"

"Almost all of the Mexican and South American cartels buy their guns from US arms dealers. Like Pogo said, 'We have met the enemy, and he is us.'"

44

B Y THE TIME MARSHAL STONE ARRIVED at Lieutenant Rosa's office, Agent Chen, Wildlife Warden Colin Dawson, and Santa Lucia Police Chief Steve Bryant were assembled and had been briefed on the airplane shooting incident.

"We've understood all along we're dealing with the Sinaloa and Jalisco—lawless and extremely dangerous cartels," said SLPD Chief Bryant, "but I never thought in a million years that they'd go so far as to openly try shooting down a plane in US air space. That's nuts."

Marshal Stone, who was leaning on the doorframe, raised his hand. "I got a close-up of the woman with black braids who I thought might be Delfina Cuera. I'll text it over to you, Lieutenant Rosa."

"Got it," said Rosa. He brushed the photo of the woman's face onto the big screen.

"This woman is Asian, not Native American," said Agent Chen. "She is definitely not Delfina Cuera."

"I just ran her image through AFIS," said Detective Jamison. "She came up pretty fast. The woman is Qi Guang Fong. She's high up in Wo Shing, a powerful triad secret black society, one of the Chinese transnational organized crime syndicates."

"It seems a stretch that a leader of a powerful Chinese triad would visit a humble pot farm in California," said Colin.

"I'm not surprised," said Stone. "The triads do business in every country. Prostitution, sex and drug trafficking, fraud, extortion, smuggling, counterfeiting goods and software: that's all routine business for them. And it's a known fact that there's a close relationship between the Chinese triads like Wo Shing, and the Mexican-based Sinaloa and Jalisco cartels. Qi Guang Fong is probably here to check up on her employees. I've been tracking her for a long time. This could be the opportunity I've been waiting for, to finally take her in."

"I want to take out that nest in the quarry now," said Rosa. "We do have the warrant for a high-risk search and seize, yes?"

Agent Chen gave a thumbs up. "Good to go."

"All right. It's estimated there are about twenty-five people up there, obviously well-armed," said Rosa. "Chief, you say you have a city police unit standing by?"

"Yes, but I want to add a team from the county's SWAT unit," said the police chief. "They have the special tactical training and the arsenal of weapons we're going to need to resolve this situation."

"I'm fine with that," said Rosa.

"I'm bringing DEA and ATF into our task force too," said Agent Chen. "From the looks of things, we'll be seizing a lot of drugs and illegal firearms up in that quarry."

"Copy that. We need to go in with enough manpower to clear the area quickly, and with minimum casualties. We don't want to send our people out to slaughter. I want a well-organized, surgical operation. We need to take alive as many of those vermin as we can, so we can arrest, indict, and lock them up."

"On the other hand," said Agent Chen, "we don't want a Waco situation. You know what the media will do with this if they get the chance. Jack-booted government thugs terrorizing poor Mexicans. Cientox may try to claim that we attacked employees who were just there doing their job."

"Agreed," said Rosa. "We've got to get ahead of the narrative that's been driving violent anti-government crime since Waco—the Oklahoma City bombing, Columbine, the Bundy Standoff, the January 6 Insurrection. Make sure everyone wears bodycams and operates by the book. Every move we make must be well documented. And evidence of whatever they're smuggling in to sell must be systematically collected and documented."

★　　★　　★

In the dark before dawn the next morning, forty specially trained officers rolled up the road to the quarry in a caravan of BearCat stealth vehicles: two ten-man SWAT units, five sheriff's deputies, three Santa Lucia police officers, two FBI agents, a four-person DEA unit, a four-man ATF unit, Marshal Stone and Warden Colin Dawson.

Lieutenant Rosa and Agent Chen remained below at the gate to serve as overwatch in a black van equipped as a mobile command post.

Each of the two ten-man SWAT squads was divided into two five-person elements. The five sheriff deputies plus the three SLPD and the two FBI constituted a third ten-person squad. The DEA and ATF units were to coordinate, and Marshal Stone and Warden Dawson were assigned to function as a two-person team.

Colin and Stone rode in a van with the DEA and ATF units. Colin felt nervous about partnering with Marshal Stone. He was an unknown. Could Stone be trusted to have his back?

As their vehicle bumped slowly along the narrow dirt road, someone handed Colin night vision goggles. He strapped them on under his Kevlar helmet and practiced moving them over his eyes and then back out of the way several times. His helmet was equipped with a night vision video camera and a communication system. His body armor made him sweat. He held his rifle across his lap.

The men who were packed shoulder-to-shoulder inside the vehicle with Colin rode in silence. Each was armed with a Sig Sauer, Glock, Beretta handgun, or an UZI plus a submachine gun or a semiautomatic AK-47 plus a shotgun. One agent had a shotgun mounted under the barrel of his submachine gun. Two of the ATF agents carried long-range sniper rifles equipped with laser and optical sites. Marshal Stone wore a Colt .45 in a holster low on his hip, and he carried a modified bolt-action hunting rifle fitted with a cutting-edge scope and other high-tech sniper add-ons.

These guys all looked like military combat vets. Colin's stomach churned at the thought of the bloody violence these weapons foreshadowed. He felt like he was back in Afghanistan. He had no doubt that the people they were going to arrest were really bad hombres, but he hoped no one would be needlessly killed or injured on this mission. Would everyone in this van survive until dawn?

Would he be able to keep it together without having some sort of PTSD meltdown? A firestorm of intense emotions raced through

Colin's mind. His heart raced. He felt flushed. He visualized sitting next to Delfina in her garden. He started his breathing protocol and silently chanted his mantra until he regained control.

Colin's squad leader spoke into his ear, asking for everyone to verify that they could hear and be heard. Agent Chen and Lieutenant Rosa added their voices, updating the entire unit—all four squads—on the recon from the stealth drone hovering above the quarry camp site.

From Stone's aerial picture file and these drone images, they had a good idea of the layout of the land, weapons involved, number and disposition of suspects.

Chen and Rosa, serving as overwatch, reviewed the details of the assault plan and ran through a few quick and dirty contingency plans.

"Be warned that the perimeter is probably booby trapped," advised overwatch.

One kilometer away from the drug dealer's encampment, the vehicles stopped. The assault teams disembarked as silently as shadows. Night goggles on and weapons ready, officers hustled toward the target, each of the ten-man teams approaching from a different point of a triangle around the camp.

As a Wildlife Warden and a former Army Ranger, Colin was accustomed to night vision technology. He moved stealthily toward the perimeter of the camp, scanning for trip wire and other booby traps.

"Stop!" Colin spoke through his headset, pointing to a wire stretched across the ground. Stone halted just in time. The wire connected two tin cans, each holding a live grenade. If Stone had stepped on the wire, the grenades would have been pulled out of the cans and detonated, blowing Colin and Stone to smithereens.

Colin had a moment of vertigo. He took a deep breath, fighting off a flashback. The last thing he needed right now was to black out.

His mind cleared. He moved forward.

The unit leader gave the command to form a snake: a single-file line. Carrying his rifle in a sling, Colin racked his Glock and fell in behind Stone. The point man at the front of the snake gave the "Go" command. The snake rushed into the drug camp, immediately meeting hostile fire. The snake broke apart. Colin and his team found cover and returned fire. Someone on his team shot a man in the chest. Colin watched blood spray out, then heard the shot strike. More bodies were hit, and fell.

Colin was aware of the other units moving into their areas of responsibility. Coached by Overwatch, officers adjusted their positions to cover the entire camp. They tossed flashbang grenades into the compound to disorient sleeping suspects and met all hostile fire aggressively.

Dodging bullets, Colin and Stone ran toward a tent. They threw a flashbang inside, then rushed in.

They startled awake two men Colin recognized as the dealers who sold drugs to kids at the gate.

"Drop your weapons! Down on the ground!" Colin aimed his weapon at the dealers as he shouted commands. "Hands behind your back!"

The dealers complied, lying face down on the floor. Stone kept his Colt .45 aimed at the suspects while Colin collected their weapons and cuffed them.

Suddenly, an assailant rushed into the tent.

Stone spun and fired his Colt before the man got off a shot.

The assailant fell, bleeding from the leg. Stone grabbed the assailant's Uzi.

Colin cuffed him and reported through his coms, "Three suspects contained."

The wounded man was thrashing and howling in pain.

Colin tore a strip off the assailant's shirt and tied it around his leg to slow the bleeding.

Leaving the prisoners bound and secured to pick up later, Colin and Stone rushed out of the tent into the firestorm.

A chaos of smoke, fire, shouts, screams, and blood enveloped them.

Stone shouted that he was going to look for Qi Guang Fong and ran off.

Colin took cover behind an old pickup truck.

He recognized the truck as the one used to abduct Johnny Taylor.

He racked his rifle to defend his position. A round ricocheted off the truck, just missing him.

Colin shot, winging his assailant in the shoulder.

The man dropped his gun and fell.

Colin rushed in and kicked the gun away from the suspect, who held his bleeding shoulder and moaned. Colin cuffed him.

"Suspect down," he reported.

His eyes blinked tears as he peered through the stinging, acrid gun smoke rolling through camp. The smell of blood and spilled bowels sat like iron on his tongue.

The whirling haze cleared momentarily. Colin spotted Marshal Stone firing his rifle at a helicopter just taking off.

Two agents with long-range sniper rifles joined Stone.

The helicopter got away.

Sounds of shooting slowed, like the last popcorn popping in the pan. Finally, it stopped.

Medics bandaged the wounded. Two dead suspects went into body bags. None of the law enforcement personnel had sustained serious injury.

A rescue helicopter arrived to take injured suspects to the hospital. All of the uninjured suspects—growers and drug traffickers—were assembled in handcuffs in the center of the compound. The suspects were loaded onto police vans and driven to prison for booking.

While waiting to board the departing SWAT van, Colin glanced over his shoulder at the old truck. A hundred baby spiders danced in his brain.

He stepped out of line and approached a handcuffed pot grower waiting to board a van bound for prison.

"Hey, Señor, do you know who that old truck belongs to?" Colin asked in Spanish.

"No one knows. My friend found it parked with the keys inside, up on that road above the quarry. It seemed abandoned, so he drove it down here for us to use."

★　　★　　★

That evening, Lieutenant Rosa, Agent Chen, Colin, Deputy Jamison, and Marshal Stone gathered in the lieutenant's office at sheriff's headquarters to debrief.

"We didn't get her," said Marshal Stone. "I don't even think Qi Guang Fong, the Dragon Master of Sam Gor, was on that helicopter we fired at. She must have made it out before our raid, right after those yahoos shot at the Puma Project's plane."

"I'm sorry to hear that," said Agent Chen. "Nevertheless, I think we're going to check off plenty of boxes on the FBI's most wanted list once all of our arrests are processed."

"I wonder if Ramona Cuera's killer is in the bunch we picked up," said Detective Jamison.

"I'll tell you who would have made my day, despite missing out on Qi Guang Fong," said Marshal Stone. "Catching Al Kozel."

"Why would a racist like Kozel be hiding out in a camp full of Mexicans?" asked Deputy Jamison.

"It's true he hates Mexicans," said Marshal Stone, "But he needs money to finance his activities. AFT and DEA want him as the leader of a *drug and firearms trafficking* conspiracy. A few years ago, he got in bed with the Sinaloa cartel to fund his Oath Keeper Chapter in San Diego. He supplies Sinaloa with guns; in exchange, they give him drugs to sell."

"Wait," said Jamison. "He hates Mexicans, but he sells guns to the Mexican cartels, then uses the money he makes from doing business with Mexicans to fund his racist activities. Ironic."

"Kozel is just unprincipled," said Rosa. "We have to find him before he blows up the Cougar Creek Coast Ranch substation."

45

T HE NEXT MORNING, Wednesday, May 18, the hush of waves breaking on shore across the highway wafted in through Colin's open kitchen window.

At dawn, he'd gone surfing for the first time since the beating by the Fresno cops. Sky and ocean were calm, and the waves were breaking in perfect, glassy four-foot tubes. Colin caught a few sweet rides before anyone else arrived, then walked back home across the highway and rinsed off at his outdoor shower, feeling a hundred percent in the pura vida zone.

His shoulder and ribs ached a little, and the almost-healed cuts and abrasions stung from the salt water, but ocean was a powerful healer. He felt strong, fantastic.

Barefoot, with a towel wrapped around his hips, he stood at the kitchen counter pouring boiling water from his glass kettle through a coffee filter loaded with fresh-ground fair trade Peruvian Oro d'Cacao.

He transferred the fragrant brew from the carafe to his favorite hand-thrown mug, savoring the coffee. Outside the window, a hawk made slow circles above the strawberry field.

A day off! He'd already worked beyond his forty-hour shift: six eight-hour stints, plus ten more hours of overtime. There was not a single thing he had to do today but relax.

It crossed his mind that he should go put some clothes on before Delfina got up. The thought of her turned him on. He'd been having sex dreams about her every night.

Before he could act on his intention to get dressed, Delfina appeared, smiling. She was barefoot and wearing a braless pink camisole and thin cotton pajama shorts. Her long shining hair fell gracefully over her shoulders.

Colin blinked in amazement. His flagpole stood at full mast.

"Good morning. That coffee smells great." Delfina poured herself a cup and casually sat down at the kitchen table.

Colin stepped behind the waist-high butcher block table. "Good morning." He sipped his coffee nonchalantly.

"You went surfing?" Delfina asked. "Looks like you're feeling better in spite of last night."

Colin smiled and nodded.

Delfina helped herself to a strawberry from the bowl on the breakfast table. "Is this a frittata? It looks delicious." She cut a slice, put it on a plate, and tasted it. "Oh my gosh. This is so good. You're an amazing cook, Colin." She helped herself to guacamole and salsa and ate for a minute, then frowned at Colin. "You're not eating?"

"I'm not that hungry," said Colin.

"What's bugging you?"

"It's nothing."

"I know you had a really intense week, Colin. When we met, you told me that you were done with war and violence, and now you've let yourself get involved with a big raid, with SWAT and a massive amount of weapons. I've seen the scars on your back. What's the deal? Any PTSD symptoms, flashbacks? Want to talk about it?"

"No. Yeah, okay. The scars are from shrapnel during that firefight in the 'Stan I told you about. I got lucky: no internal organs were hit, and my spine wasn't damaged. Just flesh wounds, really. I got pumped up with morphine in the hospital, though, and it was hell getting off that dope. That's where my aversion to pharmaceuticals comes from. And yeah, it bothered me, being part of that raid last night. But I mean, obviously, even though it was violent and ugly, it was necessary to take out that drug dealers' camp in the mountains. My mind stayed clear and focused, like it just remembered what to do."

Standing at the butcher block table, Colin took a few bites of his frittata and sipped his coffee. "It definitely brought up old trauma from Afghanistan. But I didn't get triggered. No nightmares. No flashbacks or hallucinations, no bad nausea. Just one brief minute of vertigo. And surprisingly, I'm not exactly depressed either. It's just that afterward—I don't know—I feel numb and disgusted with myself, with the whole situation. Kind of like I have a hangover from the violence, the adrenaline rush. I mean, why do the cartels and all the trafficking in drugs, weapons, and humans even exist? Obviously, going after them with military force doesn't get rid of them. It may even make them stronger."

Delfina wrapped her hands around her coffee mug and nodded. "I'm pretty sure that if we legalized drugs, treated addiction as a mental health issue, and provided appropriate care, the drug cartels would go out of business. But guns and human trafficking, I don't know. It might help to shut down the NRA. I'd like to see that happen, but honestly, I think that as long as humans are unhappy, even if the NRA went away and we had the best gun regulations possible, some people would still find a way to get into violent, twisted shit. And the more stressful any animal's environment gets, you know—like, overcrowding, food and water or other resources in short supply, or the climate's too hot—the more likely the animal will become violent."

Colin studied Delfina's face. "Something is bothering you, too. I mean, beyond the obvious fact that they still haven't caught your mother's killer, and he may be stalking you. There's something else. What's going on?"

Delfina cast her eyes down and twisted her bracelet, a sure sign that she was conflicted about something. "I still haven't been able to reach Hawk. Yesterday I went by the rental house where he's staying."

"And?"

"I don't know. The house is one of those beautiful big old Victorians in town. There were six people living there. I've stopped by several times, and no one's been home. Yesterday, the front door was open, so I went in. Colin, the place was completely vacant. Not even any furniture. I don't know where he is, what's going on. But I'm worried. I'm going to try calling him again."

Delfina picked up her phone, pushed away from the breakfast table, and walked to the front screen door, where she could look out at the ocean. Light poured through the screen, backlighting the contours of Delfina's body through the thin fabric of her PJs.

Hawk's number rang. He picked up.

"Hawk! I've been so worried about you. Where are you? Are you all right?"

Delfina put the phone on speaker so Colin could hear.

"Sorry, Cuz. I should have called sooner but it's been so hectic. I'm up in Bellingham. Our Playa Azul landlord gave all of us only a week to move out. I think that short of a notice is illegal, but none of us was in a position to fight it. Our landlord sold the house to a big real estate development corporation that's buying up blocks of historical homes in downtown Playa Azul. They're planning to bulldoze the houses, the historic library, the downtown farmer's market, and heritage trees, and build multilevel parking structures and twenty-story high-rises—five times higher than any existing building in the city."

"Oh hell no. That's definitely illegal," said Delfina. "The city has development ordinances, including height and size limits, protection of historical buildings and heritage trees. New parking structures? What about the city's climate action plan? They're supposed to be planning for *less* cars. How can they get away with that?" Delfina pushed the screen door open and stepped out onto the front porch where she could breathe the sea air and get a better view of sparkling ocean and blue sky.

"Big money got control of our city planners and city council, Cuz," said Hawk. "They rewrote the ordinances. They're even planning to build high-rises along the San Lorenzo River, with twenty-four/seven lights shining on the water. That's going to really mess up the endangered salmon trying to migrate upstream into the mountain creeks to spawn."

"But we have strong local, state, and federal environmental protection laws, especially for the endangered native wildlife. Our salmon and the riparian area are priceless."

"All those laws take vigilance to enforce," said Hawk. "The old hippies and progressives who used to actively defend our natural environment and our way of life are aging out and dying, or being priced out and moving away. People who live in Playa Azul now only care about themselves. That's why I'm up in Bellingham, checking things out. I can't afford to rent in Playa Azul or anywhere in Santa Lucia County anymore.

I don't want to end up homeless, sleeping on the street. It's cheaper to live here, and hopefully safer for people like me. There's more support for the arts here, too."

"Please stay safe, Hawk. I miss you. Let me know right away when you get a permanent address."

"I will. I promise to stay in touch. I'll text you at least once a week. And Delfina, I'm happy that you're with Colin. You two are good together. Love you, Cuz."

"I love you too. Bye."

Delfina ended the call. "Whew," she said. "I'm so relieved to know he's all right."

Colin had followed her out to the porch and was standing at her back. She turned, into his waiting arms.

He pulled her to his chest, and she gasped in surprise. He pressed her closer, not even trying to hide the erection under the towel threatening to slip off his hips.

All he wanted was to lose himself in her. He could tell by her scent that she was turned on too. The things they'd just been talking about, which had felt so desperately important minutes before, now seemed insignificant. Making love with Delfina was all that mattered.

"Delfina, I want you so much."

"Yes, but—"

He breathed her in like a drowning man desperate for air.

"Yes?"

Her lips were slightly parted. The sweet warmth of her breath pulled him in. He brushed her lips with his. Gently, he drew her closer. Her breasts, pressing against his chest through her whisper-thin camisole, ignited a wildfire that blazed up his core.

She raised her arms over his shoulders and laced her fingers around his neck. Her pink tongue darted out and moistened his bottom lip. Then she kissed him.

Colin's knees buckled. He sat down on the big wicker porch chair behind him, lifting Delfina onto his lap.

He caressed the flawless skin of her cheek and brushed her sensuous lips with his fingertips. Her face shone with unaffected beauty. He wound his fingers in her fragrant, silky hair. For a long moment of tingling silence, he searched her eyes, and read what he needed to know. They kissed, gently at first, then hungrily, with unrestrained passion.

46

S TILL HOLDING HER on his lap, he slid his hand across her breasts, veiled by the diaphanous camisole. His fingers made slow circles, as he teased each nipple, erect underneath the silky fabric. All the while, he kissed and nibbled her neck, and under her ear, burying his face in the faint strawberry warmth of her.

Eyes closed, he slid his tongue into her mouth, more aroused with each of her sweet, delicious moans. Mind swirling, Colin tumbled into a universe of exquisite pleasure.

Floating motionless while the stars realigned, he listened to the infinite silence between notes in the music of the spheres. He had entered a new reality. He knew that his life, and hers, were about to be forever changed.

His hands worked their way under the camisole. He kneaded her breasts, until she cried out for his kisses. He bent to the call with gentle lips, and then with his tongue.

Her mouth sought his. Their kisses were deep, wet, wanting.

Answering the desire in her eyes, he slipped his fingers lower. Her hips lunged to meet his hand.

He rose from the chair, lifting her. Her legs wrapped around him.

Still kissing, he carried her into his bedroom and gently settled her on his bed.

He knelt over her, watching her breasts rise and fall.

She threw her arm across her eyes, and began to cry.

Startled, he sat next to her on the bed. He knew intuitively not to touch her.

"What's going on, Delfina? Can we talk?"

She opened her eyes, still welling with tears, and frowned at him.

"Would you like to sit up?" He piled a couple of pillows against the headboard.

She pushed herself to sitting and leaned against the pillows.

Colin studied her face, and chose his words with care. "I learned from my shrink in Afghanistan that when strong emotions get triggered, it helps to name them. You've been through a lot, Delfina. Your mom was murdered, you're being stalked, you were raped when you were thirteen. Maybe we stirred all that up just now. Want to talk about it?"

"Name my emotions? Oh, God, there's so much confusion swirling inside me." Delfina gazed out the window, twisting a lock of hair around her finger.

She turned back to him, anxiety clouding her face. "Mostly I feel shame, Colin. Shame and self-loathing. I know it's wrong, but I feel dirty and stupid that I was raped, like it was my fault."

Colin shook his head. His forehead wrinkled; his emotions roiled. He knew Delfina's was a common reaction among rape victims, and nothing he could say would help. The best he could do for her right now was to compassionately listen.

"Years have passed since the rape, but I still have nightmares about it. I've kept my sexuality locked away, shut down all these years since then, afraid to reopen the memories and feelings. But somehow just now, it was like my body remembered the assault. Because I was drugged, I only have glimpses of memory in my mind of what happened, but my body remembers everything, including the terror and horrible pain. It makes me afraid to—to try."

"It breaks my heart that that happened to you, Delfina. I promise I will wait as long as you need, for you to heal and for us to work through this. No pressure. Nothing has to happen here. You are in control. Just tell me what you need."

"I feel like part of me is broken. I know sex can be a beautiful thing, but I wonder, is all this shame always going to rise up and overwhelm me whenever you touch me that way? When you carried me in here, I felt the same stabbing pain I felt when I was raped, then my body went numb."

"My shrink in Kandahar talked to me about somatic memory and trauma. I don't have a lot of answers, but I know you are absolutely not broken, Delfina. You are perfect. I love you deeply, with or without sex. I see you and I respect all of who you are. If you don't want to make love, I'm fine with that. If you do want to make love, tell me how I can give you the pleasure you deserve."

"I honestly don't know. I know nothing. I've never had an orgasm, Colin. I've never even touched myself."

As she spoke, Delfina unconsciously ran her fingers over her inner left thigh.

Raised red scars, like the claw marks of a large beast, violated the perfection of Delfina's smooth skin.

"Delfina, what happened there? How did you get those scars?"

Delfina's tears wet the scars. She sighed deeply. Then, like water breaking through a dam, her words flooded out.

"I've already told you about my mother arranging for me to have a traditional Soul Retrieval after the rape."

Colin nodded, forehead furrowed.

"That helped me cope with the initial trauma. But after my best friend's suicide, I fell into a deep, deep depression. I just wanted to die. I hated myself for being alive. I didn't think I deserved to live when my friend was dead. I was so ashamed, so full of self-loathing and emotional pain, that I started secretly cutting myself. I guess I was trying to make the pain and ugliness on the outside equal the pain and ugliness on the inside. God, I was so young, so confused, so messed up. I thought that by cutting myself in such an intimate place, my mother wouldn't see it, wouldn't figure it out. But Mama never missed a thing. She confronted me about the cutting, made me start working with a psychiatrist, and enrolled me in a teen psychiatric counseling group for suicide prevention. Eventually I got better, or so I thought until a few minutes ago. Now you know the whole truth. You know how damaged I am."

"You are perfect, Delfina. I've never known a more beautiful, perfect woman in every way as you. I think I'm in love with you."

"But what if we can't ever have sex?"

"You're in charge, love. Just being with you here right now is enough for me. You are my world. It doesn't matter if we have sex or not. Let's just try to relax and enjoy whatever pleasure we may give to each other, day by day, in any way that feels right to you. Listen to yourself, to your body. Tell me or show me what you want. Take as long as you need. We don't need to worry about orgasms, as if it's a goal to achieve. That's only a small part of what being in love means."

"Really?" Delfina cradled Colin's cheek, her fingers dabbling in his new beard. Her eyes reflected back his love.

"Just one thing," said Colin. "If you ever decide to have sex with me and you get triggered, I hope you don't all of a sudden turn into a mountain lion and maul me."

Delfina laughed. "I know you think you're making a joke, but you'd better watch out, Colin Dawson. You have no idea who you're dealing with."

47

O N THURSDAY, MAY 19, Sheriff Rosa received an alert from Saint Francis Hospital. Johnny Taylor had expired at 3:15 a.m., nearly two weeks after he was rescued. The boy had remained in a coma until the end.

Rosa shared the news with Detective Jamison and Agent Chen.

"Sorry to hear that," said Jamison. "I thought he might pull through."

"He was out in the mountains all night in a freezing cold windstorm," said Chen. "Hypothermia, dehydration, exposure, massive levels of chemicals in the boy's system. It was all just too much for his body."

"Once he started buying fake Adderall from that bunch up at the quarry, the poor kid didn't stand a chance. I feel for the whole family," said Jamison.

"So do I, so do I," said Lieutenant Rosa.

"Remind me, what were the chemicals Dr. Sandow found in his system?" asked Jamison.

Rosa skimmed the pathologist's report. "Dextroamphetamine, amphetamine, fentanyl and a small amount of xylazine."

"Xylazine. The animal sedative also found in Ramona Cuera's body. Makes sense they'd find it in Johnny's lab workup," said Chen.

"Xylazine is one of the cheap additives used on the black market to adulterate pharmaceuticals, like Adderall."

"Johnny's death was no accident," said Chen. "Marshal Stone's surveillance video shows that Johnny was abducted when he went to buy that adulterated Adderall at the gate to the quarry. Who snatched him, and why?"

"Maybe he saw something he shouldn't have," said Jamison.

"Where do we stand with the arrests made?" asked Rosa.

"Everyone rounded up in the quarry bust has been arraigned, sir," said Jamison. "No bail set for any of them."

"Good." Rosa stroked his moustache. "Hopefully they'll stay in custody until trial."

"I was thinking," said Jamison, "even though none of them fit the profile of Ramona Cuera's killer, we did catch some really bad guys. If any of them had gotten their hooks deeper into the Clark's Landing community, Johnny Taylor would've only been the beginning. I don't even want to think of the evil they could have caused."

"True that," said Chen.

Rosa stared at the digital murder board. "George, can your investigators locate Matsen's Proud Boy chat room on the dark web? Matsen and Kozel's prints and DNA were all over Delfina Cuera's home. Presumably they broke in with the intent to abduct, probably even harm her. Right now, Matsen and Kozel are also our prime suspects for the Ramona Cuera murder. We need to know if they were acting alone, or if someone else contracted Matsen and Kozel to dispose of Ramona Cuera and her daughter. Who else had motive?"

"Yes, sir. We're already on it."

Rosa flipped through the pages of his pocket notebook. "I can't help but wonder if Johnny witnessed Ramona's murder on one of his ramblings around Cougar Creek Coast Ranch."

"I've thought that too," said Chen. "Johnny didn't fall down that cliff."

"Someone pushed him," said Jamison.

Rosa tapped a pack of gum on his desk.

"That boot print found by the quarry gate near where Johnny was abducted—did it match the print at the murder site?"

"We haven't heard from forensics about that yet," said Jamison.

"Tell the lab we need that information ASAP," said Rosa. "Did anyone think to look around on the cliff where Johnny was rescued for boot prints matching the ones at the murder scene?" asked Rosa.

"No, sir."

"Probably futile," said Rosa, "what with Rafe and his horse and the helicopter rescue disturbing the scene, but let's have someone go up and look around anyway. You never know."

"Yes, sir," said Jamison. "Consider it done."

Rosa turned to Agent Chen. "George, have your cyber forensic agents managed to open Johnny's phone and computer yet?"

"Yes. I got a text yesterday afternoon that all of Johnny's data is now available to us."

"Good. We need to comb through the boy's photos from the day of Ramona Cuera's murder. We have his sketchbook here in evidence to examine, too."

Rosa turned to Detective Jamison. "We need to go back up to Agua Pura Farm and take a look at that kid Frankie's drawings. Should have done that weeks ago, but looking at children's artwork just wasn't a high priority, until now."

"Maybe those two knew each other," said Jamison.

"Good thinking." Rosa wrote himself a note to ask Frankie about Johnny Taylor.

Then he thumbed through the pages of his pocket notebook. "Here's another thread we need to pick up: the warrant that authorized us to search the Vadim home expired ten days after it was issued. We need to get a new one and search that place thoroughly."

48

ON FRIDAY, MAY 20, at six a.m., Sarah Amari arrived as usual from Agua Pura Farm to set up her booth at the Lockland Village Farmers Market. Lockland, a picturesque mountain community, is nestled among the redwoods in the San Lorenzo River Valley, a major watershed that cuts through the coastal mountains down to the beach town of Playa Azul.

At ten o'clock, Sarah smiled at her customer as she gave him change for a quarter pound of snow peas and bunch of arugula. She glanced over his shoulder just as two men across the street exited Grizzlies Liquor.

They looked familiar, especially the hefty one with a bushy red beard wearing a camo shirt and ballcap. Where had she seen them before?

Sarah watched the men strut down the sidewalk. A slight breeze blew red beard's unbuttoned shirt aside, revealing a dirty white "Don't Tread On Me" rattlesnake logo T-shirt stretched over a fat belly, and a barely concealed handgun.

Sarah had never seen anyone but the police carrying a firearm in California. It was illegal in this state to carry a gun without a permit, virtually impossible for a civilian to obtain a concealed-carry permit, and it was absolutely not part of the culture in California's deep blue coastal communities, not even in the somewhat more inland rustic redwood mountain hamlet of Lockland. Sarah felt revulsion, as if she were watching man-sized globs of viral contagion ooze down the street like they owned it.

A light bulb went on in her head, and she remembered where she'd seen them: on posters in the Santa Lucia Post Office. They were wanted for the murder of Ramona Cuera.

With shaking hands, she opened the photo app on her phone and took video of the men getting into an old beat-up green Honda. She shot close-ups of the license plate as they drove away, then she called 911.

★   ★   ★

Detective Jamison knocked on Lieutenant Rosa's office door, then entered. He nodded to Warden Dawson, who had been discussing the Ramona Cuera homicide investigation with the lieutenant.

"Sir," said Jamison, "we just got a hit on that wanted poster for Kozel and Matsen."

"Tell me."

"A woman named Sarah Amari called it in, got the plate number. She said they drove north on Highway 9 up the mountain toward Dead Man's Gulch. She emailed photos and a video she took. Should be in your inbox."

"Get those images up on the board. Were there any security cameras in the area?"

"Yes, sir. We have surveillance from Grizzlies Liquors coming in, as well as from the gas station next door and the post office down the street."

Video streamed onto the smart board. There could be no question that the men in the pictures were Al Kozel and Bert Matsen, suspects wanted for the murder of Ramona Cuera and for conspiring to blow up an electrical substation.

"Get a drone in the air," said Rosa. "Track them."

"Yes, sir."

"I want a SWAT team after them on the ground. Now. Warden Dawson, you're on the team. I'll notify Agent Chen."

★   ★   ★

At twilight, the SWAT team vans pulled up to the run-down cabin. A single AK-47 fired out of a broken window. The rifle's distinctive loud booming report echoed through the darkening woods of Wild Horse Gulch.

Colin jumped out of the van and hit the ground hard. The whiz of a 7.62mm round missed his ear by an inch, followed by the sickening thud of impact and a choked cry. Officer Miller, right behind him, crumpled to the dirt, a crimson bloom spreading on his tactical leg-panel.

Without a second thought, Colin pivoted, a surge of adrenaline overriding the ringing in his ears, and dragged Miller's limp weight behind the ballistic shield of the armored van. A storm of automatic fire hammered the vehicle's reinforced side, rocks and dirt spitting from the nearby ground. Colin clamped a field-dressing to Miller's femoral artery, the familiar metallic tang of blood thick in the air, until a medic, already sprinting from the rear, took over with a quick, practiced handover.

Colin joined the stacked formation moving towards the cabin, a silent, disciplined serpentine of dark-clad figures. The rhythmic thump of the stealthy advance reverberated through his chest, a primal drumbeat. Dodging suppressed rifle fire that chewed at the tree line, Colin's mind flashed back to the dust and claustrophobia of Marjah in Helmand Province.

★   ★   ★

He tripped, rolling instinctively behind a gnarly oak, the impact jarring his body armor. He blinked, sucked in a ragged breath that tasted of gunpowder and dry earth, and shook his head to clear the ringing. Another line of men, precise and swift, flowed past him, flanking the cabin's western wall.

From the cabin's shattered window, the buzzing roar of an AK-47 furiously ripped across the woods, the muzzle flash momentarily silhouetting the cabin against the twilight gloom. An acrid, biting smell of propellant hung thick in the air.

Colin circled, low and fast, towards the rear. He tested the back door, a quiet click of his hand on the handle. Locked.

His comms unit crackled: "Overwatch reports single target, cabin. Take target alive if possible. Fugitive two, still at large. Repeat, fugitive two at large. Proceed with extreme caution."

Enhanced by his helmet-mounted night vision, Colin swept the forest understory, searching for any movement. Nothing.

He focused back on the lock and executed a rapid series of precise movements with his breaching tools. The lock mechanism gave a soft, almost imperceptible click. Weapon at the ready, Colin eased the door open, stepping warily into a cramped, shadowed back room, assessing the space in a fluid sweep.

Clear.

Aware that the second fugitive could strike from any shadow, Colin pressed himself against some rough wooden boxes, seeking cover. Rifle shots tore through the air from the next room, the concussive blasts ringing in his ears even through the muffled protection of his ComTac headset. He drew a steadying breath, shaking his head to clear the lingering echoes and steeling himself against the rising tide of a flashback, then edged closer to the main room.

Through a chink in the wallboards, Colin spotted Matsen's back.

Suddenly, the front door splintered inward, two officers bursting through, followed by the rest of the squad. Weapons leveled, they aimed at Bert Matsen.

Growling and hissing like a cornered hyena, Matsen cursed and leveled his rifle at the line of armed officers. His trigger finger twitched, eyes fixed in a frozen glare on the SWAT team.

Seizing the instant, Colin stormed into the room, tackling Matsen from behind.

Fighting the urge to recoil from the fugitive's repulsive stench, Colin wrenched the rifle from Matsen's grasp. It clattered to the wooden floor.

Colin kicked it across the room toward his squad. An officer secured it while the others maintained their ready stance, prepared to assist Colin but adhering to orders: bring in the suspect alive; lethal force a last resort.

Matsen squirmed out of Colin's hold, a Bowie knife flashing into his hand from his boot.

Colin's brain shut down. Muscle memory took over.

Matsen carved the air around Colin, the blade aiming for eyes and throat. *Fighting dirty. No surprise.* Colin ducked and spun, narrowly evading the hungry steel.

Over and over, Matsen's long sharp Bowie knife sliced wildly through the air. Colin danced, a blur of motion, escaping the blade by mere inches, his skin tingling with the near misses.

Snarling, Matsen drove Colin up against a wall, thrusting his sharp blade toward Colin's groin with an evil laugh. Colin grabbed a piece of firewood and parried, blocking the knife, then leapt over a wooden crate, spun, and landed at Matsen's back.

Matsen cursed, pivoted, and lunged. Colin kicked the crate under Matsen's feet, disorienting him, then seized Matsen's knife arm, leveraging his weight to throw the larger man off balance. Matsen grunted in surprise, staggering backward, his grip on the Bowie knife momentarily loosening.

Seizing the opening, Colin delivered a swift, powerful kick to Matsen's knee, sending a shockwave of pain through the fugitive's leg. Matsen howled, dropping the knife with a clatter as he clutched his injured limb. Before Matsen could recover, Colin was on him, twisting the man's arm behind his back and forcing him to the ground.

Matsen screamed, swore, and wriggled free, recovering the knife.

Colin lunged, grabbing Matsen's filthy shirt.

Matsen twisted, his shirt ripping away, then slashed at Colin with the blade.

Colin whirled Matsen's torn shirt over his head, roping Matsen's knife with the fabric, and yanked. The steel clattered to the floor.

Matsen turned and ran. Colin threw a piece of firewood, hitting the fugitive in the head. Matsen fell. Blood poured from the wound, seeping into the old floorboards.

Matsen cursed and moaned, his hand groping for the fallen knife.

Colin pounced on him, held him down, and punched him in the face, hard. A direct hit. Matsen passed out.

The rest of the squad moved in swiftly. An officer secured the fallen Bowie knife, while two others cuffed Matsen. They lifted him off the floor and hauled him out of the cabin to a waiting van.

Colin clutched his side, breath rasping. Rifle smoke mingled thickly with the coppery scent of blood in the air. His tongue scraped over his teeth, metallic saliva a bitter taste in his parched mouth. *Blood and iron.*

He was pretty sure he hadn't been cut. He hoped he hadn't reinjured his ribs. His recently dislocated shoulder burned like hell. He rubbed his wrist. That weird scar throbbed and itched.

Outside, frantic shouts of "Kozel! In the woods behind the cabin!" cut through the darkening night as officers gave chase.

A search inside the cabin yielded four AK-47s, a thousand rounds of ammo, two explosive grenades, an unregistered rifle with the identification number sanded off, and a sawed-off shotgun.

In one of the wooden crates, the SWAT team found a homemade bomb powerful enough to destroy the Coast Ranch substation. Detective

Jamison observed while a demolition expert prepared the bomb for safe removal.

"Good Lord." Lieutenant Rosa rubbed his wrinkled forehead. "This place is a tinder box. One stray spark from all that gun fire, and this cabin could have blown."

"Yeah," said the demolition expert. "And that could have started a forest fire with the potential to wipe out the whole San Lorenzo Valley."

"Well that's one ticking time bomb we no longer have to worry about," said Jamison.

"We've still got at least one more live one to neutralize," said Lieutenant Rosa.

"Sir?"

"Kozel eluded capture. He is still at large."

★　　　★　　　★

Later, in the interrogation room at the Sheriff's Headquarters, Detective Jamison questioned Proud Boy Bert Matsen, while Rosa, Chen, Colin Dawson, and Marshal Stone observed through one-way glass.

"We found your prints at Ramona Cuera's home," said Detective Jamison. "We've got you dead to rights for breaking and entering the house and smashing things up. We know you were looking for Delfina Cuera, that you chased her and shot at her and her mother in San Diego," Jamison bluffed. "What were you planning to do to Delfina? Why did you kill her mother?"

"Okay. I admit we were on the trail of Ramona Cuera and her bitch-spawn back in San Diego. A few years ago, we got a contract to take them out, okay? The dude was gonna pay us a lot of money. So yeah, we almost got them, once, in the hills above the city. But a fuckin' Santana wind came up all of a sudden and blinded us. It was a goddam witches' dust storm. We lost 'em. The dude that wanted them to disappear gave us a big advance. He was threatening to do something real bad to us if we didn't deliver. It's taken us years. But finally, we tracked them up here. So you're right. I tossed the bitch's house, okay? But I didn't murder Ramona. Hell no. That cunt was killed with a crossbow. I don't even own one of those things. They're for pussies. That's not how I roll. I would have shot her with a rifle."

"Who hired you to kill them?"

"Hell if I know. It came from the Dark Web. I was pinged while I was on a Proud Boy chat room. Some anonymous dude reached out.

Never saw him and don't know his name. I took the job and invited Kozel to get in on it with me."

"Where were you from midnight until four p.m. on Thursday, April 14?"

Matsen's thin Aryan lips spread into a self-satisfied smile. "That's easy. On April 14, I was at the Motel 6 on Second Avenue in San Diego, trolling cop reports on my laptop. That's when I saw that Ramona Cuera had been killed, and I called Kozel to let him know somebody else already horned in on our job. We caught a red-eye on Southwest Air right away. We wanted to see if it was true that somebody else took out Ramona. Got to San Jose at the ass-crack of dawn on April 15. We bought a used piece of shit Chrysler beater and drove to the murder site on the coast north of Santa Lucia. We got to the Sheriff's Command Center at that new so-called national monument late that afternoon, April 15. If my information serves me correctly, the bitch was shot on the fourteenth. We weren't even there yet. Only thing you got on me is a measly B and E."

Matsen's smug grin made Rosa want to reach through the one-way glass and punch him.

"We'll check out your alibi," said Jamison.

"You go ahead and do that."

"Where is Kozel now?" Jamison asked.

Matsen hissed through his teeth. "You think I'd tell you if I knew?"

"Why were you in the Cuera home on June 10?"

"I already told you. Me and my compadre, Al Kozel, we're on a mission. We signed a contract and took an oath."

"What kind of oath?"

"To cleanse those filthy squaws, and all the other non-whites, Jews, ragheads, retards, woke libs, and queers from our country before they spawn more of their kind. We white men are a dying breed. Anglo-Saxon culture is under siege in the USA. We patriots gotta stand our ground." Matsen made his hand in the shape of a gun, aimed his index finger at Rosa, Chen, Colin, and Stone observing behind the one-way glass, and pantomimed pulling the trigger. Then he blew imaginary smoke off the tip of his pretend gun. His thin lips stretched into a grin, and he pointed to the insignia on his ball cap— a badge with a yellow rooster and the word, DEFEND.

"What would you have done to Delfina if she had been in the house? Did you plan to murder her?"

"What do you think?"

"I don't know. Enlighten me."

"Nah. We didn't plan to kill her. We were gonna lock her up and cock her up. Use that sweet piece of ass 'til we got bored, then traffic her to the highest foreign bidder and finally collect the rest of our contract fee. Double dipped. Cherry on top." Matsen licked his lips.

"If you trafficked her, would you still get paid by whoever hired you to 'take her out'?"

"Yep. Our employer just wanted those Cuera women to be silenced and go far away from the US forever. Like maybe to a harem in the Middle East."

★　　★　　★

An hour later, a deputy informed Rosa, Chen, and Jamison that Matsen's alibi checked out. Colin Dawson and Marshal Stone had already departed.

"Matsen and Kozel came up from San Diego on the same plane," said the deputy. "They didn't arrive in Santa Lucia until the day after Ramona Cuera's body was found."

Rosa frowned and opened a new pack of chewing gum.

"These are really bad guys, Boss," said Jamison. "Please tell me that Matsen's not just going to walk. Think he'll get off on bail?"

"Absolutely not. He alibied out of the murder charge, but we have his confession, on video and in writing, to the home invasion with intent to rape and traffic. We'll hold Matsen until arraignment. At the arraignment, we'll request that no bail be set due to the fact that he has a history of violence and presents a flight risk."

"What about Kozel?" asked Jamison.

"Priority number one now is finding Kozel. When we arrest him, we already have him for impersonating a federal officer, as well as for breaking and entering the Cuera home, along with Matsen, with intent to rape and traffic."

"By the time Matsen and Kozel go to trial," said Agent Chen, "I think the prosecutor will have a solid case against both of them for domestic terrorism as well. The federal government takes such allegations seriously and prosecutes those cases aggressively to the full extent of the law. If convicted, penalties can be from three years to life in state prison."

"I don't see either of them going free for a good long while," said Rosa.

"But first we have to catch Kozel. And we still don't know who murdered Ramona Cuera," said Jamison.

"Or why," added Chen.

"Something's been in the back of my mind, nagging at me," said Rosa.

"What's that?"

"Whoever shot Ramona Cuera is an ace technical sniper, an adept user of an unusual tactical bow and arrow. He's smart and cunning. Meticulous. And he evidently traversed a wide area of rough terrain on foot, so we can assume he's in very good shape. Athletic and tall. I should have realized a long time ago that Matsen and Kozel don't have the stature, physique, cunning, or skills to be Ramona's killers."

Rosa's phone rang and he answered Colin Dawson's call.

"What is it, son?"

"Sir," said Colin, "I forgot to tell you. When we raided the drug compound in the quarry, I saw the truck used to abduct Johnny Taylor parked up there. I recognized it from the video. Maybe someone should go back up and examine it for evidence."

"Good find, Dawson. I'll send a forensic team up there today."

49

I N THE MIDDLE OF THE NIGHT, Colin woke to the full moon's light breaking through his window.

Delfina stood framed in his open bedroom door. Moonlight shimmered seductively over her graceful, bare shoulders, and her beautiful face, open and vulnerable.

Colin sat up and leaned against the pillow propped against his headboard. *Am I dreaming?*

He watched the moonlight pour across Delfina's perfect breasts, rising gently with deep, even breaths. As she stepped toward him, the moonlight spread over the feminine curve of her belly. Colin's desire rose.

Delfina had been sleeping in Colin's spare bedroom every night since she'd returned from San Diego, almost a week ago. He'd fallen asleep each night alone in his bed, yearning for her. *Is this real?*

She stood at the edge of his bed. Her scent overwhelmed him. He reached for her. Their hands met, entwined.

She knelt on his bed. He threw off the sheet covering his naked body, and pulled her down on top of him.

With a playful growl, she scratched her fingernails lightly across his chest. He shuddered. She gently bit his shoulder.

He rolled her over so that he was on top of her, then took a breast in each hand and licked and sucked her bright red nipples. "Can you feel this?"

She arched her back and whimpered and lifted her hips. She wove her fingers in his hair and gently tried to nudge his head down toward the promised land.

He released her breasts and moved his hand onto her belly. She tried to coax his hand lower, but he resisted. He drew circles on her perfect round belly and then kissed it. She writhed and softly moaned under his kisses.

"Show me what you want me to do," Colin whispered.

She moved his hand down between her legs, over her silky pajama shorts.

"Wait a minute," he said. He kissed her on the tip of the nose, rolled off of her, and leaned over to his bedside table.

He opened a drawer and pulled out a pack of condoms and new bottle of high quality intimate lubricant. She sat up and he showed her the bottle. "I will never, ever force you, my love. But just in case the day ever comes, I want to keep you safe and pain free. This will make whatever we do feel better."

She held his face in both her hands, looked into his soul, then kissed him on the mouth, opening to him, trembling, but eager.

"You're a goddess," he said.

Delfina rolled off the bed and stood facing him. He sat on the edge of the bed, watching her slowly pull down her pajama shorts and step out of them as gracefully as a dancer. She came closer and straddled his legs.

His cock stood straight and tall, quivering. Delfina met Colin's eyes. He smiled and raised a questioning eyebrow. She nodded.

He swooped her up and lay her on her back on his bed, sidling on his belly toward her open legs. He ran his hands along her soft inner thighs, lightly caressing the old scars, then teased across her mound of Venus. She moaned.

Then he covered the same territory with kisses.

Frantic for more, she grabbed his hand and tried to force it between her legs.

"Please. Touch me, here."

He teased around her inner thighs with light licks and gentle tickles, while she panted and thrashed. Lightly he slipped a finger into the crease between her legs. She gasped.

He pulled away, moistened his finger with lubricant, and wriggled it back along the crease. "Oh, yes," she whispered.

He kissed her swollen vulva, parted the lips, and lightly tongued a circle around her clitoris.

"Oh mmmmn …"

He softly grazed her pearl with his tongue.

Delfina cried out.

"Did I hurt you?"

"No. Don't stop. Please. Don't stop."

"Yes, ma'am, but just push me away if you quit liking it."

Colin took his time, gauging Delfina's state of body and mind by listening to her breathing, feeling her heartbeat, monitoring the sounds she was making, and feeling where there was tension in her body.

He was entirely in the moment, with no goal but to give her pleasure.

He raised his head, and looked into her eyes. "I love you, Delfina. I love the way you smell. I love your taste. You are beautiful. Exquisite. My goddess."

He poured lube on his fingers, licked her clit, and gently eased a lubricated finger into her vagina. She pushed against his finger, forcing it deeper, and moved her pelvis up and down in a rhythm Colin matched with his hand and tongue. Her yoni opened like a flower. He gently added a second finger, not disrupting their rhythm. He curled his fingers up toward her G-spot, pressing slightly harder on her clitoris with his tongue.

Delfina threw her head back and cried out. Her yoni contracted around Colin's fingers. His hand was wet. He felt euphoric, swept up in the tidal wave of her awakened sexuality.

With an urgency that matched his own, her voluptuous lips sought his kisses.

She wrapped her legs around his hips with utter abandonment, passionately lunging with her hips.

"I want you inside me, Colin."

"Are you sure?"

"Yes. Now."

He slipped on a condom, slathered it with lube, and gently pressed his cock against her opening. She pulled away as if it hurt her.

"Should I stop?"

"No"

He fingered her and kissed her. She wrapped her hand around his cock and rubbed it against her yoni. He moved his hips slightly. His cock suddenly pushed inside her. She screamed, grabbing his ass, pulling him in closer, lifting and pumping her hips. The feeling of her vagina contracting around his cock almost made him lose it.

He eased out a little and, very slowly, pushed in again, just a little way.

She moaned. He gently circled his fingers over her clit while they rocked together. They gradually found a rhythm, going deeper, deeper, in the timeless dance of life.

A multicolored bouquet blossomed at the point of their connection. Its center opened and opened, consuming them as it expanded like a kaleidoscopic hologram. Their pleasure grew ever more intense, their lovemaking wrenched cries of ecstasy from their very souls.

In flames, they spiraled away from earth, escaping gravity's hold. Time stood still.

The agony of desire burned, squeezed, clamped, and reshaped them, wringing out every drop of who they were; the heat of their passion vitrified the simple clay of their humanity, transforming them into pure crystal, to diamond. They lost all consciousness of their individual selves and became One, exploding in a luminous supernova, scattering light, colors, and love all across the universe.

At last, inexorable gravity recaptured them, and they tumbled to earth like gentle rain.

For a long time after, the two lovers lay still, joined together, the embers of passion's heat a simmering pulse between them.

Colin floated at sea on a boat made of swan feathers. He memorized the delicate color of his lover's lips and cheeks, and every curve and highlight of her face, still aflame with intense emotion.

She smiled at him languidly. They gazed into one another's eyes, sharing without words the warmth and peace of true connection.

Delfina's voice startled him when at last she spoke.

"Colin, you said, 'I love you.' Is that something you always say during sex?"

Colin pulled apart from her then, like unplugging from an electrical socket, leaned on his elbow, and looked into her eyes. "That was for you, Delfina. Only you. I love you."

He caressed her face and kissed her lips, circled her perfect breast with his fingertip.

"I feel the same about you, Colin. I've never been interested in any other man. I love you more than the stars in the sky."

They kissed tenderly, with their lips and tongues and teeth and breath, and with their full, open hearts.

Colin cupped his hands around her cheeks and gazed deep into her eyes. He rubbed noses with her and gave her another soft kiss on the lips, then on her forehead as if bestowing some kind of baptism or sacred blessing.

"Delfina, if you wanted to, you could live with me while you go to grad school next year. My place here is farther up the coast than your house in town, so you'd have an easier commute."

"I think for now, we'd better take it one day at a time, lover. I just don't feel ready to talk about the future. There are still too many things to sort out."

"Lover? Call me that again, please." Colin felt disturbed that she had demurred on his invitation, but thought it best to let it be, for now.

Delfina laughed and rolled on top of him. He slid his hand over the curve of her hips and her perfectly smooth round bottom.

Later that night, she rolled over in her sleep, and he snuggled his arm around her waist. His knees bent and cradled her. Still asleep, she wriggled against him, and his body was ready to make love again, although he didn't want to wake her.

He glanced at the floor by the bed, where moonlight illuminated the puddle of silky pajama bottoms Delfina had stripped off a few hours ago. It felt like a lifetime ago.

Colin's growing love for this woman spread from his heart through his entire body, from head down to his toes, radiating a warm protective glow that blanketed him and his lover. He slid his hand from Delfina's waist to her breasts, and sighed. With a sensation of deep peace and satisfaction, Colin fell asleep.

At five o'clock, the moon had set, the house was pitch black, and Colin and Delfina were both sound asleep.

Neither of them heard the doorknob rattle.

Or the lock being picked.

Or the man sneaking through the front door into Colin's house.

The man stood in Colin's dark living room and scratched his thick red beard. He slipped his hand under his flak jacket, wriggled his fingers around the belly sagging like an inner tube over his belt, dug under his camo shirt and filthy undershirt, pushed his hand down his pants, and scratched an itch in his crotch hairs.

He pulled his hand out, sniffed it, and rested it on the butt of the SIG Sauer holstered on his belt. He licked his lips, muttering under his breath. "Gonna get me that dirty little squaw pussy this time."

He spit a glob of chew on Colin's mother's rug, then turned toward the open bedroom door.

As he turned, his elbow winged a pottery vase, and it crashed against the wall.

"Fuck."

Colin and Delfina woke at the sound.

Wordlessly, they slipped from bed and hid in the deep shadows behind a tall chest of drawers.

★　　★　　★

Kozel stood in the dark at the side of the bed. He drew, cocked, and pointed his gun at the lumps under the covers.

"Got you this time, you little cunt. Don't think that boyfriend of yourn can help you. He's already a dead man. I been watchin' this house since you disappeared, figurin' you might come to him once you seed your house were trashed."

Kozel switched on the bright light attached to his gun, flipped back the bed covers, and his jaw dropped.

Colin pounced at him from behind. Kozel spun away from Colin's grasp and fired wildly.

Delfina screamed and fell to the floor.

A scarlet splash of her blood flooded Colin's psyche.

His Army Ranger training flipped into high gear.

He grabbed Kozel's fat neck in a chokehold from the rear and slammed a knee up into his balls.

Gasping and gurgling for breath, Kozel dropped his gun.

Colin kicked the backs of Kozel's legs, forcing him to drop to his knees.

Grabbing the SIG off the floor, Colin planted the gun barrel in the hollow at the base of Kozel's skull. "Hands up. Don't move."

Colin glanced over his shoulder at Delfina.

A bullet had grazed her arm. She was standing, watching wide-eyed, not bleeding too badly. She had pulled Colin's T-shirt from the pile of clothes on the floor and was pressing it to her wound.

"Delfina, there are zip ties in my uniform pocket, in the closet. Grab them!"

Kozel cursed, twisted, and tried to seize Colin.

Colin pistol whipped Kozel in the face. His jawbone made a crunching sound and blood gushed from his nose. He fell face first on the floor, in a fetal position, holding his jaw with his hands.

Pointing the gun at Kozel's head, Colin drilled his knee into the base of Kozel's spine until he was lying prone, face down.

"Hands behind your back." Kozel drooled and wailed, blood pooling on the floor from his nose and mouth.

Delfina handed Colin a plastic zip tie, and Colin fastened it around Kozel's wrists, pulling the zip so tight the wrists were inseparable.

Kozel lay on his belly wailing and writhing.

Colin restrained the assailant's ankles in the same manner as his wrists, then pulled the ankles up to meet the wrists, forcing the fat man lying on his belly into a backbend, like a trussed pig.

With the SIG still pointing at Kozel, Colin shouted to Delfina, "Find my phone!"

She ran to the front room, snatched the phone from its charger, rushed back to the bedroom and handed it to Colin.

Colin hit speed dial. "Lieutenant Rosa, we've got Kozel. Hurry!"

While they waited, with Kozel cursing, wailing, and writhing on the floor in a pool of his own blood, Colin took Delfina into the bathroom, and—with the door open so he could keep an eye on Kozel—he washed and bandaged Delfina's wound.

"Just a surface wound, but I know it hurts." Colin held Delfina close.

Within fifteen minutes, Lieutenant Rosa's deputies were hauling Kozel off for booking. Rosa took Colin's and Delfina's statements.

At the kitchen table, they sipped water with fresh lemon and talked while the sun rose.

"Now that we're finally safe from Kozel, I feel like a dark shadow has lifted." said Delfina.

"We're not in the clear yet," said Colin. "We still have to find your mother's murderer."

"It isn't Kozel?"

"It doesn't appear so. But at least now we've got the men who've been stalking you and broke into your house. I heard Matsen admit that he and Kozel were the ones who chased and shot at you and your mom in San Diego. They were contacted on the dark web and anonymously contracted to eliminate you and your mother."

Delfina shivered.

Colin pushed his chair away from the table, rose, and wrapped his arms around her. "We'll catch him, Delfina."

Delfina took a deep breath. Standing to face Colin, she placed her hands on his shoulders. "How are you feeling right now, Colin?"

Colin closed his eyes and did a whole body assessment. "Well, first of all, I finally feel like I can really own the fact that I'm a warrior. I'm not sickened or afraid of being violent anymore. Amazingly, I've completely come to accept the fact that some of us have to be protectors, and I'm grateful I have the strength and skill to fight for and defend what and who I love. I finally feel free, Delfina, and not ashamed, or judging myself for who I am."

Delfina gently brushed a wayward curl away from his eyes. "You should be proud of yourself, Colin. You're a hero. One of the good guys. So, how are you doing physically? It's only been a month since those cops beat you up."

"My injuries are healing pretty well, except for minor aches, especially this morning, thanks to Mr. Kozel. But that bite wound from the day I found your mother is itching and throbbing again." He held his wrist up in the dawn light and examined it. The strange scar, like a tattoo in the shape of a puma, was raised and rippling.

Delfina studied Colin's wrist, her forehead wrinkled. "I wouldn't worry about it. Are you using that salve I gave you?"

"Yep."

"Just give it time." She placed her cooling fingers over the wound.

"Ah, that feels better," said Colin.

Delfina stood on tip toes and kissed him on the cheek. "Have any nightmares lately?"

Colin smiled. "While you were missing, I went through the Soul Retrieval ceremony you arranged for me. I was sick with worry about you, and I thought the Soul Retrieval might bring me closer to you, or help me find you."

"I guess it worked. Here I am." Delfina sat back down and took a sip of her lemon water.

Colin pulled his chair close to Delfina's and took her hand in his. "Seriously, Delfina, it changed me. Since going through the ceremony, the nightmares have pretty much stopped. I feel much less overall anxiety, and I definitely sleep better. And now that you're back, I've actually experienced moments of pure joy for the first time since I was a little kid, like sunshine cracking through dark clouds."

"Good news! What was your Soul Retrieval like? What do you remember?"

"Not much. Honestly, I don't think I was supposed to remember it consciously. It was like a dream. I feel like I slept through a lot of it. I remember the sound of a drum beating, and the Kuseyaay Cha'ak blowing funny smelling mist through a reed whistle. I remember the sensation of running around in a place that seemed strangely familiar, like we were chasing a little kid playing tag. There were some friendly animals, and the feel of the Cha'ak touching my head and heart. That's all.

"But when it was over, I felt more complete, psychologically and even physically stronger, more balanced and at peace with myself. He told me he'd found several fragmented, frightened pieces of my psyche hiding in the spirit world. He brought them back and reintegrated them with my soul. He told me to trust my spirit guides, especially mountain lion. Since then, I've had complete certainty that my life is on the right path. I know who I am—that I was born to be a wildlife warden, a protector of people, animals, and the natural world, and to be with you. You and I are meant to be together. I'm sure of it. I feel like we've always been together. I love you, Delfina Cuera. Completely, with my whole self."

"I love you too. But—" Delfina's eyes had a haunted look. "I'm still feeling up in the air about things."

"What things?"

"For one, I'm worried about the general state of the world, and our country. I'm starting to feel uneasy about the presidential election coming up next year, in '24. I know it's crazy to think that a failed former president and adjudicated rapist with thirty-four felony convictions who incited a violent insurrection and tried to overturn the 2020 election could ever come close to getting back in the White House, but

I'm really starting to fear that, with Putin and Musk behind him, he could take over the country. I think if he gets back into the Whitehouse, we could be living under an oligarchy before the end of his first year as president."

Colin shook his head. "That's never going to happen. Don't waste your time thinking about it. What else has you spooked?"

Delfina stared out through the kitchen window. A long line of pelicans glided across the early morning sky. Her eyes alight with determination, she turned back to Colin. "Colin, I need to see the place where my mother was killed."

"Of course. I'll take you there tomorrow. I've worked more than a forty hour stretch, so I need to take a few days off. Oh, hey. Speaking of nightmares, I just remembered I had a strange dream about you last night, right before Kozel attacked us."

"Tell me."

"You were in a foreign city, with heavy snow all around. You were dressed in gray and white striped pajamas, a big yellow star sewn over your heart. I stood in the falling snow, a mountain lion by my side. We watched soldiers force you into a black 1940s limousine. A man who seemed somewhat familiar to me, wearing a heavy wool coat and a fur cap, got in after you. A chauffeur drove the limo away. I felt powerless to help, like a piece of my soul was being torn out and taken away. Do you believe in reincarnation, Delfina?"

"Of course."

"Do you think that dream could have been a memory from a previous lifetime?"

"Hmm."

50

MONDAY MORNING, MAY 23, platinum gold sun blazed blindingly off the ocean under a cloudless blue sky. Delfina drove her classic 2019 VW Bug, with the top down, south along the wild Pacific coast toward Cougar Creek Coast Ranch.

Colin leaned back in the passenger seat, a hive of happy honeybees humming inside him. He closed his eyes and savored the sweet moment. He couldn't remember when he'd felt such a profound sense of well-being.

On the day after the Kozel home invasion, the Monterey Bay's Mediterranean climate held steady in the comfortable mid-seventies. Delfina tuned her Spotify Car Play station to classical guitarist Isaac Albéniz' bright and triumphant Suite Española Asturias.

She turned off the coast highway onto a byway that took them under a leafy arch of old eucalyptus trees. As they motored under the archway, fragrant eucalyptus leaves twisted in the breeze and sparkled with a million gold lights in the sun. Monarch butterflies fluttered overhead. Albéniz's music swelled, evoking passionate emotions of exuberance and joy.

Delfina pulled up to the padlocked Cougar Creek Coast Ranch gate.

All of a sudden, Colin's bite wound started throbbing painfully. He held his wrist up in the light and examined it. The strange scar in the shape of a puma, with red veinous lines running through it, was spreading up his arm.

The cops no longer guarded the gate. Sheriff Rosa had packed up his tent and the crime scene circus had left the ranch. The area was deserted. Not a soul around. Even the surf was quiet today.

All was silent, as if waiting.

Colin hopped out of Delfina's VW, opened the lock, and pushed open the gate. Delfina drove through and waited for Colin to close and relock it.

Before he got back in her car, he stood, stretched, and gazed up the road. It seemed to lead all the way to the sky. Every time he came up here, the land showed him something new—a landscape as changeable as Delfina—always breathtakingly beautiful and as complex as the matrix of flora and fauna, biotic and abiotic features, that composed this watershed.

Colin could hardly separate the woman from the land. Today, she wore a light spring sundress, dotted with black cows grazing on a coastal prairie that stretched for miles, in a field of topaz sky and ocean that matched her eyes—sultry under a ridgeline of dense redwood forest, populated with deer, fox, coyote, bobcat, wild turkey, quail, mountain lion …

Colin's heart felt like it might burst with love for both the woman and the land.

He ducked back into the VW, and Delfina drove twenty miles an hour up the steep, narrow, winding mountain road, navigating around deep potholes in the old asphalt.

After an especially treacherous S-curve, the road opened to the spacious landing next to the oak grove.

This was where Ramona Cuera had been murdered.

"Park here," said Colin.

Delfina pulled over and parked.

"This is it, right?"

"Yes."

"Show me."

Colin led Delfina under the oaks. Stepping out of the intense sunlight, they were temporarily blinded by the dark shade of the ancient oak grove. Colin took Delfina's hand.

"This was a sacred place to the Natives who once lived here," said Delfina. "I feel it. Show me. Exactly where did you find my mother?"

Colin led her deeper into the oak forest. All the while, his hand and arm painfully throbbed.

"This is the place," he said.

Delfina knelt, placing her hands on the ground. She spoke in a language Colin didn't understand.

A respectful distance away, Colin sat on a fallen limb the size of a bench, cradling his throbbing arm on his leg.

"What's wrong, Colin?"

Delfina sat beside him. She winced at the sight of his pulsing scar.

"Colin, it's time I tell you something. I hope you can hear this without wanting to leave me, but however you take it, I have to say this."

He dug a water bottle out of his pack and drank, then offered it to Delfina, and she drank.

"I'm listening, my love," he said. "Open heart, open mind. Nothing you can say would make me love you less. Tell me."

"I'm not supposed to tell this to anyone. But I trust you, and I think you need to know. So—yeah, you were afraid that I'd think you were crazy for thinking my mom was a mountain lion when you first saw her? Well, listen to this. Here it goes. Ready?"

"Yes. Go."

"Colin, the reason you thought you saw a wounded mountain lion when you first found my mother is because she really was a mountain lion."

Colin flinched in surprise, but Delfina continued holding his hand.

"Hawk thinks it's something genetic in my people," she said. "My mother took me to a cave the first time I changed, when those men in San Diego were hunting us with guns. In the cave, she showed me ancient paintings that depict our people changing into mountain lions."

Colin laughed. A short burst. "Is this a test? Yeah, I have PTSD, which sometimes comes with hallucinations. But I've hardly had any for quite a while. And—" The look on Delfina's face stopped him.

"Colin, trust me. I love you. I would never set you up for some mean mind game."

"You're serious?" Colin put his head in his hands. "Oh, my God. Maybe you're the one who's unhinged."

"I know. It's fantastical, unbelievable, impossible, but—"

"Hold on," said Colin. "I have a university degree in environmental science. I trust science. I've got to tell you, after all the insane conspiracy theories that have been floating around since you-know-who got elected in

2016—the QAnon stories about libs eating babies, Jews using space lasers to start the California forest fires, Covid vaccines with implants so the government can track us … my bullshit meter is tuned to high alert. You're trying to mess with my head, right? Forget about it. I can't believe you."

"Remember what you saw when my mother died. Recall what you know about climate change. The natural world is undergoing major habitat disruptions. Wild animals' habitats are being encroached upon and diminished, due to the exploding human population's rapid settlement of increasingly scarce wilderness. Humans are moving into close proximity with species of animals and insects they've never previously come into contact with. A bite, a scratch, a flea bite by an exotic insect or animal has become more likely. Humans are also amplifying the possibility of exotic species contacts through the so-called wet markets where people can buy bats, pangolins, other rare animals. Changes in temperature and food supply are triggering massive migrations of all lifeforms on Earth. Recent alterations in the environment and in human and animal behaviors have affected the way our genes work. And thus enters the theory of epigenetics."

"That all sounds vague and disconnected. Please don't hate me for not believing you, but I've worked hard for years to claw my way out of the cloud of PTSD hallucinations, nightmares, brain fog, vertigo, and flashbacks to find mental clarity. I think I finally have a strong grasp on reality, Delfina. Far as I know, epigenetics is just some fringe theory."

"What I'm saying may sound vague because it's complicated. Everything is connected. Epigenetics is the theory that novel RNA codes are spreading, imbuing us with new genetic information. Viruses can transfer DNA from organism to organism, sometimes inserting it into the germline, where it becomes heritable. Known as horizontal gene transfer, this is a primary mechanism of evolution, allowing life to evolve together much faster than is possible through random mutation. Could the viral pandemic we've just experienced have triggered epigenetic mutation?"

Colin shook his head. "Just another crazy conspiracy theory like space lasers, Delfina. I'm a scientist. Show me the proof."

"Read the scientific literature on climate change and pandemics. Think about the rapid intensification of human-caused climate havoc that the planet is experiencing right now. Try to understand. Researchers know that the environmental changes we've brought about have made frequently recurring global pandemics inevitable. The COVID-19 virus wasn't an anomaly. One of the consequences of climate change is that more global pandemics are coming, bringing more mutated viruses. More than seventy percent of all emerging infectious diseases are zoonotic—that is, they jump from animal to human. Viruses that can transfer DNA, or novel RNA, from organism to organism can be transferred with a scratch or bite from animal to human."

"What does all this have to do with your mom?"

"Legend has it that the DNA of our bloodline has an epigenetic marker, long dormant, that causes shapeshifting to occur if triggered. It explains the werewolf legends, the mythical animal/human creatures depicted on ancient Sumerian pottery, Inuit art. According to our oral tradition, it was foretold to my people centuries ago that humans would manufacture a crisis that could cause all life on Earth to go extinct. At that time of crisis, according to our legends, a mutated seed would activate our shapeshifting gene, and we would be able to assume the form and enter the psyche of wild animals, forging alliances with nonhuman creatures, and together overcoming the Evil Two-Hearted Ones bent on destroying Mother Earth and all her children."

Colin's eyes opened wide, his cheeks puffed up, and he exploded in laughter. "Nice fairy tale, Delfina, but I can't believe any of that. Sorry, but …"

Delfina dropped Colin's hand. "Okay. Just forget it. You're right. I was only trying to make you feel better about that bite wound. Should have known you'd be too smart to buy that."

Abruptly, the pain in Colin's wrist grew unbearably sharp, stabbing, the scar rising, pulsing, spreading. His body was wracked with pain. He doubled over, collapsed on all fours, opened his mouth, and caterwauled like a mountain lion.

His feet became large paws. His body grew fur the color of California's summer hills. He collapsed on his back on the brittle fallen oak leaves and writhed in pain and terror.

He heard her voice inside his head: "Colin, take deep slow breaths. It's going to be all right. Don't fight it. Look at me. I'm here with you."

Delfina was a mountain lion, standing above him.

"Don't be afraid," her voice said. "Your grandma was right. You must have some Native blood, or else you've got some other lineage with the epigenetic marker. It was triggered when my mother bit you. You're a shapeshifter like me, Colin. Follow me."

★　　　★　　　★

Terrified and confused, Colin followed Delfina. Together they ran—away from human roads and trails, up beyond the oaks, deep into the redwood forest and up to the top of the coastal mountain range.

Colin followed Delfina into a grotto. She revealed a hidden spring, the source of the Agua Pura headwaters. They drank until they were refreshed. Then she led him into a cave, where they fell into deep, dreamless sleep.

They woke in their human forms.

Delfina had obviously visited this cave before. There was a neatly folded stack of blankets as well as stacked wooden crates that served as a pantry, with canned and dried food, candles, a full jug of water, and utensils.

Colin and Delfina talked for a day and a night and another day.

By the third day, Colin had started to come to terms with his new reality.

That night, in their human form, they made love at the mouth of the cave, under the stars.

Planet Venus' light shimmered up and down the curves of Delfina's exquisite body, her face, her graceful neck, breasts, belly, her hips, her perfect ankles, feet, and toes, her strong legs opening, welcoming him. Delfina's long black hair, spread out over the blankets as she lay under him, glistened with blue highlights. When her arms reached for him, her hands seemed full of stars. Reflected starlight twinkled in her eyes and on the moist, sensuous lips covering him with kisses.

Venus, you did not pass me by, after all. Here you are tonight, shining your light on my true love.

On their fourth day at the cave, Colin and Delfina shapeshifted into pumas. Cautiously, they made their way down the mountain on secret paths. Back where they had first transformed, they shifted into their human bodies and found their clothes and Colin's backpack under a thimbleberry bush where Delfina had hidden them. They returned to Delfina's car and drove back to Colin's house in silence, pondering the profound experience they had just shared, adjusting to the fact that their lives would never again be the same.

51

A GENT CHEN ARRIVED with coffee and quiche on Friday morning, May 27.

"What? No Starbucks?"

"I noticed a quirky coffee house in the neighborhood and thought I'd give them a try. Support local business for a change. Let me know if you like your latte."

Lieutenant Rosa sipped. He smiled, his black mustache white with foam. "Umm. Good. Thanks. What's this? Another departure from the usual?"

"Sometimes oatmeal gets boring. I felt like we could use some eggs. A little morning protein. Variety is the spice of life. Hope you're okay eating eggs? This is a spinach, cheese, and bacon quiche."

"Bacon? Man, you're living dangerously, old friend. This is out of character. What's gotten into you?"

"Well, I've enjoyed working with you on this case, Carlos. We've accomplished quite a bit: busting a major fentanyl trafficking operation, capturing Kozel and Matsen—two domestic terrorists on the Agency's Most Wanted list, and I think we may be getting close to solving the Ramona Cuera murder. I just felt like celebrating. TGIF. Happy Friday morning."

"This quiche is delicious," said Rosa. "But I hope you're not jumping the gun here. Don't start celebrating yet. In the matter of finding Ramona Cuera's killer, we're nowhere."

"Sir," Detective Jamison entered Rosa's office with a paper in his hand. "We have our renewed warrant to search the Mikos Vadim home."

"Excellent. Assemble the search team. Ready for a ride up the mountain and down another rabbit hole, Agent Chen?"

★   ★   ★

Lieutenant Rosa knocked at the grand front door, with FBI Agent Chen at his side. A team of deputies led by Detective Jamison stood by at a discreet distance.

The same maid who'd answered the door last time greeted them again. "Yes?'

"Is Mr. Vadim home?" asked Lieutenant Rosa.

"No. He's went mountain biking with the BLM manager, Mr. Budalo. He won't be back until after dark."

"How about his personal assistant, Mr. Qiao Sung?"

"No, sir. He is gone for the day as well."

"We have a warrant to search the premises. We're coming in."

"No, sir. I don't think …"

"Excuse me, ma'am. We're coming in." The maid stepped aside, and Rosa strode through the door. Agent Chen, Detective Jamison, and the search team followed Rosa into the house.

The team had been instructed to avoid property damage, so they handled priceless vases, Haviland teacups, and drawers full of ironed and neatly folded Swiss table linen with care. The house was large. Their search was thorough.

An FBI cyber forensics unit sat at the bank of computers in Vadim's office, sifting through Vadim's files.

"Sir, we've located evidence that Vadim sold stolen semiconductor software to a Chinese wind turbine corporation. We've traced the recipient of the sale and their payment in bitcoin to an offshore account belonging to Vadim. It looks like there have been multiple fraudulent financial transactions run through that account."

The team packed up Mikos's computer equipment to take back to the FBI's Transnational Organized Crime (TOC) group.

312

In a safe they found an external hard drive they determined to be Vadim's crypto wallet.

Rosa was investigating the spacious room downstairs that he'd seen on his earlier visit—the one with wildlife trophies and glass cases full of weapons, including crossbows and exotic knives. He headed down a hall that opened into another large room, a portrait gallery.

A grand oil painting dominating one wall caught Rosa's attention. It obviously depicted the sire, the sanctioned oligarch of the house. Rosa studied it.

Something familiar. The eyes.

Next to that painting was a portrait of two young men lounging by an infinity pool. One of those men was clearly Mikos Vadim, only younger. He had the same eyes as his oligarch father. Rosa deduced that the other man was Mikos's younger brother, Kiki.

In Mikos' bedroom, Jamison and his deputies turned up a small amount of cocaine and marijuana.

In the younger brother's bedroom, in a desk drawer, the search team found a party pack of cocaine. In Kiki's massive walk-in closet, they discovered camo gear: tactical pants and a hunting jacket with a hoodie, wadded up in a laundry bag. The search team opened a box tucked away in the back corner of a bottom shelf and pulled out Belleville steel toe tactical boots.

Rosa entered Kiki's room and ordered his squad to open the six-foot-tall safe hidden behind a wall tapestry. They pulled out a crossbow and a pack of arrows.

"This could be the murder weapon," said Rosa. "Handle it carefully. We don't want to lose any trace evidence. Let's get these things to the lab, pronto. Put a BOLO out on both Vadim brothers."

52

THE FOLLOWING MORNING at the sheriff's headquarters, Kiki Vadim sat handcuffed to the interrogation table, crying.

"Your prints are on that crossbow." Detective Rosa glared across the table. "Why did you kill Ramona Cuera?"

Agent Chen observed behind one-way glass.

"I told you. I don't even know who that is." Kiki spoke in a high-pitched blubbering whine. His face dripped with tears and his swollen lips frothed with snotty foam. "I was hunting a mountain lion. I wanted to get a trophy kill for my da-dad."

"Where did you go after you shot the woman?"

"I didn't shoot a woman." The shrill pitch of Kiki's denial climbed an octave. "I would never!" Kiki dropped his forehead in his hands and sobbed.

Rosa sat patiently, waiting.

Gradually, Kiki stopped bawling. He straightened his shoulders and wiped the tears from his eyes. Rosa handed him a tissue, and Kiki blew his nose.

"Listen, Lieutenant. I swear I didn't see any women when I was hunting that day. I shot at a mountain lion. I knew I'd hit it because I heard it scream.

But when I was walking toward my kill to take trophies for my dad—the head and paws—I spotted a game warden approaching, so I took off." Kiki's face crumpled, his shoulders shook, and he finished his statement in a gasping wail. "I never even saw whether or not I bagged my lion."

Rosa let Kiki snivel for a while, then said, "You knew you were hunting illegally."

Kiki raised his face, a new defiant spark in his eyes. His features had hardened in anger; his mouth twisted in a cruel grin. "Sure. So give me a ticket. How much do I owe you?"

"According to Warden Dawson, you owe the state a ten-thousand-dollar fine, and your right to hunt in California has been permanently revoked. There may be a prison sentence for the wildlife violation as well."

"Whatever." Kiki shrugged and glanced at the expensive watch on his wrist.

"Where did you go when you saw the wildlife warden approaching?"

"I ran to the creek. Boulder-hopped all the way down to the fence at the Coast Road. Climbed through the hole in the fence. Walked to the road, to my car. And took off."

★　　★　　★

After the interrogation, Chen and Rosa sat in the lieutenant's office and shared their thoughts.

"I went over and over it with him," said Rosa. "His story never changed."

"And it seems to jive with what Frankie, the kid from the farm, described," said Chen.

"It's plausible that he was tracking a mountain lion, or thought he was. Apparently, Ramona Cuera was walking close enough to the mountain lion's path to lead to visual confusion."

"Visibility wasn't great." Rosa flipped pages in his pocket notebook. "Tall grass and foliage probably obscured the view. Kiki could be telling the truth."

"I agree. Kiki has daddy issues. Big brother Mikos is successful, important."

"Handsome, a ladies' man. Well respected. Daddy's chosen elder son."

"Kiki wants to prove himself. He goes out and tries to bag a lion for his father."

Rosa nodded. "We should send a couple of deputies up to the hole in the fence by the creek where Kiki claims he parked his car, to corroborate his story. My bet is they'll find prints that match Kiki's boots. Maybe even tire tracks that match Kiki's car."

"We're still waiting for the lab report on Kiki's boots," said Chen, "but I have a hunch they will not be the same as the boot print found at the spot Ramona's killer stood."

"Agreed. As I see it, Kiki just doesn't fit the profile of Ramona's murderer."

"Even if his boot matches the killer's print," said Chen, "it would be difficult to prove he intentionally murdered the Cuera woman. Nothing indicates that he ever met her. I see no motive for murder."

"So, we charge him with involuntary manslaughter?"

"Maybe hold him on suspicion of," said Chen.

"We're not done here. If the shoe prints and murder weapon are a fit with the killer's, we should call in a profiler."

"Investigate Kiki's motives for murder. Dig deeper for any connections with the victim."

"All right. We hold him," said Rosa.

"And if further investigation turns up nothing else, maybe he does time for violating state hunting laws."

"Meanwhile," said Rosa, "thankfully, big brother Mikos Vadim was easy to locate. He's so arrogant, he saw no need to try to avoid us. My deputies report that he laughed when they arrested him for his theft of semiconductor software, his fraudulent charity, and his Chinese wind turbine scheme to defraud the government."

"Mikos will go away a long time for the theft and sale to a hostile government of protected infrastructure critical to the US," said Chen. "FBI's TOC Division is very happy about the intelligence we acquired during our search of the Vadim mansion. We provided them with evidence they needed to wrap up an investigation they'd been conducting for quite a while. Counterintelligence is prosecuting Mikos for espionage."

Rosa popped a stick of gum in his mouth, put his feet up on his desk, and leaned back with a satisfied sigh.

Detective Jamison knocked on Lieutenant Rosa's office door and entered.

"Sorry, sir. I have bad news. Kiki Yadim's crossbow is not the same kind as the murder weapon. Also, forensics has determined that his boots do not match the ones worn by Ramona Cuera's killer. Wrong size, and Kiki's don't have the unique marks, dings, and striations on the sole we're looking for."

Agent Chen raised an eyebrow and shrugged.

"All right," said Rosa. He glared at the digital murder board, then pulled his notebook out of his pocket and flipped through the pages, crossing out a note here and there.

"Let's see if the kids' artwork can tell us anything," said Chen.

"All right. Good idea. I'll phone Agua Pura and ask if Frankie can meet with us this afternoon. So many moving pieces to this puzzle. Now, where did I put Johnny Taylor's drawings and photos?"

53

T HAT AFTERNOON, Saturday, May 28, in front of a barn at Agua Pura Farm, Wildlife Warden Colin Dawson sat at a picnic table with Lieutenant Rosa and Frankie. Frankie's drawings were spread out on the table along with Johnny's sketchbook and a laptop loaded with Johnny's and Frankie's photos from the day of Ramona's murder.

"Like I said, the guy looked like Rambo," said Frankie. "You know, like Sylvester Stallone in Rambo: First Blood Part II, where he loses his guns and has to fight the bad guys with a bow and arrow? I admit, I smoked a doobie before I went for my walk. But still, I know what I saw."

"Can you put these drawings in chronological order for us, Frankie?" asked Rosa.

"Okay. This one is where I first spotted the mountain lion. It was fire! Totally amazing! This was only, like, the fifth one I've ever seen. I love these animals. Then I saw Camo Guy with the crossbow stalking the puma. He seemed like a total Sus, dude. It grossed me out to think that he might kill that beautiful cougar. That's when I phoned the Fish and Wildlife CalTIP line to put in the anonymous report. I also texted Rafe the cowboy."

"Thank you for doing that," said Colin.

"Fo'sure. So here's the drawing where the guy looked all Rambo. Totally pumped and—oh, wait. I forgot. He wasn't wearing camo then. Couldn't tell what he was wearing, he was in dark tree shadows. And his bow was different—not a normal crossbow, more high-tech. I don't know. It's kind of fuzzy. Shit. Maybe there were two guys stalking the lion."

"Let's go through your photos," said Rosa.

Rosa scrolled through the images on the laptop. "This looks like your camo guy, right?'

"Yeah. That's him. And there's the puma. OMG, that's Johnny. I didn't even realize Johnny was there too. I was standing over there on a knoll. I guess Johnny was just out of my field of view until I randomly swung around and took that shot on accident. I feel so bad that he died. We were friends."

"What's this?" asked Colin, pointing to a dark shape in the trees in the next photo.

"Hey, that's Rambo. Dude, look at him," said Frankie. "Total jungle warrior. He's taller than Camo Guy. He kind of looks like a vampire, lurking in the shadow of the trees."

"Frankie," said Colin, "do you think you'd be able to take us on that walk, and show us exactly where you saw Camo Guy and Rambo and the puma?"

"Yeah, yeah yeah. Fo'sure. Let's do this."

★   ★   ★

It was a pleasant spring afternoon in the mid-seventies, a good day for a hike. Over the rolling prairie flowed waves of canary yellow—a super bloom of dainty tarplant sunflowers. Three newly fledged peregrine falcons swooped and wailed overhead. Rosa, Frankie, and Colin walked through the tall grasses and endangered native wildflowers. Invasive milk thistles, bursting with brilliant magenta blooms, caught their clothes and pricked their legs as they passed. The uneven ground made walking a challenge.

"Watch out for snakes," said Colin.

"Yeah, I totally love snakes," said Frankie. "We've got all kinds around here: kingsnakes, San Francisco garter snakes, rubber boas, ring necks, gopher snakes, and yellow-bellied racers. But don't worry. The only poisonous ones are rattlers. They're awesome."

Lieutenant Rosa glanced around anxiously.

Colin stopped walking and held up his hand. "Would you say this is about where you spotted the puma, Frankie?"

"Yeah," said Frankie. "I was right about here when I first saw her up there on that sandstone rise. She was so beautiful! I watched her stumble, then kind of claw and slide down the sandstone to the bottom, right here."

Colin bent to examine a perfect print in the dried clay. "Was it muddy that day, Frankie?"

"Oh, yeah. We've got a lot of natural clay in the soil around here. I still haven't got all the caked mud out of the soles of my boots."

"These are your puma's prints," said Colin. He placed a flag next to the paw prints and took photos with his phone.

"Way cool," said Frankie. "You're a tracker."

"Show us where you remember standing, Frankie," said Rosa.

Frankie strode uphill to the rise, their gangly arms swinging.

"I was here."

Colin planted another marker flag.

"Where was Camo Guy?" asked Rosa.

"Hmm. The puma was down there where Colin found her prints, walking along the edge of that coyote brush. Camo Guy was a little below where we are, over there. He was totally obvious. Not much of a hunter if you ask me. Total cringe. This is where I called in the CalTIP. Lucky I had cell service."

Colin dropped a pin on his GPS map. "Sir, we may be able to establish a geofence and determine what cell phones were here that day."

Rosa smiled at Colin and nodded. "Good idea. I loaded Johnny Taylor's photos from that day onto my phone. Let's see." Rosa scrolled through the images and then pointed to a stand of oaks nearby. "Judging from the point of view where he took his photos, I think Johnny was watching from over there."

Colin studied the photos and nodded. "Tell you what," he said, "how about if I go check out those areas and see if I can pick up Johnny's and Camo Guy's shoe prints, while you two wait here. I think the fewer people walking around, the easier it will be for me to find the prints we're looking for."

Colin hurried to the oaks and easily located what he surmised were Johnny's shoe prints. He flagged and photographed them, dropped another GPS pin, then tracked over to the area where Frankie had first seen Camo Guy. Colin found, flagged, pinned, and photographed prints he expected would match Kiki Vadim's boots.

On a hunch, Colin looked over his shoulder at the oaks sprawling across the rolling terrain where Johnny had stood. Those could be the trees where Rambo Vampire Man had lurked in the shadows. Colin triangulated the puma prints with Frankie's, Johnny's, and Camo Guy's lines of sight, and determined Rambo Man's probable position. It was worth taking a look.

He called to Rosa and Frankie, who were standing on a rise about two hundred yards away. "I'll be right back," Colin shouted.

It didn't take long for him to find the familiar boot prints—the same as those found at Ramona's murder site under the oaks.

He flagged and photographed the prints, dropped a marker on his GPS, and recorded a voice memo on his phone: "Frankie's Rambo Vampire Man is the murderer. Johnny was standing close by. Was the killer aware of the boy, and vice versa?"

Colin reunited with Lieutenant Rosa and Frankie.

"Tell us what happened next, Frankie," said Rosa.

"Well, I followed the Camo Dude, who was following the cougar. I was careful to keep a safe distance."

"What about Rambo Man?"

"That's where it gets confusing. I think I only saw him that one time, when I took that picture, kind of on accident."

Frankie, Rosa, and Colin hiked downhill to within a hundred yards of the murder site.

"Where were you when Camo Guy shot the puma?" asked Colin.

"Here. This is where I was standing when I saw the puma run behind that coyote bush. No, wait. I—I think I lost track of the puma for a minute. That's when I saw the nude woman. She was walking fast. She looked over her shoulder, then ran behind that manzanita. A puma ran out the other side. Camo Guy shot his arrow, and I heard screams."

"Did you see Camo Guy's arrow hit the puma, or the woman?" asked Rosa.

"Nah. I just I turned around and ran all the way home. Speaking of which," said Frankie, "this has been fun, guys, but I really need to get home. I have homework, and I've got the munchies. Are we done now?"

"We're good, Frankie," said Rosa.

"You've been tremendously helpful. Thank you," said Colin. "Are you all right getting home all by yourself?"

"Oh hell yeah. I'm totally good to go. Check ya later, dudes. Peace out."

Frankie sprinted away.

★   ★   ★

Rosa shook his head as he watched the child go. "Frankie clearly doesn't grasp how much danger she was in, or how deadly serious the situation is. What's wrong with kids these days?"

"Frankie's a good kid, Lieutenant," said Colin.

"Noted," said Rosa. "And she did give us some vital information. Not one, but two bow hunters were out here the day Ramona Cuera was murdered."

Colin nodded. "My bet is on Kiki Vadim for Camo Guy."

"I'm guessing his boot prints will lead away from here out to the hole in the fence by the highway, where he claims his car was parked. My deputies are already checking there for tire tracks and prints."

"Sir, do you mind waiting here just a minute?" asked Colin.

"Go ahead." Rosa sat on a nearby large, flat rock, and opened a new pack of gum, conscientiously putting the wrappers in his pocket to toss in the trash later.

Carefully observing the ground, Colin paced to the coyote bush Frankie had pointed out, and dropped a pin. He tracked puma prints leading behind the bush and discovered human barefoot prints going away.

She shifted to human here. Colin scuffed the dirt, obscuring evidence of the shift.

Then he followed the human footprints to the manzanita thicket. He dropped another pin at the manzanita. The footprints led behind a twisted tangle of red manzanita branches with peeling skin and berries the color of dried blood. There, in the soft dirt, prints confirmed that a barefoot woman had shifted back into a puma. *Ramona.*

Colin shuffled his boot over the ground, again erasing evidence of the shapeshift.

So far, no one had questioned his story about having a hallucination that a dying puma changed into a woman. Luckily, most people won't believe what they see with their own eyes, if that truth conflicts with their socially programmed beliefs about reality. Everyone knows that tales of therianthropy—shapeshifting—are only myths.

But why take a chance of discovery by leaving evidence around?

Following the puma's tracks out from behind the manzanita, Colin came across an arrow on the ground. He marked the find with a flag, photographed the lay of the projectile, then placed the impotent shaft in an evidence bag and recorded a voice note of the find. It was not a high-tech arrow. It most likely belonged to Camo Guy, Kiki Vadim.

Continuing to follow the puma's tracks a few yards farther, Colin arrived at the spot the lethal high-tech sniper's arrow had struck the wildcat. The flag he'd placed the day of the murder was still there. A brown, rust-like blood stain discolored the ground and spread around in a spatter pattern. From here, the trail of blood from the wounded puma led to where Colin had found Ramona dying.

His heart broke for Ramona all over again. He dropped another pin on the GPS map.

He looked back in the direction he'd come, to the position Johnny's photograph showed vampire man standing in the tree shadows. Colin estimated the distance to vampire man was about the length of a football field—a hundred-twenty yards away from the kill shot. Even the most highly skilled sniper with a technical crossbow and arrow would have moved in closer to take his shot. Colin paced to where he estimated Rambo may have shot Ramona, in her puma form.

He searched until he found the killer's telltale boot prints, then dropped another pin.

Returning to where the lieutenant waited, Colin handed the evidence bag to Rosa.

"This arrow is probably Kiki's," said Colin. "I left an evidence marker where I found it. I also dropped pins at several more key locations, including the place Ramona was hit and fell, and the probable location of the kill shot. Boot prints that will most likely match the murderer's were all over the area where the fatal shot was fired."

"Good work, Colin. I've been thinking about your idea of identifying who was here the day of Ramona's murder by geolocating the cellphones present that day. I contacted Chen and he's set the process in motion with the Agency's cyber forensic unit. Chen said once they receive your data, it may take them a day or so to identify the people who were present that day. Can you email them your GPS pins now?"

"Done," said Colin, hitting send on his phone.

54

THE NEXT DAY, Sunday, May 29, Lieutenant Rosa opened the folder labeled Missing and Murdered he'd found in Ramona Cuera's filing cabinet. He spread the papers out on his desk.

Ramona had been searching for a missing Kumeyaay girl named Stella Osuna, age fifteen. She'd last been seen at the Cherry Coke Dance Club, San Diego, August 20, 2017.

Something niggled at Rosa's mind. He opened his pocket notebook and flipped pages back to the day when he and Detective Jamison had visited Ramona's home.

There it was: a reminder to himself to check back with Delfina for the key to Ramona's locked file drawer.

Delfina picked up her phone after a couple of rings.

"Good morning, Delfina. Colin tells me you made a trip to San Diego to take care of some of your mother's business. We're all so relieved to have you back safely. How are you feeling?"

"I'm fine. Thank you, Lieutenant. What can I help you with?"

"I'm hoping you were able to locate that key to Ramona's locked file drawer."

"Oh, my gosh. I forgot about that. Workmen have been clearing away all the broken furniture and debris from Mama's house. You're welcome to go by and check. If that filing cabinet is still there, feel free to break the lock and take whatever's inside."

★　　★　　★

Rosa and Detective Jamison inched across town through the heavy Memorial Day weekend tourist traffic to Ramona's house.

When they arrived, workmen in overalls were just returning to the house from a lunch break.

Rosa flashed his badge. He and Jamison entered and found their way to Ramona's room.

Rosa breathed a sigh of relief at the sight of the dented file cabinet lying on its side. He asked one of the workmen to crowbar the drawer open.

Inside, he found nothing but one bulging accordion file organizer, sitting on its end, securely fastened shut by an elastic band. Rosa pulled it out, stuck it under his arm, and he and Jamison drove back to headquarters.

★　　★　　★

The front section of the organizer contained a thumb drive, plus files, photos, newspaper clippings, and a police report on Stella Osuna, the fifteen-year-old Kumeyaay girl missing since 2017. Another section contained information on the unsolved 2010 rape of thirteen-year-old Delfina Cuera.

Rosa texted FBI Agent Chen and Warden Colin Dawson: *Get over here as soon as you can. I may have found the key to Ramona Cuera's murder.*

Connecting the thumb drive to his laptop, Rosa opened the Stella Osuna files and played a video taken from a surveillance camera outside the Cherry Coke Dance Club in San Diego, at 11:56 p.m. on August 20, 2017.

Rosa and Detective Jamison watched on the wall-sized digital murder board as Stella left the club alone. She was underage, but with the fashion get-up and all the makeup she was wearing, she could have passed, with a fake ID, as a legal adult.

Stella walked along a deserted sidewalk. A man dressed in black, with a black ski mask, sprang out of an alley, grabbed her, and put a rag to her face. She went limp, and he dragged her into a car with no plates.

"Looks like he chloroformed her," said Rosa.

Colin arrived and studied the digital murder board where video of the Osuna abduction was looping.

Rosa projected the Cuera rape file on the murder board and scrolled through it. "The Osuna assailant appears to have used the same MO as Delfina's rapist."

"Do you think it's the same guy?" asked Colin.

"There were years between the assaults, but perhaps Ramona suspected the unsub was the same," said Rosa.

"You know what other case had a similar MO?" asked Jamison.

Colin's eyes opened wide. "Johnny Taylor's abduction in that old truck."

"CSI should have examined that truck for evidence by now," said Rosa.

He pulled up the report on the SWAT drug cartel bust at the quarry and skimmed through. "Here it is: The truck had smudges from multiple hands, but no useful fingerprints. They did, however, find Johnny Taylor's DNA."

"What kind of DNA?" asked Colin. "Blood?"

"No. Urine on the passenger seat upholstery. The poor kid pissed his pants."

"What if Ramona Cuera's killer knew that Johnny witnessed the murder and wanted to silence him?" suggested Agent Chen, who'd arrived not long after Colin.

"And if Ramona's killer is the same man who raped Delfina and her friend thirteen years ago, and abducted Stella Osuna four years ago, then—?" asked Rosa.

"If Ramona was getting close to identifying him, he'd need to take her out," said Chen.

"If all that's true, something here in Ramona's files might lead us to her killer," said Jamison.

55

"I'VE GOT AN ALTERNATIVE to digging through all those files," said Agent Chen. He pulled a thumb drive out of his pocket. "Here's the information from the geofence."

Rosa inserted the flash drive into his laptop, and a short list of names scrolled onto the wall's digital murder board.

As they appeared, Rosa read aloud the names of the cell phone users who'd been at the murder site: "Frankie, Johnny, Kiki Vadim, and—oh Holy Mother of God!"

"Marshal Kurt Stone?" Jamison whispered in amazement. "But he's a good guy, isn't he?"

"Honestly," said Colin, "I've had a bad feeling about him since the first day I laid eyes on him."

"All right," said Rosa. "Let's dig in. What do we know about Stone?"

Jamison pulled up the research his deputies had done. "He's definitely legit. He's been a US Marshal in good standing for decades. He's made some outstanding busts and received commendation for his work on fentanyl trafficking. Sir, I just don't understand how Stone could be our murderer."

"Stranger things have happened, Detective," said Rosa.

Chen nodded grimly. "A man gets a taste for young girls and gets away with it; it can become an addiction. It happens."

"We need to trace where he's been working over the years," said Rosa, "and then reach out to local law enforcement in those areas and see if they have any records of assaults, rapes or missing girls during the time Stone worked there that match the profile of the Stella Osuna and Delfina Cuera cases."

"That's a good idea," said Colin, "but I'm afraid it will take a long time to implement."

"Not so, Colin. The Agency sees this case as a top priority. They should be able to accomplish the research pretty fast."

"All right, George," said Rosa. "Ask your people to do a search of local police records of abductions, rapes, and disappearances around the U.S. since the Cuera rape of 2010 that coincide with Stone's movements. Make it happen."

★ ★ ★

Two hours later, Rosa, Chen, Colin, and Jamison reconvened in the lieutenant's office.

"I'm impressed, George," said Rosa. "That was fast, even for the FBI."

Chen cleared his throat and adjusted his Hermès tie, which was already positioned with mathematical precision. "We do good work. Here's the map of Marshal Stone's known whereabouts across the US over the last thirteen years."

A map appeared on the digital murder board on the wall.

"Each county where he stayed for more than six months is highlighted. Look at this." Chen pressed his presentation clicker, and a star appeared in the highlighted county of San Diego, with the descriptor next to the star: "2010, D. Cuera."

"This star indicates the rape of Delfina Cuera in 2010. Stone was there at the time, working on a fentanyl investigation. Now, watch this." Chen pressed his laser clicker again. Ten more stars, including the disappearance of Stella Osuna, appeared in highlighted counties.

"This is the thirteenth year since the Cuera rape. We found ten cases identical to the Cuera MO, in locations and in the timeframe where Stone lived and worked."

"Let's pay Marshal Stone a visit," said Rosa.

"Sir," said Jamison, "one thing I don't understand. If Stone is the rapist and Ramona's killer, who contracted Matsen and Kozel, on the dark web, to murder Ramona?"

"I'll have our cyber forensics unit see if Stone was active on the dark web. If we can locate his handle, we'll be able to determine whether or not he was the one who contracted Ramona's hit."

★   ★   ★

Rosa deployed a county SWAT unit to accompany his team to Stone's residence of record, a motel just off the freeway in midtown Santa Lucia.

When officers arrived on scene, his room was empty. Maids were cleaning it. The desk clerk confirmed that Marshal Stone had checked out the previous day.

Officers searched the motel dumpster. They found size thirteen Belleville steel toe tactical boots manufactured within the last year. The boots were bagged and sent to the forensic lab.

In the sheriff's van on the way back to headquarters, Colin turned forlornly to Rosa. "Now what, Lieutenant?"

Rosa's steely eyes stared straight ahead. His jaw clenched. "We'll find him, son."

56

T HE FOLLOWING MORNING, the last Monday in May, FBI's forensic lab issued a DNA report confirming that the boots found in the motel dumpster belonged to US Marshal Kurt Stone. In addition, the unique gouge in the outsole of the left boot, and the residue in the Vibram sole from the cow patty where one of the murderer's boot prints had been found, were a match. The boots would provide prosecutable evidence that their wearer, Kurt Stone, murdered Ramona Cuera.

Homeland Security issued a BOLO to all agencies.

At noon, Lieutenant Rosa received an alert from TSA: the suspect had purchased a plane ticket to Mexico, and his car had been located en route to the San Francisco airport, about seventy miles up the coast from Playa Azul.

Rosa, Chen, Jamison, and Colin, along with FBI and sheriff's deputies secured a Golden Gate Division CHP helicopter and in less than fifteen minutes converged with San Francisco police at SFO.

It was Memorial Day, the first major holiday in three years that travel was not restricted due to the pandemic. The airport was packed with record crowds.

TSA confirmed that Marshal Kurt Stone had already cleared security for an international flight.

In the first-class lounge of the Harvey Milk Terminal, Marshal Stone sat calmly, reading a newspaper and sipping scotch. He crossed his long legs and flicked a speck of dust off his immaculate black chinos, then straightened the leather bolo tie around the collar of his black shirt, and stretched his toes inside his custom bison Tecavos boots. The wide shovel brim of his black felt lawman's hat shaded his face.

The Scotch was as smooth as warm silk. He held his palm over his glass and swirled the amber liquid, then smelled his hand, stirring memories. He put his nose over the glass and, with parted lips, breathed in the smoky, peat aroma. Finally, he sipped, holding the Scotch in his mouth a few seconds to feel the burn before letting it slide down his throat.

Closing his eyes, he let memories wash over him.

Stone felt proud of his tenure as a US Marshal, despite his regrettable little mistakes. *My addiction,* he admitted to himself.

He leaned back and recalled each one of his pretty girls, growing hard as he relived the sensual delights of each—the sweet and acrid scents, the taste on his tongue, squeals of fear, tender juicy private parts wetting his fingers, slick with blood. One at a time, he summoned the pleasures of his senses, starting with the first—that ripe Cuera girl, and her almost-ripe friend.

Once he'd finally decided to give in to the urge, he'd calculated it would be safest to choose Native American girls. No one paid attention to what happened to the brown ones. Rape and disappearance of Indians, Mexicans, and Blacks was rarely investigated with any rigor.

Too bad that Cuera mother, Ramona, was such a smart cunt. It was her fault my problem spiraled. She got too close. She made me reckless. I should have stopped; never should have touched the Osuna girl.

Stone took another sip of his whiskey.

And then those incompetent imbeciles I contracted to take Ramona out completely botched it. I ended up having to do it myself. Couldn't leave that bitch free to keep digging. She was too close to IDing me.

Finally tracked Ramona to Santa Lucia and took care of it, just in time. But that fucking Taylor kid. He screwed it up. Saw everything.

Then that twat Kozel shows up at the sheriff's command post at Cougar Creek Ranch, completely oblivious that the man he's talking to, namely me, US Marshal Kurt Stone, is not only the killer, but also the very same person who hired him and Matsen on the dark web to get rid of Ramona and her daughter. What a fucking shit show.

Stone took another slow sip of whiskey, letting it roll with a slight burn on his tongue before swallowing.

And what was that supernatural Indian magic juju of Ramona's with the mountain lion? Almost seemed as if she could change into one. Those Indians. Stone shook his head. *Jesus Christ. She was a strange one.*

Well, now that Matsen and Kozel are in custody, it's only a matter of time before Rosa comes for me. This is the end of the line.

A wave of aching regret swept through Kurt Stone. He'd miss his work as a US Marshal. The prestige, the power, the respect. The sense of doing good. All that was over. He had to disappear.

He flinched when his name was called.

57

THE GATE AGENT ANNOUNCED that his flight was boarding; his boarding number flashed on the marquee. Stone folded his newspaper, swallowed the last of his Scotch, and placed his empty glass on a mirror-topped table in front of him. He tipped his hat to a pretty young girl he'd been watching, and exited the lounge.

One of the first to enter the Aeromexico Boeing 737 MAX to Mexico City, he settled into his roomy seat at the first row window, which afforded a view of the crowd still waiting to board.

Stone's throat was dry. Take off couldn't be soon enough.

Colin and Detective Jamison moved rapidly through the airport, shoulder-to-shoulder with the SWAT team.

They elbowed through the throng and made their way up the boarding ramp into Stone's plane.

Colin was one of the first to enter the 737. All one-hundred-sixty-two seats had been sold, but only a few passengers had already boarded.

Colin did a quick visual sweep of the cabin.

Stone was not in his assigned seat and was nowhere to be seen.

Colin and the other officers searched every possible hiding place, including the restrooms.

As Colin rushed toward the back of the plane, he heard a woman crying.

A stewardess, bleeding from the mouth, pointed to the back exit door, which was gaping open.

"He made me open it," she said.

Colin held on to the sides of the door and leaned out over air. No ramp. A ten-foot drop.

He glimpsed Stone running across the tarmac toward the terminal.

Through his coms, Colin alerted Rosa and Chen, who were stationed in SFO's TSA coordination center—the airport's watchful eyes gathering, analyzing, and evaluating data inside and outside the airport.

"We see him," said Chen, standing in front of a bank of surveillance monitors. "He's heading to the baggage claim exit doors that lead out to the passenger pickup area on the street. We're deploying officers to intercept him."

Colin glanced toward the front of the plane.

The aisle was plugged with SWAT officers. Behind them a throng of frightened passengers were stuck, unable to back up or move forward.

No! The man who raped Delfina is not going to escape. Not if I can help it.

"I'm on my way!" Colin shouted.

He leapt through the back exit.

Falling through the air, Colin's body started changing.

He fought with all his will to resist the shift.

Hitting the tarmac hard, he rolled and landed upright on two feet.

Still human, he took only seconds to reorient himself. Adrenaline masking the pain of the fall's impact, he raced after Stone.

He slipped through a service entrance into the crowded terminal, threading his way around an ebullient Scottish soccer team and a family trying to quiet a screaming infant in a stroller.

The stairs and escalator to baggage claim were clogged with a wall of people.

Colin slid down the banister.

Halfway down, he spotted Stone disappearing through the exit.

Colin's boots hit the ground, and he ran through the exit in pursuit.

Out on the street, airline traffic cops and city police blew whistles and waved their hands. Sirens sounded in the distance.

Colin scanned up and down along the busy passenger pickup curb.

Stone was pointing a gun at a driver in a black Dodge Charger Hellcat. He forced the driver out of the car, jumped in, gunned the motor, and sped away.

A departing jet roared overhead.

"Colin! Get in!"

Screeching to a halt in front of Colin, Delfina gripped the steering wheel of his candy apple red Mustang Shelby GT350 Voodoo V8. The 'Stang's convertible top was down.

Colin dove into the passenger seat and Delfina stomped on the gas.

She ran through a red light and sped toward the black Hellcat that was fishtailing around a corner.

"What are you doing here, in my car?"

Delfina downshifted, taking the sharp turn flawlessly.

"Hawk called me. He saw all this in a vision and told me to come."

The Dodge was just up ahead. Delfina shifted into high gear and stepped on it. The 'Stang shrieked forward like a Ferrari.

"Fuck, Delfina! How did you learn to drive like this?"

"One of my cousins is a race car mechanic. He taught me."

Colin gaped at her in awe.

Delfina was a flaming goddess in blue jeans, a tight white halter top, a black ball cap with the word NATIVE embroidered in red along the crown, and turquoise earrings. Her gleaming blue-black hair hung in a braid down her back; the abalone shell at her neck shimmered like opal. As the convertible raced along the street, feathery wisps of Delfina's hair escaped, flying around her fierce face.

A hawk's raspy scream drew Colin's attention. A redtail soared above.

"Speaking of cousins, that's Hawk, right?"

Delfina smiled and nodded as she executed another hairpin turn, onto Highway 101 North.

They raced up the Bayshore Freeway. San Francisco Bay glinted like a strobe light through gaps between trees lining the highway.

Weaving in and out of heavy traffic, the Mustang began to gain on the Dodge Charger.

The Charger went into overdrive, crossed two lanes of speeding cars, and merged onto I-380 West.

Delfina almost missed the turn. Barely avoiding a truck, the 'Stang spun, screeching to a stop on the painted divider at the interchange. A fierce swarm of cars whooshed past.

On a light pole arching over the interchange perched the red-tailed hawk.

Colin and Delfina stared at each other wide-eyed for an instant, before Delfina shifted into gear and merged onto I-380, resuming the chase.

A mile up the interstate, the black Hellcat turned onto the I-280 exit toward San Francisco. Delfina pursued.

The five-lane freeway was choked with holiday weekend traffic. Traffic crawled to a stop. Colin stood up on his seat and searched the cars ahead.

"I see him!" said Colin. "He's two lanes over to the right. Looks like he's planning to take the Nineteenth Avenue turnoff toward Golden Gate Bridge."

Delfina worked her way to the right. When the Mustang was in the far right lane and still barely moving forward, she turned to Colin with a questioning look. He nodded and winked.

She cranked the steering wheel hard right, bumping onto the dirt shoulder, and sped toward the Hellcat Charger.

Stone spotted her coming in his rearview mirror and swerved the Hellcat onto the shoulder, racing away toward the turnoff.

Delfina chased Stone onto Junipero Serra Boulevard, into the heart of the city's Sunset District.

Passing San Francisco State University, Delfina slowed, careful not to mow down the droves of students walking, biking, waiting for buses and trolleys, and looking down at their phones as they stepped obliviously into traffic.

Up ahead, Stone was stopped at a red light.

Sirens sounded in the distance.

Colin, still dressed in tactical gear, had Lieutenant Rosa in his ear coms.

"Colin, this is Lieutenant Rosa. Do you copy?"

"Yes, sir."

"Is that Delfina driving?"

"Yes."

"She's good!"

"Yes, sir."

"We're tracking you and Stone via street cams and a drone. The San Francisco City Police and our SWAT team are making their way toward you. We think Stone is heading for Golden Gate Park."

"Roger that."

"Colin, there's an annual free concert in the park today; it's the event's first time back since the pandemic. Before the pandemic shutdown, this concert, Hardly Strictly Bluegrass, attracted more than half a million people every year. The crowd is expected to be even bigger this year. Keep your weapon holstered, Warden. With all those people, we can't have any shooting in the park if it can possibly be avoided."

"Copy, sir."

One stop light behind the Hellcat, the Mustang crept toward the park.

Sirens and police horns blasted. Vehicles inched out of the way. Two SWAT BearCats maneuvered in front of Colin's Mustang.

Horns, sirens, and a megaphone screeched louder. Up ahead, vehicles cleared to the sides. A lane opened.

The SWAT BearCats sped toward Stone's Charger, Delfina and Colin trailing inches from SWAT's bumper. Five San Francisco police vehicles followed the Mustang.

Up ahead, drivers made way, giving Stone the opportunity to speed up the open street, into Golden Gate Park.

Pulling a fast right, he turned under the cover of the park's thick woods.

The SWAT vehicles followed, with Delfina and Colin and the SFPD close behind.

The park was crawling with concert goers heading on foot to Lindley Meadow.

The stolen Hellcat screeched to a stop in the middle of the road.

Stone leapt from the car and ran, shoving people aside. Startled shouts rang out over the music blaring from the meadow beyond.

The SWAT BearCats, Colin's Mustang, and police cars slammed on their breaks behind Stone's black Dodge. Colin, Delfina, and all the officers poured out of their vehicles, taking chase on foot.

Colin had never seen so many people packed so close together: old people, Millennials, Gen Zs and Gen Alphas, families with young children and babies, people of every skin color, people wearing face paint and outrageous and beautiful costumes. Festival goers were standing, sitting in beach chairs and on blankets on the grass, mulling around, and respectfully stepping over one another when necessary. Perfect spring weather in this lush meadow surrounded by trees, plus the cloud of cannabis smoke hanging in the air, contributed to the mellow vibe of this twenty-three-year-old San Francisco music festival.

A fleet of Blue Angels flew overhead and tipped their wings in unison.

"It's the Blue Angel Memorial Day air show!" Colin shouted to Delfina over the music.

An old hippie sitting on the grass nearby commented, "Whoa, trippy, dude. I'm no fan of the evil military-industrial establishment, but I gotta say these Blue Angels are way far out."

Everyone was smiling, laughing, friendly, and accommodating, as if they were all part of one big happy community—dancing, sharing food and weed, watching each other's kids, helping the disabled and elderly.

Colin glanced at a poster detailing the impressive and eclectic line-up of world class rock, pop, folk, and bluegrass performers here to share their music with the people, absolutely free. The sound system was phenomenal. Even with tens of thousands of people seated on the grass between him and the stage, Colin could hear the music perfectly.

He and Delfina paused to catch their breath and orient themselves, while Steve Earle sang "Copperhead Road." Colin put his arm around Delfina's waist. She rested her head against his chest.

The crowd's easy vibes seemed undisturbed by the police wading through.

But how were they going to find Stone in this throng?

"Colin, do you copy? Come in."

Colin adjusted his earpiece to block out ambient sound. "I hear you, Lieutenant Rosa, sir. Loud and clear."

"The drone has located Stone. He's in that grove of trees up behind the stage. Look at your phone. I'm transmitting the image to you now."

Colin showed the image to Delfina.

"How are we going to get through all these people?" Delfina asked.

"Not we, Delfina. Stone is too dangerous. You've done enough, race car driver. Stay here. Be safe. Enjoy the music. I'll find you later."

Colin kissed her on the forehead and was gone before she could argue.

He picked his way toward the stage, stepping over and around people who didn't seem to mind.

"He's gone into the trees," said Rosa over the coms. "The drone has lost visual."

"I'm in back of the stage, heading for the trees with five SFPD officers," Colin spoke into his mic.

Colin and the other officers spread out. Colin unsnapped his holster and rested his hand on his gun grip, keeping low and staying under cover.

Branches rustled. Colin looked up. A hawk perched above him. "Hawk?"

The raptor ruffled its feathers. Inside his head, Colin heard Hawk's voice: "I know where he is. Follow me."

Colin nodded and Hawk flew low through the trees. Colin followed. The SFPD officers fell in behind him.

"Stop," said Hawk. "He's just ahead."

Colin signaled the other officers that he was stopping, then he drew his Glock.

Crouched in the shadows wearing black, Stone was hard to see, reminding Colin of Frankie's photo of "Rambo Vampire Man."

The officers rushed the Marshal.

Stone ran.

The police chased, yelling at him to stop and surrender.

"Go around to the left." Colin heard Hawk's voice in his head.

Colin made an end-run.

Coming out of the bushes straight at Stone, Colin froze.

The barrel of Stone's gun pointed at Colin's mid-center.

"Drop the gun," said Stone.

Colin placed his Glock on the ground.

"On your knees."

Colin knelt.

Marshal Stone adjusted his weapon, aiming at the center of Colin's forehead.

Colin swallowed.

He heard the trigger click.

Stone's arm jerked wildly.

The bullet cracked and roared.

Hissing and whining, it whizzed inches from Colin's head, into the treetops.

Crying out, Stone fell to the leaf-covered ground, dropping his gun.

He moaned and writhed, holding his thigh.

Police rushed toward the killer, weapons drawn.

An enormous Western rattlesnake slithered away into the bushes.

"He's been bitten by a rattlesnake!" shouted one of the officers.

"Radio medevac!" yelled Colin. "Get them here ASAP!"

Colin threw Stone's gun out of reach, and pushed the writhing marshal onto his back.

He removed Stone's expensive watch so it wouldn't cut into the wrist already starting to swell, then yanked off Stone's boots. Using his pocketknife, Colin cut Stone's chinos away from the bite wound.

Lacking soap, he rinsed the wound with filtered H2O from his water bottle, then dried the skin around the wound with his kerchief. With his pen, he marked the leading edge of the redness and swelling on Stone's skin, and wrote the time alongside it.

The Medevac helicopter arrived.

"We need to keep him prone while we move him," said Colin.

One of the medevac officers produced an emergency cloth stretcher. Eight men lifted Stone into the transport unit, and they flew him away.

Three Blue Angel Hornets whistled over the trees, their white jet trails snaking across the sky.

Lieutenant Rosa spoke through Colin's earpiece. "Excellent work, Warden Dawson. Suspect apprehended, no shots fired by our officers. Congratulations. Take care of yourself. I'll call you next week."

★   ★   ★

Colin found Delfina where he'd left her. Someone had loaned her a blanket to sit on and had given her a bottle of water. She smiled up at Colin and patted the blanket. Colin sat down next to her.

"Hawk told me what happened," she said. "He said he'll see you later. He's already on his way back up to Bellingham. Do you want to go home now?"

"I'm pretty wiped out, Delfina. Do you think we could just chill and listen to the music for a while?"

"I was hoping you'd say that." Delfina threw her arms around Colin and kissed him.

Six Blue Angels flew overhead in formation, splitting into two three-jet arrows. Each jet rolled upside down above the meadow, then all six jets came back together and screamed away, contrails catching sunlight in their wake.

"Maybe we should stay in the City tonight," said Colin. "Get a hotel room, go out for a nice dinner?"

"Yes, definitely," said Delfina.

The Indigo Girls and Willie Nelson finished a set.

All of a sudden, Delfina stood and pointed. "Colin, look! OMG! Can I believe my eyes?"

Taylor Swift pranced across the stage to the microphone amidst swelling music and roars from the crowd.

58

TWO DAYS LATER, Colin stood on his front porch with his arm around Delfina's waist and his cell phone to his ear.

"Good morning, Lieutenant Rosa. I have Delfina with me. Do you mind if I put you on speaker phone?"

"Not a problem. I'm glad you called, son. I want to thank you for all your help not only with Stone's capture, but also with the investigation. Your geofence idea turned the tide for us."

"I'm glad to hear that. I didn't know for sure, but as I mentioned before, I've had a spooky feeling about Marshal Stone since that first day I laid eyes on him. What gall to walk straight into the Cuera homicide investigation on the day of, and then later to show up at your office with a video of Johnny Taylor's abduction."

"I have to say," said Rosa, "it threw me off when we watched the video of Johnny's abduction, and Stone was dressed like one of the drug dealers instead of in his usual all-black clothes."

"That was cunning. Stone's hubris is unreal." Colin shook his head.

"But when we took a closer look at that video," said Rosa, "we determined that the unsub with the truck who abducted Johnny was the same height and build as Stone, significantly taller than the drug dealers," said Rosa.

"And Stone's motive is clear. He knew Johnny could identify him."

"That's right. We've got strong prosecutable cases against Marshal Stone for the murders of Johnny Taylor and of Ramona Cuera. The boots with his DNA on them, found in a dumpster at the motel where he'd been staying, matched the boot prints from both murder scenes. Besides the boots, we have motive. Added to that is a photo we discovered that Johnny took of Stone actually drawing a sniper's bow and aiming at a woman. The image was blurry, but forensics was able to enhance it enough to positively identify the woman as Ramona and the man as Stone."

Delfina trembled in Colin's arms.

"There's more," said Rosa. "We definitely have him for the 2010 rape of Delfina Cuera. His DNA is a match with the evidence in her rape kit."

Colin choked back curses.

"We also have the files we found at Ramona's house, implicating Stone for the 2017 abduction of Stella Osuna. We think he targeted Ramona because she was onto him. San Diego PD has sent us all their records on that cold case, and we're reopening it. When we find out what became of Stella, I think we'll have another murder to pin on Stone. His attack on Delfina and her friend was his first, and at that time, rape was enough for him. We now have evidence that over the last thirteen years, Stone may have raped a young girl in every location he worked. But by the time he got to Stella, he seems to have escalated to murder.

"The man is pathological," said Colin. "All those years he was a serial rapist, and he worked in plain sight as a US Marshal."

"He didn't even bother to disguise himself when he was trying to make his getaway at the airport," said Rosa. He stuck out like a sore thumb in his all-black wild west lawman getup. If you ask me, it's as if he wanted to get caught. You won't believe what we found in his checked luggage."

Colin took Delfina's hand. "Tell us."

"The murder weapon. The son of a bitch ditched his boots, but he packed his high-tech sniper crossbow along with some arrows. I guess he couldn't stand to leave that bow behind. Forensics has determined without a doubt that it's a match for the weapon that killed Ramona Cuera."

Delfina sat down on the wicker front porch bench.

"Wow." Colin put his hand to his forehead and closed his eyes. Recalling his close contacts with that arrogant, cunning murderer, he felt sick. He sat next to Delfina on the bench and took a deep breath.

"How confident are you that you'll be able to make the charges stick? Will he get a long prison sentence?"

"Here's exactly where it stands, son. Police are guarding him twenty-four seven in his hospital room. Once he's discharged from the hospital, he'll go to jail, where we will be holding him without bail. He hasn't confessed to anything yet, but I'm confident we have sufficient motive, means, opportunity, and evidence to convict Marshal Kurt Stone at trial of Ramona Cuera's first degree murder. The murder of Ramona Cuera is solved. Not only that, since there is no statute of limitations for rape in California, I'm certain we've got him for the 2010 rape of Delfina Cuera. The case we're building against Stone for the abduction and murder of Johnny Taylor is very strong. And with time, I have no doubt that we'll also be able to make the case for Stone's abduction of Stella Osuna and the rape of at least ten other girls. I'm confident that Kurt Stone is going away for life, without parole. He'll never hurt anyone again."

59

T HE FOLLOWING SATURDAY, June 4, Delfina steered her VW Bug over a rutted dirt road on Agua Pura Farm, and parked behind an old barn. She switched off the engine, unlatched her seatbelt, and turned to Colin.

"Ready?" Delfina's smile was as bright as the June sky.

Colin's forehead furrowed. "Are you sure we can leave the car here?"

Delfina gently smoothed Colin's creased forehead. "I told you, the Agua Pura folks have given us permission to leave my car here while we go 'camping' for a month. No worries. I'm positive it's fine."

Colin freed himself from his seatbelt and turned to face Delfina. "Are you sure you want to do this?"

Delfina put a reassuring hand on Colin's knee. "Stop worrying, love. I feel my mother smiling. I know she's at peace now. Her killer has been caught. He's going to prison for life. I'm finally free from him. And I know that Stella and all the other girls he hurt, and their families, can find peace now too." She leaned in closer. "What about you, Colin? This is big for you. Are you sure you're ready?"

"Oh, I'm so ready." Colin took a deep breath. "Haven't had a vacation since I started this job. I've accumulated four weeks off from work." Colin kissed Delfina's hand. "And now that your stalkers, Kozel, Matsen, and Marshal Stone, are behind bars and you're safe, so much pressure has lifted."

Delfina gazed toward the forested mountains rolling up from the coast. She imagined she could see the faces of her ancestors looking down from the puffy, cotton ball cumulous clouds drifting above the trees. "And the Cougar Creek Coast Ranch is going to be truly protected into the future?"

Colin nodded with satisfaction. "Mikos Vadim has been arrested for his theft of semiconductor software, his fraudulent charity, and his Chinese wind turbine scheme to defraud the government. We'll no doubt have good sustainable wind energy projects developed in California in the future, maybe even at the Cougar Creek Coast Ranch Monument, but not by Chinese cyber thieves.

"Plus, Mikos's brother, Kiki, lost his hunting license permanently and has a big fine to pay for wildlife violations, and Mikos's 'bike bro' Bob Budalo has been fired as BLM Central Coast Field Office Manager. Their bike trail building project on Cougar Creek Coast Ranch land has been put on indefinite hold while all the lawsuits make their way through the system. Before the park opens to the public, qualified ecological scientists will collect baseline data on all the sensitive species in the monument, and will finally get to do an EIR, which can guide management and mitigation going forward."

"So BLM's primary management focus has shifted from recreation to conservation—the original mandate of the monument?"

"Yep. Everything is settled. I'm ready. You good?"

"I don't have to start law school until August 18. I'm more than ready."

"Honestly, Delfina, I wonder if maybe we should just go off the grid permanently—change into mountain lions, disappear into the wilderness, and leave this toxic human race behind for the rest of our lives."

"I've thought about that, too." Delfina took both of Colin's hands in hers. "I absolutely understand the impulse to just give up and drop out. I really do, Colin. But that's not what I want." Delfina kissed Colin's hands and released them, then turned her gaze again up into the mountains. "I choose a path of hope. I choose to stay in the struggle. I want to fight with everything I've got, including a science degree and a law degree and license to practice, as well as my indigenous knowledge—and my 'special' gift."

Delfina felt the heat of the cougar rise through her body. "There's so much at stake: the fate of women, and people of color and divergent genders, the protection of all our wild brothers and sisters, conservation of biodiversity and all the unique habitats on our priceless Mother Earth, the fight to stop the climate crisis before we go completely over the tipping point cliff and turn this exquisite, sacred earth into a dead rock floating in space."

Delfina searched deep into Colin's eyes. "I'm excited to retreat into the mountains with you as pumas for a whole glorious month this summer, Colin. I want to show you some of my favorite places—secret waterfalls, mysterious forests, and meadows more pristine and beautiful than you can imagine. But then I want to come back down the mountain and work every day alongside you to protect all that I love. I believe you feel the same way."

"You know I do, my love. I also choose hope. And I choose you." Colin kissed Delfina on the forehead. "I love you forever." He stroked her hair, his brow creasing. "But I've gotta confess something's still worrying me, Delfina. I just can't quite seem to shake this fear that some bad thing might happen, and I'll lose you."

Delfina cupped Colin's cheeks, scuffed up his new beard, and leaned in close. "Hear this, Colin Dawson. Even if one or both of us dies, we don't have to worry. We will always find each other again. We're soul mates. We're destined to be together, always."

Their kiss said more than any words could.

"All right then. Let's go."

★   ★   ★

They left the car, carrying nothing with them, and hiked up into the mountains.

On a ridgetop rich with the fragrance of summer redwoods, far from any scent or artifact of humans, they stood watching the sun slowly sink toward the tree line. Light began to fade into the gloaming.

"Look," said Colin. "Even before it's completely dark, Venus is so bright it's already visible."

"Twinkle twinkle little star, how I wonder what you are," Delfina recited the nursery rhyme. "Up above the world so high, like a diamond in the sky."

Colin continued. "Star light, star bright, first star I see tonight, I wish I may, I wish I might." Delfina joined in and they finished the rhyme together, "have the wish I wish tonight."

"Even though Venus is technically a planet, not a star," wondered Colin, "do you think we can make a wish on it?"

"Definitely. I can see the light of Venus shining steadily in your eyes, Colin," Delfina teased. "The Goddess of Love is blessing you."

Colin blushed. "There's always more to wish for. But honestly, love, I've already got the most important wish of my life." Colin took Delfina in his arms and kissed her tenderly.

They held hands and watched the sky transform into an ever richer kaleidoscope of colors and patterns. Sun turned into an orange paper lantern, poofing bubbles off its top that flashed brilliant green, like magic, until the last remnant of orange vanished over the western horizon.

Spinning in the vastness of space, Planet Earth cast a blue shadow band on its atmosphere in the east. The band widened, then deepened into black night.

Constellations blinked into sight like stage lights coming on in a darkened theater, one by one, until thousands of diamonds spilled over the black velvet curtain of night.

Colin and Delfina took off their clothes, folded them neatly, and hid them next to a large boulder, under a bramble of wild rose.

The change was easy for both of them now.

Venus shone brightly above the two pumas, guiding their way as they trotted off together into the wilderness.

Haawka
May the fire burn bright in you.

ACKNOWLEDGMENTS

I gratefully acknowledge those who helped me tell this story.

All mistakes are mine! I humbly ask to be forgiven for any factual errors, and for my fantastical flights of imagination.

- ❖ The Sycuan Band of the Kumeyaay Nation
- ❖ Kumeyaay teachers Dr. Stan Rodriguez, Martha Rodriguez, and Jaime LaBreak
- ❖ The people of Molino Creek Farm Collective
- ❖ California Fish and Wildlife Captain Steven Schindler
- ❖ Santa Cruz Puma Project Director Dr. Chris Wilmers
- ❖ FBI agent George Fong
- ❖ Forensic Pathologist Dr. Terri Haddix
- ❖ Santa Cruz County Sheriff's Office
- ❖ Dana Isaacson and Penni Askew, my brilliant editors
- ❖ My book cover designer Niki Lenhart
- ❖ Beta Readers: intrepid educator & swim buddy Melanie Coon; mystery writer & avid bicyclist Nancy Wood; psychologist (trauma-based therapies specialist) Rachel Pfotenhauer; environmental warrior Mark Lipson; organic farmer Judy Lowe; green builder Ray Newkirk; poet Anna Citrino; author & patron of the arts Nancy Jarvis; fierce environmental attorney Gary Patton; and my dear life partner "Cosmic" Joe Jordan.

DEDICATIONS

to the memory of

- ❖ Delfina Cuero, author,
  Diegueño Indian of the Kumeyaay Nation, 1900 – 1972

to the defense of wilderness and biodiversity:

- ❖ Puma Project
  https://www.santacruzpumas.org
- ❖ Center for Biological Diversity
  https://www.biologicaldiversity.org

to the Water Protectors
of the Standing Rock Lakota Sioux Tribe and their allies
and the 1,000 Hummingbirds Council
"Water is Life (*Mni Wiconi*)"

and to **Justice** and **Hope**
for families of missing and murdered Indigenous people

Coalition to Stop Violence Against Native Women
https://www.csvanw.org/resources
Native women face murder rates more than 10 times the national
average

Learn More, Take Action

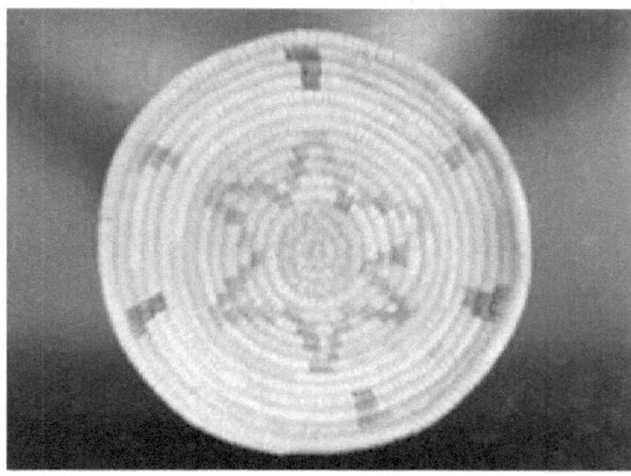

basket made by Kummeyaay artist Martha Rodriguez

Love

ABOUT THE AUTHOR

Mary Flodin's debut novel, *Fruit of the Devil*, published in 2019, was a finalist for the PEN/Bellwether Prize for Socially Engaged Fiction and the Pacific Northwest Writers' Competition. Her newest cli-fi romantasy, *Incident at Cougar Creek*, came to her in visions while hiking nearly daily in the Santa Cruz mountains during the covid pandemic. Imaginary characters and even a real live puma appeared to her and asked her to tell their story.

Before settling into the writer's life, Mary taught k-12 environmental education, English language arts and literature, social studies, digital media, and art in California public schools. A native Californian, she lives on an urban micro permaculture farm on the Monterey Bay coast with her husband—a retired NASA climate scientist—and their dogs, koi, feral cat, chickens, 1,000 hummingbirds, and gopher herd. Learn more about Mary at *https://shorturl.at/NTdAi* and *https://linktr.ee/maryfloiam*.

ALSO BY THE AUTHOR

FRUIT OF THE DEVIL
Mary Flodin

Ms. Aurora Bourne would do anything to protect her students from harm ... even if that means going up against the most powerful corporation on the planet.

Available from Paper Angel Press in
hardcover, trade paperback, and digital editions
paperangelpress.com

YOU MIGHT ALSO ENJOY

DUE DATE
A Shelby McDougall Mystery
Nancy Wood

Surrogate mother Shelby McDougall just fell for the biggest con of all—a scam that risks her life … and the lives of her unborn twins.

MARGERY
Jeffery Penn May

Introverted backpacker Jeremy wanders off trail and discovers an eccentric, otherworldly town nestled in a mountain basin.

PIOUS REBEL
Jory Post

After her partner dies suddenly, Lisa Hardrock realizes how little she knows about the life she's been living— and starts exploring her questions in a blog that unexpectedly goes viral.

Available from Paper Angel Press in
hardcover, trade paperback, and digital editions
paperangelpress.com